The Ballad of the LOST DOGS of East Nashville

A NOVEL BY
JOHN J. THOMPSON

Enthusiasm For The Ballad of the Lost Dogs of East Nashville

Like a few of the central characters in this book, singer-songwriter John J. Thompson may seem a bit tardy in offering his best gifts to the world. He's an experienced storyteller and serial author, but *The Ballad of the Lost Dogs of East Nashville* is his debut as a novelist. The timing is perfect, however. Thompson infuses a lifetime of unique challenges and experiences into a relatable story of redemption, personal reinvention, community, and music. This uplifting story of a band of unlikely local heroes works as entertainment, but stands ready to inspire anyone to overcome self-inflicted roadblocks in pursuit of whatever form their own art may take, at any stage of life. Among other things, this a musical fable about what makes America truly special. It may open your eyes to see beauty in unexpected places and family in unexpected people…

…I'm confident that Mr. Rogers would like what he finds in this neighborhood. As elderly accordionist Cesar says of the Lost Dogs' musical blend of Latin, soul, gospel, country, and rock 'n' roll, the rapidly changing East Nashville becomes the crisol or melting pot that produces a marvelous feast by unifying what everyone brings to the table, all in due time.

 —Jeff Elbel, *Chicago Sun-Times, Illinois Entertainer*

The characters jump right off the page and into your heart. If you're a fan of second-chance stories, this is for you! It's all about the power of music to unite people from all backgrounds. A beautiful song of a story.

 —Sam Wade, *Producer, Songwriter, and "Hadestown" band member*

A charming book with likable characters and a story that isn't rushing the reader along. Thompson has created a cast of characters you start caring about as soon as the pages turn. That's because it seems likely that the author cares about them, too. Maybe it's because I read the book during the holiday season, but *The Ballad of the Lost Dogs of East Nashville* has all the feel-goodness of a timely holiday movie.

 —Phil Madeira, *Songwriter, Producer, Musician with Emmylou Harris,
Buddy Miller, etc.*

I found *The Ballad of the Lost Dogs of East Nashville* invigorating and capable of not just entertaining me but also serving as a catalyst for how I might live in the new year.

    —Pastor Matt Staniz, St. Luke's Lutheran Church, Philadelphia PA

The Ballad of the Lost Dogs of East Nashville is a wonderfully written testament to what it means to be human in a broken yet hope-filled world. Thompson's characters come alive as they form a community that is a taste of heaven on earth. East Nashville is where we all live, between now and eternity, dwelling in the relationships we create…

    —Quentin Schultze, *Professor of Communication Emeritus, Calvin University, author of* You'll Shoot Your Eye Out! Life Lessons from the Movie 'A Christmas Story

John J. Thompson did much more than create a fictional band on these pages; he invited you and me to join one. And any book that features Bono & the Beatles, a benefit concert & Bonnaroo, Bobs Dylan & Marley, and the Beatles & biscuits, is for me. Stevie Wonder famously sang, 'Music is a world within itself, with a language we all understand.' Thankfully—for all of us—JJT speaks it fluently.

    —Rob Birks, *Salvation Army Kroc Center, San Diego*

The characters in this compelling story are people I'd love to hang with. This book sprang straight from the creative heart of the Nashville music scene. It's multigenerational, multicultural, full of energy and pain and possibility. Best of all, it's a page-turner. You fall in love with these folk and must find out what happens to them. A great read I want to revisit.

    —Gwen Moore

John Thompson spins a yarn here that covers a lot of my favorite themes: music, social movements, and the deep territory of the human heart. The story carried me along with intricately developed characters and musical descriptions only an insider could know. I'd say it was a page-turner if I had turned any pages, which I didn't. I listened to the audio version, which I highly recommend.

—**Don Chaffer**, *Singer/Songwriter with the band Waterdeep & Professor of Music, Lipscomb University*

The Ballad of the Lost Dogs of East Nashville by John Thompson is a rare treat of a novel--it is fun, wise, and inspiring. You'll love the characters and feel the Nashville setting. Lost Dogs is music to your ear and a bright light to your soul.

—**Bishop Todd Hunter**, Author: What Jesus Intended)

The Ballad of the Lost Dogs of East Nashville is the first book I've ever read that truly captures the core of the magic of East Nashville. Thompson has created unforgettable characters who perfectly match the various folks I have come to learn about, listen to, and fully appreciate in real life while living in East Nashville for almost 20 years. East Nashville is an epicenter of creativity that is more of the creative foundation of Nashville than any other part of Music City. This story is a wonderful example that gives outsiders a real picture of what has been going on here for over 25 years. It also provides a community blueprint for how the essence of what is loved most can be maintained and grow for the locals who refuse to leave (or get kicked out due to the 'progress' of a city growing faster than it is ready for). I can't recommend this book enough, and I'm excited to read it again and stay tuned with the magic that John Joseph Thompson will continue to create with everyone, young and old, who choose to make Nashville their home, too.

—**Chuck Beard**, *Metro Arts Nashville*

First Edition

This novel is a work of fiction. Any resemblance to actual persons, living or dead, is purely coincidental. All characters, events, and incidents portrayed in this book are products of the author's imagination or are used fictitiously. The names of real historical or contemporary individuals or businesses mentioned herein are for contextual and entertainment purposes only and should not be interpreted as implying the participation, endorsement, consent, or actual actions of those individuals or entities.

Text ©2024 John J. Thompson / Gyroscope Productions (http://www.LostPerros.com)
First Date Of Publication: Oct 1, 2024
Publisher: Gyroscope Productions, PO Box 60401 Nashville TN 37206
Cover Illustration: Kreg Yingst (kregyingst.com)
Front Cover Design: Andy Zipf
Design and Typesetting: Marc Ludena (BasslineShift.com)
All rights reserved.
Printed in the United States of America.
No part of this book may be reproduced, stored in a retrieval system, or transmitted in any form or by any means, electronic, mechanical, photocopying, recording, or otherwise, without express written permission of the publisher.
ISBN: 979-8-9916862-0-4
Distributed by IngramSpark

Library of Congress Control Number: PENDING (Case# 1-14304666561)

I dedicate this book to the wonderful people of East Nashville, our family's home since 2007, and the neighbors we miss from the east side of Aurora, Illinois, our home for many years before that. This also goes out to the arts community in one of my favorite cities, Asheville North Carolina, which was devastated by flooding in the fall of 2024. Actually, I dedicate it to people living in, creating in, and getting pushed out of the funky side of cities everywhere. Here's to the artists, the lovers, and the working-class dreamers struggling to gather tribes around something good, true, and beautiful. May our various creative hopes and dreams be realized as we love our way back to the garden.

-JJT

Track Listing

The Ballad (Intro)

It only makes sense that a story set in a community as steeped in music as East Nashville, Tennessee, would take the form of a ballad. Ballads tell stories—stories that reveal things about who we are individually and collectively. The best stories ask questions and then trust the audience to discern the answers. Ballads may give us something to dance to or simply something to contemplate as we stare into a roaring campfire. They may be sung slowly, but that is never a prerequisite of the form. The tempo isn't really the point. It may even change throughout the song.

Folks weren't in a hurry when the old ballads reigned. No one cared how many minutes could fit on one side of a record or whether a deejay might play it on the radio. The audience, young and old, wanted to get lost in the story and the sound.

This ballad is about music, and music is about people, and people love and hate each other with a passion and talent that is truly astonishing. This song is about unlikely heroes overcoming long odds and being overcome by them. It is about a new community being built upon the rubble of an older one without losing the memory of what had come before. It's about songs we've heard before—some of us too many times—ending in slightly different ways. It's about the mystical power that dances between the beats and through the notes, drawing some folks together and pushing some folks apart. It asks some old questions, setting notes in tension with each other and allowing the characters to decide how those chords will be resolved.

This ballad is a fable set in a real place, inspired by real people, who get caught up in a fantastic new melody that stretches their artistic sensibilities, challenges their cultural limitations, and leaves them spinning and breathless on a brand-new dance floor.

As our story begins, you will get a glimpse of the end of the song (kind of like starting with a chorus). Then you will get a closer look at our primary balladeers and hear about the strange things that have happened over the last year or so in this rapidly changing community. In several spots we'll go much farther back on the timeline, but we'll always bring you back to the porch where most of the song is being sung.

And now, we'll have the drummer count us in.

Count Us In

Present Day

How could something as thrilling and completely unlikely as making music he loved with some of his closest friends, in front of thousands of people, in his own neighborhood, in a way that generated real, tangible benefits for his community, be filling Jerry Wesley with so many conflicted emotions and complicated thoughts?

Something truly miraculous had happened—was happening—and instead of being able to just enjoy it, Jerry was wracked with anxiety. The stakes suddenly felt very high. Thank God he wasn't in this alone.

He ran his middle finger over the lip of a nearly empty coffee cup and stared blankly at a picture hanging on the wall of the Nashville Biscuit House. As he usually did when he felt himself getting overcome, he made his way to this spot. As hard as it would be to explain to anyone else, there was an almost meditative presence to this booth.

Everything about this diner was familiar. His aging body knew the feel of the vinyl bench. The smells of coffee, syrup, bacon, and griddle smoke combined into a sort of calming incense. The kitchen workers, other customers' conversations, and the drawl of the servers cascaded over a bed of tinny WSM background music, creating a near symphony of sound. It all wove together into a multisensory comfort field for one of waitress Sharon's favorite patrons over the last five decades.

She freshened Jerry's coffee with a genuine smile. "Where are you this morning, sweetie?"

"Huh?" Jerry snapped back into the moment. "Oh, I'm right here. All's well. I'm just a little overwhelmed, I guess. Gotta say, I never saw this coming. I'm not sure what to think of it all."

"Well, try to enjoy it a little bit," she teased. "But I don't want to see you coming in here with a handlebar mustache and suspenders any time soon." She waved her forefinger at him. "Oh, but you do have to sign something for us."

Jerry played dumb. "My check?"

Sharon dropped a Sharpie and a morning copy of *The Tennessean* on the table and patted him on the back. Above the fold was a sweaty picture of him with a retired African American trolley driver, a Mexican American landscaper, one smart-looking grandmother, as well as a few college students, and some other friends from the neighborhood who had gathered backstage after their inspiring concert in the park next to the Community Center the night before. Just above the picture read this headline:

Is This Band of Retirees and College Students Bonnaroo Bound?

Jerry shook his head and smiled. He was surprised the news of the offer was already out there. Now he had to get back to his house a few blocks away to meet the others. They had some decisions to make.

He got up from his booth and made it over to the counter with a bit more of a limp than usual. His leg was acting up this morning. He figured it was probably just barking at him from overuse the night before. He paid for his meal and signed the newspaper on his way out the door—his first autograph.

To Sharon and the Biscuit House Crew; Keep It Real!
—Jerry James Wesley

He was pretty sure that was really stupid.

The Dogs Begin to Howl

Jerry found it very hard to believe that he was sixty-eight years old. It seemed that it was just last week that he had been a teenager working his family's tobacco fields, fiddling with cars on the weekend, and kicking up dust with his friends when there was nothing better to do in small-town Tennessee. Had it really been almost forty-five years since he had returned home from Vietnam? Thirty-eight since he'd stopped drinking?

Jerry was the quiet type, generally, and would rather keep himself busy than get too introspective, but the old man who had greeted him in the mirror that morning forced a different kind of reflection. He saw a story in his own green eyes that he could somehow sense was about to tell itself.

Jerry made his way home from the Biscuit House to get ready for the big meeting. He usually preferred the walk, but with time—and his leg—not exactly on his side, he was glad he had taken his old truck. Though he had just played a mind-blowing concert with these people, one that he knew would alter the course of all their lives, he was truly more excited to have these friends back in his home. Against all odds, they had become a kind of family. He smiled. How silly it was that he could miss people he had only been apart from for a few hours.

Despite his exhaustion when he had finally made it to bed at around 2:30 a.m., he had woken early—excited about what the day might hold.

He hadn't felt this fidgety in a long time. He couldn't actually remember the last time. He checked his watch five times over a span of three minutes. He paced between his front porch, where he scanned up and down the street for familiar cars, and his kitchen table, where he never quite managed to sit down and relax. The others were attending church with family or attending to other duties. They had all agreed to meet at 1:00 p.m.

He had gathered with a few of the guys a couple hours earlier for "something like church" in his own kitchen. It was really just coffee, a little bit of reading from the biblical book of James, some talking, and some quiet, but it was the closest several of them had been to church in a while and it felt good. They had then scattered to take care of different things before the meeting.

Jerry was alone with his thoughts for a few minutes. He took a deep, cleansing breath and smiled. He was simply coming down from an adrenaline high from the night before. His addict brain was trying to play some tricks on him, but he was wise to it. He let out half a laugh and shuffled to the bathroom.

After washing his face and running his wet hands through what was left of his now almost entirely silver hair, Jerry made his way to the kitchen. When he wasn't forced to see the truth in a mirror, he still pictured himself with light brown—almost blond—hair. Though it had lost its color, it still hung a bit past his collar. It was nothing too radical compared to what a lot of guys in East Nashville had growing out of their heads, but if his old man could see him, he'd holler at him to get a haircut.

That made him smile again. He was in pretty decent shape, all things considered. Sure, he had a bit of a hitch in his giddyup. He could stand to lose a few pounds, but his weight wasn't out of control. He was healthy overall, his mind was sharp, and considering some of the things he had done to his body, that was more than he should take for granted at this point.

He poured some coffee from an impossibly old Mr. Coffee brewer into a mug that had followed him home from 'Nam in 1974. He worked his way over to his favorite chair by the front window and sat. The front room of his small, simple East Nashville home was humble but nice. There was an older couch and a small dinette set on one side of the room. A small bookcase sat just inside the front door. An old Martin acoustic guitar rested on a stand in the corner, next to his chair.

He reached over to his 1950s Admiral Bel-Air record player, turned it on, and dropped the needle carefully on an old LP. Through some scratches and pops coming both from the vinyl and the old man listening to it, the warm tone of John Prine's "Fish and Whistle" filled the room as Jerry picked up the old photo album and a leather-bound journal from the coffee table.

He savored the simple, rootsy, acoustic sounds and the coffee as he looked over the photos. The midday sunlight angled through the front window, and he could see out onto his front porch and beyond to his small yard, his little picket fence, and Boscobel Street. So much had happened out there.

Jerry was generally satisfied with small stuff, like his coffee and his records. But the lines on his face told him that there were still some things left to do with his life and a finite amount of time in which to do them. His precious routine had been obliterated. The volume knob on his life was being turned up. He felt a definite loss of control happening.

In some ways it was thrilling. In others, however, it scared him. He understood how his mind worked and the events of the last few months had raised the stakes for his physical and emotional health. As exciting as it all seemed, he was entering several minefields at once. He had some difficult decisions to make.

But not before he finished enjoying some music and a cup of coffee.

As he continued flipping through the old photo album, a gentle knock sounded on the frame of his screen door.

"Whoever that is, you should know by now you're welcome to just come on in."

He had assumed it would be Louis, or Cesar, or Alex, or any of the others, but when a young woman walked through the door, looking more than a little bit uncomfortable, Jerry sprung to his feet, an apology already forming in his mind when she interrupted him.

"Hello," she said somewhat tentatively, almost as if it was a question. "My name is Marisol Knudsen. I'm a blogger, and Alex invited me to come over to meet the group. He said I could maybe ask a few questions for a story I'm working on about everything that has been happening with your music in the community."

"Oh," Jerry said, surprised and feeling bad about his greeting. "I'm sorry for not coming to the door. I thought you were one of the gang. I should have known none of them would have knocked. I do remember Alex mentioning something about this. Sure, come on in. Happy to meet you. The others aren't here yet, but they should be soon."

Marisol was a twenty-three-year-old Latina, with fiercely curly, mostly black hair that revealed shades of henna where the sunlight hit it directly. She had pulled it back into a smart-looking ponytail and wore nice jeans and a black buttoned blouse. She layered an Army-issue shirt over it like a light jacket. Jerry recognized it right away. She carried a well-worn leather satchel full of recording equipment and well-organized papers and books. It was clear to Jerry that she was confident, prepared, and seemed to have at least a bit of radical in her.

"I think I got here a bit early. I knocked at Alex's next door, but no one answered. I tried calling and texting, but he hasn't responded. I saw that your door was open so I decided to try here."

"I'm glad you did. Tell you what. Let's go sit out on the front porch. I can fix you a cup of coffee if you want."

"That would be great. It was a late night last night, wasn't it?"

"You were there?"

"Oh yes. I've been following this whole story since the beginning. I wouldn't have missed that for anything. But wow! It was so much bigger than I expected."

"Yeah." Jerry rubbed his head. "It was pretty huge. That's part of what we have to talk about this morning."

"Wow. I can't wait to hear about that. While we're waiting, though, would you tell me your story? I've heard a little bit here and there, but I'd love to know more about your roots. Where do you come from? How did you get here?"

The two settled into seats on the front porch. Jerry realized he still had the photo album in his hands. He laid it carefully on the railing. "Sure. I'm still not good at interviews and such, though. I'm not sure how much of my story will be interesting to a journalist or anything. I'm pretty average, I guess. But I'll tell you what I remember and try to be honest. But would you tell me a bit about yourself first? What do you write about? What makes a kid like you interested in an old guy like me? Seems you'd be more interested in talking to Jamie or Alex."

The young woman looked a bit taken aback. "Um, of course. I'm not sure where to begin. Alex and I have known each other for a while, I guess. When we were younger we went to the same church youth group for a while. I stopped going to church once I got to college, and we lost touch. Alex wasn't much of a church kid as I can recall, either. But we reconnected last year and caught up a bit."

"Why did you stop going to church? If that's not too personal."

"Not at all. I don't think it was a specific thing, really. It was just that as I got more concerned about community issues and started to learn more about history and justice, it felt like my church didn't have much to say about those things. What they were talking about, constantly, just kind of… well…I guess I just drifted. My parents still go and I will attend with them sometimes, but based on some of the things the denomination is part of, I don't think I'll be back."

"I hear you. That's too bad. I can relate, though. Definitely. We're all on a journey, aren't we? I'll be right back with your coffee."

Jerry stepped into the house to fetch her a cup while Marisol settled in. She noticed the photo album, lifted the cover, and stole a glance at a couple of striking, small, black-and-white prints on the first page. One was of a beautiful young woman in what looked like a small town some time ago.

The other was of the same woman, but with two babies. She had a scarf on her head and wore a worried, forced smile.

As she heard her host returning, she allowed the cover to fall back into place and looked up toward the door. Jerry handed her a warm mug and she inhaled the aroma. "Thank you. The smell reminds me of the coffee at my father's favorite diner."

"Wonderful. So, tell me a little bit more about who you write for."

"I have my blog, and I occasionally write for local papers or magazines. I am particularly interested in the stories of people making a positive impact in their community. I think I had my fill of bad news a while back."

Jerry nodded. "Sounds good to me. I think I have allowed bad news, mistakes, and blind spots to form too much of my life. I'm hoping I can spend whatever years I have left invested in something that brings light and life to this place. But I gotta tell ya, I've spent years and years fixing things and trying to make myself useful. I never, in my wildest dreams, imagined anything like all this attention."

"That's probably what makes this so fascinating," Marisol offered. "Many people plan and invest and work and experiment, only to have their efforts fall flat. I've seen it over and over—from well-meaning nonprofits to the church I grew up in. They build programs and hire consultants and everything else—and when it's all done, not much has happened. But you people just start doing something, seemingly without even trying, and now people all around the world are talking about it."

Jerry was shaking his head, rubbing his chin, and looking off into the trees that lined his street. "Well I don't know about all that. I can tell some folks are excited, but I don't think it's about us, entirely. I think it's maybe about something deeper."

"Are you aware of the impact this story is having on people?" she asked. "Have you been following the media reports on this at all? Do you know how rare something like what happened last night actually is?"

"I guess not. I mean, I know what happened last night was very special. But I haven't paid too much attention to the stories about it. Alex did set up a Facebook account for me, so I'm not totally in the dark. I just don't think it's really about me, or even us."

"Well I'd like to know what you think it's all about, then, because this is about the most hopeful I've been about this community in a long time." Marisol started her recorder and sat poised with her pen and paper.

She was starting to think this old man's humility was genuine. She took a deep breath and offered a gentle smile as this man she was quickly coming to regard as a hero shared his life story with her.

"How about we start at the beginning?" she said.

Jerry's Theme

1950 — 1966

Jerry was the child of parents often referred to as part of the "Greatest Generation." They had been born in and formed by the American South. His father, Hank Wesley, was a decorated World War II veteran who returned from the Pacific Theater to farm the land that had been in their family for several generations. He worked hard and he held his demons close. Even as an adult, Jerry knew very little about his father.

Hank and Jerry's mother, Evelyn, were deeply religious in that Southern way—which meant church every Sunday and Wednesday night, formal clothes, and never talking about doubts, fears, or questions that demanded anything beyond the politest, clichéd answers. Drinking was strictly forbidden by their church, so Jerry's dad only drank at home. He only swore when he drank. He only lost his temper when he drank. Thus the outside world never saw the side of Hank that Jerry did.

Jerry was a typical baby boomer kid for that part of the world. He worked the fields in Crossville, Tennessee, played football at school on Friday nights, knew his way around an old car, and had gotten hooked on Chesterfields by the time he was sixteen. But where most of his friends loved listening to pop music, Jerry started to feel a deeper connection to the songs of artists like Johnny Cash, Merle Haggard, Hank Williams, and even Bob Dylan.

When he was alone with a radio or a record player, which was rare, he would sing along, the songs resonating somewhere deep down in his gut. In one music class, he even dabbled with an acoustic guitar, learning a few chords. The first time he felt the magic of playing a simple folk song it nearly brought tears to his eyes. He kept those feelings to himself.

One hot June Sunday that Jerry tried hard to forget but never could, he overheard his father talking to one of their neighbors outside of church just before they went home. Jerry was already sitting in the backseat of that old '55 Chevy with the top two buttons of his shirt undone when Mr. Chester Clark stopped his old man.

"You need to come to the meetin'," Mr. Clark had said, just a little too intensely for Hank's liking. "This stuff's important, and if we don't do something about it now, it'll be too late!"

Hank was irritated. He took his hat off, wiped his brow with his handkerchief, and tried to pack as much intensity as he could into his voice without hollering. "What, exactly, do you suppose men like us can do, Chester? These politicians don't care about us. I got fields to tend. I don't got time for no meetin's."

"Well, you're doggone right about that! They don't give a damn about us, that's for sure. That's why we have to take care of this shit for ourselves. I don't want no Washington men from up north telling me who I gotta hire at my company or where my kids have to go to school. God made us how he made us, Hank. These folks are just godless!

"We're gonna lose our way of living—our way of worshippin'—our way of doing business. But if we come together and take care of it like men, they can't stop us. You just come to the meetin'. It'll make sense then. Pastor James'll explain it better'n me anyhow."

"I'll think about it, Chester. I'll see what I can do."

Jerry wanted to ask his father what that was all about. He had an idea, but at just twelve years old, politics was still a bit over his head. He had almost worked up the nerve to ask when they pulled into the driveway at home, and his father opened his car door and walked toward the house with a kind of frustrated determination that could only mean one thing.

He wasn't in the mood for talking.

Sure enough, Hank found his silver flask and stomped out the back door. "I gotta check something out in the barn!"

It was pretty early for Dad to be grabbing the flask on a Sunday. This wasn't likely to end well. Jerry decided to make himself scarce. He grabbed his transistor radio, a notebook, and a pencil from his bedroom and slipped out the front door to sit out on the porch. He'd listen to some music quietly and do some writing and some sketching. He could get lost that way for hours.

He found a radio station playing Gospel music out of Nashville and liked what he heard. This was different than the Southern Gospel quartet music he'd heard in his church. He could tell from the sound that this was coming from a Black church. It captivated his attention immediately. He turned the volume low, set the radio on the porch railing, and set to writing some words that might have been a poem or might have been lyrics to a song. He wasn't sure.

After about a half hour, his father exploded through the screen door, nearly tearing it from its feeble hinges. "What are you doing out here? We got no time for idlin'. Get your sorry ass out there to that shed and get busy."

It took his father a few seconds of relative silence to hear the music coming from the radio. Jerry was making his way to it, trying to turn it off before his father noticed. Too late.

"What the hell is that?" he demanded. "What is it with you and this damned jungle music all the time? And THIS? Not even listening to anything decent. You gotta listen to a bunch of race music? Do you even know what those people are doing to our country?"

Hank spit a stream of tobacco juice toward the radio. It splashed on the railing, trailed onto the floor, and dribbled onto his own shirt. That set him off even more. He took a swing at the little blue Windsor and sent it flying into the bushes. "Leave it! And get your ass out to that shed."

Jerry knew that his father no longer remembered, or cared, that it was Sunday. His mother had somehow vanished to find some chores to do.

Jerry went out to the shed to find something productive to work on since his father had, in fact, never given him any specific assignment. As screwed up as the situation was, if he could find a piece of equipment to repair, or some blades to sharpen, or maybe if he cleaned and organized some part of the place his dad had left a mess, he'd likely get at least a begrudging "Good job," in the morning. At least he'd avoid a beating.

Jerry repaired the wiring on a broken work light, removed four wasp nests, and cleaned out a gummed-up carburetor on one of the mowers. None of it prevented him from taking one last lick upside the head from the old man a couple hours later. Hank had sobered up enough to drive himself to whatever meeting they had been talking about, but not enough to realize that he was, once again, enraged at Jerry for no particular reason.

Jerry seethed. His face hot, his teeth clenched, he practically held his breath until he heard the Chevy pull away. That night he found his father's Jack Daniel's and helped himself to a swig or two for the first time. It didn't take much for him to feel that knot in his chest start to loosen.

***

As the Sixties wore on and Jerry saw images of social unrest around the country, flickering on his family's black-and-white television, he was confused. The race riots and antiwar demonstrations and integration struggles seemed to be a million miles away from his small town. His father became more and more agitated about the threats to "our way of life," but Jerry heard the voices of "the other side" coming through the speakers of his radio. He started to notice a significant disconnect between the message of peace and grace preached by Jesus and the anger and fear being preached by the religious community he had grown up in, so he slowly lost respect for the church.

Jerry was frustrated by the lack of understanding he saw everywhere. As he prepared to graduate from high school, he wished the world could work like the songs he was listening to. Those chords resolved. Those lyrics made some kind of sense.

After finding and repairing a damaged old Brownie camera, Jerry developed a quiet passion for photography. He was especially compelled to capture images of things out of their element—buildings, vehicles, equipment, and people in need of repair, or in some kind of precarious condition. Jerry rarely showed his photographs to anyone, and only kept the ones he liked the most. He curated his collection relentlessly and mercilessly. He found an old photo album at a secondhand store and pressed it into service as his own personal archive. Only his best images made it into that book.

Jerry met Susan Sheehan in the tenth grade, and they connected right away. She was drawn to his quiet nature and sensed that something interesting was happening beneath the surface. She was mildly concerned about his brooding side—the way he got so deeply into his thoughts and had such trouble sharing them. She assumed that she would be able to tame his Saturday-night drinking once they were out of school.

Jerry loved taking pictures of Susan. She wasn't broken down, misplaced, or even the slightest bit odd, like most of his subjects. To his eyes she was as pretty as a peach and perfectly put together. He had a couple of simple photos he could sit and study for hours. Her dark-brown hair was sleek and shiny, like mink fur, and her skin was fair and flawless. She didn't fuss over herself overly much, but she was no slouch. She got as much attention as any of the girls at school.

Jerry tried sketching her, but it never looked right. She was too perfect for his pencil. She was also much more confident than most of the kids their age. As one of their friends said about her once, she "didn't take no lip from no one." He could never capture that self-determined presence in a drawing without making her seem angry.

The first time Jerry trusted Susan enough to share with her a song he had been trying to write, she fell for him hard. Her reaction to his first attempt as a songwriter was enough to get him hooked on both her and the craft. She became his safe place and his muse.

His creative side was utterly useless to his father, but Susan treasured it. The two got married right after high school, in the summer of 1967. Jack was born ten months later, and Marianne came fourteen months after that. Jerry was not yet twenty years old when their second child was born. Adulthood hit him like a runaway train.

Jerry worked the tobacco fields on his family's farm during the season, then at a local processing plant as he chased a dollar in support of his young family. He had precious little time to pursue music or anything else he enjoyed about life. He could barely even see his babies, and the pressure of poverty and the reality of life was already driving a wedge between Susan and him. Infatuation turned into the worst kind of resentment, and both Jerry and Susan started searching for some kind of escape.

One night, Jerry got home from his second job around eleven o'clock and crept through the back door, removing his work boots and his jacket before tiptoeing across the creaking wood floors. He got himself a beer from the icebox and was trying to make it to his chair in the front room when he heard his baby daughter start to fuss.

Since Susan was already asleep, he went into the baby's room to try to calm her down. She wouldn't respond to his words or his gentle back rub, so he picked her up awkwardly. As he held her and rocked her back and forth, he sang a simple song to her. For several days the ditty had been stuck in his head—taunting him. His distance from music gnawed at him as he worked. But here, in the small hours, in hushed tones, he offered it as a lullaby just for her. It wasn't done yet, but he sang what he had.

Oh sweet Marianne
Breathe it out and breathe it in
Don't be afraid there's nothing to fear
You're not alone
I'm not much, I know
But I'm right here

At the sound of his voice the little girl calmed right down. He sang the simple refrain a few more times, kissed her lightly on the head, and placed her back into her crib. Then he crept back out of the room, sank into his chair, and cracked open his beer. The work he was doing was not enough. The bills were mounting. The farm was struggling. He did not know what to do.

He saw his guitar sitting in the corner and realized it had been weeks since he had even touched it. He both longed for the release that music offered and feared what might happen if the emotions he was barely containing came uncorked. He knew that to be good as a musician would take a significant investment of time and effort, and he had not been able to afford either. He resented that as he sucked down the rest of his beer and exhaled a bitter breath through his teeth. *"I'm not much, but I'm right here,"* he sung to himself disdainfully.

The next day Jerry enlisted in the U.S. Army.

1969

It was possible that because of his family commitments he may have been able to avoid the draft, but there was no guarantee. His father had been pressuring him to enlist for a few years. Although Jerry never sensed that his father even liked him all that much, he sure seemed to want to see him follow in his footsteps. "Serve your country like a man!" was a mantra at the dinner table. And as distant as he felt from his old man, some part of him still felt drawn to earn his respect. Plus the opportunity to learn some new skills that might lead to better work back home was also compelling.

Ultimately, though, his decision was much more practical and immediate. The pay he would receive from the Army would be more consistent than seasonal or shift work. As frightening as the war was, Jerry felt that he had no other choice. Enlisted men were supposed to have much better options than conscripts. After some brief reluctance, Susan agreed.

After an abbreviated boot camp, Jerry shipped out, fresh meat for the grinder of war. He applied to become a medic, because it appealed to his need to be needed and especially because he believed it would somehow keep him out of harm's way. The opposite turned out to be true. Jerry was assigned to a helicopter unit that was sent out to gather up the wounded and dead, sometimes while battles were still underway and shells were still flying.

The jungle ate him alive.

Jerry adapted to the insanity, as most young men did. Although he bonded with the various platoons he was assigned to, he kept to himself. His taste for beer evolved into an increasing need for whisky.

He carried his small camera whenever possible and took photos when he dared. He wrote letters to Susan and the kids and sent home pictures of beautiful vistas, nature, and exotic people—never pictures of the carnage and violence he so frequently encountered. He also leaned hard into music, discovering a much wider world of soul, protest music, and even psychedelic rock and more. Music became his main escape. He started trying to write lyrics, storing his attempts in a leather-backed journal, sharing them with no one.

One afternoon, after his chopper delivered a load of wounded to a medical camp, he and his crew were forced to wait for a while before they returned. He saw an old guitar leaning up against some supply crates. "You mind?" he asked, nodding in the general direction of the beat-up instrument. Its weary owner shrugged.

After an attempt to tune it, he groped out the few chords he remembered and strummed out a simple folk-styled song. A ragged and raw version of "Sweet Marianne" wafted over the wreckage of the pain-soaked field hospital. As wounded soldiers had shrapnel removed from their bodies and limbs amputated, Jerry strummed feebly and sang his simple song. It had a prayer-like feel. Tears formed and then fell, and not just from Jerry's eyes. Something sacred seemed to be happening.

The moment was shattered by radio squawks and rushing men. Another group nearby had just been hit, and Jerry's unit needed to get there fast. He hastily replaced the guitar, threw his helmet back on, and ran to the chopper.

When he and his troops dropped from the chopper to the seemingly abandoned battlefield, they found a large pit, at least ten feet deep, with around a dozen U.S. troops lying in it, dead or dying. The enemy seemed to have set some kind of trap and then dumped these men in the hole. The mission for Jerry's crew was to extract these soldiers out of this pit and load them onto the chopper to be evacuated.

They began the gruesome work, finding a few still alive among the dead. Getting each man out of the hole was difficult and painful. About halfway through the job, the chopper started to receive significant surface fire and had to bug out. Enemy troops were back, closing in from all sides.

Not knowing what else to do, Jerry and his remaining fellow medic, his buddy Sean, jumped down into the pit and buried themselves beneath the dead bodies. Then they waited under the pressing weight of their comrades, the dripping of unidentified blood, and the increasing heat of the day. Pungent smells they had been able to dismiss amidst the distraction of activity now stabbed mercilessly into their sinuses. Nausea and pain wrestled for primacy in their minds.

After about fifteen minutes the Viet Cong soldiers made it to the pit and peered in. Wanting to make sure that all of the soldiers at the bottom were in fact dead, they shot into the pile of bodies, firing hundreds of rounds. Most riddled the bodies of the men already dead.

A dozen or more ripped through Sean and ended his life on the spot. One found its way through one of the bodies Jerry was hiding under, piercing his right thigh. The pain seared, but Jerry remained stone silent and still.

The Viet Cong poured gasoline into the pit before the American troops returned, forcing the enemy's retreat. Jerry lay there in that pile, bleeding and smelling the stinging odor of gasoline, for just under an hour before being rescued. He was evac'd to the same M.A.S.H. unit that had dispatched him. That mission would prove to be Jerry's last as a medic.

After over a week of unconsciousness, fever, and multiple surgeries, he finally woke up to a level of pain, nausea, and confusion he had never experienced before. Between the blood loss, the fume inhalation, and the infection that had set in, the head medic told him it was a miracle Jerry had even survived.

Within minutes he started scanning the area to see if anyone had left a sidearm lying around. He could not imagine living in this kind of hell for another hour. Before his suicidal fantasy could gain a footing, though, someone came by with some more medicine and he was sent back to the Sandman.

His wound would keep him off that leg for months. He was heading home—defeated in more ways than he could comprehend. But not before being introduced to the powerful effects of morphine.

The injury to Jerry's leg was serious, but nothing compared to the damage done to his mind. The muscles and tendons eventually healed, leaving him with a slight limp that would linger for the rest of his life. But the mental trauma was something he could never quite explain to himself or anyone else. And while the morphine was prescribed for the pain in his leg, it also provided a short-term escape from the panic and dread that was his near-constant companion.

"Kind of funny when you think about it," one of his buddies two cots over said one night when none of them could sleep. "They say smack is illegal if we buy it on the street, but when they give it to us here and call it morphine, it's all good."

"This stuff and heroin ain't the same thing," another soldier said. "I tried heroin and it flat took me away. This stuff ain't helping much at all."

"Trust me," the first guy said assuredly. "It's all the same stuff, just different strengths." He pulled out a small plastic bag full of what looked like brown putty. "I just doubt it's gonna be as easy to find this when I get back home."

That guy was from Chicago. Jerry had never heard of heroin, or "smack," being available on the streets of Crossville.

Unfortunately for Jerry, the war wasn't done with him once he got home. Reentry into Tennessee was a slow-motion nightmare. In the two years he had been gone, his babies had grown just enough not to know who in the world he was, and Susan had carved out a survivor's life that had little room for a convalescing veteran. Jerry's relationship with whisky had deepened, darkening his skies and dulling his senses. He spent as little time at home as possible, and when he did walk through his door, it seemed that something always made him lose his temper on a dime. Any last shred of affection Susan had once held for him was long gone. She barely tolerated his presence, mostly wishing he would just leave.

One night around two o'clock, Jerry stumbled home after connecting with another discharged war buddy from the V.A. Loaded on Jack Daniel's and cocaine, Jerry crashed through the back door in a frenzy. He heard the sound of gunfire and chopper blades from somewhere in the darkness. "Cover up, soldier, you're on your own!"

All lines between memory, imagination, and the present were gone. Jerry was in survival mode in his own kitchen. Pain scorched his leg.

Susan was awakened from a deep sleep by the slamming of the kitchen door. As she transitioned between confusion, fear, and anger, she quickly became infuriated with her manic husband. "You're stoned, Jerry!" she screamed. "You're out of your mind! Just get out of here and sleep it off!"

Enraged, Jerry trashed the kitchen as if he was trying to escape a prison camp. He threw over the table, tossed a glass through a window, and slammed a chair up against a wall. Something about that cut through the fog for a split second. What was his guitar doing in a war zone? And when did it get crushed?

"You stay out of this!" he bellowed, pointing a finger in Susan's face and sending spit all over her. "This is all your fault!"

Susan was having none of it. Her adrenaline was fully engaged and she had seen enough. She moved closer, intending to force Jerry to see that this entire disaster was all in his warped, sick mind.

"My fault?!" She stepped right up into Jerry's face. "You bust in here in the middle of the night, high on who knows what, and it's my fault? You get out of here right now!" She moved to push Jerry back toward the door behind him.

Jerry responded defensively, as if Susan was somehow a threat. He shoved her away from himself, across the room, where she landed on the floor, slamming her head against the edge of a cabinet hard enough to draw blood.

But the sight of her on the floor, holding her head with hands smeared red, cut like a knife through the chemical fog that cloaked his brain.

With the babies screaming and crying in fear and Susan threatening to call the police, Jerry stumbled out the back door into the darkness.

His chest heaved with grief so palpable he thought it might kill him. In that moment he would have welcomed death with open arms. His head was on fire. Everything was broken. The sound of that screen door slamming created an echo in his mind.

It was the sound of an M16 in the jungle.

It was the sound of an old tractor backfiring on his father's farm.

It was the sound of the screen door of his childhood home being slammed by his old man.

It was the brutal sound of being smacked upside the head.

How could he have become this messed up? Jerry wandered into his neighbor's field. He collapsed into the dirt, wept, retched, vomited, and wept some more. Eventually he lost consciousness in the mud.

The next morning Jerry woke up in the mud, bitterly disappointed that he could remember everything. He found a pump and hose to roughly clean up with and then made his way back to his car. As he drove to his parents' house, his mind recalibrated. He found a way to frame the story that, while still unpleasant, felt more like a misunderstanding and an overreaction.

He would apologize profusely to Susan, of course, and promise it would never happen again. But he knew it was too late. Even through the intoxicated fog, he could see it in her eyes—a look he had never seen in his own mother's eyes.

Susan had had enough. Some kind of instinct to protect herself and her children had kicked in, and he was dead to her.

By telling himself that earning her forgiveness was hopeless, he believed that he was saving himself a whole lot of trouble.

Susan filed for divorce that day.

Jerry had picked up a few skills in the Army as both a technician and as a driver, and he found ways to put those skills to use in the greater Crossville area. He had also learned how to pace his drinking so he could still wake up in time to make it to his job. His tight finances forced him to move back into his parents' house. He settled into a sad routine that allowed him to earn enough money for his own meager expenses and send the rest to Susan and the kids every other week.

It took him about three years to dial in the coping skills of a functional alcoholic. Then he decided it was time to explore Nashville, where there were more opportunities for work (and for drinking). An old Army buddy turned him on to a gig with a trucking company that paid pretty good money to guys who could work on big engines.

Susan didn't want him to see the kids, and he knew he was in no condition to be a dad, so in 1975 Jerry moved to East Nashville. Nashville offered new scenery and relative anonymity. Plus, it was Music City, after all. Though he hadn't sung a note since that day in Vietnam and hadn't touched a guitar since the night he destroyed his own in the kitchen, he still told himself that he was some kind of a musician.

Jerry found a small, run-down house on Boscobel Street to rent for a hundred and fifty dollars a month and sublet one of the bedrooms to another guy from the shop. He put a blue, vinyl-covered bench seat from a 1970 Ford Econoline van on the front porch and used it as a sort of couch. His furniture consisted of an old record player, an overstuffed and threadbare recliner, a small Formica dining table, two chairs, and a bed. The house had no air-conditioning and used a wood-burning stove for heat in the winter. It was a nice enough neighborhood, full of eclectic houses, rolling hills, and lots of trees.

Most of the White folks were leaving, or had left, because of the increasing presence of minorities and rumors of rising crime rates. Jerry didn't care about all that, and anyway, he had nothing worth stealing. He pretty much did his job each day and then came home to drink, listen to records, and look at old pictures before he passed out. Some nights he slept out on the porch on the van seat; some nights he even made it to his bed. Folks said the outlaw Jesse James had once lived in a house a few doors down. Jerry liked the thought of that.

Jerry also liked to take his breakfast at the diner just a few blocks away. The staff knew him when he walked in, and his normal plate was often sitting in front of him within a few minutes. The smell that hit his brain when he walked in the door was the closest thing to a smell of home that he knew. He couldn't afford to eat there every day, but you could find Jerry at the Knife and Fork at least a few times a week.

1978

Jerry's then-roommate Bruce occasionally played guitar, especially when that occasion involved drinking. One Friday night after work, he brought a couple friends over to the house, and a very loose and highly lubricated jam session broke out on the front porch. The booze was flowing and everyone involved, including Jerry, sounded much better in their minds than they sounded to anyone unfortunate enough to be subject to the caterwauling. The grimy band of drunk mechanics butchered songs by Neil Young, Bob Dylan, Gram Parsons, and Johnny Cash until the wee hours of the morning.

Jerry, all shyness long surrendered to Old No. 7, perched his best sunglasses on his nose, a ragged trucker cap on his head, and proceeded to do his best Merle Haggard impersonation for the crew before passing out right in the middle of "I'm A Good Loser." He didn't fall over, though. He simply stopped singing, balanced perfectly where he sat, with his mouth hanging open about half an inch.

"Is he alive?" Bruce asked, half urgently, half laughing. Once they confirmed that he was, in fact, still breathing, the gang burst out into laughter and continued the song without him.

Late the next morning Jerry was still out on the porch, sitting in the exact same position, mouth still agape, sunglasses on his nose. Everyone else was gone, but Jerry had kept an unconscious vigil over his front porch and yard, his mouth and throat bone dry and his day about to start off in a very strange way.

Out on Boscobel Street, two long-haired "hippie types" were walking purposefully through the neighborhood. From a distance, you couldn't tell that one was a girl and one a guy, but the beard on the person on the right was a dead giveaway once they got close. Their bell-bottom jeans, frayed T-shirts, and fringe jackets made it clear these two were from the counter-culture. In this East Nashville working-class neighborhood, these kids stuck out like sore thumbs. If Jerry had been conscious, he would have seen them coming a block away and would have gone inside to avoid them. As they strolled along from door to door passing out flyers, they noticed Jerry sitting on the porch and assumed he was awake.

"Good morning!" the young man said. "My name's Glenn Kaiser, and this is my wife, Wendi, and we're in a group called Resurrection Band. We're going to be playing a concert down in the park later on this afternoon and would love to have you come hear us. Are you a music fan?"

Somewhere through the fog in Jerry's mind, he started to hear voices. Now, that was nothing new, but these voices were friendly and enthusiastic. As consciousness slowly and brutally forced its way across his brain, he realized that this was no dream. It was time to open his eyes and figure out where he was. It was quite a surprise, once his pupils adjusted, to see these two widely smiling youngsters sitting on the railing of his front porch, talking directly to him. How long had they been here? That boy just went on and on. Jerry had no idea who he was or where he had come from. They seemed not to know that the object of their conversation had been asleep until now.

"…And man, that's just the thing about Jesus," the fellow said. "It's not about religion or rules or anything like that at all. It's about a personal relationship, and man, that relationship totally changed my life! So we have all these songs, and we're going to be playing some pretty loud rock and roll down there at the park with some friends of ours. We'd sure love it if you'd come listen. What did you say your name is, Brother?"

Jerry, completely flummoxed by the conflicting image of a long-haired hippie freak literally in his face talking about Jesus, began to offer his name, but due to his parched vocal cords, when he tried to speak, nothing came out but a sad, slightly terrifying wheeze.

The young girl backed away a step or two. Glenn's eyes got a bit bigger. "Are you okay, man?"

"Water," Jerry coughed.

Wendi offered a sip from a metal canteen, the kind Jerry used to carry in the war, and he sucked it down. It started to dawn on her that they had just woken something like a hungover sleeping bear.

"Thanks." Jerry passed the water back to her. "I gotta go inside. Not feeling well. Good luck to you guys."

"Sure thing," Glenn said. "But hey, can we leave you a copy of our record? Maybe you can listen to it later. If you dig it, you can come down to the park and hear us play."

With that, the kind-faced kid set a copy of the LP inside Jerry's front door and turned to go.

"I didn't get your name, Brother, but we'll be praying for you. Jesus loves you!"

Jerry stumbled through his house, filled a tall glass with water from the tap to chase down four aspirin, and then fell on his back on his bed.

"What the hell was that?" he asked no one and then fell back to sleep.

About three hours later Jerry woke up again, still nursing a nasty head-ache. Was the cheerful Jesus-hippie incident all a dream? But when he made his way to his chair in the front room, he saw the record leaning up against the wall next to the front door. "Son of a gun," he muttered.

He picked it up and looked it over. It was colorful, that was for sure. He went ahead and pulled the record out of the sleeve and put in on his turntable. He set the needle down, with little care, and turned the player on. Those kids could definitely rock. The music was heavy—like the stuff he had listened to in Vietnam. It had elements of Jefferson Airplane and Cream. But the songs were clearly about the kind of crazy Jesus stuff the smiling kids had been talking about when Jerry was still half asleep.

He sat there in his chair and let it play. He had no idea what to make of it. This was not the kind of religion he had heard about in church back in Crossville. That kid Glenn looked to be about his age.

One lyric in a very Zeppelin-like song really caught his attention.

> *But all along I realized*
> *That if I had to choose between love and my old sweet lies*
> *Love was bound to lose*

That one gave him chills. It made him think of Susan and his kids. His old photo album was leaning up against some other records, and it seemed to call to him, but he knew better than to open it up. He thought about music and what he thought his life would be like when he was a boy. Maybe he could have been a songwriter or an artist. Maybe a farmer. He remem-bered when he was sure he would be a family man, or maybe someone who would make a difference in the world. He remembered thinking that he would be different than his old man. But that was a door best kept closed. Whenever he started thinking about things like that, bodies and bullets weren't far behind. He'd listen to the rest of this record later. It was time to go out and get something to drink.

1980

Eventually Jerry transitioned from mechanic to driver. First it was trucks, then buses. Nashville, it turned out, had a ravenous need for tour bus drivers in the late seventies. Jerry became a favorite of several major acts. Stories spread of his ability to both drive the bus all night and to fix it when it broke down. (And buses always broke down at some point.)

By the time he turned thirty years old, as the 1970s were making way for a new decade, Jerry had grown thoroughly fed up with his own existence. He would drive the bus all night, usually rolling out from some kind of venue around midnight and driving until eight or nine in the morning. Then he would find something to eat, go to his hotel room, black out the windows as best he could, drink a pint of vodka, and go to sleep. He was lonely. He was miserable. He was good at what he did, and the bits of pleasure he found in life were clearly connected to his work, but those moments were few and far between.

Susan had remarried and wanted nothing to do with him. His kids were nearly eleven and twelve, and they seemed to wish he had never existed. He sent cards for birthdays and Christmas, maybe an occasional gift, but never heard back. He continued to send as much money as he could and asked Susan to use it wherever it was needed.

Some mornings, in the hour when the liquor started to flow but before sleep came, he thought about taking his own life—just ending it all. He still had nightmares about that pit in the jungle.

He drove all kinds of musicians on his bus. From Southern Gospel groups to big-time country acts—even famous rock bands—he'd seen them all. At first, he was surprised at how listless some of them appeared after their shows. They really didn't seem to enjoy what they were doing, either. He also found it almost humorous that some of the craziest rock-and-roll bands were really rather conservative, eating health food and drinking nothing but fruit juice, while some of the most religious groups were the wildest out there. He started to think that for most performers, everything was part of the act.

Jerry had developed pretty well-defined musical tastes, though—that many hours of "windshield time" allowed for lots of listening. He studied the greats in several genres; the best songwriters, the best instrumentalists, the best singers. He liked to think he had a good ear. He noticed that what he thought of as the best music seldom got to be the most popular. He had some theories on why that might be.

One night as he was driving a heavy metal band from Chicago to Cleveland, he couldn't help overhearing a few of them when they gathered toward the front of the bus for what he soon realized was a recovery support meeting. Jerry had never been to a twelve-step group, but he'd seen a few on TV. These guys were serious. They greeted each other by name, even though it was obvious they had known each other for years and had been together all day.

"Good evening, brothers," one of them said, somehow with both a playful and serious tone in his voice at the same time.

Jerry snuck a peek in his mirror and saw that it was the bass player. He was pretty sure his stage name was "Cheese," but he introduced himself by his given name. "My name is Tommy and I'm an alcoholic and a drug addict." The other members nodded, patted him on the back, and one even snapped a towel at him.

"I haven't had a drink or any drugs in six months as of midnight tonight," Tommy said. With that he got a rousing bit of encouragement, applause, and sweaty hugs. "I gotta say," Tommy continued, "I never thought I'd make it. And if I wasn't out here with you old ladies, I probably wouldn't!"

More joshing commenced, and Jerry noticed that even though their spirits were light, Tommy's eyes were wet. Jerry stared straight ahead and wished to God he had some headphones to drown this out.

"Well, bro," the lead singer, Mike (who the fans called Knife), said as he stood in the aisle of the bus, gradually getting everyone's attention and causing the easily riled-up group of kids to calm back down. "As it is your official six-month anniversary and I am your sponsor, I am super stoked to give you this fresh six-month sobriety chip!" He pressed a dark-blue poker chip into Tommy's left hand and gave him another hug, as did everyone else. "You got anything you wanna share?"

"Yeah," Tommy said, as they all calmed back down again. He took a swig from his water bottle, wiped his face with the towel that hung around his shoulders, and seemed to steel himself for the words to come.

Jerry didn't even have to look in the mirror to feel the intensity of the bus change.

Tommy took a deep breath, then exhaled through lips puckered so tightly he almost whistled. "I feel like I almost lost it today. From the minute I woke up I just felt like shit. My head hurt, my body hurt, and I was just tired of being in my life."

The others nodded quietly. They all knew what he meant.

"I know you could tell I wasn't feeling it during sound check," Tommy continued. "I'm sorry I was snapping at you guys, but man, I could not stop thinking about my little girl and my ex and all the stuff I left back there in LA. And as soon as I start thinking about that, I start blaming her for taking Sissy away from me, and I blame her parents for poisoning our relationship, and then I start blaming my parents for making me feel like a loser and making me want to get high all the time. And before I know it, I am seriously thinking that I just need to 'go for a walk,' you know?"

They all nodded and agreed. They knew what he meant. They had all wanted to "go for a walk" or to "get some air" several times a day, but they all knew that every walk away from their little unit of accountability was a walk toward a dealer somewhere or a groupie with a flask.

"I started to feel like I was going to have a panic attack at dinner time," he continued. "All I could think about was my little girl. Her face was like, right here!"

Jerry was gripping the wheel far too tightly now. He so wished he could leave.

"I started to imagine feeling like that for the next thirty years, or even thirty minutes, and I decided I couldn't do it. I needed a little break. Just to get my head right. But right then you saw me." He pointed up at Mike, who was looking down at him like a little brother. "You saw it all in my face and asked if we could take a walk together. You didn't get in my face or nothing. You just hung out there with me. We shot some hoops!" They both chuckled a little bit.

"And then you asked me about Sissy. You asked me what kind of person I thought she might be when she grew up. That got my mind off my own crap just long enough to realize that I was about to do it again. I was spinning out. We talked about her—and about beautiful things. Man…" Tommy started to break down in tears. His bandmates—obviously his brothers—encouraged him to let the tears come. "It's cool, man," someone said. Jerry could not believe that this was some scary heavy metal band.

Tommy continued, with a bit of a sulk in his voice but a clear sense of victory as well. "So I did my breathing. I said my prayer. I told you what I was thinking. And I decided not to give in today." The clapping started again.

"One day at a time, dude," Mike said. "One damn day at a time."

Tommy was still wiping his eyes and blowing his nose. All Jerry could think about were his kids, and Susan. What if he had found a group like this back there in Vietnam or back in Crossville? He'd heard of this recovery stuff. He'd just never thought about it. But every second he sat there, he got more and more agitated. He didn't even want to imagine a life without liquor. But a worm was in his head now, eating away at what was left of his consciousness. These kids were beating back demons that Jerry had allowed to crawl all over himself. And he wasn't the only one suffering. His family had paid the price.

He spent the rest of that drive trying to decide between death or giving in to this voice in his head that seemed to be calling to him more and more.

The other members started talking about what their abuse of drugs and alcohol had cost them. Jerry's face got hot, and the lines on the road started to blur through tears. He blinked them away.

In many ways Jerry was right back in the jungle, on that surgical table, coming in and out of consciousness every day. He was medicating the pain, but the medication wasn't working. He was scanning the M.A.S.H. tent for a revolver. He started to realize that he could just end it now if he wanted to. He was pretty sure no one would miss him. He was just a broken, useless mess. Maybe it was time.

But as he heard these kids tell their stories, something started to awaken in him. They were so young and had screwed things up just like he had, but they were finding a way forward. He had never heard men be as transparent about their secret thoughts. It shocked him way more than any partying rock stars ever had. As they talked about their parents, their fears, and the things that set them off, Jerry wanted to climb out the window of that bus. He was disgusted by the whole thing. But on another level he wanted that kind of freedom for himself.

The band members closed their gathering by reminding each other of the twelve steps to sobriety to which they had each committed, and they renewed their promise to support each other. Those steps sounded pretty sensible to Jerry. He was a fixer, and though nothing in him wanted to admit that his life was broken and in need of repair, something about the logic of that plan sounded right.

He hated it.

Then one of the musicians put a cassette in the tape deck and the speaker on the tape shared tips and strategies about the value and power of personal honesty while the drummer stumbled toward the front of the bus to use a mirror to remove his stage makeup. The whole thing made Jerry uncomfortable. If he hadn't had his hands on an oversized and very important steering wheel, he would have excused himself. But he couldn't un-hear what he had heard.

The next morning, while he was checking into his motel room in Cleveland, Jerry noticed a small flyer hanging on the bulletin board.

Recovery Support Group
Weekdays 8am and 8pm
Next Door at St. Mark's Church

That morning, April 5, 1980, Jerry James Wesley admitted to himself and to the world, for the first time out loud, that he was an alcoholic who was powerless to help himself. Though he made sure that the three older gentlemen and one woman at the meeting understood that he was in no way ready to sign up under one particular version or understanding of God, he was willing to accept that somewhere there was a God and that it was not him. He would lean on whoever God was as he started this journey. Jerry hadn't prayed since Vietnam, and he wasn't sure that the words that fell from his mouth next counted as much of a prayer, anyway. But he meant them from the bottom of his broken heart.

"God, help."

1990

The most challenging aspect of recovery for Jerry was the lack of experience he had with people. He wasn't used to having close friends. He was no good at sharing his feelings and thoughts. He struggled at first, and though no one would likely ever refer to him as the gregarious type, he could be a good listener, and it was nice to be known by a few folks. He even found himself darkening the door of a church in town on a regular basis. One of the artists he had driven for had invited him one Sunday, and he didn't hate it as much as he had expected to. When one of the church leaders asked for his help with some electrical problems they were having at the soundboard, though, he was hooked.

Sober Jerry's new "drug" was the feeling of being needed.

The folks in that nondenominational church needed him, he figured, so he'd keep coming around. He fixed whatever was broken. Since the church met in an old theater, something was always broken.

Something had gnawed at Jerry during his first decade of sobriety and beyond. A big part of the twelve-step program that had helped him get—and stay—sober focused on making a "fearless moral inventory" of himself. Extended sobriety had opened his eyes to the pain he had caused Susan and, no doubt, his kids. Marianne and Jack had been teenagers in the late 1980s, and they had never responded to his gifts or letters. Jerry assumed they hated him, and he couldn't really blame them.

All he could think of was the way he had deserted them.

He had long told himself that he had left for their good—that he was unfit and his behavior that night twenty-one years ago was proof that they were better off without him. But with some extended time of reflection and the benefit of learning from other people's stories, he started to see that he had taken the easy way out. Instead of apologizing, in all sincerity, for causing Susan's injury that terrible night, admitting to himself and everyone else that he had a problem, and then dealing with that problem, he had left her and the kids to fend for themselves.

Sure, he had sent some money, but that meant little compared to what his family had needed: for him to man up. He just hadn't had it in him to do that back then, and now it was too late.

His shame and failure weighed on him as if it had just happened yesterday. When he'd tried to reach out to Susan to sincerely apologize yet again, he was rebuffed with a stinging letter that insisted he never reach out again.

"If you've stopped drinking, that's fine," she wrote. "But we have moved on and it's been hard. The best thing you can do for us is to stay away!"

Jerry couldn't—and wouldn't—argue with her bitterness. But it left him unable to fully complete the eighth and ninth steps.

Step 8: Make a list of all persons we have harmed and become willing to make amends to them all.

Step 9:   Make direct amends to such people wherever possible, except when to do so would injure them or others.

He longed to let his kids know how sorry he was not to have been a part of their lives. He was stuck.

Jerry continued to drive tour buses throughout the 90s. He got several jobs driving for artists in the newly popular "Christian rock" world, which he found rather interesting. He wanted to like the music more than he did. It had some decent moments, and a few of the artists piqued his curiosity. Most of those involved with it, from the stars on down, were good folks. With a couple of notable exceptions, he enjoyed driving for Christian artists. Still, he was glad to find out that most of them listened to "normal" music on the bus.

In 1993, he was shocked to run into one of the Christian artists he had recently driven for at an AA meeting. Afterward, the two agreed to get together for coffee at a diner near a spot where many of the tour buses would load and unload. The kid's name was Kyle, and with several songs playing on Christian radio he had a lot to lose if word got out that he had a drinking problem. He seemed downright terrified to have seen Jerry at that meeting, and Jerry was determined to put his mind at ease. He motioned him to a small booth near the back of the diner, and they seated themselves.

"I guess I'm glad for the 'anonymous' part of AA," Kyle stammered as he looked sheepishly at Jerry. "I mean, I'm really glad to see that you're at a meeting, man. But I just tried to choose one I thought no one would know me at. Dang, Nashville is a small town!"

"Look," Jerry said in the calmest, quietest, Crossville accent anyone has ever heard, "you do *not* have to worry about me. I don't understand why you have to be so secretive, but I see that you do. Heck, when I tell people I'm a recovering alcoholic I get pats on the back and congratulations. Folks buy me sweet tea! In your world you have to act like you're perfect. That's a burden I'm glad I don't have to bear, and I wish you didn't have to. I think it might make staying between the lines that much harder for you.

"Here." Jerry slipped Kyle a piece of paper. "This is my phone number and my address over in East Nashville. If you ever feel tempted or frustrated or you just need to vent, call me—any time. And if you're out and about and need to go somewhere safe, come on over. I promise you." He smiled. "I haven't seen anyone that looks like a Christian music fan in my neighborhood in the two decades I've lived there. They're terrified of the 'transitioning'!" He laughed, using mock air quotes.

"Seriously," Jerry added, "if I'm not there, you can find a key under the cement cat by the back door. Just let yourself in, make yourself some tea, and put on a record or something. What you're doing here is hard work, but you can do it. There's nothing to be ashamed of, son. You've got a long life ahead of you. How old are you, anyway?"

"Twenty-one," Kyle said, noticeably more relaxed than when the two had first sat down.

"Shit! When I was twenty-one, I had two babies and was getting loaded in Southeast Asia. My problems were just taking root. You're way ahead of the game here, Kyle. You've got this."

It occurred to Jerry in that moment that his son, Jack, was just a bit older than Kyle. Did Jack wrestle with addiction? Did he have people in his life who he could talk to like this? Was he alone like this kid? If he was, Jerry was sure it was his fault.

Kyle exhaled deeply and looked into Jerry's eyes with genuine relief. "Thanks, man. You have no idea how much that means to me. This whole thing is terrifying. Church is hard. It feels like there's no one I can be honest with there. I can't go very often now that I'm on the road so much. My parents have no idea. And every night I get up in front of thousands of people and sing these songs that I absolutely believe in—about how good God is—for people that I suspect would run me out of the building on a rail if they knew I was a drunk. And God help me if they ever found out about my pornography problem!"

Jerry's eyes bugged a little. He wasn't ready for that one, but he recovered. "I don't know what to say about all that," he offered lamely. "I've never been much of a religious person, and I have no patience for hypocrites, especially myself. But I guess it's kinda like your family, and if that's your family and that's who you're here to serve, then you gotta serve them as best you can. I've driven plenty of country singers who hate country music, but they sing those songs every night. I guess they give the audience what it wants. It'd sure be nice if we could all just be real, though, wouldn't it?"

Jerry allowed the waitress to refill his coffee and took a careful sip. "But my offer stands. You call anytime."

Kyle did call. Often. In fact, he darn near made Jerry his exclusive driver whenever he could. On those rare occasions that Kyle met other artists in recovery, he told them about his secret weapon on the road: the bus-driving twelve-step partner who could fix anything. Jerry loved offering that kind of support to these young folks. It helped him on his journey, too. No number of these Nashville kids could make up for his own children, but he'd help as many as he could.

At some point in the eighties Jerry had been able to switch from renting his little house on Boscobel to buying it. It was still nothing fancy, but over the years he had fixed it up pretty nicely. Plus, it was darn cheap. The important stuff worked well. He kept it clean and decorated it in an understated style. He stashed the van seat in the garage out back and got a proper swing for the porch. He kept that old record player working, too. He replaced the threadbare recliner with a slightly less worn—but still second-hand—chair that could have been its twin. He couldn't seem to let loose of the old chair. He dragged it out to the porch and covered it with an old blanket. It was mostly out of the rain, at least.

Jerry's record collection grew slowly, as did his collection of photos, the best of which made it into the beat-up photo album that sat on the coffee table in the front room. Kyle, in particular, loved to flip through those old pictures. So Jerry had started just leaving the book out for him. He still had the old camera he had carried around Southeast Asia. He used it to take interesting pictures on the road. There were still plenty of buildings, vehicles, equipment, and people who were out of their element, in need of repair, or in some kind of precarious condition.

One night in the mid-nineties, when Jerry had just come off a particularly long tour with Kyle and his band, he walked into his little home, fixed a glass of tea, and went to his record collection. Thumbing through it he went deeper into the stacks until he found the record from those smiling hippies he remembered from all those years ago—Glenn and Wendi Kaiser, and that group called Resurrection Band. He wondered what had happened to them.

He pulled the album out and put it on the old turntable. It was called *Awaiting Your Reply*. As the seventies classic rock came pouring forth, he sipped his tea and listened, deeply. He smiled. As for that proposition in the lyrics—the choice between love and the old lies that used to run his life—he was pretty sure he'd make a different choice now than he would have then. He felt good about that. He wished he had made the walk down to the park that day to see their band instead of walking the other direction to the bar.

Just as Jerry drifted full off into the music, someone made an abrupt knock on his front door. It startled him enough to spill a bit of his tea on his shirt. He got up, wiped himself off, and made his way to the door. There on the porch was Kyle.

"Three months wasn't enough?" Jerry joked. "You need some more? Come on in."

"Actually, I have something that I forgot to give you when we unloaded the bus. I found it when we were in New York."

He pulled out a smallish acoustic guitar case and handed it to Jerry. "I heard you messing around with one of my guitars one night before sound check, and I remember you mentioning that you used to play. I checked and this little Martin will fit right up in the storage shelf over your head on the bus. You can bring it with you whenever you drive and then play when you have a break. Anyway, it seems you had something taken away from you back then, and I wanted to try to give it back."

Jerry was speechless. He took the guitar out of the case and strummed it a few times. It was old but solid. It had some definite wear on it but great tone. Jerry had been around music and musicians enough to know that an old Martin was something special.

"It's from the early sixties I think," Kyle said. "Maybe even older, I don't know. But I saw it, played it, and it just sang out to be yours. It's got a lot of music left in it."

"I don't know what to say. It's beautiful. It's perfect."

"She's yours!" Kyle beamed. "Now get to know her." He gave Jerry a meaningful hug and then turned for the door before either man could see the other's tears.

1998

Jerry spent the rest of the nineties driving tour buses, fixing things at the local aspiring megachurch, and encouraging young artists in their recovery. But as the church became more political, Jerry became less and less interested in Sundays. He stuck around, though. When they put out the word that someone needed help moving, Jerry would usually be one of the first to volunteer. He was on the road a lot, but he had cultivated a special kind of friendship with artists in recovery from addiction. He even took a couple of support classes at an East Nashville Community Center in order to be a better sponsor. He read books on theology, spiritual formation, and general wellness.

He often had a guest or two crashing in the guest room of his little house on Boscobel. Kyle often referred folks who were new to town to Jerry. It was helpful for him to have roommates so the house was occupied when he was on the road, if nothing else. East Nashville had gone through quite a shift since he'd moved there back in the mid-seventies. Back in the eighties the general opinion was that the neighborhood had taken a dive, and in the nineties crime rates continued to rise and property values continued to fall, which seemed to be the only way people considered the value of a community.

By the mid-nineties, it felt to Jerry like he was one of the few White guys left on his street. He didn't think of himself as a racist, of course, and when he was on the road, he was very comfortable with folks of all ethnicities. He had become quite a fan of Gospel music over the years, too. But there, on his own street, he still pretty much kept to himself. He couldn't tell you the names of any of his Black neighbors and tended to cross the other side of the street when he saw a group of Black teens or even children on the street.

His community was a fascinating example of tacit segregation. The races often self-segregated into their own restaurants, grocery stores, and even parks. He rarely saw a Black face at his diner, for instance, unless it was one of the workers. Once he decided to go to a movie at a theater north of downtown Nashville only to discover after he got there that it was now frequented by a predominantly African American crowd. He never went back. It wasn't a conscious decision not to. He just never thought about it.

By 1998 Jerry had lived in the same house for nearly a quarter of a century and still knew almost none of his neighbors. It had never even occurred to him to introduce himself. Though there were several predominantly Black churches within walking distance of his house, he still drove across two bridges to get to the church he attended and to visit friends around town. He even attended recovery meetings a couple miles away. He just never thought much about his neighborhood. It was just the place where his house sat.

That changed on April 16, 1998. Jerry happened to be at home because most of the bands he had been driving were in Nashville for a big Gospel music convention. Never much of a TV watcher, he had been enjoying the off day by listening to records and playing his guitar when suddenly, and with almost no warning, the skies grew dark and he started to hear screaming and panic in the street.

In a matter of minutes, several tornadoes tore through his neighborhood, ripping off roofs, destroying one church, yanking trees from the ground, and filling the streets with broken glass, splintered wood, and twisted metal.

Jerry was absolutely unprepared for a tragedy that day. But in a matter of seconds his mind went from peaceful and relaxed to full-blown panic. As the wind picked up and the trees bent, he saw debris flying through the air. Something yellow, maybe a kid's playhouse, flew down the street about four feet off the ground.

Jerry's fight-or-flight instincts kicked in and it was like he was back in Vietnam. He didn't even have time for his rational mind to catch up to his reactions. He would not have been able to tell if he was hiding from incoming mortar fire or an act of nature—he was simply trying to survive. The sound was deafening. As if a Huey had landed in his living room.

When the storm ripped through, Jerry barely had time to lie down on his bathroom floor, and when it was done he came out to find a couple of broken windows, a decent amount of dirt and gravel in his living room, most of someone's magnolia tree on his front porch, and a tree lying across his car. In the aftermath Jerry joined his neighbors as they walked the streets, dumbfounded by the destruction. He had gotten off easy. People two doors down had lost most of their home. The folks across the street had lost their entire roof. The convenience store down on the corner was devastated.

Another storm blew through a couple hours later, as if to add insult to injury. News reports were declaring it one of the worst disasters in Nashville history. One young man later died from injuries he had sustained during the storm at a park across town.

After the second storm had passed, Jerry took just a minute or two to breathe and regain control of his heart rate and his emotional state. He walked down the street to see if he could help anyone. Just two doors down he met Lamont, a Black man he had seen countless times, even done the casual wave and smile on the street, but had never spoken to.

"Everyone okay here?" Jerry asked Lamont.

"Don't know where my dog is," Lamont said, unable to hide the break in his voice. "Wife's all broken up. She's sitting inside, but she ain't hurt. We lost almost everything."

Lamont was in shock. Jerry wasn't sure what to do, but he felt he needed to do something.

"I just lost a couple windows. Why don't we get your wife over to my place? We can set her up there with some tea or something, and then you and I can look for your dog and whatever of your stuff we can salvage. You guys can stay at my house tonight if you want."

The words came out of his mouth because they needed to be said, but part of Jerry was surprised that he was saying them.

"You serious?" Lamont asked. "Thanks, man. I'll go get her. She's a mess."

Lamont emerged from the wreckage of what had been their home with his wife, Gina, wrapped in a blanket, sobbing. Jerry walked them over to his house. Once in the door he swept the debris off his couch and from the floor around it and had her sit down. He went to the kitchen to fix her some tea, only to find out that the electricity was dead.

"I'm afraid all I can offer is some lukewarm sweet tea or some water," he apologized.

"She likes sweet tea," Lamont suggested. Gina still hadn't spoken.

Lamont helped Jerry tape some plastic over the broken windows and clean up the broken glass. He put some crackers and cheese out for Gina in case she got hungry and gave her a battery-operated radio to listen to.

"We're going to go look for your dog and any of your valuables we can salvage," Jerry told her quietly. "We're just over there if you need anything. Just holler. We'll hear you."

Gina nodded, offered a pained smile, and took her tea. She saw the photo album on the now-dusty coffee table and opened the cover absentmindedly.

Jerry and Lamont did eventually find their mixed-breed pit bull, Chelsea, but many in the neighborhood did not. Lost dog flyers were ubiquitous. They were all almost the same. A picture, with the dog's name, "Answers to

Junior," and then ten or twelve little pre-torn tabs along the bottom edge with the owner's phone number on them.

Lamont and Gina managed to salvage about four plastic tubs' worth of valuables. They were renters, so after two days with Jerry they were off to find a new place. The impact on Jerry was profound, though. He kept searching for more people to help. He got his house fixed up as quickly as possible and then kept offering it to neighbors who needed a place to stay. After twenty-three years, it had taken a nightmarish tornado to bring him closer to his neighborhood. Though some folks had left, the ones who stayed felt a new kind of bond.

Jerry had just gotten his first cell phone, and soon he had dozens of new friends' phone numbers programmed into it. East Nashville, a neighborhood known for crime and poverty, had received a near fatal blow from Mother Nature. If that blow had been meant for evil, however, it had backfired. Jerry had never felt more connected to his neighborhood or his neighbors.

In the process of helping people fix their roofs and their windows—and even a couple of cars—Jerry started to hear their stories. While helping one neighbor repair his garage roof, he noticed boxes of old soul, R & B, and blues records.

"What this?" he asked. "What are these doing out here collecting dust?"

His neighbor, a sharply dressed, older Black gentleman named George White, lit up when Jerry noticed his vinyl.

"Those? Oh, those are my old records. I haven't had a record player in decades. I don't even know if these will still play."

"I bet they will," Jerry insisted. "Come help me with something."

The pair walked over to Jerry's, picked up his record player, and carried it back to George's driveway, placing it carefully in the shade. They ran an extension cord to it and fired it up. Jerry started flipping through the records until he found the perfect candidate. The smooth sounds of Marvin Gaye's "What's Going On" were soon serenading the men as they worked. Neighbors were smiling and grooving as they walked by. One friend of George's looked like he wanted to join in.

The tornadoes of 1998 transformed East Nashville in numerous ways. Some said it was the influx of all that insurance money. Some said it was the dive in property values that summoned poor artists looking to start a sort of colony. Others said the neighborly spirit that gripped the area was so powerful that it acted as a sort of beacon. People wanted to be a part of that kind of caring and enthusiastic community. Whatever the reason, in just a few years East Nashville went from being a "no man's land" to being thought of by many as one of the coolest places in the country. Jerry was a part of that. But he did not understand it at all.

Throughout the 2000s, as the dust settled from those storms, Jerry continually felt himself drawn to help people. He started going out of his way to find places to volunteer. His introverted nature never changed, but his heart for his neighbors definitely did. He became much more intentional about meeting folks when they moved onto his street. He started attending recovery meetings at the Black Baptist church right near his house instead of the Community Center two miles away.

He also played his guitar. A lot. Although he never played in front of people, he kept it with him. When he was driving, it rode just above his head and he ended every day with an hour or more of practice. When he was home, he spent more than an hour a day playing. He played along with records by Ry Cooder, Eric Clapton, Stevie Wonder, Sting, John Prine, and Santana, as well as some younger artists.

Comparing himself to the best musicians in the world as he played along made Jerry feel like he was never quite good enough. But he had no idea just how skilled a musician he was becoming. This old dog was learning something new.

Jerry also began writing letters to his son and daughter once a month. Even if they never read them and if they never replied, he was determined to do anything he could to break through the wall he had built.

What Happened on Boscobel?

Present Day

Jerry was startled out of his reminiscing by a familiar voice. Brother Louis. Of course, everyone in town called him that, but over the last year Jerry had come to feel that this man, with skin of a very different color, was every bit his family.

"Good afternoon, Brother!" Louis called, as he strode up the walkway from the street. He could see Jerry up on the porch, but due to a trick of the midday shadows had not seen Marisol sitting there until he got closer.

"Well hello," he said to her.

"Hello, Mr. Williams." Marisol rose to her feet. "It is such an honor to finally meet you."

"Marisol here is a *blogger*," Jerry offered as Louis got to the bottom of the steps. "She's a friend of Alex's and is working on a story about us. I just got done boring her to death with much more detail than I imagine she ever wanted to hear about an old fart like me."

"By no means," Marisol insisted. "I'm so glad we had the time."

Jerry greeted Louis with a warm hug and a somewhat-weary smile.

"A lot has happened this year, hasn't it, my friend?" Louis returned the smile, leaving a hand on Jerry's shoulder as he looked toward Marisol. "I've been on this planet a long time, and I don't think I can think of a more eventful year in my life than this one."

Jerry nodded. "I'm not sure where we go from here. But I'll tell you this much. I wouldn't change a thing. If all this happened just so you and me could get to know each other, that'd be enough."

It was hard for Jerry to say those kinds of things. But he was getting better at it.

They both noticed the sound of Los Lobos' "Kiko and the Lavender Moon" blaring from some car speakers pulling up. Cesar had arrived. They stepped toward the street in time to see their favorite old Mexican getting out of a freshly vandalized F-150 pickup truck.

"Cesar!" Jerry waved. "You liking that Los Lobos record?"

"*Sí!* Very interesting. Good accordion. Good singing. I like them very much. Some songs are kind of strange, but even those are good."

"I figured the way you latched on to 'The Neighborhood,' you'd find plenty to love with those guys," Jerry added. "I wish I could say your truck looked better in the daylight than it did last night."

Cesar waved it off. "Ain't no thing. I've already had a couple of different people offer to help clean up the paint, and Nadia connected me with a guy who took care of the tires."

Marisol was curious about the story behind the vandalism. She suspected she'd get her answer soon enough.

Louis greeted Cesar with a hug and walked him the rest of the way to the porch. He looked a touch more chic than usual, with a new cream-colored linen guayabera-style shirt and black slacks. His sunglasses sat regally on his nose and a straw Panama hat perched on his head.

Catching the inquisitive expression his threads elicited from Louis, Cesar attempted to preempt any commentary with a sly grin. "I came straight from church, *mi amigo*," he said under his breath.

"I approve." Louis nodded, as he put his arm around his friend's shoulders. "Cesar, this is Marisol. She is a friend of Alex's and a writer. She'd like to stick around and write about what we are doing if that's okay with everyone."

Cesar shrugged, removed his sunglasses, smiled widely and offered Marisol his hand with a slight bow. "That is a lovely name. Where is your family from?"

"My grandparents were from Guadalajara," she replied, beaming.

Cesar nodded knowingly. "Beautiful place!"

Jerry smiled. Cesar was making much more of an effort with his English than he had when they'd first met. Jerry really wanted to learn Spanish. He'd even picked up an audiobook to start trying.

It was nice enough outside that Jerry decided that they could continue the conversation on the porch. He brought out some lemonade and some tea. As Cesar made his way up and they exchanged hugs, Jerry remembered something he had always wanted to ask him.

"Cesar. While we're waiting for the others to arrive, would you be willing to tell Marisol about the first time you came over here and played with us? I've heard different tellings of it, but can you give her the accurate version? Did your wife have something to do with that?"

"Oh *sí*. I would be nowhere without Irma. Nowhere at all." Cesar proceeded to, in his best attempt at English, tell Marisol, Jerry, and Brother Louis all about it.

Few things in life brought as much pleasure or peace to Hector Cesar Jimenez as when his entire family gathered for a meal. It was a large *familia* at this point, always growing and never without a significant number of challenges and drama. But when the Jimenez people gathered and the house was filled with noise and aroma, Hector's heart was full. At seventy-eight years old, he didn't take these moments for granted.

Actually, since his parents had died, Irma was the only one who called him Hector anymore. His seven children, twenty-four grandchildren, and eleven great-grandchildren all called him Papi—the ones who could speak, that was. His friends and coworkers had called him by his middle name since he had immigrated to the U.S. in 1959.

Earlier on that fateful Sunday of the group's first meeting, the Jimenez family had been celebrating several things. The gathering had included extra friends, dates, coworkers, and neighbors. Because of the expected crowd, and some lovely early spring weather, they had moved the celebration from their home to a picnic shelter at a local park. Well over sixty people had already gathered by noon, and more were on their way.

They would have at least three piñatas, lots of food, and some live music. It was a big day, after all. Two little ones were celebrating birthdays, one baby had just been born, one of the grandkids was celebrating her first wedding anniversary, two of the grandkids were celebrating their recent confirmations, and Papi and Mami's sixtieth wedding anniversary was coming up. Plus there was a date Cesar made a point to honor every year: November 6, the date President Ronald Reagan had granted amnesty to three million undocumented Mexican immigrants, including Cesar and Irma, who were able to prove that they had been in the country since prior to 1982, had committed no crimes, and that they had an understanding of U.S. history, laws, and some English.

That day in 1986 changed their lives and set the stage for the amazing, thriving family to celebrate their blessings. As proud as Cesar was of his Mexican heritage and culture, he had made sure to include plenty of American flags at that party. It was their family's Independence Day, he always said. A congested family calendar had prevented a proper celebration back in November, so they had added *that* to the spring celebration as well. It was quite a party.

"That," Cesar said to Jerry, "was when that kid—I think he was a friend of one of my grandsons—came and said that I should come to this garage and bring my accordion to play music with a White man and a Black man and some kids." He shook his head.

"My father had told me that when I got to working age and had to support my family, I needed to 'put away childish things,' like my accordion. But Irma told me, just that day, that sometimes we needed to pick up childish things." He smiled, shook his head, and shrugged in pleasant resignation. "I decided to go with my granddaughter and see if maybe I could play some music for her at this 'jam session.' That sounded pretty childish!"

Jerry and Brother Louis both laughed. This whole story was bordering on insane.

"I'm glad you did, Cesar." Brother Louis put his arm back across Cesar's shoulders. "I'm sure glad you did."

Finding the Tune

Alex and Jamie, the two college students from next door, showed up and found their friend Marisol already hard at work documenting stories and getting to know these amazing older folks. Alex never tired of hearing the tale, and, using one of his favorite musical metaphors, he kept reminding people that they hadn't even "gotten to the bridge yet."

"That's true enough," Louis replied. "But how does a nice, smart, young woman like Marisol here get mixed up with riffraff like you two?"

Alex feigned offense. "Hey, Louis. You're supposed to make me look good here. I'm still trying to impress her!"

Marisol smiled but tried to get the subject off of herself as quickly as possible. "I've known Alex too long for him to impress me at this point."

That got a good laugh out of the group. She was starting to feel comfortable, and they could all see that she and the boy did have some history.

"She'll never say it about herself," Alex gently moved the photo album from the ledge to the porch floor so he could sit where it had been, "but Marisol has a way of talking about important, complicated issues in a way that the average person can follow. She's an excellent communicator about these things. She's got me thinking about stuff like immigration and the environment and criminal justice—and I am *not* political."

"That's wonderful," Louis said. "What was it that inspired you to get so involved in these issues?"

Seeing that there wouldn't be a quick escape from this attention, she settled into it, set down her recorder, and looked thoughtfully out onto Boscobel Street. "I think that as I started to become aware of the complicated, systemic problems baked into our communities and our institutions, my first response was fear. I felt powerless. Then I went through a time of cynicism and apathy. I felt like it was all hopeless. The politicians, the church—they were all failing. I just gave up on it all."

Louis nodded and offered an almost-imperceptible smile.

"But last year I decided that even if it was futile, I just had to start looking for examples of goodness and stories of things that were working, or I might lose hope altogether. I needed to invest my energy and whatever talent I had into something productive and positive. So I started searching for these stories and sharing them—at first for my own sake. It didn't take long to find out that I wasn't alone in my frustration."

Jerry could not wait for her to meet Nadia.

The group sat around, and as they waited for one more key member of the group to arrive for their big discussion, they recounted the events of the last several months for the benefit of the young reporter.

The Past Year

Early that year, the tour bus company that had employed Jerry for decades decided there just wasn't enough business to keep him on full time anymore. Everyone in Nashville knew about the declining sales of music, but Jerry had seen that tours were still doing pretty well in most genres. He suspected that there was an effort to push him out to make room for a younger driver they could pay less.

The Christian music market had shrunk over the previous fifteen years. Kyle was off the road and leading worship every Sunday at a big church in

Oklahoma, but he often came to town to write and then crashed in Jerry's spare bedroom.

But Jerry never cared about musical styles—he'd drive for anyone. He had enjoyed the friendships he had made in the Christian music world much more than he ever enjoyed the music. Some bands he found pretty compelling, but most of the ones who had a big enough platform to need a tour bus had to fit into a pretty tight creative mold. He saw that it wasn't different in country, pop, or rock music though. When it came to popular entertainment, the masses weren't often looking for much in the way of innovation or adventure. Contemporary Christian music just wasn't made for people like him. He didn't take it personally. He had plenty of records.

Over the past ten years, though, many of the Christian artists Jerry had known were exiting the game. Christian music—or at least what was played by the most prominent artists in that genre—had all gone "worship." Most people of faith who wanted to make something other than worship music were duking it out in the mainstream—many as independents. Jerry had met several of them along the way—some in recovery meetings, some at local shows in the various small venues that had popped up around his neighborhood.

People were exploring spiritual, and even specifically Christian, ideas in music all over the place. Just not so much in "Christian music" anymore. He thought that might be better in some ways. He remembered back when rock and folk bands talked about Jesus in normal music. Maybe that could happen again.

Jerry didn't need a lot of income. He had lived pretty simply, paid off his house, and stashed some money away. But he hoped to be around for a while, and his savings wouldn't last forever. Plus, life in East Nashville had gotten more expensive than he had ever expected. His property tax bill alone cost more each month than he had paid for rent when he'd first moved in. Besides the financial part, though, Jerry was definitely not ready to retire. He needed stuff to do. Though the idea of not being up all night and away from home all the time had a certain appeal. What kind of work was a sixty-eight-year-old going to find—especially one with no formal education?

Jerry found himself wondering what to do. He even wondered what he wanted to do. He was pretty adept at recognizing what other people needed or what needing fixing, but he was realizing that he had a significant blind spot when it came to himself.

One morning in March the weather in Nashville was beautiful. Winters were mild in Music City, and anyone who said otherwise just hadn't been around. Most years only saw a handful of truly cold days. But winter was wet—and gray. It could be overcast for weeks on end, and then in the summer it got so hot and humid that it could be unbearable outside. But in the spring and fall, on the days when it wasn't raining, Nashville could be the most beautiful place on earth.

Jerry liked to think that the weather didn't bother him, but on that morning, with the sun peeking through the tree branches, dappling his front porch with light, and the thermometer reading a perfect sixty-eight degrees, he decided to take his morning coffee on the front porch for the first time that year. That was always a good feeling—almost a little victory. Spring was in the air. Everything felt clean and new.

He sat there, sipping from his cup and watching over his small yard, noticing a few small projects he would now have plenty of time for. He started looking up and down the street at his neighbors' houses. He remembered a time when he wouldn't have known any of their names. Now he knew the Martins next door and the McCarthy family across the street. In fact, he could name at least ten families or individuals just on his block. He remembered that he needed to return a Bill Withers record that he had borrowed back over to George White later that day. It would give him an excuse to check in on his old friend. None of them were getting any younger.

Lamont's old home, and a few others on Jerry's block, were now Airbnb houses. Those hosted new people every week. They were fine for the most part, but there was no real way to get to know those folks. But down on the next block there were the Jacksons and the Millers, and there was a gay couple who had been two of the first to move in after the tornadoes. He sat there and felt momentarily overwhelmed and grateful to be a part of such a community. He knew that all of those people could have easily been sitting and looking at his house, and they knew him as its resident as well. And he knew that as eager as he would be to help any of them if they needed it, most of them would be glad to be there for him as well.

Something moved Jerry to do something he had never done before. He put his coffee down on the porch railing, went inside, and got his old Martin guitar. He took it to the porch and sat there and played. As he strummed and picked, he realized that something felt different. He had played almost every morning and evening in his front room, just a few feet away, but he always stayed inside. He noticed this because of the difference between the acoustics in his front room, where the sound of his guitar bounced off three walls, a large glass window, and hardwood floors, and the porch, where the notes just floated out into the world. It wasn't an unpleasant sound, but it was definitely different.

So why had he never brought the guitar outside? It's not that anyone was listening, but someone might have heard him. The houses on Boscobel were pretty close together. And it's not that anyone would have minded. The neighborhood was full of music. The kids next door were constantly practicing in the basement, and everyone could hear and feel the bass and drums for a couple hundred feet. His neighbor Noble played the French horn at the most random hours. Jerry had heard a mariachi band a few Saturdays earlier and thought nothing of it. East Nashville was full of music, and about the only time people complained was when the music from the amphitheater downtown caught the wind just right and blasted through the neighborhood so loud that people couldn't hear their TVs in their own living rooms.

But Jerry was still self-conscious about playing for others to hear so had never done it. He wasn't good enough, he thought. He knew some amazing guitar players and felt like a pretender. For him, the instrument was part of his therapy—his prayer life. It was part of his recovery. He wasn't performing. But that morning, he let go of his musical shyness, just a bit, and sat there on the front porch, picking out a simple little lullaby he had written for his daughter fifty years earlier.

The accompanying chords were more sophisticated now. He had learned different voicings and inversions. And the melody had taken on some new shapes and tones. But beneath the layers it was the same basic lullaby he had sung for her when she was a baby. Though he never opened his mouth, he sang the lyrics in his mind and played them with his hands.

> *Oh sweet Marianne*
> *Breathe it out and breathe it in*
> *Don't be afraid there's nothing to fear*
> *You're not alone*
> *I'm not much, I know*
> *But I'm right here*

He expanded on the melodic theme. It kept going, growing. Jerry was improvising, but his skills on the instrument had gotten to the point that whatever he conjured in his mind would come through his fingers. He never hit a bad note.

Marianne had two kids now—his grandkids—that he had never even met. He tried not to think about that too often because when he did, the grief took his breath away. But that day, he allowed those thoughts to take root and grow. He played their melody, an offshoot of Marianne's theme, praying a blessing over them. As he played, he lost himself in the song, and he didn't even notice his college-aged neighbor Alex standing down by the fence listening.

As Jerry resolved the final chord, he opened his eyes and saw Alex, still by the fence, his eyes wide and his mouth agape. He was awestruck. Jerry broke what felt like several seconds of holy silence, sensing that Alex wasn't going to utter a word.

"Mornin', Alex. Hope I'm not disturbing the peace this morning. It's just so nice today, I thought I'd do my practicing outdoors. How long have you been standing there?"

"Long enough to hear one the most beautiful songs I've ever heard." Alex's voice held a strange amount of nervousness, considering he had known his old neighbor Jerry since he was a little boy. "I'd always seen that old Martin sitting in your front room, but I had no idea you could play like that. That was unreal! What was that song?"

"Oh that? I don't know if that's really a song," Jerry demurred. "It's the melody of a little ditty I wrote for my daughter when she was just a tiny little thing. I've had it stuck in my head for darn near fifty years. I just started making some stuff up around the melody there."

"Could you play it just like that again? I mean, if you wanted to?" Alex asked.

"Probably not." Jerry chuckled. "At least not exactly the same way. I really was just messing around. That's all I do with this old guitar. I don't really play the way you young guys play. For me, it's just something that helps me pray—helps me feel something quiet and good."

Alex was suddenly in awe of an old man he had barely paid any attention to before. He had always liked Jerry. Everyone liked Jerry. But he was just another nice older guy who helped kids when their bike chain fell off or had the extra key when somebody got locked out of their house. He was the one Alex's father was always asking car questions. But at that moment Alex realized that Jerry, this gray-haired old man, was like a stranger to him. There was a side to Jerry that Alex had no idea about—and it was a side he now felt compelled to know.

"Jerry," Alex said, with a new tone of respect bordering on reverence taking over his voice. "You know my brother and I are always practicing over here. He's gotten to be a very good drummer. I don't know if you know that, but Jamie is getting noticed. He's super talented. And I'm getting pretty decent on the bass. And the two of us are pitching ourselves to different singer-songwriters as a rhythm section. Like a two-for-the-price-of-one, turnkey deal. We've gotten some decent gigs and had some good experiences, but what we need is some extended practice time playing with a guitar player and maybe a singer. Would you be willing to play with us some time? Just casually. Just for fun."

Alex could see the surprise on Jerry's face all the way from the sidewalk. He opened the little gate and let himself through and started making his way up the walkway toward the porch.

"Gosh, Alex," Jerry began. "That sure is nice of you. But I don't think you boys want to be playing with some old fart like me. You're *good*. I've never played a note with another person in my life. Not with a singer, definitely not with a band. I think you boys would just be more frustrated with me than it'd be worth."

"I doubt it," Alex said with 100 percent honesty. "Look, Jerry, I'm not blowing smoke here. I've been playing bass for years. I've been studying it in school. I've even done a few recording sessions. I mean, I'm no Victor Wooten, but he's the kind of bassist I aspire to be. I've played with all kinds of musicians, but I've rarely heard the kind of heart and soul in a song that I just heard in that tune you say you were just improvising. One of my teachers always told me that one of the most critical ingredients of great music is the story behind the notes. When you were playing I felt that story. I just want to play with you, man. I *need* to play with you. It will make me better at what I do. Jamie will feel the same way.

"Tell you what," Alex continued, sensing that he was getting somewhere with Jerry. "What if Jamie and I come over to your place tonight at about seven, he'll bring a few percussion things and I'll bring my acoustic bass, and let's mess around and have some fun. No pressure—just fun. How about that?"

"I guess that couldn't hurt anyone, could it?" Jerry offered.

"No!" Alex laughed. "No one will get hurt. I promise. Awesome. Seven o'clock. See you then!" Alex practically skipped away.

Jerry started rubbing his chin. He took a sip of his coffee and found it had gone cold. He drank it anyway. "What have we gone and gotten ourselves into now?" he asked his guitar.

Jerry spent the rest of that day trying not to think about how nervous he was to do something as simple as playing acoustic music in his front room with neighbor kids he'd known all their lives—and how stupid it was for him to be so worried.

He went to the diner to get a late breakfast and was annoyed that his favorite waitress wasn't working that day. He told the replacement girl what he wanted to eat and then realized how nice it was to be a regular somewhere and have people just know what he wanted without having to say it. His breakfast was fine, but something was different about the grits.

He went to the YMCA to do a little workout. Afterward he tried to go to a coffee shop he had heard about but got overwhelmed at the long line and left. The modern coffee shops that had sprung up in the area were mystifying to him. They were beautiful—and he could not deny that their coffee was good—but their prices were so high, and their menus made no sense at all. Their equipment looked like chemistry sets in the laboratories of mad scientists, and about three-quarters of the patrons seemed like they were auditioning for a fashion magazine or a music video.

He knew his attitudes about these places made him a relic, but every so often, he tried one again. But he just didn't get it. He should have gotten coffee back at the Y. They had the best coffee in town. It was hot and it was free.

He decided to go for a walk in the park for a while. That often helped him focus his mind, and it was a good way to prevent his leg from getting too stiff. The weather just got nicer and nicer. It was the kind of day made for superlatives. A nice early spring Saturday like this brought folks out to the Greenway. He saw some kids getting ready for a baseball practice and some others playing a pickup soccer game. There were plenty of runners, bicyclists, and dog walkers. Several couples strolled arm in arm, and he tried unsuccessfully not to let those sights trigger his feelings of loneliness.

After a couple of hours, he went back by the house to get the Withers record and return it to George. He valued George's friendship and still couldn't believe that it took a tornado for them to meet. On the surface, he and George White didn't have a lot in common. George was about ten years older than Jerry, Black, a deacon at the Main Baptist Church, and was very formal. George wore a tie every day, even if he wasn't going anywhere. Jerry had five snap-front Western shirts, a few dozen T-shirts that various bands had given him over the years, about ten different tour jackets, four pairs of blue jeans that still fit, and one suit for weddings and funerals. And although he had never aligned with any denomination, his sense of spirituality and theology was shaped by his recovery from addiction, his network of relationships, and the massive number of books he had read while on the road.

George was like a pastor to Jerry. He challenged him with provocative questions, encouraged his growth as a man of the community, and held him accountable in his recovery. Jerry listened to the record one more time as he fixed himself a simple sandwich and a glass of tea, then slipped the LP into its sleeve and began the walk to George's house to return it.

Jerry strolled up to George's front door and used the proper brass knocker. A few moments later, the owner's broad, smiling, but somewhat languid face appeared in the open doorway.

"Jerry Wesley, my friend," he boomed. "Have you come to return my long-playing record or to make sure I am still to be counted among the living?"

"Does it have to be one or the other?" Jerry grinned and accepted George's gesture to come inside.

"What did you think of the record?"

"I liked it quite a bit," Jerry said. "Withers is interesting. He has some amazing songs, but he kind of falls between genres, doesn't he? It's soulful, but it doesn't follow all of the standard soul music rules. Then he dabbles in folk music styles but strays from their rules, too. And sometimes he throws these symphonic strings all over the tracks in the same way some of the Nashville producers did."

George nodded. "Old Bill played by his own rules but also seemed to know how to write songs everyone could sing along with. By not fitting into one camp or another, he came up with a handful of songs that managed to bless everyone."

"I do like how constructive his songs and attitude tended to be," Jerry added. "Obviously I knew his big songs before, but it was fun to hear the album cuts. I didn't realize how much acoustic guitar he used. It was fun to play along with his record."

"I'd like to hear that sometime," George said as the two of them took their usual seats in George's formal living room.

"Speaking of that. Something interesting has come up and I'm having some mixed feelings about it." He told George about his accidental morning concert and the fact that Alex and Jamie were coming over to play music with him in a couple hours.

"I'm not sure why the thought of playing music with those kids makes me so nervous," Jerry said. "Especially considering how incredible it felt to play that song this morning, before I knew Alex was listening. But to be honest, today I have felt extreme beauty, true peace, and intense anxiety and fear. And today has been the closest I have come to wanting a drink in a couple of decades. I have no idea what's going on in my head."

"Ah," George said. "I think you may be opening a new door."

Jerry looked up at him but didn't need to say anything.

"That's how growth works sometimes, Jerry. We face one challenge for a while, work through it, it works on us, we do our wrestling. And at some point, we learn what we need to learn, and we overcome what we need to overcome—but often not without taking on some new kind of limp or pain."

George leaned forward and looked straight into Jerry's eyes. "Then we move on to our next challenge. The thing is, our hearts and minds carry memories of the pain from our previous experiences. Like the limp Jacob had after wrestling the angel. Sometimes a challenge today might unconsciously remind us of some kind of pain from a long time ago."

George leaned back into his chair and stared up toward an abstract painting that hung on the wall over his mantel before he continued his thought. "That's just how pain works sometimes. The important thing, though, is to be present—to be awake for it. To know what it is you are feeling and not to reflexively try to relieve it or medicate it." He looked back at Jerry. "You know all about that."

Jerry nodded.

"What's interesting about this," George continued, "is that there is something about performing this music that is resonating in a painful way with you, when it should be bringing you pleasure. I suppose that's worth some reflection. I think that sometimes our emotions, both positive and negative, tend to live together in the same box. You might be opening that box a bit when you play, and mostly good feelings come out, but those feelings about your kids and your ex-wife and the war— those feelings are in that box, too. The mystery of great art is how some folks are able to allow those things to wrap around each other in the service of something that is ultimately beautiful, even if in the short term it might involve some darkness.

"I suspect," George continued, "that just being aware of this association might be enough to defang it a bit, but this might be something worth talking about at a recovery meeting, too. Other than that, I'd just go for it. I have a feeling you're going to have a good time tonight. I'm excited for you. And I'm excited for those boys. They will get a lot out of this, too. It's nice to see some youngsters treating their elders with respect."

"Well," Jerry said, "they are coming by at about seven o'clock tonight, so if you happened to stop by at about eight, who knows what you might hear."

George smiled. "Well, neighbor," he said wryly, "it sounds like you are trying to trick me into taking a walk!"

Jerry went back to his house and got ready. He brewed a fresh pot of coffee and a batch of sweet tea. He felt like he was hosting the ladies' auxiliary. He even laughed at himself a few times. There was nothing else he could do to prepare and it was only five thirty. He put a John Hiatt record on, took out his photo album, grabbed a new stack of prints he had just picked up from the Walgreens, and spent some time culling them for his collection.

The most recent batch of photos were from a tour he had been the driver for out West. The trip had taken him through most of the southwestern states and even into Mexico. He still had his old Brownie camera, and it still worked, but it sat on a shelf in the front room, waiting for special occasions. He had bought a digital camera several years ago. It had a million features he didn't understand or use, but because it didn't use film, he could take as many pictures as he wanted. He was pretty diligent about deleting the extraneous ones as he went, but he still ended up with a pile of close to fifty prints that day. He was determined to only add ten from that batch to his photo album. Only the best and most interesting made the cut.

The Southwest had really captured his imagination. It had felt like most scenes were worth photographing there. He had enjoyed the days in Austin, San Antonio, El Paso, and Laredo. He had spent an off day in Nuevo Laredo, Mexico, and wanted to get back there some day, maybe traveling deeper into the countryside. The recent violence and corruption had taken a significant toll on the community, and on the other extreme was the tourist and commercial growth that seemed to be trying to crowd out the historic charm and character of the old city.

But the beauty of the people and the place still poked through here and there. He found one picture he had snapped of a city sign that said *Nuevo Laredo* and had a beautiful young girl playing with what looked like an injured pigeon on the ground just in front of it. He decided to add that photo to the album and then continued through the stack.

The guys knocked on the open door at about ten minutes to seven.

"Hey, Jerry, you good?" Alex came through the screen door. "We're a couple minutes early. Is that okay?"

"Sure. Come on in. I'm just messing with this old photo album." He set the book on his coffee table and got up to shake their hands and welcome them in more appropriately. "Can I get you boys anything? I've got coffee or sweet tea. I could make you up a glass of water, too, I suppose."

"Water's fine," they both said. "Thanks."

As Alex and Jamie set up their simple gear and Jerry fixed their drinks, the John Hiatt record continued to play. It was an album from 1988 called *Slow Turning* and was one of Jerry's favorites. He had discovered Hiatt through some friends in AA. His blend of country and rock—the younger ones were calling it "Americana" now—was perfect. His lyrics clicked with Jerry on a very personal level. They were just the right balance between humorous, introspective, sarcastic, and confessional. When he read some interviews and learned that Hiatt was also a recovering alcoholic, he felt an even deeper kinship with his music. He couldn't begin to guess how many miles he had logged listening to John Hiatt's music.

"What's this?" Jamie gestured to the record player. "That drummer sounds amazing."

Jerry proceeded to tell them about John Hiatt, but before he could get very far, Jamie had found the credits on the vinyl jacket. "Oh, that's Kenneth Blevins. I think he played with John Prine not long ago."

Jerry looked up. "You know John Prine's music?"

"A little bit," Jamie admitted. "I'm at the front end with Prine. I have a long way to go, but man I love the new record. I'm working my way back through his catalog on Spotify. I've heard of John Hiatt but haven't heard much of his stuff. I'm always listening for these players who find these patterns and rhythms from country and blues and Cajun music and bluegrass and bring them back in fun ways."

Jerry started to think this would work out just fine. He was still nervous, but now at least he knew that these boys listened to more than just pop music and rap. He picked up his Martin and tuned her up. Again.

"So, how do you want to do this?" Jerry asked. "I gotta warn you boys, I've actually never—ever—played my guitar with other musicians in my whole life. I pretty much play on my own or with records. And I don't know if you've noticed, but I'm sixty-eight years old. I'm not sure how quickly I'll take to something new like this."

Alex had been preparing for this. "Jerry, let's just flow, man. Let's not overthink it. We have no plans—no agenda. You got any songs you've been digging? Something you're writing? Some tune someone else wrote?"

"How about 'Ain't No Sunshine' by Bill Withers? You boys ever hear that one?"

Jamie looked at Alex with a big smile. They loved that song.

"Perfect," Alex said. "Any key you want. You start it and we'll kick in."

Jerry took a breath and started playing the main riff in A minor. After about four times through, Jamie kicked in with a rhythm part on the percussion box he sat on. Alex dropped in at the top of the very next measure, and just like that there was a groove. No one was singing, but Jerry somehow managed to pick out most of the melodic elements while still playing the main rhythmic groove.

It sounded flawless right out of the chute, but after a couple minutes of jamming, it found a flavor and tone all its own. When the verse pattern completed and returned to the top, Jamie would drop the rhythm out just a touch, and Alex felt it just right. Then, without missing a beat, they would filter right back in for the next stanza. Jerry could tell they were brothers; they were tight; they were dialed in.

The impromptu three-piece acoustic band riffed on "Ain't No Sunshine" instrumentally for a few minutes, and then Jerry tried singing some lines. He lost the timing of the pattern and the groove just a few bars later. Everybody laughed a little bit as the song careened into momentary chaos. Jerry had a good sense of melody. He could sing but his voice was rough. He liked to blame it on the Chesterfields he had only gotten around to quitting when he came off the road, but it was also just how he sounded.

"Don't sweat it," Alex said reassuringly. "Singing and playing at the same time is a different animal altogether. Do whatever you feel."

Jerry felt like somebody needed to be singing. They decided to move to another song. Jamie suggested "And It Stoned Me" by Van Morrison. Jerry didn't know the chords right off the top of his head, so Alex showed him. It only took a couple minutes to dial in the groove on that one. Jerry swore he could hear the horns coming from somewhere in the ether.

And that's how the evening went. Song after song after song. Each one started with Jerry mapping out the changes and making sure he understood how it went. But once he did—once the "chart" was in his head—things came alive. The brothers had never played with anyone like him. He had a sense of the rhythmic pocket that many professionals never mastered. He covered elements of rhythm and lead guitar without leaving anything out. He had a delicate touch but was never weak.

Alex and Jamie lost count of how many times they caught themselves giving each other "the look" that said, "Can you believe what's happening right now?"

At about nine o'clock, someone knocked on the screen door, and a large Black man with a fedora and a tie entered and moved right behind where Jamie sat on his cajón.

"George!" Jerry shouted. "You've gotta hear this. Come on in."

After some quick introductions, the band kicked in to "Stand by Me" and then revisited "Ain't No Sunshine." George sat on one of the dinette chairs and beamed. They sounded much better than he expected them to. He saw the sweat on Jerry's face and collar and the way his hair was matted down and stuck to his forehead. He noticed his rolled-up sleeves and the wider-than-usual smile. The music was doing what it was supposed to do.

He also noticed the way the two young men stared at Jerry with awe. George was surprised at how good they were, considering how young they seemed. He sat there for about fifteen minutes and then prepared to make his exit.

"Well, gentlemen." George replaced his hat. "I must say that these proceedings fill me with great joy, but it is past time for my repose. I look forward to whatever future endeavors you may pursue. And if this particular ensemble were to release an LP, I would certainly appreciate the opportunity to procure a copy."

Everyone laughed but George, and they all stood to shake his hand. Just like that, their first audience had left the building, and it seemed a reasonable moment for a short break. "Seriously, guys," Jerry said as they moved the few feet from the front room to the dining room table. "I can take it. Honestly…how do you think I'm doing?"

Alex shook his head. "Okay. Jerry, now I think you're just fishing for compliments, and I'm gonna lay some truth on ya. This has been the most fun I've had playing my bass in a while—and we're just jamming on cover songs. It's just the way you play. There's something so different about it. On one hand it's deep and soulful, and on the other it's fresh and lively. I can't put my finger on it."

Jamie nodded. "I can't believe you've never done this before. Why the heck not? You obviously love it and you're amazing. I don't get it."

Jerry took a deep breath, rubbed his head, and took a big gulp of his tea. He wasn't sure what to say, but the music had gotten his blood pumping and an improvisational buzz was humming in his head. His normal filters were down.

"When I was a kid, I loved music," he said. "But we were poor farmers, and my father did not see how stuff like music or art had anything to do with surviving in this world. Then, just as I started to get a feel for writing some songs and playing guitar, I got married, had two kids just like that, and started running away from poverty full time. Then Vietnam and Jack Daniel's took care of whatever little bit was left in there."

The boys did not expect such a vulnerable answer. You could hear a pin drop in that little house.

"Music was like a little trickle of beauty," Jerry continued, now looking off into space somewhere, "into some very dark places. But sometimes all the trickle does is remind you how black the darkness is. It's hard to explain."

"What about that song you were playing this morning?" Alex asked. "You mentioned that you wrote that a long time ago—like fifty years ago."

"It was 1969," Jerry said. "I remember the night."

"Wow," Jamie interjected. "You remember the night all those years ago that you wrote that melody? There's got to be a story there."

"Oh yeah." Jerry looked down, rubbing his chin. "There's a story there alright."

He told them about the night that he composed that song to comfort his crying baby girl. He shared the few lyrics with them. Then he explained that his family wanted nothing to do with him and why. He told them all about his drinking years and the night he knocked his wife across the kitchen. He talked about getting clean from his addiction and how music had come back to him in waves, but that it was still so hard for him because of how he associated it with his kids and his wife.

"Could we try to play that song"? Jamie asked.

Jerry looked up with his eyes wide. "Well, you don't beat around the bush at all, do you?"

"No, man. I don't. Alex has been talking about that song all day, and now that you've told us the story behind it, I feel like we have to play it. It's almost like when someone tells you a house is haunted or a closet has a monster in it. You have to go into it just to prove that it's safe. That song is your trickle of light, man. And you have follow that trickle back to the source—not off into the darkness. Maybe that was your problem back then. You just walked in the wrong direction."

Alex took a breath and then offered his perspective. "Jerry, I don't want to push you into something you don't want to do. But if you want to walk into that old house, I'd like to go in there with you."

Jerry stretched his arms out to his sides and then rubbed his head. It almost looked like he was stretching his way out of an invisible straitjacket.

He exhaled, put his glass of tea on the table, and looked up at the brothers. "Well, all right, boys. Let's go."

They moved back over into the front room and got into their positions. Jamie surreptitiously started the voice recorder on his iPhone and set it on the table. Jerry tuned his Martin and Alex tuned his bass. Then Jerry decided to recite the lyrics instead of trying to sing the melody.

Oh sweet Marianne
Breathe it out and breathe it in
Don't be afraid there's nothing to fear
You're not alone
I'm not much, I know
But I'm right here

And with that Jerry started playing.

Jerry could barely sleep that night. He was both physically exhausted from hours of playing music and mentally and emotionally exhilarated. He first tried to go to bed at about 1:00 a.m., not long after Alex and Jamie went home. But after several minutes staring at the ceiling, he gave up and headed back into the kitchen. He was glad not to have a houseguest that night.

He'd never been a journal keeper, but his mind was racing, and he remembered someone at a meeting once mentioning that journaling was a good way to bring cascading thoughts under control. He dug out his old leather journal, wrote the date at the top of the first page, and then started scribbling.

He filled five pages with recollections and observations of the day. His hand was cramped up from all the writing. At the bottom of the page he made a bullet-point list of a few things he wanted to make sure not to forget, a few things he needed to do because of today:

- *Set up a regular schedule to play with Alex and Jamie*
- *Spend more time writing original songs*
- *Find a friend who can sing?*
- *Connect with my kids*

The writing process did help calm his mind. His physical exhaustion took over his brain and he made his way to bed. He dreamed of playing his guitar, of tuning his guitar. He had one funny dream about trying to sing while he was playing. It involved a juggler, an auctioneer, and an axe-throwing clown with exactly four axes that kept coming at him over and over again in perfect rhythm.

In the morning he cleaned up, got dressed, ate a quick breakfast, and went for a walk. He decided to pop in at George's church, even though he wasn't dressed quite well enough. The truth was, most of the folks there dressed to the nines, but they never made anyone else feel bad for coming as they were.

He looked for George and joined him in his pew. As usual, Jerry was one of just a few White faces in the sanctuary at Main Baptist. It didn't bother him, though. A growing handful of people, mostly from his street, knew him and were glad to see him. He tended to visit Main once or twice every couple of months. George told him there were lifetime members who had poorer attendance records than that.

George leaned over to give Jerry a welcome hug. "How late did you boys play last night?"

"They left after midnight. I could have gone longer. I'm a little sore this morning, but oh man, that was amazing. Those kids are good!"

"That they are. As are you. You surprised me, Brother. You should have seen the way those boys were looking at you. You'd have thought they were playing with Stevie Wonder!"

Jerry laughed and then turned his attention to the hymn. He had to follow along in the hymnal. He didn't have these songs memorized the way most of these folks did.

After the service as they were walking out, George (known as Deacon George to the folks here) was shaking hands and giving hugs like a politician at a picnic. Jerry could tell that he was beloved in that community, and he knew why. Jerry was enjoying standing back and watching him do his thing, but George kept pulling him over to meet people.

A few minutes later, though, as Jerry was making his way down the steps to leave, he heard George's booming voice one more time. "Mr. Jerry Wesley, there is one more man you must meet." Jerry turned around with a smile and returned into the scrum.

"Jerry." George clapped his hand on Jerry's shoulder. "This is Brother Louis Williams. Brother Louis, Jerry Wesley." George was beaming, like a proud papa watching his son take first place in a big race. "Brother Louis, Jerry here is the man I have been telling you about for several years. He and I have been trading long-playing record albums since the tornadoes came through, and he helped me fix the roof on my garage. He noticed my record collection and that I was no longer listening to them, so he procured for me a functioning and beautiful record player while he was on the road. Now I can listen not only to my records but his! Each week, he brings me one of his records and he takes one of mine. We listen on our own and then get together to talk about them. It's been quite a wonderful experience. I had no idea how soulful some country music could be!"

Brother Louis laughed. "I remember hearing about you, Mr. Wesley. In fact, I have a memory, if I'm not mistaken, of maybe seeing you two out there working on that roof with an old record player in your driveway."

"Yep. That was us," Jerry said. "I ran a long extension cord and we brought the player from my front room over. Boy, what was that, almost twenty years ago now?"

"I wanted to join you gentlemen that day," Brother Louis added, "but I had to get to work. I used to drive the streetcar-style bus up and down Gallatin Road."

"No kidding," Jerry said. "I was a bus driver for most of my career. I usually drove tour buses. Just now being forced to retire."

"I'm sure you gentlemen have plenty more in common," George interrupted, "but there is one very pressing thing I simply must interject at this time. I hope this is not too forward for either of you, though I am certain that it is. But, you see, Brother Williams is possibly the best singer in all of East Nashville. If you don't believe me, just arrange to be in the locker room at the YMCA any weekday morning at about eight. And Brother Williams, Mr. Wesley here has just started an auspicious new band that is in desperate need of an excellent singer."

And there on the steps of Main Baptist Church, Jerry and Brother Louis both stood in complete shock. If not for their mutual respect of Deacon George, they might have simply run away. Louis was mortified at the idea of singing in a band. Jerry was terrified at the thought of bringing the "best singer in East Nashville" into his house to sing with two kids who had not in any way agreed to be a band. They hadn't even confirmed a second time to get together. Jerry was feeling dizzy. This was so unlike George.

Louis thought he might throw up. His wife noticed the small circle forming around the three men and started to make her way over to see what was going on. And there in the middle of it all, with his fine apparel and a Cheshire grin, was the giddiest Baptist deacon in Davidson County. George White, in his heart of hearts, was confident that he had just lit a fuse.

Jerry and Brother Louis exchanged pained facial expressions, shrugged, and shook their heads. They communicated in every possible nonverbal way that Deacon George had lost his mind. But somehow, their mutual discomfort in the moment seemed to draw them together. When Louis's wife, Kelly, heard that this conversation had to do with her husband singing in a band, she could not have seemed more shocked. Louis furtively waved off the suggestion as her smile started to grow. He could feel this thing taking on momentum. He had to get ahold of this fast.

"What an interesting idea, Deacon George." Louis forced a smile. Not wanting to embarrass his friend, he decided the public moment needed to end so this train could be derailed in private. "Mr. Wesley, I would love to get your phone number. Maybe the two of us could get together and talk about all of this soon."

"Absolutely," Jerry agreed. "I'd love to hear you sing sometime, but I think Deacon George here may have an elevated opinion of both my skills and the ensemble that came together last night at my home. But yes, let's get together and talk."

When Jerry saw the address that Louis wrote on a church bulletin with his phone number and name, he stopped. "Is this where you live?"

"Indeed it is," Louis said. "I grew up in that house. Lived there all my life."

Louis lived one block over and two blocks down from Jerry.

"We're practically neighbors," Jerry said. "I'm just over on Boscobel, a few doors down from George. What are you doing later this afternoon? Want to come over for some tea?"

Present Day

Marisol was so caught up in the story, she had stopped taking any notes. She glanced at her recorder to confirm that it was still functioning and stared down the street, imagining the stories it could tell. Even though everyone here knew the basic details of what had happened, things had been moving so fast they were all enjoying this relaxed reflection on what had brought them to this point.

"So," Marisol interjected. "You two got together later that day?"

"We did," Jerry said. "I think we both sensed a need to put a lid on something George was trying to stir up." He chuckled.

"Little did we know!" Louis added sarcastically. "Little did we know."

"Brother Louis showed up to my house at about four o'clock that afternoon," Jerry recalled. "I was on my front porch, strumming my guitar and enjoying yet another beautiful spring day. I was pretty nervous about what he would expect about this supposed band that George had promised, and I was using my guitar to help me kind of calm down a little bit. I'll never forget, when I saw this handsome brother striding up my sidewalk, my stomach started to get all in a knot. Then he said, 'That sure was an interesting meeting this morning, wasn't it?' I started to feel more relaxed right away. I could tell he thought George had lost his mind too!"

"I was nervous myself," Louis added. "In fact, it took some doing for me to even make that walk."

Jerry continued. "I explained that I did not have a band and described what had happened with the boys, and we had a good laugh."

"Jerry was a perfect gentleman," Louis added. "He offered me a glass of lemonade and told me his story. About his struggles, his regrets, and how the war had wounded him. He was surprisingly open with me. We started to discover how much we actually had in common. We had both been bus drivers, of a sort. We had both been in Vietnam. We both loved music."

Louis reached back over and put his arm on Jerry's shoulder. "As I look back, I think that was the first time I had shared so much of my story with a neighbor. Here, this White man I had just met was interested in how I wound up driving that trolley and what the war was like for me. He wanted to hear about my family, my kids, this neighborhood. I just talked and talked. I started to find a brother that day—a brother I didn't even know I needed so badly."

"Would you share some of that story with me?" Marisol asked.

Louis took a deep breath and let it go. The memories were becoming clearer now. He shared many of the same things with Marisol and the gathered group that he had first shared with Jerry months earlier. In the intervening time, he had experienced something powerful about the power of story and place.

He looked down and saw that Jerry had already refilled his glass of lemonade. "Alright. I guess it's my turn. Here we go. Someone turn me off when this gets boring."

Brother Louis's Theme

Marisol pulled a copy of a local magazine out of her bag. It had published a short profile on Brother Louis, and she wanted to check some of the claims with him directly. According to the magazine, the prevailing theory around the East Nashville YMCA was that Louis Anthony Williams was known as Brother Louis because everyone assumed he was some kind of minister. Inadvertently speaking for everyone who knew the man, one of the front desk workers said, "He just has that pastoral presence. I assumed he was a reverend or a deacon or something."

"I have no idea why folks assume that," Louis insisted after Marisol read the quote. "I mean, I appreciate it, I guess. I go to church. I consider myself to be a man of God. But I ain't never been to seminary. I ain't never been ordained to nothing. I ain't even been able to decide if I'm Baptist or Methodist! I just try to treat people right."

"Then why does everyone call you Brother Louis?" Marisol asked.

"You know," Louis pondered, "that goes back so far I have to stop and think about it. I'm seventy-four years old now, and I do believe I've been called Brother Louis since I was in about the seventh grade. I think it was either one of my teachers at school who started it or another student that maybe started it as a way of teasing me. The thing is, I always liked it. So I just let it ride."

Louis was born in East Nashville in 1945 while his father, Gregory Williams, was helping the Allies clean up Europe. His mother, Cynthia, was known in their Historic Edgefield neighborhood as an amazing cook and an excellent pianist and organist. She would often step in at the Main Baptist Church of East Nashville to accompany the choir if needed.

Young Louis loved to sing as a child, but his singing was limited to church or hymns around the house with his mother. He was the oldest of a brood that eventually totaled six Williams kids. That role instilled a sense of responsibility into him that had lasted his whole life.

His youngest brother was born when Louis was thirteen, which was the same year that Louis's voice changed. From that point forward, no one ever heard him sing unless he was in the shower. His mother had said that was the year he became "Mr. Self-Conscious" around people, but he somehow seemed unaware of how thin the walls in the Williams' house were. When it was his turn for a shower, his whole family could count on a rousing rendition of whatever song was stuck in his head. No one told him they could hear him. They didn't want him to stop.

Louis grew up in the Jim Crow South, and as a young man he attended segregated schools until he reached high school. The famous *Brown v. The Board of Education* court case rocked the country when Louis was nine years old, and though the landmark ruling in that case meant that segregation was no longer legal, Nashville adopted a "slow and gradual" plan to integrate their schools, and it seemed Louis was going to miss out on any benefits. The only schools to integrate immediately, in fact, were the Catholic schools.

Sensing an opportunity, Louis's father enrolled him at the Nashville Catholic High School for Boys. That the family was not Catholic was a minor concern compared to Gregory Williams' commitment to making sure his sons had every possible opportunity for success. His father had once told him, "I'm sure you can learn as much from the Catholics about Him as you can from the Baptists if your heart is after Him good. We're all just doing our best to figure it out, anyway."

Louis did well in school. He enjoyed it. He was blessed with the kind of disposition few men had and fewer still could sustain under pressure. He was pleasant, comfortable in his skin, amiable, positive, and humble. And al-though he was always unassuming, he possessed a certain kind of charisma. It wasn't a salesman or preacher kind of charisma, though. It was the kind that drew people close, made them feel comfortable, and assured them that what they were saying—at that moment—was the most interesting thing in the world to him. This all came naturally to him, too. He didn't have to conjure it. His parents saw it in him and encouraged him. His father feared that the darkness in the world would soon snuff out the beautiful light burning in his son's eyes. His parents adored him, as they did all of their children.

In 1960, when Louis was just fifteen, he talked his father into taking him to Fisk University to hear Dr. Martin Luther King Jr. speak. Four thousand people were packed into that auditorium, and a young Louis Williams sat transfixed by the reverend's words. A local civil rights attorney named Z. Alexander Looby had just seen his house bombed, and King's response gave Louis chills. "We will say, 'Do what you will to us,'" he boomed, "but we will wear you down by our capacity to suffer."

Our capacity to suffer?

Louis's life was as challenging as any young Black man's was in Nash-ville at that time, but as he sat there next to his strong, protective father, with food in his belly and decent clothes on his back, Louis started to think about real suffering. Something started to click in his mind about the power of joy and the potential for nonviolent change. He became a student of the leaders of the movement but also of the spiritual principles that guided them. He thought about the Jesus so many Christians claimed to follow and how much that Jesus was willing to suffer for the sake of love. The more Louis learned, the more grateful he felt. His positive dis-position strengthened and grew—tethered to a growing sense of responsi-bility for his community.

Marisol's eyes were wide and her expression revealed a combination of reverence, awe, and curiosity. She had learned about Nashville's role in the Civil Rights era, but to be sitting with someone who had witnessed it all firsthand was almost overwhelming to her in a way she did not expect.

"You saw Dr. King in person?" she said. "That's incredible. What kind of impact did that have on you? I can't even imagine."

Louis noticed that everyone was leaning in now. He offered an amiable smile as he settled into the rest of his story. "Dr. King said that he came to Nashville because he was inspired by the peaceful, civil disobedience going on here. I was, too. I watched Black ministers sit with college students at segregated lunch counters downtown. These protesters were well dressed, respectful, and extremely disciplined as they defied the unjust and illegal segregation practices happening in Nashville.

"I also watched in horror as these conscientious men and women were treated like animals by police, security guards, business owners, and neighborhood bullies. I wanted to get on one of the buses John Lewis was taking straight into the heart of darkness in Alabama, but I was just a bit too young. But I kept up with his reports, and when he said, 'If not us, then who? If not now, then when?' it just lit me up! I got as involved with the movement as a teenager could.

"John Lewis was a bit shy of five years older than me—which made him just old enough to be inspiring as a role model and just young enough that I could relate to him. I loved hearing him speak, and I spent time with him whenever I could. I so wanted to be one of the Freedom Riders with him. If I had been just a few years older, I'd have been right there with them on those buses, taking those cruel beatings and making the hate, hypocrisy, and lies of the protectors of Southern apartheid plain for all good people to see."

Louis used the excuse of a sip of tea to marshal control over his rising emotions. "Years later, I was amazed, but not surprised, to see my hero speaking on the National Mall at the March on Washington right before Dr. King delivered his famous 'I Have a Dream' speech. What a day."

Louis began to believe that it was true: Change was on the horizon. He dared to hope that Dr. King's vision of a land where a man would be judged not by the color of his skin, but by the content of his character was coming to pass. Louis was determined to be a man of character. He committed to dress professionally, speak articulately, apply himself diligently to his studies, and make himself an agent of positive change in the world. He outgrew his father by the time he was seventeen, eventually topping out at a strapping six-foot-two-inches tall. He was fit, upright, and he recognized the positive response his wide smile and gentle expressions evoked from people.

"And I'll tell you what," Louis continued. "When I heard John Lewis talk about the spiritual impact that Billy Graham, this White Southern preacher had had on him, it had an impact on me. I saw that we didn't have to be as divided as we were and that there is a spiritual element to these racial struggles. I started to listen to some of Graham's talks on the radio and they were powerful."

Louis stayed close to his church family and saw no line of demarcation between church and civics. He continued his studies at Tennessee Agricultural & Industrial State College, where he focused on engineering and history classes, before he settled on an engineering degree.

Louis was looking out toward the street, and beyond—his gaze anchored on nothing physical. "I was twenty-two years old when Dr. King was assassinated. I was about to graduate from college and was looking forward to engaging in the struggle for civil rights as a gainfully employed adult. But it was as if James Earl Ray's bullet traveled all the way to Nashville from Memphis after it had left the reverend's body and landed squarely in the deepest part of my heart of hearts." He took another sip of tea. He had not shared these feelings in many years.

"Several of my friends as well as a couple of my brothers and cousins started to become more interested in radical ideologies than in Reverend King's nonviolence. After the assassination of JFK, Malcolm X, and then Dr. King, I could understand why. And I could respect a lot of what groups like the Black Panthers were doing in the community. They had a powerful vision, and they did some good things for sure. But I just could not handle that violent attitude. I got close a few times, I guess. I got so angry that I could feel the temptation to repay violence with violence, but ultimately I just couldn't go there. Instead I think I just kind of lost faith in all of those people and parties. I started to just detach."

With little opportunity for work around Nashville, and wanting to avoid the rumored upcoming draft, Louis enlisted in the U.S. Army Corps of Engineers in the spring of 1968. He spent four years in the service, mostly in and around Vietnam, regularly being recognized for his excellent critical thinking, his strong people skills, and his creative problem-solving abilities. One of his fellow soldiers called him the most spiritually uplifting nonchaplain in the entire Army.

Louis continued to sing in showers, from Vietnam and Laos to Germany and Japan. One Army Corps buddy estimated that there might have been over a thousand GIs who had the privilege of attending a Brother Louis Williams concert between 1968 and 1972.

When he returned to Nashville in 1972, with excellent military credentials and recommendations, exceptionally marketable skills, and a winning personality, Louis confronted the brick wall of American opportunity for young Black men in the South. In his first four months, home he applied for over two hundred jobs—literally every job he found that had anything to do with engineering, advanced building, or project planning. Time after time he saw those jobs given to less-qualified, younger, fairer-skinned applicants. When his mother heard him come through the front door after a day's worth of interviews around town, she called to him from the kitchen.

"Is that you, Louis? Come on in here and tell me how it went."

Louis took a breath, installed his smile, straightened his back, and walked into the kitchen, giving Cynthia a kiss on the cheek from behind as she stirred a pot of soup simmering on the stove.

"They were all perfectly polite," he said. "They all said they'd keep track of my application in case anything opened up. But, Mama, I think I'd be much more likely to land one of these jobs if they had to hire me over the phone. There seems to be something about me that they can't get over once they see me." He was smiling sarcastically, squinting as if he was searching for the answer and didn't know what it was.

"Someone will see what an amazing talent you are. Even if just out of pure greed, one of those old buzzards is going to snatch you up!"

"I don't know, Mama. I think I've hit every single place that is hiring or might someday be hiring, and the best job they might offer me is on their janitorial team."

Louis eventually picked up a temporary job driving a streetcar-style bus and spent his evenings with his ailing father watching television and talking about the world. Though he never let it show, the constant rejection crushed him. The military had seen the value of his mind and put it to use, but back home all people seemed to see was another Black man on the street. The pleasant demeanor Louis presented to the world was no longer connected to an internal reservoir of joy and hope. It was becoming an act. He was good at projecting positivity and he kept it up because he knew people appreciated the spirit, but over time he started to forget that he didn't feel it anymore.

In those days, Louis and his parents attended church together two or three times a week. One Wednesday evening he was moved by a message the preacher gave. He was thundering about the fact that all creation testified to the glory of God—even when that testimony was one of rebuke.

"When we see the birds of the field," the preacher implored, "don't we see God's loving-kindness and concern for the least of these?"

"Yes" and "Amen" rose from the pews.

"When we see the beauty of creation, don't we sense his handiwork?"

The "Amens" rose again.

"Sure we do. When we see a little baby or the face of someone we love, or when we see acts of courage or great sacrifice—works of great beauty— we're seeing reflections of the glimmer of God's goodness in this world. Are you with me?"

Louis was nodding alongside everyone else.

The pastor interrupted the crescendo of agreement and brought it all to a sudden halt with a slam of his palms on his podium—his voice exploding through the building as he nearly wailed, "Then what about when everything is wrong? What about when all we see is injustice and suffering and corruption? Does that mean that God is dead? Is he gone? Were we wrong?

When we feel alone, like Daniel in that den of lions, does that mean that God has forgotten us?"

A handful of sisters were quietly saying, "No, sir," but most of the congregation was waiting to see where Pastor was going with this.

"Church. When we don't feel God's presence, we need to *be* his presence for someone else. When we don't see his hand, we need to *be* his hand. When we don't sense his purpose, we need to walk in his ways anyway. And when we feel deep in our bones that this world is not the way it's supposed to be, we need to remind ourselves that we are in good company. Brother Paul is right here with us. Brother James is right here with us. Brother Jeremiah is weeping right here with us. And Jesus himself is right here with us!"

The "Amens" were back.

"Remember, our sense that things are not the way they're supposed to be is in us because God has planted the eternal in our hearts. He is inviting us into his Kingdom and the Kingdom of this world will always be at odds with God's Kingdom. So, we will continue to work. We will continue to lift our brothers and our sisters up. We will continue to pray that his Kingdom comes and his will is done—because we know that it will get better than this and we want to be on the side of love!"

Now Louis remembered why he needed church. When the closing hymn kicked in and the congregation started singing "This Is My Father's World," Louis let himself sing a little louder than usual. With his mother on one side and his father on the other, he felt the sound rising in his chest and throat. Because he couldn't hear his own voice as loudly as the congregants around him, his self-consciousness didn't limit him, and he let fly.

His parents, for the first time, got to hear their oldest son in full voice and it nearly brought them to their knees. His was no longer the gangly, humorous, enthusiastic voice of a nervous teenager. It was now a strong but sensitive liquid-smooth elixir. Louis felt his mother reach behind his back to grab hold of his father's arm and gave it a strong squeeze.

Louis continued his streetcar job, driving up and down Gallatin Road six times each day, picking up workers, schoolkids, and tourists and delivering them where they needed to go, all the while keeping an eye open for a job that would better utilize his specialized engineering skills. While he never found that elusive job, he learned more about the people of that community than he ever could have imagined. He heard stories from senior citizens, disabled veterans, schoolkids, and local politicians. He heard every conspiracy theory, sales pitch, political angle, and weather prediction before anyone else. He always had an encouraging word for everyone and seemed to have a sixth sense when it came to zeroing in on what was bothering someone. His streetcar was like a roaming chapel and his dark-blue uniform a liturgical vestment. Many in that East Nashville corridor confided things in Brother Louis that they wouldn't dare share with their own pastor.

He traded recipes, books, and photos with the regulars, and often had young ladies pass him their phone numbers. He was too much of a gentleman to ever call any of them, of course. Then one afternoon he noticed a familiar face step onto his streetcar, give him a courteous smile, and sit in the seat just behind his. It was Kelly Malone, a young woman from his neighborhood and church that he didn't recall seeing since she had gone off to Bennett College in Greensboro, North Carolina, four years ago. She was at least four years younger than him, and even though she used to run around with his little sister, somehow he'd never paid much attention to her before.

As he glanced at her, he wondered why. "Miss Malone? Is that you? Welcome back to Nashville! How long has it been? Are you back to stay or just for a visit?"

"I didn't think you'd remember me, Brother Louis. I've graduated from college, and I'm trying to figure out what's next. You have any ideas?"

"Well, I just might!" Louis enthused. "We'll have to think on that. Where are you heading on my streetcar today?"

"I don't know. I actually just got on because I wanted to see you."

Suddenly Kelly seemed a bit older than Louis remembered her, and he was a bit embarrassed. With those few words he noticed how attractive she had become and how well dressed she was. He saw that her hair was arranged in one of those nice styles that took quite a bit of effort to arrange.

It framed her face so nicely, though. Her brown eyes seemed gentle, intelligent, and playful, and he realized that he would like to keep looking into them for a while. The more he noticed these things, the less he knew what to say next. His usual reserve of charm was suddenly coming up empty.

"I hope that's okay." She sensed that she had made him uncomfortable. "I know I was more friendly with Sally than with you, and you honestly don't know me from Adam's house cat. But to be frank, since I was a little girl I've always felt that somehow you had answers. When I got home yesterday and my mom mentioned that you were driving this streetcar, I immediately knew what I was doing today."

"You did, huh?" Louis said in his least charming way ever. "I guess I have no idea what to say to that. I just don't know what to say at all. Except maybe one thing."

"What's that, Brother Louis?" Kelly asked with the cutest grin she could muster.

"How about you just call me Louis?"

Louis and Kelly were married seven months later. The whole street and half of the residents of the Cayce Homes housing project came to the reception in the park. Everyone tried to get Louis to sing at the reception, but he wouldn't do it. But later, when Kelly and Louis settled into their little apartment and she heard him sing in the shower, she couldn't believe how good he sounded.

She then joined the chorus of people trying to get him to sing in public. "You've got a serious gift, Louis. It's pretty selfish of you to deprive the world of that voice of yours."

Louis spent the next several decades driving that streetcar during the day and teaching beginning engineering classes at the local community college at night. Kelly became a beloved teacher in the local elementary school. When she had given birth to their third baby, the complications were serious enough for them to decide that would be their last.

His father, Gregory, passed away shortly after Louis's thirtieth birthday. Before he died, he asked Louis to sing at his funeral. That was a request

Louis could not turn down. He sang "His Eye Is on the Sparrow," his first public performance at the cemetery, and the gathered friends and loved ones, grieving though they were, could not believe they had never heard Louis sing before. Cynthia could almost feel Gregory's arm in her hands as she squeezed Louis.

Louis and Kelly decided to move their crew in with Cynthia. She needed the company and help with the old house, and they needed more space. So Louis was back in the house he grew up in on Fatherland Street. Kelly's mother was five doors down, and her aunts and uncles were spread around the neighborhood. Everything was close enough to walk to, though the gangs and drive-by shootings made that a risky venture. Louis was glad he had daughters and not sons. But he felt a deep burden for the sons in the neighborhood who seemed so, so lost.

Things got bad in the nineties. Their daughters moved away as soon as they were old enough and would barely even come back to the old house for holidays. They loved their mom and dad, but East Nashville was just getting too nasty. Their once-vibrant street was so close to the housing projects that it now looked like a war zone. Shootings were common.

Louis spent time volunteering with a local mentoring program, but he was becoming more and more discouraged about the lack of opportunity, especially for young men. He thought about selling the old house, but when he looked into it, he was dissuaded. It was paid off, which was a huge blessing financially. But the real estate prices in the area were so low, he realized that if he sold it, he wouldn't get enough to move into anything anywhere near the area. He was stuck.

Then over the span of two days in 1998 a slew of tornadoes had their way with Nashville. The Williams' house, like so many others, needed a completely new roof after all was said and done. Louis, seeing an opportunity, decided to add some tall dormers and make a third-floor apartment up there. Kelly thought he was crazy to sink more money into a house that already felt like a trap, but Louis had a vision.

"Someday one of the kids might come back and want to live here," he said. "Or maybe when we do go to sell this place, that extra floor will add some value. I don't know. Maybe I am crazy, I just have a feeling that this is the right thing to do."

The workmanship was excellent. He hadn't had a chance to use those skills in a long time. When it was finished, he set it up as an office and used it as a place for his constant reading and studying. Kelly took to calling it The University.

After the tornadoes, Louis got caught up in a sort of neighborhood revival that gripped Historic Edgefield and the wider East Nashville area. "I'd certainly never seen anything like it all my days," Louis explained. "I saw White folks helping Black folks fix their roofs, and Hispanic folks helping White folks paint their fences, and Black folks setting up day-care centers to watch over multicolored gaggles of kids so their parents could work on repairs together. That was all lovely. But then I also saw many people of color who were renters lose everything they had. They didn't see any of the benefits at all."

"I remember one night at dinner, telling Kelly about a ragged-looking White man a couple blocks over on Boscobel, playing Marvin Gaye records in the driveway while he helped old George White fix the roof of his garage! She kinda rolled her eyes like I was spinnin' a yarn, but I promised I was speaking the truth. That man," he pointed at Jerry, "dragged an old record player into the driveway and was playing George's old records while they swung their hammers! 'Course I didn't know him yet, but if I hadn't a been on my way to work I would've joined 'em."

"A close call I guess," Jerry interjected.

Over the next couple of years, Louis and Kelly noticed some major changes taking place in East Nashville. On one of their evening walks, Kelly brought it up. "What do you suppose is actually going on around here? I don't know what to make of it all. I'm not complaining, but I just never thought I'd see the day."

Louis nodded. "People are moving into East Nashville, not out of it. And it's all manner of people: artists, old people, young families. But not very many Black people, that's for sure."

Kelly pointed to a small little neighborhood restaurant down the block. "Like that place. Little fancy restaurants like that are opening up all over the place. That's fine, but wouldn't it make sense for at least one of the new places to have the kind of food our community likes?"

Her husband hadn't stopped nodding. "Did you ever imagine that this part of town would start drawing White people with money?" He laughed. "It sounds like a gag. If you were to have told me five or six years ago that there would be a fancy grocery store with organic food within walking distance of our house, I would have laughed you into next week!"

"Six years ago I doubt you would have known what organic food even was."

That was true. Louis remembered asking his daughter why some bananas cost so much more than others.

"It seems like crime is down," Kelly added. "That can't be bad, right?"

"I guess not. But I would like to see the facts behind the data."

Kelly didn't know how to respond to that. "I wish this had all happened before the kids all moved away. I'm glad to be able to stroll through the grocery store and not get tailed by a security guard, and not to worry so much about you going on your evening walks."

"Plus we get to celebrate tomatoes at a crazy art festival every summer now," Louis said. "What else could we want?"

The public schools were getting better results, and that made Louis especially happy. East Nashville was making the national news as one of the biggest neighborhood turnarounds in the country. Folks were moving there from around the world. But the housing projects were still there and still in need of repair, and minorities were never surprised to hear about the latest police-involved shooting. There was a certain amount of generational cynicism and hopelessness that permeated the minority communities around issues of equality, law enforcement, government representation, health care, and education. What looked like progress on Gallatin Road, Eastland Avenue, and at Five Points, didn't feel like progress to communities of color. While all the fancy restaurants and retail stores seemed to benefit from the new residents who could afford the rapidly escalating prices, the largesse was not evenly distributed.

Louis started to hear from friends whose rent had skyrocketed to levels none of them could've imagined. Marcus, a stocky, short, second generation Cuban American, who had been a butcher at the grocery store for as long as anyone could remember, got on Louis's bus one morning with an uncharacteristically sour look on his face.

"Good morning, Mr. Marcus. Are you alright this morning? You don't seem yourself."

"G'morning, Brother Louis." Marcus attempted to manage his mood in that moment, but he came up short. "I just found out that my rent is going up from seven hundred dollars a month to thirteen hundred dollars! They might as well evict me. I've never been one day late with my rent, and I've been renting that house for seventeen years. They just want me gone."

Louis was no longer shocked by news like this, but the empathy he felt for his friends and neighbors was intense. He shook his head and squeezed the steering wheel. "Well, that just don't sound right at all."

Marcus continued. "I was up all night searching for another place, and it looks like the closest I can afford will be at least a half-hour drive, and there's no bus lines that go out that far, so I have to buy a car too."

His positive disposition was getting a workout. How could a couple of tornadoes and a bunch of nice new folks coming into a rough neighborhood be good news for some and such bad news for so many? Louis wondered if his old hero John Lewis might have any ideas. He had been in the U.S. Congress representing Atlanta for years. Maybe he'd drop him a line.

Louis noticed it on Sunday morning, too. As the Black folks were being pushed out of the neighborhood, attendance at Main Baptist was dropping in a big way. Several big historically Black churches that used to be packed on Sunday mornings were now dwindling to nothing or selling their property to developers and moving away. Where was everyone going? Some had moved over to the north side of town. Some to the south side. Families were getting separated.

One Sunday, he and Kelly left church and went to grab something to eat at a café, until they found out they'd have to wait an hour for a table. "So," Kelly thought out loud, "now that the neighborhood's not scary anymore, the churches are empty but the diners are full? That doesn't seem right."

The city shut down Louis's route shortly after the tornadoes. He drove a city bus for the Metropolitan Transit Authority for a few years until he could officially retire. When that day came, however, it just meant a different kind of work. His pension was nowhere near enough to keep up with the rising cost of living in their suddenly "cool" neighborhood. He picked up some part-time work with a developer he had met during the tornado-recovery season. He spent about half of each day overseeing small-scale construction projects and the rest of his time either volunteering with the mentoring program or teaching at the college.

Kelly's plan was to teach as long as she could. She was in good health, was constantly learning new skills, and though her hair had some significant gray in it, she looked at least fifteen years younger than she was. They were happy that their daughters, two of whom now had kids of their own, were much more comfortable coming to the house to visit. But in their mid-sixties, neither Louis nor Kelly felt old enough to slow down. Louis's mind was always racing. Kelly, on the other hand, though active, was centered, self-confident, and possessed of a kind of inner peace that both enchanted and mystified Louis.

One afternoon, Louis and Kelly's oldest daughter, Andrea, stopped by and found him sitting at the dining room table, surrounded by papers and drafting materials and concentrating on a complicated problem. She slipped into the room to hug his neck while he worked.

"You just don't seem to understand what 'take it easy' means, do you, Dad?"

"Well hello, honey! Oh this? This *is* me taking it easy. I'm just studying some expansion plans that the community center is considering. I think they may have gotten some bad advice from someone. But when you look at this new kind of construction and you think about how they're going to use this, and then you look at these groups over here who have been searching for space…"

He started riffling through another pile of papers, searching for something to argue a point his daughter was not interested in.

"That's fine, Dad. If it makes you happy to help those people, then help them. I just don't understand taking on all that stress if you're not even getting paid for it."

"Well." Louis took off his reading glasses for a moment and looked at his daughter. "Honestly, sometimes I feel that I just have to do something—to feel like I am fixing something or making something better. It's the only way to keep the wolves at bay."

"Wolves?"

"Sure. Wolves. The anxiety. The fear of what's happening to our community. And somehow, even though some of the obvious problems around here seem to be getting better, some deeper, more hidden problems are being allowed to fester. I can't quite put my finger on it yet, but I have this feeling in my bones that I'm supposed to do something about this. I was put here for something. And I am an engineer, so I will help by building. It's all I know how to do."

"Wow," his daughter said. Her father had just become a bit more three-dimensional to her. The strange thing was that though she knew he had trained as an engineer and was a very talented builder, when she thought of her father, that was not what first came to mind.

"I guess we all just gotta do what we are put here on Earth to do, right?" she said. "Someday maybe I'll figure out what I was put here to do other than to clean up after your monster grandbabies!"

Louis pushed himself away from the table and walked with his daughter out on the porch to catch up on the latest goings-on with her family. His project could wait. They both greeted a couple from Norway who were just arriving for a week in Music City.

It turned out Louis's idea to add that third-floor apartment might have been the only thing that allowed them to stay in East Nashville when the property taxes jumped again in 2015. With a few minor adjustments, Louis was able to turn "The University" into a short-term rental. Folks from all over the world booked it online and paid good money to stay so close to downtown.

Now in his seventies, Louis's body was starting to wear out a bit. His back was his biggest problem, no doubt due to all those years sitting in a terrible seat in that streetcar. The East Nashville YMCA soon became Louis's home away from home. He was there every morning no later than seven for the seniors' swim class. He'd join the group in the pool, do the workout his young chiropractor had given him for his back, and then hit the shower before he joined his normal crew for coffee in the hallway upstairs for some important social time.

One morning as he swam his laps, he tried to estimate how many times he had driven past that building on Gallatin. Twelve times a day, five days a week, fifty weeks a year, for forty years…120,000 times. And that was just when he was on the job. When he had been a kid, the pool at the YMCA was still Whites-only, and now it was one of the most warm, generous, and welcoming places for people of all colors and backgrounds he had ever experienced.

Change was happening, but oh so slowly. He thought back to that day he had sat with his father at Fisk and listened to Dr. King. He thought about the long arc of history and how Dr. King had promised that it was bent toward justice. Louis didn't want to give up hope, but had he just been keeping himself busy to avoid asking himself the harder questions? What if King was wrong? Was the light flickering? He remembered how his father had talked about seeing a special kind of light in his own young eyes. Had it gone out long ago, but he had become so good with his smile that he had fooled even himself?

He contemplated these things as he slowly swam his laps. Back and forth—over and over—getting nowhere. Kelly was away visiting a friend in North Carolina for a couple of days, so he was in no rush to get back to their big empty house.

When he made his way back to the showers, he did what he always did. He didn't realize it, of course, but he did it anyway. As soon as the water was running, he started singing. On this day it was Bill Withers' "Ain't No Sunshine." He didn't know all the words, so he kind of looped the first verse over and over, but boy, did he feel that thing. He always thought of this song when Kelly was gone, but that day the sense of longing seemed to point to her, and through her, to something deeper that he was missing.

Within a few minutes he was singing so loudly and fully that the sound carried all the way into the locker room next door. Louis was in another realm. He had no idea. But there on the other side of a glass door three men sat slack jawed by what they were hearing, while a fourth just shook his head and smiled.

"Who in the world is that?" one twentysomething kid asked. "That has to be a famous singer. It sounds like Al Green or Donny Hathaway or something."

"Ha!" Mack Smith, a large, older gentleman some folks called The Mayor for no apparent reason, said. "That's Brother Louis. Man, that boy can sing, but he only sings in the shower. If you make any kind of comment, he'll shut right up. But if you stay quiet and just listen, you can get quite a little concert some days. When the mood hits him, you might hear a random medley of Wilson Pickett, James Cleveland, Marvin Gaye, and John P. Kee. Then again, some days you might hear the same seven words from some children's song on repeat like a broken old record!"

Louis stopped singing for a second. Mack laughed a little too loudly and thought Louis might have heard him. But he picked up again on the "I know, I know, I know" part, and everyone knew the song would continue.

"He's so good!" a second man said. "I produce records. You think I might be able to get him to sing for me in the studio some day?"

"I'd love to see you try!" Mack laughed. "Hell, half of old East Nashville would kill for a Brother Louis record. That boy could sing the ingredient list on a box of grits and I'd buy it. Many have tried. Good luck to you."

As the music producer, also in his twenties, waited for the owner of the remarkable voice to come in from the shower, he prepared his pitch. He even dug a business card out of his gym bag. But when the steamed up door opened and a seventy-three-year-old man walked through with a towel around his waist, the kid just about fell over.

"Was that you singing in there?" he asked like an eager fan.

"Oh," Louis said sheepishly. "Could you hear that? I keep forgetting how sound travels in here. I'm sorry. I sure don't want to bother nobody."

"Bother! Are you kidding me? That made my day. That was some of the best singing I've heard in months—and I'm in the music business—or at least what's left of it. My name is Michael Thomas, and I have a little studio out behind my house and spend most of my time making records either out there or in other rooms around town. Is there any chance I could talk you into coming over and recording a song with me?"

"Oh, I'm no singer. Nashville is full of singers. I like to sing in the shower, that's all. I can introduce you to a dozen better singers than me."

"All due respect," Michael said, "I work with a ton of studio pros. But I've never heard anyone quite like you. You've just reminded me why I got into music. I'd love to get you on tape—just to do it! Maybe we make a little record for your family or something, or we can just mess around and see what happens. But seriously, this has to happen! It's meant to be, man. With a voice like that, singing *must* be your calling."

"I don't think so," Louis said. "Unless you can set up your studio in that shower stall, I don't think it would work. I have a hard time singing when I know folks are listening. But I thank you for your kind offer."

The young man was shocked. His gaze searched for witnesses or backup from the friend on his left, who was simply looking down and shaking his head, then to The Mayor on the other side of the locker room, who replied wordlessly with a shrug and a grin.

As Louis finished getting dressed and made his way upstairs to take his coffee with the regulars, the offer from the producer kid was sitting in his head in a funny way. Kelly had also been bugging him to record something—anything—so the family had some kind of record of his voice. Why did he feel so weird about singing in front of people? Was it the attention? Something about the thought of it just made him feel like he was going to faint. He couldn't explain it.

But that day, between the thoughts he had been having in the pool and the reaction from the kid in the locker room, he started thinking maybe seventy-three was the right age to start facing his fears and getting over himself. He took his coffee and his bag and headed out to his car. He had some work to get to at home.

It was about a week later that George had introduced him to Jerry after church. After sharing the highlights of his life's story on Jerry's porch that Sunday afternoon, Louis turned the attention back to Jerry's music and whatever it was that George had misunderstood to be a band.

"So tell me about the music you're doing," Louis said, "but before you do, please know that as much as I appreciate that folks like my singing voice, I've never sung in public. I'm just a casual, sing-in-the-shower kind of guy. I don't really have any ambitions to do anything else. Folks are often trying to get me to sing here and there, but I haven't felt comfortable. In fact, the other day I met a kid at the Y who wants to record me. That seems crazy. So, no pressure from me! I'm not looking for a singing gig. But I am interested to hear about what your band does."

"That's the funniest bit." Jerry laughed. "I don't have a band at all. What I have are two talented college-aged neighbor kids who play bass and drums—great kids, mind you. I've known them since they were tiny. They are still in school but have already been on stage with some excellent artists and have played on some good records.

"Anyway, they came over last night and played some songs with me, and that was the first time I've ever played my guitar with any other musicians. We had a great time. It was so much fun. But it's not a band. George misspoke. I don't have any idea what got into him."

"Well," Louis said, "it sounds like we have yet one more thing in common." Both laughed again.

Jerry and Louis sat out on the porch for a couple of hours just talking. They talked about their families. They talked about regrets and getting older. They talked about the music that inspired them most. They talked about how the neighborhood was changing. They even talked about the weather. It got dark. They couldn't believe that they had lived so close to each other for so long and had never met. How was that even possible? After two hours on the porch, Louis felt like he could hang out with Jerry all the time.

"Well," Louis said, "I'd best be getting home. Kelly's gonna have some kind of dinner on. I tell you what, though. If you and those boys play music again, I'd love to hear it. Do let me know, will you?"

"I will indeed," Jerry said. "I will indeed."

When Louis got home from his visit with Jerry, Kelly did a pretty poor job hiding her curiosity about what had gone down.

"That you, Louis?" she hollered when she heard the door.

"Indeed it is, my sweet."

"How was your visit with that nice friend of Deacon George?"

Louis had a playful tone as he found Kelly in the kitchen. "Well now. How do you know that he's a nice man? He could be a very nasty man for all you know."

"Oh hush." She snapped her kitchen towel at him. "Why in the world would Deacon George introduce you to a nasty man?"

"That's a good point," Louis conceded with a nod. "Good point indeed. But I am afraid that old George White may just have lost his mind today. After dinner I might need to call on the good man to see if he has a fever or something. How many years have we been knowing George? It has to be thirty years now. Have you ever seen him like he was today? I think the man busted a valve or something."

"Now why in the world would you say that?" Kelly set their plates on the kitchen table. "He was just excited to introduce you two. That doesn't seem crazy to me. Wash your hands now and come to the table."

Louis had already been on his way to the sink when she gave him those instructions.

"Everyone knows I can't sing in public," Louis continued. "And he said that Jerry over there had a band, when the truth of the matter is that Jerry had one evening of playing songs with two young men who live next door and that was the first time the man ever played music with other musicians in his life. He's sixty-eight years old, Kelly! Last night he had some kind of jam session with some college kids and George White calls it a band? Jerry Wesley told me himself, it ain't no band. And George knows I ain't no real singer, let alone the 'Best Singer in East Nashville.' Shoot!"

Kelly was smiling, and Louis was half laughing, but she could tell that something about this was getting under his skin. They sat at the table and held hands as they always did before saying a blessing over their food. Louis was on a roll, though. He had to finish this thought, and Kelly was not of a mind to interrupt him.

"So what kind of man is he, then?"

"He does seem like a good man," Louis said as he recounted the basic details of their conversation. "I found it easy to sit there and talk to him. He's kinda lonely. But there's a good heart in there—he really wants to help people. He has no idea what George was thinking this morning either, so we have that in common, too. I can't believe we've lived this close to each other for nigh unto forty years and ain't never met 'til today. That seems like a shame."

"Hmm." Kelly still held Louis's hand. "So here you have found a man who's close enough to your age, has all kinds of stuff in common with you, who you say has a good heart. He's supposed to be a great musician, according to a friend we trust, but he's nervous about playing in front of people and he's waited until he's a ripe, old man to even think about using his God-given musical gift to bless other people. And you wonder why Deacon George was so giddy about introducing you two this morning? Sometimes, oh love of my life, you can be as thick as a brick. Now say the blessing, Brother Louis, so we can eat this food before it gets cold."

Louis obeyed.

Lightning

Present Day

Marisol was transfixed by Louis's story. She wasn't the only one, either. As Jerry heard the tale retold, from Louis's perspective instead of his own, he started to think that this time of reflection might help the group as they considered what to do about the decisions they had to make. After the incredible, life-changing experience that had happened the night before, it was good to recalibrate by looking backward a bit. Although he could not be sure, he suspected that Alex and Jamie were getting something out of this time as well.

Marisol picked up her recorder, hit the Stop button briefly, and then hit Record again. "Sorry. I just need to do that every so often to keep the file sizes from getting too big."

Jerry nodded as if he had the slightest clue what she was talking about.

"So, where were we?" she asked the room.

The day after he met Louis, Jerry called Alex and asked if they wanted to set up another time to play. They agreed to get together that Thursday. Jerry asked if it was okay with the boys if he invited Brother Louis to come hang out but didn't mention anything about him being a singer. No one had a problem with that. With the extra bodies, Jerry thought it might be better to hold this in the garage instead of the house. He spent the next couple of days getting it cleaned up and ready.

When the boys showed up on Thursday they brought a small PA system with two speakers and an amplified mixer. They had a microphone and a special pickup for Jerry's guitar. They wanted to try to have Jamie play with a small drum set and figured they might need a bit more sound reinforcement for that. They also had a microphone in case anyone wanted to sing.

Jerry invited Brother Louis and George White and both showed up right on time.

"Now this is no concert," Jerry assured them. "Don't let the microphone fool you. The boys just brought some extra equipment over." George was smiling and it was making Louis nervous.

They started with a sort of generic blues tune, just to set the levels on the PA and to make sure Jerry felt comfortable with everything. Once everything was feeling right Jamie piped up. "How about 'Ain't No Sunshine'?" he asked. "That one sounded pretty great the other night and might be a good warm-up."

Louis's eyes opened a bit bigger.

They kicked it in and, once again, the unique groove was right there. It had elements of both country and soul. It felt connected to the original, with plenty of R & B energy, but there was something about how Jerry played it that added something fresh and inviting to it. George started singing along in his seat. Louis just sat and took it in. When they wrapped it up, George clapped with gusto and offered several robust "bravos." Then he leaned into Louis and flat dared him to give it a shot.

Speaking to Louis quietly, so only he could hear, George made his challenge plain. "Brother Louis. I know you know this song. I've heard you sing this one at the Y. Would you please consider singing just this one song, for my sake, with these men? It's just the five of us here, and I promise you, this does not count as a public concert."

Louis was already feeling drawn to the song. He was nervous, of course, but when would an opportunity like this come again?

"I supposed I could give it a try," he said," if these men don't mind a rough go of it."

George immediately stood and raised his hands in order to get everyone's attention.

"Excuse me, gentlemen. Pardon me. But Brother Louis would like to attempt to sing that song if you would agree to play it again."

Jerry smiled. The boys shrugged. Not having any idea about the backstory, it was no big deal to them. "Sure," Alex said. "Here's the mic."

Louis stood next to the microphone and Alex adjusted it to his height. He thumped it a couple of times to make sure it was on, and then asked Brother Louis to sing something so he could check the level.

"What should I sing?" Louis asked.

"It's just a sound check," Alex said. "Sing whatever you want."

Louis started singing "Ain't No Sunshine" a capella. But he only got a few words out and then stopped. "It doesn't sound right," he said. "I can't sing with it like that."

"What's wrong with it?" asked Alex.

Louis frowned. "It just sounds bad to me. It doesn't sound like it does in the shower."

"In the shower?" Alex asked.

"Yes," George interrupted. "Brother Louis is, in many people's opinion, one of if not *the* greatest singer in East Nashville. But he only sings in the shower. So he is used to how his voice sounds in the shower. Can you make his voice sound more shower-like?"

Alex grinned. "Reverb! You want reverb. Unfortunately this PA doesn't have built in reverb. Can you just sing without it this time and I can try to figure out something for next time?"

Louis made a few vocalizing sounds into the microphone but then abruptly stopped. "I'm so sorry. I just can't. It's hard to explain, but it's almost like it hurts when I hear my voice like that."

"Hold on," Jamie said. "I might have an idea." He dug through his brother's equipment bag until he found a reverb effect pedal designed for a guitar.

He found the necessary cables and ran the vocal mic through the guitar pedal and then into the PA. It took a couple minutes to get the effects set, but once he did, he invited Louis to sing. The result was the wettest, steamiest, reverbiest vocal Jamie had heard in a long time.

"Here you go, sir," Jamie said. "If you turn this knob, the signal gets more wet—think 'more shower,' and if you turn this one, the sound gets more dry."

He demonstrated what the pedal did and Louis was amazed. "It sounds wonderful."

The band kicked off the song and played through a whole verse instrumentally before Louis started singing. When he did, though, something transcendent happened. Jerry felt it. The boys felt it. Louis felt it. George was absolutely right about him being one of the best voices in East Nashville. Louis instinctively fell into the groove. As interesting as the form and pattern that the bass, drums, and acoustic guitar played was, when Louis started singing he pulled the song into an entirely different space.

No one in that garage wanted the moment to end. But it had to. When it did, the musicians sat staring at each other. What had just happened? Was it lightning in a bottle? Louis exhaled a long, slow breath with his eyes closed. Without a word Alex started playing a slightly lethargized version of the bass line for "I'll Take You There." Jamie found a drum pattern that felt swampy and yet determined. Jerry figured out the chords and played them in a crisp, simple way. And then Louis sang that first line, "I know a place..." and the chills hit everyone again.

They did another song and another. The results were the same as the previous week, but this time they had the added dimension of Brother Louis's voice. He didn't get every lyric or melody exactly right—some of the songs sounded more like interpretations than cover versions—but that made them that much more compelling. These four players were finding some kind of sacred ground that existed outside of race, age, or culture.

After over two hours of random, stream-of-consciousness song choices, they settled in on a completely improvised R & B-flavored groove. Jerry found some country-ish licks that worked right in the pocket, and Louis sang nothing but "oooh" and "mmm" and still made the song sound like a hymn.

High-fives were distributed. Backs were patted. George might have actually had tears in his eyes. Only as they began to wrap up did they notice a couple other neighbors had pulled up chairs outside of the garage to listen in. Kelly had wandered over, wondering what was taking Louis so long. She had been watching for over an hour, out in the shadows, tears flowing down cheeks that hurt from smiling for so long.

In the midst of the euphoria, Jerry spoke up. "What are we doing here? What is this? I know we all just felt something, but…what? I'm at a loss."

"I say we just roll with it," Alex said. "Why do we have to define it right now? Let's just do it again."

Jamie had, once again, secretly recorded several clips of this ensemble. "Saturday night, two nights from now, let's get together right here and do this again. Let's all think of other songs we would like to play and bring them. Let's see what happens. I feel like this is bigger than us. I don't think we could define it if we tried."

"Louis, does Saturday work for you?" Jerry asked.

"I think so. I'll ask my wife."

"She's right over there." George pointed to Kelly, still hiding outside of the garage door. "Why don't you ask her now?"

Louis spun on a dime and looked out into the yard as his wife, best friend, and biggest fan walked toward him, wiping her nose and fanning her face.

"Oh my heart!" she said as she got to Louis. "I never thought I'd see the day." She pulled Louis into a sloppy embrace, burying her face deep into his chest. "It took you long enough!" she gushed.

"Better late than never?" He patted her back.

Deacon George placed his hat upon his head and put his suit coat back on as he made to leave. "I must say," he said, his chest protruding so far that it seemed his vest might pop all its brass buttons, "this has been a most enriching evening. I would certainly appreciate a seat at your next gathering, gentle-men, and I wonder if you might permit me to invite one or two friends."

"Of course!" Jerry said. "I don't care who comes."

Jamie liked the sound of that.

Before they wrapped up for the night, Brother Louis asked if he could say something. Jerry gladly gave him the floor.

"Brothers," Louis began, with Kelly still wrapped around his side. "I thank you for welcoming me here tonight. Deacon George, I thank you for so rudely connecting Jerry and me. Jerry, I thank you for opening your home for this." He then turned his face upward, eyes open. "And God, we acknowledge that You are the Giver of all good things and that You give us only good things. We feel Your presence and grace here tonight and we ask that Your will be done with the music we perform. We thank You for our abilities. Help us never to take them for granted. Now we ask for Your blessing, Your mercy, and Your vision. May You use us to bring joy to all who hear us. Amen."

Everyone in the garage added his or her own "amen." Alex and Jamie couldn't remember the last time they had said that word as something other than a joke.

But everyone knew why they called him Brother Louis.

The Garage Gathering

The Past Year

A lot happened over the next two days. Jamie posted a few short clips of the group's rehearsal (or whatever what had happened on Thursday in Jerry's garage might be called) to his social media accounts. Alongside one of the images of the group he posted this reflection:

"I've played with some great musicians and on some big stages, but I've never experienced anything close to what it was like to play with these fine gentlemen. I feel like I fell down a well of soul and musical integrity and I hope I never come out!"

He invited a few friends to come that Saturday, as did Alex.

Alex couldn't wait to tell his good friend Marisol about this whole experience. He even showed her one of Jamie's video clips. "You've got to meet these guys."

She hadn't seen her friend this serious about anything in a long time. "I'll be there. Can I bring my friend Gabriella? She lives over on the other side of East Nashville near Cleveland Park and loves music."

"Sure," Alex said. "I think the general attitude is that we don't mind who comes."

When Marisol showed Gabriella the video and she saw Alex and Jamie playing music with those two older men, she immediately thought of her *abuelo*. "My grandfather is an amazing accordion player," she told Marisol. "Do you think he could come play?"

Marisol had no idea what this gathering was about. "Alex said they don't care who comes. I think it's like some kind of open mic."

Gabriella happened to approach Cesar at just the right time. He said, "Your *abuela* was just telling me that she thinks I should blow the dust off that old instrument. From that video I don't know if I can play that kind of music, but I'll take you, and bring my accordion, and we'll see what happens."

Deacon George spent most of Friday visiting with folks in the neighborhood, bragging about how he had put Brother Louis together with Jerry Wesley and if anyone wanted to hear some of the best music ever created, they should bring a lawn chair over to Jerry's backyard Saturday night.

Louis was more tight-lipped about it all, and Kelly was too excited to want to mess anything up. He didn't mention anything to the guys around the coffeepot at the Y on Friday, but when the producer kid approached him again in the locker room and asked if he'd reconsider singing outside of the shower, he decided to invite him.

"Young man," he said politely. "I'm sorry, but I cannot remember your name."

"Michael, Brother Louis. My name is Michael Thomas."

"Yes, well, Michael, first I wanted to thank you for your encouraging words the other day. You really got me thinking—and let me tell you, that can take some doing for a fellow my age! Anyway, a few days after we spoke, some things started to happen, some people came into my life, and—well—to get right to the point—I found some people in my neighborhood and actually sang with them last night."

"You did?" Michael said, probably a bit too loudly. Louis tried to calm him down and Michael could tell that he was trying to keep this somewhat of a secret.

"Yes, I did. And you know, it was pretty special. Anyhow, this little group—we are going to get together in my friend's garage tomorrow night and try it again. If you'd like to come and listen, I'd be happy to have you come."

"Sir," Michael said with great reverence and excitement. "That would be an incredible honor. Give me the address and I will be there."

Louis gave him the address and the time, and Michael chimed in with one more question. "I have one idea—and feel free to say no. But would you mind if I brought some very simple recording equipment? You'd not even notice it, and I'd never release anything or even let anyone hear it unless you gave me permission, but I've got the ability to record things on location and I'd be happy to try. If you want. No pressure!"

"Well," Louis said. "I don't see why not."

Jerry went to a recovery meeting at the church on the corner that Friday morning. He was feeling much less anxiety than he had twenty-four hours earlier, but he knew that intense emotions, positive or negative, were important to process. Plus, he was just excited to talk to some folks. He'd been up half the night.

When he was asked to share, he talked about the strange feelings all this music had been stirring up. He talked about the old song he had written and the feelings that resurfaced about his family. He talked about his fear of playing with the boys and how that had turned into such exhilaration.

After managing a vibrant conversation, one of the more experienced members of the group offered Jerry a perspective based on his own experiences. "Stay connected to your feelings," the old biker offered. "I have had some very exciting opportunities that led directly to some of my biggest challenges. The key for me has been to moderate my expectations and maintain my mindfulness." They all nodded in agreement.

Everyone was excited for Jerry, though. He invited them all to come over to his house Saturday night.

On Saturday afternoon Alex and Jamie came over and added a little bit of equipment to the PA they had set up. They also repositioned all the gear so if people came to listen, they could sit in the driveway and the garage would work like a small stage area. Once the gear was all in place and sounding tight, they sat down with Jerry and talked about some new song ideas. Between the three of them, they already had over a dozen songs ready, with chords and charts at hand, including tunes from Ray Charles, Merle Haggard, Tom Petty, The Beatles, John Prine, Marvin Gaye, and another couple by Bill Withers. Alex wanted to try playing "Sweet Marianne" again, too.

Brother Louis arrived at about a quarter to seven, wearing some nice blue slacks, a silk shirt, and a light jacket. Jamie noticed that Louis was a much better dresser than they were. Louis also had some song ideas, including some Sam Cooke, Wilson Pickett, and a new gospel song from a kid in Chicago he really liked.

"By the way," Louis told Jerry and Alex, "I invited a young man I had met at the Y last week. He was very encouraging to me after hearing me sing in the shower and said that he wanted to record me sometime. I think his words kind of set me up to be willing to sing with you all. Anyhow, I invited him and he said he'll be here."

"That's great," Jerry said.

"Good," Louis said. "And one more thing. He asked if he could set up some simple recording equipment and that he would not let anyone hear anything if we didn't agree. Oh, and his name is Michael Thomas."

Jamie looked up with a start. So did Alex.

"Michael Thomas?"

"Yes, that's what he said," replied Louis.

"Umm," Jamie said. "Michael Thomas is a Grammy-winning producer. He's one of the hottest young guys in town. He's had hit pop and country records. Oh, man!"

Right then another group of people walked up the driveway, so the brothers didn't have much time to process their shock. George and some other neighbors filed in, followed by at least a dozen younger folks—all friends of Alex and Jamie. Then a beat-up F-150 pickup parked at the curb and an older Mexican man got out with a few younger kids. He had some kind of case with him. Another group of teens walked up the sidewalk from the south, while six or seven of Jerry's friends from AA showed up from the other direction.

"What the heck is going on?" Jerry asked no one in particular.

"You said you didn't care who came," Alex reminded him with a smile.

Michael Thomas strode up the driveway with a backpack and a small case on wheels. "Hey, I'm Michael. Is this where Brother Louis will be singing?"

"Yeah. I'm Alex Palmer, I play bass. This is my brother, Jamie, he plays drums, and this is Jerry. This is Jerry's house and he plays guitar."

Everyone in the small group shook everyone else's hand.

"I'm really excited to meet you guys," Michael said. "I'm not exaggerating when I say this, but when I heard Brother Louis singing at the Y, it just lit me up. It reminded me about what I love about discovering new music. I have no agenda here other than to help encourage that man to sing. The world needs to hear his voice."

"You won't find us disagreeing with you there," Jerry said.

Michael went about setting up his recording gear. Jerry watched him with a bit of concern but decided there was no time to worry about it right then.

He strolled around the growing crowd of folks gathering in his driveway and backyard, welcoming them and trying to find out who they were and, when possible, why they were here. After talking to a handful of folks, he started to sense a theme. Everyone just wanted to see and hear something "real." Jerry was afraid this might be a bit *too* real for some of them.

When he got to Cesar's group, he was a bit taken aback. "I'm Jerry. Welcome to our little gathering. Who are you fine folks? How'd you hear about this?"

Marisol spoke up first. "I'm a friend of Alex's."

Jerry nodded. He'd heard about her.

"And this is my friend Gabriella." She tilted her head and placed her arm around the young woman to her right. "We've been friends since grade school and when she saw Jamie's video of your group, she thought it might be something her grandfather would like."

Cesar sat to Gabriella's right, behind his ever-present shades, expressionless, through the whole explanation. Jerry hadn't thought of this as an open mic night, but he also didn't want to seem rude. He wasn't sure how much English Cesar understood or spoke, but Jerry worked out that the case held a small accordion.

"I tell you what," he said off the top of his head. "If you hear a part for the squeeze box, you just jump on in, okay?"

Cesar gave a slight nod, but Jerry couldn't tell if it was an affirming nod or simply an acknowledgment that he recognized that Jerry had stopped talking. Jerry thought there was a certain risk in the offer he had just made, but he also did not expect his new acquaintance to take him up on it. The whole exchange was awkward, to say the least.

When it got to be seven o'clock and the musicians were ready, there were already more than fifty people sitting in the driveway and backyard, not knowing what to expect. None of them had expected this to be a concert, and Louis, in particular, seemed to be feeling a bit agitated at the idea. He kept saying, "This is quite interesting," over and over again.

Being the owner of the garage, Jerry felt it must be his job to say something to the audience. As he approached the microphone, he realized how little he wanted to ever become a front man.

"Well." He moved instinctively away from the microphone when he heard his voice come through the speakers. "I'm Jerry and this is my driveway. These are some friends of mine and we've played music together as a group one time, two nights ago. We felt like something special happened, so we decided to do it again tonight. We've never practiced, and we didn't expect this to be like a concert, but if you're here that must mean you're supposed to be here, and I'm glad you are."

That last idea had just occurred to him as he said it. But it felt very true.

"We don't know exactly what we're going to do here tonight. And Brother Louis here has never sung in public, so the more we can make this feel like a group of friends hanging out and the less we can make it feel like a show, well, that'd probably be good."

And with that, Jamie and Alex kicked off "Ain't No Sunshine."

The magic was back. Louis overcame his nerves within just a few minutes and the gathered folks started to interact with the musicians more like members of the band than as an audience. A couple of them moved their chairs into the garage and sat very close to Alex and Jerry. Several sang harmonies with Louis once they figured out his lines. A small chorus evolved. A few found percussion instruments with which to contribute. One kid ran home and came back with a mandolin he played quietly along with the group.

They moved through several songs on their "set list." Someone on the lawn shouted out a Ray LaMontagne song that neither Jerry nor Louis had ever heard. Alex and Jamie knew it, though, and the chords were simple enough, so Jerry played along and the girl who requested it sang it. As the song grew on him, Louis came up with some backing vocals.

The whole evening was like that. There was little divide between "band" and "audience." But the music was definitely in charge. No one wanted to do anything to interrupt the incredible flow that was happening.

When it felt like it might be time to wrap up, Alex got Jerry's attention. "Can we try your song, man?"

Jerry's eyes widened as he glanced from Alex to the driveway and yard full of people.

"Your song?" Louis interjected. "You've written a song?"

Jerry explained how few lyrics it really had, and that it was really just an idea he had written for his daughter long ago.

Louis could see the excitement in Alex's and Jamie's faces, and something much different in Jerry's. "Let's see what happens."

Jerry felt like his stomach was going to erupt—like he was walking out on a tightrope over an abyss—but he closed his eyes and started playing. Alex waited about twelve bars so Jerry could establish the tempo and groove he was feeling that night, and then Alex came in with a bass line that was both countermelody and anchored to the rhythm. It provided just enough of a grid for Jamie to find a sweet but subtle and airy drum pattern. The three of them played through the pattern one more full time, with Jerry doing that two-at-once thing again—somehow finding most of the melody on the high strings while covering the chords with the others. Having the bass in there gave him some new options.

Louis, with the short bit of lyrics now scribbled down on the back of a receipt from his wallet, began to find the melody of this haunting, aching lullaby. His first phrase pulled the air from Jerry's lungs.

Oh sweet Marianne
Breathe it out and breathe it in

He repeated that phrase several times, adjusting the melody slightly each time and interacting with the notes Jerry was playing. Like the lyric said— the song was breathing in and out, in and out.

Don't be afraid
There's nothing to fear
You're not alone, I'm not much I know
But I'm right here

That last line, "I'm not much, I know, but I'm right here," became the refrain. Louis kept looping it, with a melody that landed somewhere between a lullaby and a romantic love song.

Then the band took an instrumental section and Louis just improvised with some random, wordless vocalizations. Maybe more lyrics could go here some day, he thought.

Then from out in the darkness, with the moon rising over the neighbor's fence and this impromptu community of former strangers bound together in this shared moment, the sound of Cesar's accordion crept into the sonic landscape and sent several people into immediate tears.

He stood, silhouetted in the moonlight, with no need for a microphone, and played his prayers for each of his children, grandchildren, and great-grandchildren. He played his memories of Nuevo Laredo, from the hot, hopeless fields to the lively dance halls with delicate norteño flourishes. He played for his long gone parents, remembering elements of the theme he played for Father Constance all those years before. Cesar incorporated elements of romance and passion for his beloved wife across town. His chords and melodies wrapped themselves around and through the simple arrangement, as he offered up a sound to the sky that was as sacred as anything he had uttered in any cathedral or chapel.

As he allowed his prayers to rise and his notes to flow, he also allowed some tears to fall. Gabriella slipped to the ground and sat at his feet, the way she had done when she was little. She wrapped her arms around his leg, never wanting the moment to end. But Cesar brought his part down and stayed in the band, adding his notes subtly and shaping the chords in yet new ways as Louis repeated the opening line a few more times as a sort of coda.

> *Breathe it out and breathe it in*
> *Breathe it out and breathe it in*
> *Breathe it out breathe it in*

On the third time, the band instinctively resolved the final chord. And then there was silence.

Long after the instruments were packed up and the garage door was closed on that Saturday night, no one wanted to leave. Just about everyone lingered, soaking in the afterglow of one of the most intense and yet effortlessly comfortable experiences any of them could recall. Pockets of people were clustered in Jerry's backyard, in his driveway, sitting along the sidewalk, and on his front porch. Several folks had even wandered right into his front room.

Jerry, Brother Louis, and Cesar were sitting at the dinette table for over an hour sharing their background stories. Jerry must have thanked Cesar thirty times for joining in on that song. "I just can't tell you enough," he kept saying, "what that meant to me."

"It meant much to me as well," Cesar replied. "We all have people to pray for."

"Would you consider joining us again?" Louis asked. "I know it might seem that a lot of the music we played tonight—especially the soul music— might not fit with your style," he continued awkwardly, "but I have a feeling that you could bring something special to the mix."

Jerry jumped right in. "And we don't have any kind of sound defined yet anyway We're just making this up! Why not come and help us build something from the beginning? Maybe we can find a way to bring the best aspects of Latin, soul, gospel, country, rock and roll—all of it—into something fresh."

Then he realized he was talking pretty fast. Cesar was just sitting there, silently watching him. Jerry thought none of this was making any sense to him.

Then Cesar said one word. "*¡Crisol!*"

Both Jerry and Brother Louis looked confused.

"Like a *crisol*," Cesar said.

Gabriella, who had been eavesdropping nearby, translated. "He says it's like a melting pot. A *crisol* is like a small pot you use for combining different ingredients when you cook, but it's also a part of a melting chamber where molten steel goes. When you say that America is a 'melting pot' you're talking about a *crisol*."

"*Crisol!*" Jerry said. "That's it. Will you be in our *crisol*?"

Cesar smiled and shrugged a bit. "Why not?" he seemed to be saying.

Michael Thomas was out on the front porch talking with Alex and Jamie, along with some other young people. They could see the elders sitting at the dinette table inside and wondered what they were talking about.

"I'm telling you guys," Michael said, "this is special. I haven't felt this way about music in a long time."

"Me either," Alex said. "And it blows my mind that it never would have happened if I hadn't walked outside right when I did a couple weeks ago. I heard Jerry sitting right where you are, playing that Martin, and I just couldn't believe it. Brother Louis wasn't even part of it yet."

"I don't know," Jamie said. "Doesn't it kind of feel like something else is going on? Like something spiritual or something?"

"I think all music is spiritual in a way," Michael offered.

"That's not what I mean," Jamie said. "I mean, like there were all these pieces sitting right here next to each other for all this time and God just said, 'Okay, enough is enough. I'm putting these people together.'"

Turning to his brother, Jamie continued. "Like, how long have we known Jerry? As long as I can remember. And I've never thought of talking to him about his life and his stories, and I never had any idea that he might be one of the most interesting guitar players I'd ever heard. To me, he was just another gray-haired guy. And he told me earlier that he and Brother Louis have lived three blocks apart for forty years and never even met each other. It just feels like we needed some kind of push to bring us together."

"Yeah, I hear you," Alex said. "I'm not very religious. I haven't thought about God in I don't know how long. But tonight, when we played that last song, I swear it felt like God was telling me that he still thinks about me."

"Man," Michael said. "You're gonna make me start crying all over again!"

They broke the moment up with some more laughter but couldn't pull themselves out of it completely.

"I'll tell you what, though." Michael gestured at the oldsters sitting inside at the table. "I'll follow those guys anywhere. If this is church, call me an altar boy."

The men at the table agreed that they would reconvene for another music night the following Saturday, but Jerry invited the two of them to come over before then, just to hang out for some peace and quiet.

Word started to spread about what had happened on Boscobel that second Saturday night. Deacon George was practically giddy when he and Brother Louis stopped over to visit Jerry after church on Sunday. They walked up and found Jerry working on his photo album.

"Jerry, my friend," George began. "I certainly hope you are filled with God's grace and peace on this lovely day. I am still simply beside myself over the wonderful evening of music and fellowship that happened here last night. I'll admit I had high hopes for you and Brother Louis to hit it off. But I would have been happy for you and the boys to have gotten him to sing a song or two. Last night, though. That was holy ground, Jerry. Holy ground."

Louis was nodding along.

"I'm not sure what to say, George," Jerry said. "I don't disagree."

"What I don't think you might be quite as aware of, however," George continued, "is all of the wonderful stuff that was happening around the music. I don't know if you could hear all of the participation while you were playing, but it really was amazing. People were singing along with you and playing their own instruments. Young people were visiting with older people and White people were praying with African American people. I can be given to hyperbole from time to time, but Jerry, Brother Louis and I have been talking about this all morning— it felt like something truly holy and beautiful. I know you gentlemen weren't setting out to do anything religious last night, but as a deacon, I'm telling you, that was church!"

"I'm glad to hear you say that, George," Jerry said. "You obviously know a lot more about church than I do. But I agree that it felt special. It felt different than any religious thing I've been a part of. I don't know how to explain it, but when I think of all the things that keep so many people divided and the things that keep some people away from church, like the politics and the hostility, and then I think about what happened last night, I wonder about what might be possible."

"I like how you're thinking," George said.

"Look," Jerry continued, "I don't think we need to do anything to try to take anyone out of any kind of church or religious thing they may be a part of. But maybe this thing can be something healing and welcoming for people of any age or race or whatever. We just let it be what it will be. We let the Spirit take it where it wants to take it. And if, along the way, someone feels they want to take it to more of a church place, we can point them to you guys or any of the other churches in the neighborhood."

"That sounds good," George said. "I think you might be surprised at how many people you can reach with love and grace, just by taking the accoutrements of modern church culture out of the equation."

"It's like our recovery meetings," Jerry said. "We acknowledge a higher power and have no problem with folks understanding that however they want to or need to. When I first got sober, I had a real problem thinking about God the way he had been presented to me by religious folks. The program didn't do that. I could approach God in whatever way worked, because they understood that God was big enough to handle my confusion. And who among us gets it exactly right anyway?"

"That's a very interesting perspective," Louis said. "I have to admit, I've not really thought that much about it, and I've never cared too much about the little arguments over details between this church or that church—the old folks used to call it 'majoring on the minors.' I just want young people to know, and to feel, that God is love—and that God loves them. When I hear great music, I feel God's love. When I was a young man I felt that in church, but these days I think many folks just can't feel that in or about church. There's just too much other nonsense stuck all over it."

"I know this is all just getting started," George said, "and I don't want to squash anything or overthink anything. But I will offer right now to help you gentlemen however I can. I have a feeling we're on the verge of something very special for our little community here. I've been trying to find a way to talk about the important things in life with my neighbors for decades and now it's happening, and I can't stop it! Our block might never be the same."

Jerry agreed with his friend George, but he had a feeling that this neighborhood thing could outgrow his driveway fast. What would happen if they had a hundred people come? How big could this get before it would cease to have the intimacy and relatability that everyone valued so much? He had seen things blow up before. He was seeing it all over East Nashville. But he would worry about that when the time came.

"You're right," Jerry said. "Our block might never be the same."

By the following Tuesday, Michael Thomas had rough mixes of a few of the songs he had recorded in the garage. They weren't ready for release or anything, but everyone was amazed at how good they sounded. Jerry and Louis had to have Alex bring a smartphone over that could play the files for them. They all sat at Louis's kitchen table and listened on a small speaker.

"Wow," Louis said. "He wasn't kidding, was he? That kid knows what he's doing."

"I told you," Alex said. "He wins awards for this stuff. People pay him a bunch of money for this, and he's just doing this because you guys are changing his life."

Jerry and Louis laughed a bit, but they took the compliment seriously, too.

"He'd like to come this Saturday and do it again, with just a little bit more equipment," Alex said. "That cool with you guys?"

"I'm holding on to all of this loosely," Louis said. "It's fine with me, as long as he doesn't release anything that we don't agree to."

What the crew did not count on was that several folks in attendance the previous Saturday recorded bits of songs on their phones and posted them on social media, raving about the experience. The buzz was building in a big way.

The whole gang was a bit more prepared when Saturday number three came around. The gear was all set up a bit earlier. Michael got his recording equipment sound checked early, including a few microphones out amongst the "crowd" to capture any impromptu contributions. Cesar came over a couple hours early and did some warming up that bordered on a rehearsal with Jerry.

Alex set out a notebook and a pen so they could get people's phone numbers and email addresses. Jerry pulled a bunch of old branches and scrap wood together so they could build a bonfire in the back yard after their "set."

And then, at about a quarter to seven, the people started showing up. By seven o'clock there were over 100 people. By seven thirty it had to be over 150. The driveway was full. The yard was full. Alex and Jamie's backyard was full. Jerry noticed a few folks with guitar cases and some with percussion instruments. He could tell that a good number of these folks were expecting to contribute. He huddled up the group and asked Deacon George to join them.

"Well, folks," Jerry began. "Here we are. I think it's pretty clear something is happening that might just be beyond us. I have two things to ask. First, is it okay with everyone if Deacon George opens us up with a prayer?"

Everyone in the huddle nodded.

"Second, I'm seeing lots of instruments out there. I think people want to contribute, and I'm of a mind to let them. Anyone have any ideas about how we can do that in a way that makes sense?"

Jamie spoke up. "What if we did a few songs the way we did last week—so we can set the tone and define the kind of inclusive atmosphere we want to have? Then we have a section of three or four songs where we invite others to come up with their instruments or just their voices and join us. That section goes for a little while and who knows what happens. But then we circle back and end with a few songs together?"

Everyone thought that sounded like a great idea.

"Will you explain that?" Jerry asked. "I'm nervous about people starting to think I'm in charge of this or something."

Everyone smiled and Jamie agreed to talk about the plan for the night. Then Deacon George gathered them up for a prayer. "Heavenly Father," he intoned in his deepest baritone voice. "We sense Your presence here tonight. We thank You for each other. We thank You for this music—Your music. We thank You for each person out there tonight. Make us one. Be honored by the sound we make. May it be a sweet sound in Your ears. Amen."

The night was incredible. Again. Cesar played through the whole night, and everyone was amazed by the diversity and range of styles and tones he could pull from his accordion.

A new kid no one seemed to know showed up with an electric guitar. He was young—maybe sixteen. Jerry thought he looked like a cross between Sly Stone, Lenny Kravitz, and Prince. His name was Beau, but he said that people called him B-Flat. He seemed to have a ton of attitude, but when the "play with the band" section came, they invited him up. He plugged his old Les Paul into a small combo tube amp and laid down some of the sweetest, most tasteful blues licks and chords any of them had heard.

There was a dad in his forties who brought some harmonicas and a few girls who brought ukuleles. At one point Louis noticed about thirty phones glowing as folks recorded the proceedings. Before the next song he decided to say something.

"Brothers and sisters," he said. "I know what I'm about to say will probably earn me the 'Grandpa' tag for life, but I have a request for you. Would everyone with one of those smartphones take it out right now?"

They did.

"Hold them up for me, let me see them."

Everyone obliged.

"Now," Louis said, "as you hold that phone up, I want you to close your eyes. Now, with your eyes closed, I want you to think about something. Think about that little thing in your hand. Think about the power you have given it over your life. Think about the people you have surrendered your identity to—the folks you hope are impressed by something you have to say, or some picture you can take, or something you're about to eat."

He got some chuckles with that last bit.

"Now, keep your eyes closed, but think about that stuff. Think about all the stuff you've recorded last month and last year and never went back and looked at. You missed the moment because you were recording it so you could show other people that you saw that thing or had that experience, but you ended up not having the whole experience.

"Now think about how long I've been talking and how bad you want to click that thing and look at it. You see, friends, I think a lot of us have allowed those little things to become like handcuffs on our minds and our hearts. They steal our attention from things that matter and our presence away from ground that is holy. Now, I'm not gonna ask you to throw your phone into the night. But I am going to invite you to look to your neighbor on your right or your left, right now, and say 'will you hold this for me? Will you take this and keep it safe until we're done here tonight so I can be fully present?' Now—what are you going to say to your neighbor?"

Several people said "yes" and and were handing each other their phones. A few slipped theirs back in their pockets or purses. Jerry looked over and saw Alex and Jamie trading phones, too.

"And next time we gather, let's commit to each other that we do it without those little handcuffs. Are you with me?"

Everyone cheered.

"Okay, now that that's done," Jerry chimed in, "let's sing a round of this Johnny Cash song 'I'm Free from the Chain Gang Now.'" Everyone was laughing, but they were into it, too. He taught the old song to the crowd and Cesar came up with an amazing accordion part. Then they transitioned into Tom Petty's "Free Fallin'," and the assembled congregation sang so loud that one grouchy neighbor called the police.

When they wrapped up for the evening, Alex went up to the mic and asked everyone to find the notebook he had set out earlier. "Look. If this thing keeps growing, we won't be able to keep doing this in Jerry's garage much longer. We need your contact info so if we find a better place, we can let you know.

Someone lit the bonfire, and the next part of the evening started—the part where a diverse group of people from a wide range of cultures and backgrounds spent hours getting to know each other, hearing each others' stories, encouraging each other, and even praying for each other.

The group agreed that this thing—this tribal gathering, or whatever it was—would happen every Thursday night from that point forward.

Alex and Jerry met for lunch the next day to talk through a few things. By the end of that evening, Alex had collected 163 names and email addresses. He also created a Facebook group, which was quite a challenge since the thing they were doing had no name and Jerry wasn't even on Facebook. After some gentle coaxing and Alex showing him that even Brother Louis had a Facebook profile, Jerry allowed the boys to set one up for him.

"I'm never going to touch that thing!" he swore. "Don't expect me to start updating my status or checking in to locations or any of that nonsense." He made liberal use of air quotes.

"I'd be terribly disappointed if you did," Alex teased. "I set you up with a grandpa account. Once a week it automatically sends a message to all of the kids in your neighborhood saying '*Get off my lawn!*'"

Jerry threw what was left of his sandwich right in Alex's face for that one, but they were both laughing. He understood the ubiquity of social media. It's just that he had heard so much about internet stuff in his recovery groups, he had decided to stay off-line as much as possible. He had an addict's brain, and as far as he could tell, the internet to the addict's brain was like Las Vegas to a gambler. Best to just stay the hell out.

But he understood the mechanics and didn't want to be unreasonable. He gave Alex some information so he could set up the log-in details, and he even posed for a reasonably nice profile picture at the deli where they were having lunch. The best part, in addition to the food and that they had a nice place to sit outside when the weather was decent, was that Mitchell Deli had a free jukebox with actual vinyl records in it. Jerry would make the drive up to Inglewood sometimes just for that!

"Hey," Alex said, as they were heading to their cars. "There was a girl at your place last night named Stephanie. She lives somewhere near us and heard about everything from a friend of a friend or something. Anyway, she was there and said that her grandmother is moving here from Manhattan and used to be both a poet and a literature professor. I guess she was a real free-spirit type back in the day. So, Stephanie wondered if maybe you'd want her grandma to come to one of our nights and maybe read some poetry or work with some kids on writing lyrics or something. I told her I'd talk to you about it, but I had no idea."

"Is that what they call a 'poetry slam?'" Jerry asked. "That could be interesting. Why doesn't this girl just bring her grandma over next week and let her see for herself. If she wants to get up and read something, I'm sure we could make some time."

"I guess she thinks that her grandma would be much more likely to come if she was expected," Alex surmised. "Like, if she was invited or something. I don't know. Maybe it's more hassle than it's worth."

"No, I get it, actually. This young lady is smart. She doesn't want her grandma, who doesn't know anyone here, to feel like she is pushing herself on a new crowd. Things were different in her day. People waited until they were asked into a place."

Jerry thought for a few more seconds. "Yeah. Send this girl my number. Tell her I'd be happy to meet her grandma. I'll get coffee with her and personally invite her to come over and read some of her poetry. If it's good and she feels comfortable, who knows, maybe she'll stick around. If not, what did it cost me? It's not like I've got so much else going on. I can make time for a little old grandma or two."

"Sounds good. I'll set it up. Oh, and I'll write your log-in info down on this piece of paper with this No. 2 pencil, so if you ever decide that you actually want to join the rest of society online, you can do so at your convenience."

That comment got Alex a face full of wadded-up napkins.

Present Day

Back on the porch, Jerry was about to get in some trouble. "There are only a couple of people on this planet who get to call me a grandma!" A stern voice spoke up from the sidewalk as Nadia made her way toward the house, guided by her granddaughter. "I hear you talking about me up there, old man!"

"Ooh, you're in for it now," Jamie chuckled. "Looks like the doghouse for you."

"I thought this *was* the doghouse!" Jerry quipped. That got the whole group going, including the sharp grandmother.

"Good morning, everyone," Nadia said in her unmistakable New York accent. "Sorry to be so tardy. I see you started having fun without me."

Louis hurried to the bottom step to escort her up, though she was familiar enough with Jerry's porch to find her way just fine.

"Good to see you, Ms. Nadia," Louis said. "We've just been visiting with young Miss Marisol here, telling her our stories. She's a writer and a friend of Alex's."

"It's so good to meet you, Ms. Morton." Marisol offered her hand. "I am a huge fan of your work. The piece you read last night was amazing."

"Well thank you, honey. But let's get past the fan thing as fast as possible and become friends. It sounds like we're both writers. No need to settle for vapid conventions like mere fandom. I do appreciate the affirmation, however."

Marisol liked her even more.

"I'm working on a story about this, well, this whole musical—cultural—spiritual phenomenon. I'd love to hear about your background and how a literature professor and poet from Manhattan got involved with *Los Perros Perrdidos*."

"Certainly," Nadia said. "It will be my pleasure to share with you my account of these auspicious days. I'm not sure any of us are the best witnesses to our own story, but I'll be as truthful as I can. Where did you guys leave off?"

New York Style

When Nadia Morton had first accepted the invitation to meet this "Jerry" character from the band, she was not sure that she wanted to follow through with it. She had first come for a visit to East Nashville from New York City when her son, Daniel, first moved there, and it seemed promising. But boy, the money was moving in fast. She was more than half blind but could still see that certain aspects of the community might have already grown past the point of no return. Back when she still had all her eyesight, she liked to think that she was a pretty sharp judge of neighborhoods, buildings, and people. Now she couldn't quite get her eyes adjusted to the coffee shop she was sitting in, waiting for some bus driver she'd only heard about but never met—and had no idea what he even looked like, not that that mattered. The whole thing was definitely not her style.

Nadia used to sketch and paint constantly and still had every book of poetry and every journal entry she had ever written. In fact, it's those poems that had brought her to this booth. Her neighborhood in the East Village of Manhattan gave her a constant source of things to draw, paint, or write about. She still wrote and tried to draw, but she could barely see anymore. The doctors said she'd be completely blind within the next couple of years. She thanked God for the voice memo feature on her phone. She would have preferred to just languish in her apartment, alone. Or at least that's what she told herself. This going out and meeting people—in this condition—was insane. How did she let her granddaughter talk her into this?

She still could not quite accept the fact that she would have to move here to live with Daniel and his family soon. It was humiliating. She knew that when these young people saw her—like that twenty-year-old who took her coffee order—all they saw was a broken-down, gray-haired, half-blind old lady that had no business taking up space in their fine establishment. She knew this because she remembered thinking the exact same thing about old folks when they would come to hear jazz in her favorite club in the Village. Nadia hated being old. How the hell did she get to be seventy?

"Excuse me," a faceless female voice said to her from the next table over. "I don't mean to bother you, but I noticed the tag on your bag looks like a transit ticket from the New York subway. Are you from New York?"

"Yes, dear," Nadia said nicely, but with a touch of attitude. "I've lived in the East Village since the sixties, and the Bowery before that. I just arrived for a visit with my son who has lived here in East Nashville for about fifteen years."

"Oh my gosh!" the girl said, as if Nadia were some kind of rock star. Nadia guessed from the sound of the girl's voice that she was a college student. She sounded a lot like her granddaughter. "I *love* the East Village. I've only been there once, but it was amazing. You've been there since the sixties? You must have some incredible stories! Were you part of the art scene there in back then?"

"Sweetheart," Nadia said, her voice now much more relaxed, "You have no idea."

1967

Nadia Louise Morton was a highly intentional participant in the counter-culture scene of late 1960s New York. She was a thoroughly put-together young woman, effortlessly attractive due to her strong sense of self. She perfected a low-maintenance sense of style, with her long, straight, dark-blonde hair often pulled back into a simple ponytail. She didn't fancy spending a lot of time fussing over what to wear or what makeup to use, but she was no slouch, either. Her look was graceful, efficient, and lively.

There were several distinct types of characters onstage in the play that was 1960s New York, and she was fascinated by all of them. Nadia turned seventeen in 1965 and was obsessed with being and becoming the best kind of world-changer. She had a sense, deep in her bones, that she had been born at exactly the right time. Everything in the universe was tilting in the right direction for a change. She was certain that her generation had the potential to leave the world in better shape than they had found it. She was wide eyed, optimistic, excitable, and irascible. She found people fascinating and saw her life as a canvas on which only the best ideas should be painted. She studied people, sketched them. She made notes. She came up with seven basic types and knew which one she wanted to be.

The Mindless Rebels. Nadia didn't find them interesting, but they were certainly entertaining to watch. They pushed against every boundary and rejected every convention without ever considering if it was helpful or not. She assumed their type had been around since the dawn of time and found that they didn't ask good questions or offer anything resembling an answer.

The Cools. They were kind of like the rebels, but they didn't want to get in trouble. Their main, two-part objective was to look rebellious and to feel comfortable. They were obsessed with symbols—fashion, physique, and cars. Everything was symbolic to The Cools. If you questioned their icons they disappeared.

The Dreamers. They were interesting because no matter what shape you presented to them, they saw a cloud. They were satisfied to live in that twilight space between waking and sleeping. She envied them. She tried to be a dreamer for several years and every so often, she would have a moment or two of solidarity with the species. It was her inability to sustain the willing suspension of disbelief that woke her up each time.

The Pragmatists. Some of them became bankers and some became socialists. Their ideology could vary wildly, but their defining skill was an ability to see things as they could be manipulated most effectively. They saw the levers and cables behind the curtains. They were the ones who organized the marches and got things done. She saw elements of a pragmatist in herself. It scared her sometimes.

The Oblivious. They had no idea what was going on and didn't want to hear about it. They wanted to be entertained and could have drowned in water that was two inches deep. The Oblivious drove her crazy. They invested so much energy in avoiding the knowledge of good and evil, even as the juice of forbidden fruit poured down their faces.

The Nihilists. They had given up on anything and everything. They tended to ask some good questions but succumbed to despair before the conversation could get anywhere productive. Most nihilists, it seemed, had been something else before their eyes were opened. Once that happened and they saw themselves as they were, they panicked and gave up on the entire pursuit.

But then there were **The Servants.** These were the people you rarely saw in the magazines or on TV. They were the ones who lay their lives down for others. They put themselves in harm's way for the benefit of someone else. They eschewed the pursuit of their own comfort as an end in itself. It was as if their eyes had been opened to some kind of hidden reality about the meaning of life, but instead of freaking out like the Nihilist, they found a way to take care of someone else.

Nadia developed a keen eye for servants. She called them "saints in the shadows." She sketched them. She wrote about them. She interviewed them. When she was twelve, she had noticed a nurse pushing an old man in a wheelchair in Washington Square Park. She followed the nurse for half an hour, learning all about her training, her background, her calling. Most people enjoyed talking with Nadia. She had written a paper in the eighth grade about a man who collected clothes for homeless veterans.

As the sixties came into full flower, Nadia did too, she found the hippie ethic compelling in some ways and off-putting in others. She went to Woodstock and both enjoyed the music and mourned the self-absorption. She became very invested in protesting the Vietnam War on behalf of the wasted lives on both sides of the conflict, but she was dismayed to find so few people her age willing to volunteer at VA hospitals to help clean and care for the young men who had returned from the war with terrible injuries and disabilities. The needs were so great she thought she might just surrender to the waves of despair at times. Instead she tried to surf those waves, constantly finding new ways to help people.

By the time she turned twenty-one, with a literature degree under her belt and absolutely no idea what to do with her life, Nadia joined the Peace Corps. It was interesting but far too bureaucratic and politicized for her. By the time the mid-seventies came around and most of the hippies were pupating into Yuppies, Nadia was working on her second master's degree, this one in philosophy, as she continued to seek the most effective and meaningful way to serve humanity. She was determined not to become a nihilist, but it was getting harder every year. The philosophy degree wasn't helping.

In the summer of 1976, as the country celebrated two hundred years of whatever the United States meant, Nadia had decided to spend a weekend upstate visiting an old friend named Melissa. They heard about a music festival happening at a farm nearby and wandered down, only to find out that all of the music was of the "Jesus Music" variety. The artists looked normal—blue jeans and typical musician-length hair—and they sounded "normal." And their songs were asking the right questions: Why were they here? Was there more to life than met the eye? But their answers, it turned out, were to be found in the words and work of a decidedly nonreligious conception of Jesus.

Nadia caught a glimpse of this Jesus on a homemade T-shirt, and he looked a lot like a friend of hers from the Village. This was "Hippie Jesus." He cared about the poor. He cared about the outcast. He wanted to bring people together. He spoke truth to power. He cared about justice, and He paid for it. A skinny guy with long blond hair and an eerily high voice got up on stage and sang a song called "I Am A Servant," and Nadia was intrigued.

She and Melissa ended up being pulled into an hours-long conversation with a group of a half-dozen people who lived in a sort of Christian commune in the area. Nadia had never heard of such a thing, but when she learned that they shared their money in order to give to people in need, she was interested. They stayed up most of the night talking about the difference between fear-based religion and relationship-based faith. Each of the other folks carried their own massive Bible and was able to find passages at will. The conversation moved from the extremely practical—almost legal definitions of sin and righteousness—to downright mystical stuff about human nature, prayer, and the "Holy Spirit."

"The bottom line," one of the commune members said, "is that it starts with a step of faith on your part and an invitation from you to Jesus. You surrender to his love and grace and submit your will to his, and then watch and see what happens."

Her friend wasn't buying it, but this countercultural Jesus made all the sense in the world to Nadia. One verse that stood out was where it said that there was no greater love in the world than when someone would lay down his life for a friend. It was as if these folks had been listening to every question Nadia had been asking the universe for decades.

She took home some books and got some information about a Bible study that met in the city. She found it the following Thursday night and never looked back. Nadia had no idea that the Bible had any of this stuff in it. She had studied aspects of it in both her literature and philosophy programs but always through a removed, critical, cultural lens. With these people, though, Jesus had become real. Radical. But the rebellion he was calling them to was one of self-sacrifice, not civil disobedience or sanctified consumption.

Nadia found that she could serve her neighbors, be it the wounded veterans at the VA, the disabled children at the hospital, the homeless folks at the shelter, or the crazy people in the park, as an act of worship of the one true God. The whole thing blew her mind. And as strange, or mystical, as it sounded, she started to feel the presence of Jesus as she served these people.

Along the way she met Charlie Morton. He was a couple of years younger than she and played guitar at the Thursday Bible study. They started spending a lot of time together and, in pretty short order, decided that Jesus wanted them to be married. Neither expected much resistance or guidance from their families. Charlie's parents were in California, and he hadn't seen them in years; they seemed to prefer it that way. Nadia's parents had divorced when she was very young. She hadn't seen her father in years, and her mother was in her sixties and living in Pennsylvania with a new man. Nadia and her mother didn't have much of a relationship, but she was looking forward to bringing Charlie to meet her. It was the first "normal" thing she had done in a long time.

Nadia's mom was pleasant enough when she had met Charlie, but she never did warm up to the "Jesus freak" aspect of their relationship. That was fine with Nadia. She had been on her own for so long, she didn't feel the need to have her mom's blessing or understanding. Before they left Pennsylvania, though, Charlie dug into her just a little bit about what "honoring your father and mother" might actually mean. It stung, but he made some good points. Nadia wasn't used to having someone push back against her like that. It was good.

"Look, Mom," Nadia said before they departed. "I know this doesn't make a lot of sense to you. I understand that. And I'm sorry that I've been so distant. I don't have a good excuse for that. Charlie pointed out to me that I haven't done a very good job of honoring you. I think it's just been easier to be on my own."

"I'm sure it has," her mother said plainly. "Your father and I didn't make anything easy for you. And you made it pretty clear that you were determined to live life on your own terms. I've tried to respect that—and I'm very proud of all the work you've done and the education you have gotten. You're an amazing young woman, honey. I just don't understand how that fierce, independent, thoughtful woman becomes this radical, religious Jesus

follower who's going to marry a Christian boy you barely know. It just…
well…it just seems kinda loony!"

Nadia laughed at that. Mom had a point. "Yeah, I can see that. You've
only seen this little snapshot. You haven't seen the rest of the scenery. I
guess I'm just asking you to trust the smart, thoughtful woman you think I
am and assume that I haven't lost my marbles completely!"

They both chuckled a bit more at that and hugged.

"Well," her mom continued, "most crazy people are not as self-aware as
you seem to be. I'm willing to give you the benefit of the doubt. But do me
a favor. You say you've heard from Jesus—that he talks to you. The next
time he reaches out, tell him to stop by and say hi to me. I've got a few
questions for him."

"I'll do that, Mom. No problem."

Nadia and Charlie got married later that year in the cutest, Jesus-hip-
pie-est, no-budget little wedding that the Village had ever seen. The members of their Bible study were there, and Nadia's mom even came over for
the event. They decorated their little apartment with Bible verses and "hippie Jesus" art and listened to records by some of the artists Nadia had heard
at that festival the previous summer.

They tried going to church on Sundays several times, but it was difficult.
Just because Nadia had accepted the Gospel message did not mean that she
could accept Christian culture. In fact, the opposite was probably true. "My
tolerance for these obvious incongruities was significantly higher *before* I
learned about Jesus," she had told Charlie after their fourth church visit.
"I just don't understand how so many of my fellow believers can say they
love Jesus and worship Jesus and believe in Jesus and respect the Bible and
yet do nothing that he says or that the Bible teaches about the poor or the
vulnerable.

"And I'm sorry," she added as they walked home from their seventh
church visit, "but giving money so people can go to a jungle a million miles
away and tell people about Jesus in a language they don't understand makes

zero sense when there are people with no coats right across the street and it's getting cold!"

Charlie had grown up in church, so he was used to the disconnect. But he found Nadia's passion refreshing. For a while. After the tenth visit he started to realize that they might never find a church that lived up to her standards. They started doing their own private Bible study on Sunday mornings and then going to hand out peanut butter sandwiches in the park.

Nadia eventually got pregnant and gave birth to Daniel. It was a very difficult pregnancy that almost cost Nadia her life. After Daniel was born, Nadia had a tubal ligation and Charlie's dream of a big Christian family was shot down. The three of them moved into a slightly larger apartment on the Upper East Side, and Charlie stayed home to take care of the baby while Nadia worked as a teacher at a local high school.

After about five years, with the gas running out of their marriage and the 1980s seeming to explode with opportunity, Charlie starting getting some ideas. Nadia barely made it in the door from work one evening when he told her he had some things he needed to share with her.

"I've got a burden," he said—and Nadia tried not to roll her eyes. "I feel like God has laid some things on my heart and I need to let you know. I'm actually really excited!"

Nadia was suspicious. She hadn't seen much of an indication that Charlie was hearing from God very clearly in years. He watched a lot of television and seemed to be hearing from some prominent teachers and speakers, but she wasn't sure that they all spoke for God.

Charlie cleared his throat and made his most serious face. "I need to be in church. Actually, I think I should be leading a church."

Nadia's eyebrows lifted as her eyes widened. She cocked her head slightly to the left. This was news.

"I feel that I am being called back to California. My parents are there, and they're not getting any younger, of course. And there are some churches out there that are growing like crazy. I think I could get a job at one of them—

probably as a youth pastor at first, but I'm pretty sure I could get on a path toward head pastor within a couple of years. I've been neglecting my calling and I just can't do it anymore."

"But California is so expensive. And I wouldn't be able to earn nearly as much out there if I had to start at the bottom and work my way back up. That is, *if* I could even find a teaching job."

"You wouldn't have to work." The look on Charlie's face revealed that he knew this would not be a selling point with Nadia. "This is my time to shine. Besides, my family will help us if we need it. They've wanted us out there for years. I've already talked to Mom, and I know they would help us with the cost of moving and getting settled."

Nadia didn't even bother to roll her eyes at that gem. Charlie's family had money. The romanticism of sanctified lower-middle class life had worn off. His family was also well connected in certain big-time Christian circles out there. He used to complain about the materialism and bad theology, but he seemed to be acclimating.

She shook her head and looked at the floor. "I don't know. This doesn't sound anything like what we agreed to or what we have committed to. In fact, it sounds exactly like the kind of acquiescence you used to find so detestable. Do you think you might be retrofitting your theology to fit your lifestyle agenda here?"

Charlie stared back at Nadia, his mouth half open and looks of surprise, confusion, and indignation building on his face. He hated it when Nadia asked him questions he couldn't answer. It embarrassed him. The conversation took a definite turn in that moment. His posture stiffened. His jaw tightened. He inhaled through his nose and tried to present what he thought was a slam-dunk case for his agenda.

"I've been hoping you would be as excited about this as I am, but in the end this may end up being one of those 'Wives, submit yourselves to your own husbands, as unto the Lord' kinda situations. The churches out there are very cool. I could walk in the door and get hired in a heartbeat with my résumé and my skills—not to mention the fact that I've been doing ministry in New York City for all these years."

"Ministry?"

"You know what I mean!" he snapped. "I have been preparing for this my whole life. This is my calling. I've done my time here, supporting you and taking care of the baby, but now it's time for you to support me while I support this family doing ministry in California!"

"Doing ministry you're not qualified to do, with people you don't know, because the money is good and you want to be famous? Oh, and you want to get back into your parents' good graces so you can get some money from them and get back in their will now that they are getting so old? This is your 'calling?'"

Charlie fumed. He was nowhere near self-aware enough to recognize the accuracy of his wife's assessment and nowhere near humble enough to receive her rebuke. He stood from the kitchen table with enough force to send the small chair he had been sitting in flying backward into the wall behind him and slammed his fists down in a rage.

"It's your choice! You can either submit and obey me as your husband, or you can rebel, but I am going to California and I am going to interview for those two jobs and see if there are any others. I have already started to make some arrangements. I will be there for the first interview within the next ten days. You're either with me or you leave me, but this is what's happening!"

Although Nadia had not been expecting this confrontation to happen on that day, nor did she expect those particular details to emerge, none of Charlie's antics surprised her. She thought about leaving, to go think somewhere else, but he beat her to it. After grabbing his coat and wallet he simply said, "I'll see you later" and stormed out the door.

It didn't take Nadia very long to sort her thoughts. She could give up everything that mattered to her and submit to what Charlie wanted (that word *submit* had become very popular with Charlie and some others in their circle around that time), or she could "reject his authority as the husband." Essentially, she felt he was trying to frame his abandonment of her and their child as *her* choice by twisting the Scripture to suit his purposes. He never seemed to consider the following verse in Ephesians, where Paul instructed husbands to love their wives the way Christ loved the church—even to the point of death. She had studied this idea of mutual submission and love and found it to be mystifying, challenging, and inspiring. Charlie simply used that one verse like a bludgeon.

Nadia was too smart for that and too independent. She was not confident in his decision-making skills, his submission to God's true call on his life, or his willingness to do the hard and humbling work required of a pastor. She also realized she would not likely be able to respect any church that would hire him as a leader. She would be happy to plug into a church when she found one that she believed took Jesus and the Bible seriously, and she'd consider a move to California if and when there was a plan and jobs and a budget. Otherwise, he knew where the door was.

Charlie left.

Nadia and Daniel stayed in New York. She did end up finding a small church that tried hard to be a positive presence in their community and worked hard to study the Bible with diligence and honesty. It turned out that she should never have trusted Charlie with the church-hunting duties. The little congregation she found was less than three blocks from their apartment. They had a children's ministry that Daniel loved, and she got involved with a Bible study group that included Catholics, Lutherans, and people from several other churches. Through her studies, and by spending time with some more mature people in the church, she started to recognize that some of the standards she had been holding the other churches to might have been a bit more informed by her stubbornness than by good theology.

Nadia kept up with her writing as well, but her constant work prevented her from even trying to get published. On very rare occasions she darkened the door of a coffeehouse to do a recitation, and a theater group in town adapted one of her stories into a one-act play, but for the most part, her poems and journal entries were for her eyes only. So the notebooks piled up. The lack of an outlet for her talents frustrated and depressed her. Her creative output slowed to a trickle.

When Daniel left for college in Boston, she started to lose the plot of her own life. At school, Daniel met Carrie, a lovely young woman from Illinois. Nadia liked her quite a bit, but it was hard to share her son with someone else. She was alone again. As fiercely independent as she liked to think that she was, Nadia needed to be needed.

When Daniel and Carrie came back and lived in New York, it was an improvement, but it still wasn't a good fit for her. After the young couple got married and then Carrie got pregnant, they started talking about settling somewhere else. Daniel was dabbling in medical technology and doing pretty well. He got some offers from companies that all had offices in Nashville. Nadia never thought much about Nashville other than when she listened to Johnny Cash. Now there was a Christian who understood what was what. Daniel and Carrie moved there in 2004. They settled in a neighborhood they promised was "transitioning." Nadia didn't know if she liked the sound of that.

"East Nashville is a lot like the East Village twenty years ago, Mom," Daniel had told her on the phone. "It was a pretty rough area for a long time, so not a lot of people wanted to live here. Then some tornadoes came through and tore up a bunch of houses and a church. When everything was being rebuilt, something happened and a bunch of young people and artists and creative types started buying up these run-down and damaged buildings and fixing them up. It's amazing."

"It's called gentrification, Son," Nadia told Daniel. "You're right. It sounds just like the Village. The sad part is that once that starts, all the people who made it such an interesting and fun place to live can't afford to live there anymore."

"Oh," Daniel said sheepishly, knowing his mom was right, as usual. "Yeah."

Present Day

On the porch, Marisol turned to Jerry. "You had just been standing there listening to her share her story with those students? What did you think?"

Jerry almost blushed. "Well." He rubbed his chin. "The first thing I can say is that she was definitely not the grandma I thought I was going there to meet. I waited for the one girl to finish talking to her, and then I think another person who had just been sitting next to them and got drawn in, to all exchange contact information before I introduced myself."

"Yes." Nadia jumped in. "I was caught off guard when this older man steps up and introduces himself and says that he had been standing there listening the whole time—and had even waved at me. Damn my eyes! He was just soft spoken and sweet and said, 'Welcome to East Nashville.' Somehow, in that moment, I had a sense that everything was about to change for me.

"It kind of ticked me off."

Fret Buzz

Nadia's story returned to the coffee shop in the moments just after Jerry had introduced himself. The crowd was thinning out for the day. Jerry stood there with his hand stretched out, smiling. He noticed Nadia's understated but sophisticated sense of style. She wore a skirt that went well past her knees, a pale-yellow shirt underneath a smart, angular brown tweed blazer. Jerry didn't often notice much about what people wore, but this lady's choice of clothes was cool without trying. At least he thought so.

"Oh!" Nadia said with a start, her expression transitioning from calm authority to marked insecurity. "How long have you been standing there?"

"Oh, about fifteen minutes, I guess," Jerry said. "I recognized you from your granddaughter's description and waved at you before I realized you were in the midst of such an intense discussion with those kids. I thought you saw me. Sorry about that."

"If I was less vain, I wouldn't work so hard to hide the fact that I am nearly blind. Advanced macular degeneration has left me with less than half of my vision, and it's fading fast."

"Wow," Jerry said, genuinely caught off guard. "That's terrible. I'm really sorry that's happening to you. But I will say that I just got so caught up in your story it never occurred to me that you couldn't see."

"I guess I'll take that as a compliment," Nadia offered. "But now I'm at a severe disadvantage. You've heard most of my story, but all I know from Stephanie is that you are a truck driver of some sort and you have an open mic jam that happens near her house. Honestly, she was so excited the other night when she got home, I couldn't make heads nor tails out of what she was saying. It sounds kind of like you folks have started some kind of a cross between a community outreach, a band, and a cult!"

"A cult?" Jerry's brow wrinkled and his eyebrows rose. "Why in the world would somebody call it a cult?"

"Oh, I don't necessarily mean that in a *bad* way." Nadia grinned. "But when you see a teenager rushing into the house raving about old people playing music and gathering hundreds of people around bonfires, some of them praying for each other and some saying they've seen God, well…it does have a certain Pied Piper ring to it."

"Ha!" Jerry laughed. "I guess it does. The funny thing is, this whole deal was a complete accident. These college boys next door heard me playing my guitar and asked if they could jam with me. I'd never—ever—played with another musician in my whole life! This was just a little over a month ago. Then, the next day, another friend introduced me to a friend of his, who many people feel is one of the best singers they've ever heard but who would never sing outside of a shower—and he agreed to come over and sit in with us. Next thing you know, over a hundred people are in my yard—including a guy from Mexico who plays accordion like it's wired into your soul! Three old guys, two college students, and a yard full of strangers, making this up as we go. That's some cult."

"What about the prayer part? What's that about?"

"Well." Jerry suddenly became more thoughtful and measured in his response. "It's hard to describe, but this whole thing has felt very spiritual from the beginning. None of us have a big agenda with it, and we all have different backgrounds and ideas when it comes to faith and religion, but it just seems that this is no mistake. This was supposed to happen for some reason. So we sort of acknowledged that with a couple of very simple, nondenominational prayers, and before you knew it, we looked out there and saw folks just praying for each other. Not everyone, mind you. But a few."

"Sounds like the Jesus Movement," Nadia said.

"The Jesus Movement?"

"Yes. Back in the late sixties and early seventies, millions of hippie kids who had kind of run the free love and drugs road to the dead end that it was turned to a countercultural, nonreligious understanding of Jesus and embraced it. It even made the cover of *Time* magazine. They were baptizing people by the hundreds out in the Pacific Ocean in Southern California, and it took root in England, New York, Chicago, Florida, and elsewhere. A bunch of Christian communes popped up. They even started making Jesus rock and folk music. That's where my faith journey started, actually. I wandered into a Jesus Music festival in upstate New York back in the mid-seventies."

That reminded him of Glenn and Wendi and the Resurrection Band record. "I think I actually bumped into a couple of them back then. But I wasn't ready yet. I had more drinking and avoiding to do."

"Well," she continued, "you'd never mistake most of the Christian music they make these days for that early stuff. There's some good stuff here and there, but I miss the simplicity and the passion of those heady, halcyon days. The message was simple and—when it was delivered by people who seemed to be living their lives like they actually believed it to be true—pretty effective. But when the Rapture failed to materialize, it seemed most of those 'Jesus hippies' did exactly what their mainstream counterparts did: They assimilated. It seems dispensationalism is an excellent primer for conspicuous consumption and the pursuit of earthly empire if you're not careful. It turns out that theology does matter."

This was starting to get over Jerry's head, but he didn't want to let on. The more Nadia spoke, even as she drifted into concepts he didn't understand, the more he wanted to hear her speak.

She kept going. "I think you guys have stumbled upon a particular hunger. Your lack of a plan, your simple authenticity, and your unfettered inclusivity is exactly what these people are starving for. Like Buechner says, 'The place God calls you to is the place where your deep gladness and the world's deep hunger meet.' I think that's exactly what has happened here."

Jerry was gobsmacked.

"Who said that?" He reached for a pen and fumbled for a piece of paper. "That's incredible. That's exactly what this feels like and what I feel I've been looking for since—I don't even know how long—my whole life, probably."

"His name is Frederick Buechner, and the quote is from his book *Wishful Thinking: A Seeker's ABC*. I have a copy I'll give you. I can't read it anymore anyway."

That last bit cut Jerry. He was beginning to understand just how painful this vision loss was for Nadia. He could tell that books were important to her, and he imagined she used them well. He had just met her but felt deep in his gut that he would do anything to help her see again. He noticed that the eyes that were failing her were blue.

"There's so much out there to discover," Jerry said. "I spent all this time with these people and I see the hunger in their eyes. They are offered so many things in this life—so many distractions or medications—to fend off that hunger. I want to help them find something that will really satisfy. I didn't have any idea that it would be through music. I truly didn't. But I guess it makes some kind of sense in a town like this."

Nadia nodded. Her face had softened considerably. In this moment she wasn't frustrated. She wasn't annoyed. It was like she had entered a different zone. Suddenly she seemed like the best kind of priest or something. "But what are you hungry for?" She closed her eyes gently, tilted her face upward ever so slightly—as if listening for something very faint—and asked, "What are you looking for when you play?"

Jerry felt his eyes warm and sting. He'd much rather think about helping other people. But in a matter of seconds, after weeks of softening, Nadia had tapped right into his deep longing for reconciliation. After he had done the hard work of confronting his own addiction, he had experienced the joy of serving others, especially those in recovery. But he couldn't serve his own family.

He had experienced the difficult joy of racial reconciliation in his community only when a disaster had forced him to confront his own apathy and distance from his neighbors. But reconciliation with his son and daughter, let alone his ex-wife, felt impossibly out of reach. And now he was experiencing the joy of music only because of a momentary lapse of self-restraint and a bizarre confluence of circumstances he suspected to be the hand of God, but it brought with it a tinge of pain.

Every note reminded him of the song for Marianne and the way Susan listened to him sing a million years ago. What was it going to take to bridge that last great divide—the gap between him and his children and his ex-wife? Was it even possible?

Nadia heard a faint sniff, and she wasn't so blind that she couldn't see what was happening with Jerry. "I'm sorry," she offered, in a warm, hushed voice. "I didn't mean to cause you pain."

"You haven't hurt me," he said in a broken voice, his head now looking downward. "I hurt myself a long time ago, and I've been trying to outrun it ever since. I've got a son and a daughter—adults now—who I haven't seen or talked to since they were tiny—because I hurt their mother when I was drunk. I feel like I've been hurting them ever since. I'm glad I can help all these people, but I'd like to help **them**. I feel like no matter how much good I do, I can't undo the pain I've caused all three of them. People are looking at me like I'm a good guy now, but I know that I'm not."

"It's not about being good, Jerry," Nadia said firmly but graciously. "It's about being loved. It's about redemption. Like Bono says, it's Grace over Karma. And this is now officially too heavy to talk about in this coffee shop. I think it's time we go for a walk."

Jerry took Nadia over to Five Points area and they walked around the neighborhood. Always the gentleman, and to help her avoid tripping on the uneven sidewalks, he offered Nadia his arm and she took it. He filled her in on more details of his story and bought her a hot dog from a stand built in an old Volkswagen Microbus. She asked him where he got his limp and he told her the short version of the story. She told him about Charlie and her divorce and how much she missed her late—and massively dysfunctional—mother.

He told her about the letters he had sent his kids and how he wasn't even sure if they had made it past their mother. She told him about how pissed she was about losing her independence, but that she was not looking forward to being a lonely old lady in New York.

Jerry explained that he drove tour buses, not trucks, and answered a long list of questions about growing up in the American South. After a very brief exchange about events and characters in Washington, they agreed to set politics aside until their friendship was sturdier.

As they walked, though, they were rarely alone. Jerry seemed to be stopped every couple of blocks by someone wanting to share a good word. Young and old, Black and White, gay and straight, it seemed that all of Jerry's friends were out for a walk that day. Nadia noticed how relaxed Jerry was with each of them, and that he never treated any one of them differently than another.

"How long have you lived here?" she asked. "You seem to know everyone."

"Over forty years. But most of the folks we've met today are relatively new. Betsy, from First Baptist, she's a lifer, but the rest are all transplants from somewhere. It's very rare to meet someone who is actually *from* Nashville."

Some thanked him for opening his home for these musical gatherings. One African American gentleman thanked him for helping to fix a dishwasher in their church kitchen. Betsy gently chided him for not having been at the Y lately. "It's not like this every day," Jerry lied. Being known, and needed, in his neighborhood was deeply important to him.

When they ducked into an ice cream shop, Jerry noticed a *Missing Dog* poster with a photo of a Great Dane he recognized. He tore off one of the little tabs in case he saw it again.

"What is that?" Nadia asked.

"Just a lost dog poster. I think I saw this dog strolling down his street yesterday. so I'm taking the number in case I see him again. You should have seen this place after the tornadoes in '98. These "lost dog" flyers were everywhere. You don't see them as much anymore. I think it's mostly online now. But back then, boy o boy. They were everywhere. This was like a city of lost dogs."

"From the sound of it, it still is," Nadia offered wryly. "That sounds like a good name for your band."

"Lost dogs?" Jerry asked.

"Yeah. Like you said, you felt like you were all meant to find each other but just needed some help. Dogs need families. They are pack animals, like people. Not meant to be alone. Maybe it's the same reason all those people are showing up in your driveway. We're all lost dogs until we find our pack."

"Hmm," Jerry grunted. "Interesting."

They walked toward Boscobel, where both her son and Jerry lived. As pedestrian traffic thinned and a modicum of privacy was restored, Nadia steered the conversation back to where they had left it at the coffee shop.

"You know," she said with an air of both insight and playfulness in her voice, "I don't think you're all that wonderful of a person. You're no saint."

Jerry wasn't sure how to respond. He looked at her with a smile, suspecting she was about to make some kind of point.

"But you're doing your best, and that's all any of us can do—other than ask for forgiveness when we screw up. You can't make anyone forgive you. All you can do is ask, and let it go. And hopefully we live our lives as people in need of forgiveness." She leaned a bit harder on Jerry's arm for just a moment.

"Unless…"

Jerry looked at her sideways again. *Unless?* Was there a way to *make* someone forgive you? This ought to be interesting.

"I wonder if you might be able to slide your apology under their door in a different way," she said. "You've tried the direct approach for, what, more than forty years? Maybe it's time to get artistic about this."

"Artistic? Like, creative?"

"More than just creative. I mean, what if you use this gift of yours—this ability to play music and gather people and help others—and craft the most authentic and artistic olive branch you possibly can?

"I've been thinking," she continued, without missing a beat, "trying to put myself in their position, and wondering what it would take for me to be convinced that repentance was authentic. Now, I'm as cynical as they come. I want to see results. I want to see consistency. I want to see the person prove it out over the long haul. Maybe they are like me. Maybe they need to see that that is what you have done. Maybe they can't understand transformation or redemption because they've never seen it."

Nadia stopped, pulling them both into a momentary pause for emphasis, reflection, or both, and then started walking again. "But there's also the fact that music, and art in general, often helps us feel something before we even understand it. Maybe," she said, "we need to show them in a song."

Jerry was getting excited now. Nervous and terrified but very excited. She had thought of this in the time it took them to walk ten blocks.

And did she just say, "*we* need to show them in a song"?

They walked up to his house right then.

He pushed open the swinging gate and gestured toward house. "Would you like to sit up on the porch and write that song with me?"

The next morning, when Jerry made his way to his front porch with his coffee, he noticed it was a bit later than usual. The hours he and Nadia had spent working on that song the night before had flown by. It had been a bit chilly out on the porch at midnight, but her East Coast blood was thick. She could handle it. She had pushed him for thoughts and ideas and had been honest about lyrics and melodies that felt interesting and ones that felt clichéd. She didn't pull any punches. She wasn't precious about the process at all. And man did she have literary references up her sleeves. The woman was like a human library.

When her granddaughter had come around wondering where she was, harping on her for not checking in, Jerry and Nadia had felt as if they had done something illicit—which was kind of fun. Nadia had seemed to enjoy it. The truth was that her phone had died, and the last thing either of them had been thinking about was "checking in" with anyone. They had found a zone. They hadn't quite finished the song, but it was close.

Jerry took a sip of his coffee as he thought about Nadia's hair color. It was a lovely light shade of silver-gray—so light that he wondered if it had been blonde or brown when she was younger. Although her hair was shorter—falling just a tad below her collar—it kind of reminded him of Emmylou Harris's hair.

When Jerry found his phone for the first glance of a new day, he could see that Alex was pretty eager to talk with him.

[J: Hit me back ASAP—you seen the socials?]

[J: That means reply to my text as soon as possible btw]

[Oh—BTW means By The Way]

Jerry was laughing out loud now. Alex clearly thought he was an idiot.

[JERRY: CALL ME!]

Jerry thought he'd really blow Alex's mind. He picked up his coffee cup and walked across the lawn to his left and knocked on Alex's kitchen door.

"Hey!" Alex said. "Good, you're okay!"

"Of course I'm okay. It's ten o'clock in the morning. I was up late working on a song. It's not like I sleep with my phone."

"You don't?" Alex asked, sincerely. "Huh. Anyway, I'm assuming you haven't checked out the socials."

Jerry scrunched up his face slightly. "When you say 'socials,' I'm assuming you are not talking about dances, ice-cream parties, or other gatherings, correct?"

"No! What? I don't even…social media! The stuff we just set up. You have to see this."

Alex pulled a chair out for Jerry at his kitchen table and produced an iPad. He called up Instagram and showed one short video post with 108,863 "likes." He pointed to the "follows" number at the top and it said 58,783.

"That seems like a lot," Jerry mused. "You sure that's right?"

"Yes it's right," Alex barked. "And yes it's a lot. And it's climbing. The Facebook group has over five thousand members and there are even some hashtags circulating."

"I know what those are from *Jimmy Fallon*," Jerry added helpfully. "What's causing all of this?"

"It's all the posting from the people who have come and then the forwarding that happens from their friends. You've got to see these things." Alex pulled up a few examples.

One was a shaky iPhone video clip from the driveway—of the whole group singing "Whenever God Shines His Light" by Van Morrison. Under the clip the poster had written a caption that explained just how meaningful the night had been for him, how real the music was, and how refreshing it was to be around people who weren't a part of any scene. His video had slightly more than five thousand views. He couldn't wait for his grandfather to come visit and hear this music for himself.

Another was just a still photo of Brother Louis, Jerry, and B-Flat standing around the bonfire with the caption "My New Familia!"

"There are over a hundred of these," Alex said. "And then there's the music critic."

He then pulled up a very impressive-looking music blog written by a freelance writer for several Nashville papers. The headline read "Maybe It's Not Too Late for Music After All," and the corresponding article raved about the unassuming grit and heart on display in a driveway on Boscobel. The article had 42,458 likes and had been up for less than twenty-four hours.

"When Will This Band-Without-a-Name Release Music?" demanded another blogger.

"Well, this is interesting." Jerry's brow was knotted. He wasn't feeling good about this at all, but he couldn't tell why. Just then his phone rang again. "Hello, Brother Louis. How are you this morning?"

"Hello, Jerry. Hey—I saw your car out front, so I thought you'd be home. I'm over at your house, but you're not answering the door."

"Well goodness! I'm just over here at Alex's. Tell you what; we'll be right over. Stay put."

In a few moments, Alex and Jerry were back on his front porch to find Brother Louis, who still had his phone in his left hand, with a quizzical look on his face. As they walked up the steps, Cesar's F-150 pulled up. "What's happening Jerry?" Louis asked. "Have you seen the, well, I guess the internet? My daughter just sent me a bunch of stuff saying that lots of people are talking about us."

"¡*Si!*" Cesar said as he came around the truck, with the biggest smile they had ever seen crossing his face. "A Spanish blogger talked about us and they just mentioned us on the radio! They even played some of the music that someone recorded on their phone. It sounded okay, but…"

Alex was smiling. He couldn't help it. He was excited. But he was also nervous. He understood better than anyone else on that porch what "viral" could mean. He was pretty sure the older guys didn't have a clue or they'd be freaking out.

"Guys," he spoke up. "Based on this buzz, I think we should probably not hold the gathering here in the garage tomorrow night. With this kind of hype we could end up with way too many people showing up. It could cause trouble."

"Where should we hold it?" Jerry asked.

"I've got a friend at a club just a few blocks away," Alex said, clearly unsure of the idea. "I know we could get in there. They can fit five hundred people."

"A bar?" Jerry asked. "Is that the environment we want? That seems pretty different than the yard." He wasn't excited about all of his recovery friends coming to a bar.

"What about the church?" Louis offered. "I could check with George."

"Yeah," Jerry said. "That's a possibility, but do we think these folks will all be comfortable going to a church? It's kind of the opposite problem of doing it in a bar but still maybe an issue. Many of these folks are not church people, and most of these songs aren't church songs. I wonder if the church folks would be cool with it, either."

"Good point," Louis said.

"What about the park?" Cesar asked. "There's a picnic shelter there we have used many times. I know the permit office well. I could call."

Everyone looked at each other. In the absence of objections the motion passed. The next event would happen in the picnic shelter at the park down the street. It was only about five blocks away and should hold at least 150-200 people, with room for overflow out on the grass. Was it the same place Glenn and Wendi had played back in the seventies?

Cesar was successful in securing the last-minute permit, and the brothers took care of moving the PA system over to the picnic shelter. They posted about the venue change online, and Jerry stuck notes on his front door and on the garage door. On social media, this event was officially dubbed "The Place to Be" on Thursday, and by seven o'clock Thursday evening over 750 people had made it to the hill with the picnic shelter in the park. If there had been more places to park, there probably would have been more. The police directed traffic. Several reporters were there, including a full production truck from the Channel 2 News.

The members of the group gathered around the "stage," shaking heads, rubbing their heads, and wondering what the heck was going on. Alex and Jamie were nothing but excited. They had done their best to set the PA up, but the folks at the back wouldn't be seeing or hearing much. They were just thrilled to see this thing sparking the kind of passion in others it had sparked in them. They had both been a part of "manufactured musical moments" before. This was different.

Michael Thomas was setting up wireless mics and would be doing his best to try to capture the audio from yet another "Wild West" musical experience. He looked like a kid in a candy store. No one would guess that he had spent his day in a two-hundred-and-fifty-dollar-per-hour studio with a Grammy-winning country artist. He looked like every other member of "The Tribe."

But Louis, Jerry, and Cesar were baffled. Louis was feeling the nerves again. How had he allowed himself to get roped into something this big? Cesar was concerned as he stared out at the diverse audience. He saw wealthy White folks, pockets of Black faces from the low-income housing projects, and more than a few Hispanic people. In his previous experience, that kind of combination was dangerous. Cesar was nervous about a fight breaking out.

Jerry was just overwhelmed. What did everyone here want from him and the group? Would they be able to live up to the expectations the internet hype had generated? He looked out and saw so many unfamiliar faces among the few he knew. As his emotions evolved into something like anxiety, he caught sight of George sitting regally in a collapsible camping chair, wearing a dark-gray suit vest and pants (no coat), a burgundy shirt, and a gold tie. He was positioned right near the front of the stage, under the picnic shelter. He must have made it there pretty early to get a spot that good.

Nadia was sitting right next to him, chatting amiably and looking in his direction. George wore the warmest, proudest smile, and it filled Jerry with peace. He had grown to genuinely love that man. "Well, brothers, here we are. Does anyone have anything to say?"

"I do," Brother Louis offered. "Gentlemen, I make no attempt to hide from you that the size of this crowd and the events of the last couple of weeks fill me with a certain amount of dread. I cannot say why, other than I am obviously a man of little faith and weak constitution."

"I wouldn't say that," Jerry said before Louis calmly raised his hand as if to insist he be allowed to finish. Jerry shut up.

"All I can say is that from the moment I met you all, I have felt that a larger hand has guided us, and I pray that hand is guiding us still. I feel a bit like a boat being cast about on large waves, but I am determined, right now, to place my faith in that hand, and in you, my brothers, and in these people. Something good is bound to happen if we let it. I propose that we let it."

Alex just shook his head. There was something about this guy. With just a few words he was reminded that this was not a viral moment. It was a gathering of human beings craving the same thing: transcendence. He was amazed and honored that he was allowed to be part of it and determined to be more like Brother Louis when he grew up.

Alex stole a glance at his brother, Jamie, who nodded in agreement, and they all grasped hands for something resembling a prayer.

Cesar cleared his throat, the closest he ever came to saying that he had something to say. "Before we start, whatever this is that we start," he began haltingly, "I must say that I am worried about a crowd this big and with so many…different kinds of people. This should be a good thing, and in my heart I feel that it is, but I worry about troublemakers. I worry about people who don't like to see things like this happen."

Louis nodded. Jerry was lost.

"I hear you, Cesar," Louis said. "And I share your concern. That's what I meant by putting our trust in that hand that brought us together. I hope that's not naïve."

Jerry was starting to understand that he, a White man in America, had little to worry about. He could not relate to what these brothers were concerned about. And that began to upset him. Alex and Jamie remained mostly clueless but in agreement with whatever their elders said or did. Alex increasingly felt like a kid who had started a snowball rolling down a hill, and that snowball was getting away from him.

"I remember when I was young," Cesar continued, "my padre, or priest, told me that God gave us these gifts, like music, and when we gave them back to him, it was a kind of worship. He told me that he even heard God in my dancehall music. I know that it felt special, but I didn't know it was God that I felt. I feel that again, thanks to you. I think these people feel it, too, thanks to God. I hope and I pray that all of the good things they feel from God are stronger than any bad things hateful people might think or feel tonight."

"I can't think of a better prayer than that," Louis said. "Amen and amen."

Everyone agreed. The circle broke and they took their positions.

The evening was amazing. The core band kept getting tighter and tighter, and there was no doubt that the excitement and energy of the larger audience focused their performance. But the crowd participation aspect was harder to pull off at this scale. Dozens of guitars lay around, and it was obvious that several people were hoping for a chance to sing. Louis did his best to turn the whole crowd into a massive, ad-hoc choir. It was impressive but not the same as the garage experience.

One older gentleman brought up a violin and added some stunning fiddle parts to a few songs. A young girl played her flute just close enough to the front row for the sound to be picked up on Louis's vocal mic. A twentysomething college student of Indian descent stepped up with a soprano saxophone and knocked everyone out with some incredible jazz sounds. An opera singer in the crowd let some vocals fly that gave everyone chills.

Nadia sat off to stage right, taking it all in. She enjoyed the music and talked with as many people in the crowd as she possibly could. After a particularly sloppy-fun version of "Stand by Me," which included a hilarious attempt at freestyle rap by a dad channeling his inner LL Cool J, Jerry stepped to the mic.

"Excuse me everyone," he said, way too politely for an MC. "Thanks for coming out tonight—and for finding us over here in the park. We know this is different, but I'm sure glad we don't have this big of a crowd in my yard right now!"

The crowd was laughing with Jerry. Someone shouted out, "Thanks, Jerry!"

"And I want to thank the police for coming out here and keeping us safe," Jerry added. The crowd applauded lightly.

"I want to introduce you to a new friend of mine right now. Nadia Morton is from New York City, and she is a poet and a professor there. Oh—and she's a songwriter. I have asked her if she would come and share some poetry with us tonight. So everyone, please welcome, Nadia!"

With some help from Stephanie, Nadia made her way to the microphone. A smattering of people offered polite applause. "Thank you. Considering you haven't heard a word yet and you didn't come here for poetry, that's very generous."

People were laughing with her now. They liked this old lady's spunk.

"I'm going to keep this short," she said. "I have just one thing to read you, and I wrote it today, inspired by you people, these musicians, this community, and what's been happening here in East Nashville.

"Yesterday," she continued, "Jerry pulled a phone number off of a flyer someone posted about their dog that was missing. He told me that lost-dog flyers used to be very common around here, but that they had mostly moved to the internet. It seems to me that a lot of things have moved to the internet over the last few years, haven't they? I mean, I'm happy if it helps people find their dogs—don't get me wrong. But there are a lot of things I used to do in person that I now do online, and I kind of miss them.

"Jerry also told me that it's rare to find people who are actually from Nashville. Who here is a Nashville native?"

About a dozen people cheered.

"Wow." She looked back at Jerry. "You weren't kidding."

"The rest of us—and I guess maybe even the natives—I imagine we're kind of like those lost dogs in some ways, aren't we? We're looking for our pack, our humans. We want nothing more than to belong. I know that I feel very much like a lost dog these days. Can anyone here relate to that?"

The crowd roared, clapped, and hands shot straight up in the air.

"So we're all a bunch of lost dogs, eh? Maybe tonight we're not so lost for a while. At least we have each other."

Cheers again.

"That's what I had in mind when I wrote this piece. This is something I call…'If Found, Call.'"

The crowd came to a complete hush. No chattering or murmurs could be heard. You could feel people leaning toward Nadia as she read.

I wander these streets
I amble and I stray
Am I running, or returning?
Been too long, I cannot say
And there's a song that draws me
A voice inside my head
Pulls me ever home
But I'm too good at distraction
And I enjoy the roam
And there's a song that draws me
I wander these streets
Insisting that I'm free
Barking about the choice I made
As you run to follow me
But still your song draws me
Are you looking for me?
Do you scan the horizon?
Am I just another lost dog
That you keep your eyes on?
If I'm lost, call my name in the dark
Take me running in the park
If found, call me your own
If found, call me your own

As Nadia dipped her head and stepped away from the microphone, the audience cheered. Jerry gave her a huge hug. "That was amazing," he said to her, up close.

"Wasn't that amazing?" he said into the microphone.

"Nadia Morton, everyone. We're going to try to convince her to start leading some poetry and lyric workshops here soon. Make sure you join our Facebook group so you hear the details when we get them worked out."

Jerry asked Louis if he would dismiss the crowd with some kind of blessing.

"Brothers and sisters," Louis began, "we once again thank you for joining with us in this holy work. This picnic shelter became a sort of tabernacle tonight, and for that I am grateful."

More than a few in the crowd looked completely confused by that but seemed willing to roll with Brother Louis.

"And now, I pray that each of you carries the blessing of Love with you tonight, tomorrow, and henceforth. May we be bound together as a community by that true love, true light, and the only song worth singing. Amen."

Some people started packing up their chairs and blankets, while others huddled in circles around guitars. Hugs were exchanged liberally, and more than a few cheeks were wet with tears.

Just then, over the faces of the crowd, Jerry and Nadia and the rest of the band noticed the first of what would become a regular feature of their gatherings: hastily made picket signs and less-than-loving protestors.

"Secular Music Is From Hell!"

"Go To Church!"

"Be Ye Separate!!!"

"Illegal Immigrants Go Home!"

Nadia clenched her jaw as Jerry read the signs aloud.

"Are those church people protesting us?" Alex asked nobody in particular. "Why in the world would they do that?"

"Oh yes," Louis said. "This part was, unfortunately, unavoidable."

Fortunately for everyone involved, the protestors at the park had little impact in their debut performance. A few well-intentioned folks engaged them, but apart from some heated voices, nothing dangerous happened. For the most part they were ignored.

One of the police officers did pull Jerry aside though. "You folks had best be careful. Mostly these people just want to show up and make their opinions heard, but lately there seem to be a few mixed in who can get really riled up. They need attention more than anything, and once you get enough people in one place, things can escalate."

Jerry thanked him for his concern and candor.

Before disbanding for the evening, the members of the group decided that they should gather as soon as possible to think through next steps in general. Jerry suggested the Biscuit House the following morning and invited spouses.

The next morning Louis and Kelly, Cesar and Irma, Alex and Jamie, Jerry, Nadia, and George White all gathered around the largest round table in the front room at the diner Jerry had called home for decades. Visitors could still see a ghost of the old *Knife and Fork* sign underneath the "new" *Biscuit House* sign from the nineties. The back wall featured one of the largest murals in East Nashville. Other than the lack of smoke, the inside felt the same as it always had to Jerry.

They had a lot to discuss and some decisions to make, but the first thing each of them realized as they entered that space was that they genuinely enjoyed each other's presence. They had only been apart for about nine hours, but to see them greet each other, you'd think it had been weeks. A few of the folks were meeting Nadia for the first time.

"You guys aren't going to believe this," Alex laughed, "but our little adventure in the park last night has somehow failed to dampen people's enthusiasm for this little musical experiment we've started."

"What's the latest?" Jerry asked, as everyone got settled into their seats.

"Well," Alex offered, "let's begin with the live stream."

"Live stream?" Cesar asked.

"Yes," Alex said. "Some enterprising friend decided to set up a live stream simultaneously on several platforms. It was quite an impressive arrangement. It both looked and sounded better than most of these things do. But the real shocker is that while we were playing, over five thousand users streamed the event live, and since then—just overnight—the archive of the event has been viewed more than fifty thousand times. Oh—and the numbers are rising as we speak."

"People are watching and listening to what happened last night," Louis clarified, "right now, on their phones and other devices? That's what you're saying?"

Jamie took a turn trying to explain the scope of this to the oldsters. "Yes, and when you add this to all of the other impressions, this 'Lost Dogs' tribe thing is closing in on half a million overall impressions on social media in just over a month!"

That number got everyone's attention.

George broke the momentary silence in a dignified way. "Well, it is not surprising to me that any fans of music would want to hear you folks, but that does seem to be a very large number for recordings on people's phones. Why, just think what would happen if you recorded a professional-sounding LP?"

"I'd love to hear a record, too," Nadia interrupted, "but I think part of the appeal of your music, for many people, is that it is not something created by the music industry. It may be the authentic, live, unpremeditated, and unvarnished nature of the music that is drawing people in. It's not that people don't value studios and good-quality recording, but I sense that what they are reacting to right now with you all is the realness. It reminds me of the way Deadheads would trade bootlegs of their shows back in the day."

While Jerry nodded in agreement, believing that Nadia—again—was making a good point, both Cesar and Louis were back at "Deadheads" trying to make sense of it.

"Let's pretend for a moment," Louis stroked his chin and looked up at the ceiling playfully, "that some people here might not know what 'Deadheads' are and what they had bootlegs of."

Alex chuckled. "Deadheads are devoted fans of the classic, hippie-rock, jam-band the Grateful Dead. They were famous for following the band around the country, from town to town, trading recordings of concerts and homemade merchandise. For them, a Grateful Dead show was as much—or more—about the live experience, including the gathering with other fans, as it was about the music."

Cesar nodded. He understood the parallel and agreed. Louis accepted the definition. "Must be nice to have the luxury of free time and income like that," he added.

Nadia cocked her head slightly and smiled. Of course Louis had a good point. "Yes. The way different cultures interact with and approach music can be very different, depending on their means. For some it is a product they consume and use to fill their free time. For others it is more like a lifeline: a source of spiritual and emotional survival. In both cases, though, it becomes a language. We can learn a lot about a people—what they value, fear, and hunger for—by listening to the music they make and respond to."

Though her professorial side was peeking through, Nadia earned the attention of the table immediately. Her experience in New York's 1960's counterculture, as well as the Jesus Movement of the '70s, not to mention her personal theological studies—all came to bear. She felt uniquely qualified to provide some guidance and context to this group, and from the looks on their faces, they were eager for it.

"I wholeheartedly agree," said George. "This whole thing started because some friends had a need. Young Alex here felt drawn to the experience and depth in Brother Jerry's guitar playing. Alex could play with anyone, but something was qualitatively different about what he heard from Jerry, and he wanted to experience it."

Alex and Jamie nodded, and George continued. "And the somewhat manipulative contrivances I employed in order to pull Brother Louis out of his shell were simply because I felt in my heart of hearts that he and Jerry should have this experience together. It was not about a public performance, I assure you, Louis," he gestured apologetically.

Louis demurred. "But the experience that first night in Jerry's garage was…well…I'm not sure how else to say this. It was holy."

Kelly spoke up at this point. "I've never felt anything like this, y'all. And I'm not just talking about how great it is to hear Louis sing. There's the music you're making, which is amazing. But then there's the air around it. It feels thick. It feels like it's pulling us all into itself."

Irma nodded exuberantly. "I don't know how well you can hear the people away from the microphones, but it's like the band just continues throughout the room. People are singing, playing, and joining in. It's like there is very little difference between what is happening up there and what is happening out here. And there are so many different sounds and flavors, it's like everyone can pick up something that tells them they belong here but not so much that tells them anyone else doesn't belong here. I don't know if that makes any sense."

"It makes perfect sense," Nadia replied. "The musical elements, from Cesar's accordion, to Louis's soulful vocals, to Jerry's country guitar elements, are all subtle cues. Those cues are all mixed up and blended but still noticeable. Then when something happens like that Indian kid adding some South Asian notes on his sax—you get more cues. Someone raps—more cues.

"Too many of one type of cue," Nadia continued, "and people who aren't used to that cue get the message that they aren't welcome. This isn't for them. But with the diversity of cues and the overarching lyrical messages you focus on—things like unity, hope, encouragement—we can then transcend our own smaller trenches and enter into a much bigger space where we don't feel so alone in our struggles. That transcendence and community is what, I think, people are so hungry for. Some people find it in very dark, hateful places. You are offering it in a very positive, spiritual, musical place. And you're doing it authentically because it is what you wanted and needed yourselves. We are all responding to your authenticity."

"But," Cesar interjected, "at the park last night, it started to feel more like a concert and less like when I first played in the driveway."

"Yes," Louis continued. "I wonder if the special nature of what we are doing can be the same if the audiences are so big. I don't see how people watching on their phones at home can ever feel what we feel when are together in that place."

"Simply put," Nadia said flatly, "they can't. I suspect many of those people are similarly hungry for something good and true and real—they want transcendence as much as we do. And compared to funny cat videos or the latest pop song, these viral moments are probably electrifying, but it's still just a tiny, digital, distant facsimile of what is actually happening. Now, if those little digital postcards draw people into a real experience, that's great. But if they settle for that stream or clip or even a good recording you might do someday, then I think you, and they, will have missed an opportunity here."

Jerry was feeling a bit overwhelmed but increasingly impressed with Nadia's insight. "I spent my career driving musicians from gig to gig on my bus for years. I saw every kind of artist you can think of, playing every kind of music, from big churches to small clubs to stadiums and festivals. And with very few exceptions, I saw them get on the bus, put on their headphones, or turn on the TV and go to the next gig. I don't remember ever seeing anything close to the kind of connection we felt when it was just a small group of people making music together with no expectations and no rules. I just don't know how big this thing can get and still maintain that feel. I'm not sure what we should do."

"A thought is occurring to me," George offered, "and anyone please correct me if I am wrong. But maybe we need to think about this the way a mechanic would think about his tools or an artist would think about his canvas and brushes. Maybe different goals require different tactics. There are some things that larger crowds and wide attention are good for. We thoughtfully and carefully address those goals with appropriate tactics. However, when we think about our other goals, maybe our overriding hopes for people to find community, and even God, through participation in music that transcends cultural boundaries and brings neighbors together, we use different tactics and tools."

"I like the sound of that," said Louis. "What are you suggesting?"

"I don't exactly know," George said with a slight laugh. The others joined in. "I just think it sounded good to say it."

Sharon came to take their orders, and the table broke into several conversations about ideas, hopes, concerns, and stories for Nadia about what East Nashville was like before it got "cool."

About an hour later, as the dishes were being cleared and checks were being paid, Jerry overheard George sharing a church-related concern with Louis. It seemed that the church building needed some expensive repairs, and George was concerned that it might cost more than the dwindling congregation could afford. "In fact," George lamented, "it may be time for us to sell the property like so many other churches have done." He had just seen another church building turned into an Airbnb hotel.

"Hold on," Jerry interrupted. "How much money do you need?"

"It's going to be close to two hundred thousand dollars at least," George said.

"You said there are some things that a big crowd is good for," Jerry continued. "What if we did a benefit concert? Maybe we get a venue big enough, and actually promote this thing, and ask people to donate. How many people could we fit in the sanctuary at the church?"

"About two hundred." Louis guessed.

Alex shook his head. "That's not enough. What if we did it at the community center? Or maybe in the park outside of the community center? We could put up a proper stage and PA. I bet we could get someone to donate that. We could turn it into a sort of mini festival."

Just as the group had been heading for the door, they all sat back down. This was feeling like a good idea.

"What if we started some music lessons, songwriting classes, and other smaller gatherings right away," Nadia suggested, "to try to meet the immediate needs of the community right here—the people who started this in the first place? We'll keep doing a smaller, almost unannounced or underground kind of live thing for the neighborhood, too. But we announce this benefit concert and promote it hard."

"Maybe Michael has some music we could release by now," Jamie offered. "He's been recording everything, you know."

"That's true," Louis said. "Maybe we could release an actual song to help promote this benefit concert at the same time. I'd like to hear what he has recorded, anyway."

"I'll call the community center," Cesar said. "I know them well."

Irma smiled. She was looking forward to getting involved with this group and could not believe the transformation she was seeing in her husband.

"Okay," Jerry said. "Cesar is on the venue. Louis and George will run point with the church and with promotions in the community once we have a date. Alex and Jamie will take care of the internet stuff—sorry, the 'socials'—and the production, and I'll work with Nadia on the local workshops and other stuff. Jamie, will you call Michael about the recordings he's been gathering and see if he can come by the house and play them for us?"

Jamie nodded. The team had a mission.

"Oh," Jerry thought suddenly. "Nadia, when are you supposed to head back to New York? I forgot that you were just visiting."

"Oh never mind about that. I already changed my ticket. I got someone to take care of my cat."

Jerry smiled. So did everyone else.

Echoes

Several Weeks Ago

It was raining lightly when Jerry made his way back home. He shook the rain from his jacket on the porch before he stepped into his front room, and he kicked off his shoes by the front door. He thought about how quiet his life had been until recently as he fixed himself a cup of hot tea and grabbed his laptop. He hadn't been much of a hot tea drinker before, but Nadia liked it and he had tried it and found it to be quite agreeable—especially once one had already had enough coffee for the day.

He took his laptop to the couch, put his tea on the table, and selected a Grateful Dead LP for the record player. He hadn't listened to it in decades and was pretty sure his old housemate left it there, but when Nadia had brought them up earlier, it reminded him that he had it in the stacks. He never considered himself a Deadhead, but he appreciated them from a bit of a distance. Once the tone arm dropped, he decided to check out the Facebook page that Alex had set up on his behalf.

The first thing that got his attention was over five hundred friend requests! As he scrolled down the list he saw many familiar names and faces. Louis, Kelly, Alex, and the rest of the crew were all there, and he quickly accepted their requests. Then he noticed faces from their gatherings and accepted all of those. He found several in the batch from old friends as well. Kyle Smith added a note to his request. "Will wonders never cease?" he said. Jerry made a mental note to invite Kyle to the benefit show. He wanted to introduce him to Nadia, maybe even have him do a song.

His old roommate Bruce was on the list. That was a surprise. Jerry hadn't thought about Bruce in a long time. He clicked on his link and was glad to see that he was married and had some kids. He remembered that night of howling on the front porch and wondered how Bruce felt about it all now.

He ended up accepting almost all of the friend requests waiting for him. A few seemed like they were from people overseas who might not even be real. He skipped those. But within fifteen minutes he was starting to understand why people were so invested in Facebook. It was pretty amazing to see all those people and to have all of them want to connect with him.

He ended up spending several hours, and three more cups of tea, going down various Facebook rabbit holes. He was surprised at how many people had already tagged him in photos and posts from the events. He also noticed that a good number of them were already calling the whole phenomenon the "Lost Dogs" gatherings. He smiled at that.

He noticed the search bar at the top of the page and got an idea. He wasn't sure if it was a good idea, and he thought about checking with someone first, but he was afraid they would advise him against it. He typed the name of his son in the box: Jack James Wesley. Several circular pictures popped right up. One of them, located in Crossville, Tennessee, could have been Jerry's 1998 doppelganger but for his slightly darker hair. He was tempted to hit "Add Friend" but held off. He wanted to make sure that his profile page projected all the right information before he did.

He did click on Jack's profile, though, and poked around a bit. He saw some pictures of his family and work. He seemed happy. There was a picture of him with his mother from a recent birthday lunch. Susan was radiant. She was older but retained her beauty. He remembered trying to draw her when they were kids. He noticed the depth of her smile. She was relishing the attention of her family. There was another man in the picture—an old guy with his hand on her shoulder. Susan was tagged in that picture.

Jerry clicked her name and was taken to her profile page. Her name was not Susan Wesley or even Susan Sheehan, her maiden name. No, her name was Susan McCaskey now. She was married to the old guy next to her. A little sleuthing told Jerry that they had been married for over thirty years. There were so many pictures of them together and with the kids. He had a couple of kids from a previous marriage as well. They appeared to be happy. They were a real family. But that guy was so old.

Jerry laughed at himself for thinking that when he went to get up off the couch and his back was stiff. "You're old, too, you old fart," he said out loud—to himself.

He took his laptop over to the dinette table, and after turning the record over, he sat back down to keep scrolling. He wouldn't bother to send Susan a friend request. She had made it clear where he stood with her. He would continue to seek forgiveness if he could but not reconciliation. That ship had sailed.

The sadness over that rose in his stomach, his chest, and his head. It started to leak through his eyes again. "What is with the damned tears, you old fool? You're not a crier. You gotta get a grip, son."

He clicked over to his own profile page and generally approved of what he saw. Alex had done a good job. The cover photo across the top was a picture of the whole group in his garage. His profile picture was the simple headshot Alex had taken at Mitchell Deli. It was nothing special, but it was fine. He looked older than he felt.

There were only a couple of posts. Alex had made them on his behalf. But the short "intro" bio needed some work. Jerry wrote and deleted several things before settling on something he had heard someone at George's church say once.

"Forgiven sinner, working on forgiving, seeking grace and giving grace as much as possible."

It wouldn't win any prizes, but it was truthful. It was intended for an audience of three.

He uploaded some pictures from his photo album by taking pictures of them with his phone. He replied with words of encouragement on a few of the posts that had been made on his "wall." But when it came back around to hit "Add Friend" to Jack's profile, he just couldn't do it yet.

He decided to search for Marianne's profile. It came right up as well. He was glad to see that she had her privacy settings set much more conservatively than did Jack. He couldn't see anything about her until and unless they became "friends." Oh, how he hoped that might someday happen! He caught a few glimpses of her in pictures on Jack's and Susan's pages, though. He started to feel like a stalker, so he clicked out of their profiles and back to his own.

He decided to make his first general post. Using a picture he had taken of one of the first musical gatherings at his home, he added the following caption:

It's hard to believe what all has happened in the last month or so. From a handful of friends and neighbors to hundreds of people in the park, this whole Lost Dogs of East Nashville thing is pretty amazing. All I can say is that this feels so much bigger than me or us. It feels like so many of us are trying to find our way home in one way or another. I thank you all for the encouraging words and the pictures and videos. But whatever happens from here on, just know that you are loved and that it's never too late to find your way back to the porch—whatever that means for you. I have to believe that because I'm still working on it myself. All of your prayers are sure appreciated. —Jerry

Cesar was in his truck, heading to a work site when his phone rang for the third time. He had just confirmed the use of the Community Center and the East Park on an upcoming Saturday and had some clients to catch up with. But the call was from Irma back at the house.

"Hector, dear," her sweet voice said, "how is everything going so far today?"

"Very busy. I just left the Community Center and am late for several things. Plus, I can't get off the phone."

"Well," Irma said, "I'm afraid I'm not going to be able to simplify things for you today. I have more to ask of you. Gabriella has a friend who makes a thing called a podcast—that is like a radio show people listen to on their phones—and he makes videos for computers or something. Anyway, he would like to talk with you, and maybe Jerry and the others, for his podcast. Gabriella brought him to the thing at the park, and he is very involved with activities that bring different racial groups together. He thinks this whole thing is really exciting and that his listeners would learn a lot by hearing from you."

"He should talk to Jerry," Cesar said immediately.

"But he asked to speak to you," Irma replied, as if she had anticipated his reaction. "His show is in Spanish and English, his audience is both Hispanic and Anglo. He wants to hear about your story as an immigrant and a businessman as well as a musician. He's kind of…a fan!"

"Oh boy. You already told him I would do it, didn't you?"

"Yes, actually," Irma admitted cheerfully. "I told him you would likely be home for dinner at six o'clock and that he was welcome to join us. I hope that's okay, sweetie."

"Whatever you say, of course." He was mildly annoyed but could not deny being excited by his wife's enthusiasm about all of this. He still lived for her approval.

"Okay, then. Feel free to invite the others if you don't want to do this alone, but just know that you are the main one he wants to speak to."

"I'll see you at six. I love you, Irma. Please don't book me on any television shows before I get home."

She was smiling as she hung up the phone.

When Cesar arrived at his destination, he sent a quick text to Louis and Jerry:

[Friend of my granddaughter is coming to interview me for telephone radio thing at 6 pm—would love for you to come help and have tacos and soup. C]

Jerry and Louis both replied that they would be happy to come by.

Meanwhile, at one of those fancy coffee shops for which Jerry had such disdain, Alex was getting together with Michael Thomas. One quick call to a production company had pulled in all of their staging, PA, and lighting needs for the benefit show, in exchange for a few promotional mentions of the company name. Now it was time to find out what Michael had, if anything, from all of his recordings.

"I'm so glad you called, man," Michael gushed. "I've been slammed with this other record I'm working on, but whenever I'm not working on that, I've been going through these other files and trying to see what I've got. And dude, I think I have something.

"This is no substitute for getting you into the studio, which I definitely want to do, but check this out. That first night I got a couple of songs, still rough but so sweet. I didn't multitrack anything, so there's no way to bring one instrument up or down, but I did set up mics in different places. I can blend in the sound from here or there and get to where it has a very natural, full tone. If you close your eyes it feels, to me anyway, like you're sitting there in the driveway." Michael put a pair of headphones on Alex's ears without asking.

"Oh—and check this out. On that song where Cesar first showed up and played his accordion. I didn't have a mic set up that far back, so you could barely hear him at first. But I met his granddaughter later and found out she had recorded the whole thing on her phone! She gave me that file and I was able to blend it with what I had and…here…listen to this…" Michael touched a button on his phone.

Alex was transported back to that first show—and the moment Cesar had shown up. "This is incredible!" Alex spoke loud enough for the entire shop to hear.

Michael gestured that he should speak a little more quietly and they both chuckled.

"These headphones are crazy!" Alex added.

"Wait. Check this out. This is from the second night—I set up more mics all around the yard. On this song you can hear people in the crowd singing, playing along, and at one point someone somewhere starts playing harmonica."

"Crazy!" Alex was transported again. "We have to let the others hear this."

Alex explained the plan for the benefit show and the various challenges and concerns the group had discussed that morning. He also added that they were interested in trying to release some kind of a recording to build excitement about the benefit.

"That's unreal," Michael said. "This is exactly what I was just talking about with my assistant. Is it possible to capture and release this stuff without killing what makes it so special? I've gone back and forth in my own head about it. But I'll tell you what: I've got some ideas. Do you think we could get everyone over to the studio to hear some things and talk about this? I'd rather do it there, so they could hear it in the right environment."

"I'm sure we could," Alex said. "Everything's just happening so fast. When are you free?"

"Well, I'm working with this country artist right now, but she snuck over to the park the other night and was part of that scene. She kind of tried to stay incognito so she didn't draw attention to herself, but she had an awesome time. I know she'd love to meet the guys. We could take a break whenever they are free. We're working over at Woodland. You tell me—but let's do it this week."

"This is awesome. I'm so glad you're a part of this."

"Man," Michael said, "I feel like this shit is saving my life! Oh…don't tell Brother Louis I said that."

They laughed, did the Nashville handshake-hug, and promised to be in touch soon.

Jerry rolled up to Cesar's home just before six. He had texted Nadia an invite a couple hours earlier, and she accepted. He wouldn't have been surprised to find out she had already been there. Something told him that she and Irma were hitting it off. He checked his texts right after he turned off his car.

[We need to finish your song, too,] she had added. [Maybe after?]

[Sure!"] Jerry replied.

As Jerry walked up the sidewalk to Cesar and Irma's home, it occurred to him that though they had been to his place many times, he'd never been to theirs. He made a mental note to think more about that later. He knew that Louis and Kelly had been here, and he had been invited once but had a conflict. He wanted to make sure that Cesar and Irma knew how much he valued them. He needed to be better about expressing these things.

When he walked in the front door, he was beyond impressed. Whatever he had expected, he now realized, was an extension of his own latent prejudice. Cesar was so unassuming in the way he dressed, the truck he drove, and the way he carried himself, that Jerry tended to think of him as a typical, blue-collar guy. Honestly, he pretty much thought of Cesar as a Mexican version of himself. He had expected to see a house that was a lot like his own place. But this home was stunning.

It wasn't flashy. It wasn't gaudy. It was beautiful, tasteful, and extremely well laid out. It felt much larger inside than it looked on the outside.

"Hello, *mi amigo*." Cesar welcomed him. "Finally, you make it to *mi casa*."

"I am so sorry it's taken me so long," Jerry confessed. "I have no excuse, but now that I am here, let me just say this is an incredible place!"

"Oh, thank you," Cesar said. "Irma is responsible for the beauty. I do what she tells me to do. She says, 'Take out that wall' and I take it out. She says, 'Change this window in the kitchen,' and I change it. I work for her. Things go better that way."

"We have been here for a long time," Cesar added. "I think the outside walls are the same, but most everything else has been changed. Come get some tea and join us out back. My granddaughter's friend is already here. He is very excited to talk to me—I don't know why—and I am glad to have some backup."

"Well," Jerry said, still taking it all in, even impressed with the glass his tea was served in, "I'm excited to hear more of your story myself."

When they made it out to the patio, Jerry saw that Nadia was already out there, sitting and talking with Irma. The patio was also beautiful. Jerry wasn't sure if he had ever seen an outdoor setting as lovely. He couldn't believe he was still in East Nashville—and in a neighborhood many would consider less than desirable.

"Hello, Jerry," Irma said in her lovely accent. "Welcome to our home. Please make yourself comfortable."

Jerry found himself reflexively looking for a seat next to Nadia, but none was available, so he moved to the other side of the table.

"You remember Gabriella," Cesar said. "And this is her friend…um…"

"Robert, dear," Irma said.

"*Sí*, Robert!"

Jerry shook Robert's hand. He was a good-looking man who seemed to be somewhere in his early twenties. It was getting harder for Jerry to tell, the older he got. Robert was of Hispanic descent but spoke English with no accent.

"It's very good to meet you Mr. Wesley," Robert said. "I'm such a fan—if that's the right way to put it. I mean, it doesn't feel like that. I've been very excited and honored to be a part of the events both at your house and at the park. I missed the first evening, but Gabriella told me all about it and showed me some video she took, and I've been at every one since then. I'm…just…not sure what to say."

Everyone laughed gently, not so much *at* Robert, but **with** him.

"That makes two of us," Jerry said. "I'm not sure what to say about all of this half the time, either. But I hear what you are saying, and it means a great deal. Thank you."

Louis, who had already been seated at the head of the table and was watching this display with a kind smile, spoke up.

"So, Robert, now that Jerry is here, would you tell us about this podcast and what exactly it is that you do? How can we be helpful to you today?"

"Yes, of course. I have started an online conversation around the subject of immigration justice, integrity, and community as a way to both build bridges between the immigrant and nonimmigrant communities and to help young people of all backgrounds develop a stronger sense of self, purpose, and pride in their heritage and their potential.

"As anti-immigration sentiment has flared up in recent years, I wanted to contribute something positive. It started with some blogs and articles and then evolved into the podcast and some live speaking engagements and events. I'm not sure where it will go from here."

"He's not telling you the whole picture, though," Gabriella interjected. "He has thousands of readers and tens of thousands of listeners to the podcast. His blog has been quoted in national press, and he has been asked to speak at major rallies. This thing is getting pretty big."

"Thanks," Robert said humbly, "and that's all exciting. But truthfully, I feel that the credit for the growth belongs to the people whose stories I am telling. I am trying to shine a light on the good news stories, as I think there are more than enough people doing the important work of highlighting all of the terrible things going on. I just saw a need and I'm working to fill it."

"Well God bless you!" Nadia said. "That's amazing. Now I'll shut up and listen."

"Thank you so much," Robert continued. "So, my main goal was to highlight Cesar's story and how he found your group. I'd like to hear his perspective on how music can bring people together and what you are all doing. But when he suggested having you join in, that seemed like a great idea."

Jerry liked the thought of not having to be the spokesman for this thing, but even more, he liked the thought of seeing the one guy in the group who was quieter than him step into the spotlight.

"Excellent," Jerry said. "Well I say let's just go for it. We barely know what we're doing anyway. What have we got to lose?"

Robert finished positioning a few microphones he had set up ahead of time and checked on two video cameras on stands in the corners of the patio.

"I've also got these video cameras, by the way, so I can try to get some shorter clips from the conversation and use those for YouTube. They tend to be good for driving people to the longer audio conversation."

Once everything was in position Robert sat back down, clicked a button on a remote control, and then directed his attention to one of the cameras. "Hello, I'm Robert Vallenziano and this is another episode of *Borderline Good News*. Today I am with Cesar Jimenez, Louis Williams, and Jerry Wesley, three of the people behind a growing musical and cultural movement that some are now calling the Lost Dogs of East Nashville."

"I didn't realize we had a name," Louis interjected, with a grin in his voice. "I like it."

"*¡Perros Perdidos!*" Cesar added. "Maybe it sounds better in Spanish." That got everyone laughing. They agreed that he had a point.

"*Perros Perdidos*," Robert continued, "a name you haven't chosen, for a group you didn't even plan. Tell me, Cesar, how did this all come together?"

"Of the three of us here, I was the last to show up. My granddaughter told me about what she had mistakenly heard was some kind of open mic session happening over on Boscobel Street. My wife, Irma, had been encouraging me to play my accordion some more, and I was in a good mood, so Gabriella and I drove over and found these two older guys—one Black man and one *güero*—and a couple of young people playing music in a garage. People were sitting around with their guitars and other instruments—even harmonicas, so I brought my accordion but didn't really plan to play it.

"Then, late in the evening, they started playing an original song they said Jerry here had written a long time ago for one of his children, and it was just so beautiful—it sounded like a prayer. I started thinking of my children and my grandchildren. I thought about my parents, who are long gone now. I thought about coming to America so long ago, and how blessed we are, but how dangerous this world can be. I just thought about it all, and felt it all, and the thoughts and prayers started to feel like the music I played when I was a much younger man. I reached for my accordion and played."

"He didn't just play," Jerry interjected. "I've said this before, but it felt like his accordion was connected directly to my heart. I was holding it together pretty well, considering how emotional that song is for me. But when I heard his notes coming up from the driveway—and all I could see was the silhouette of a man in the moonlight—I just started weeping. To tell you the truth, I kind of haven't stopped crying since that night."

Irma reached over and squeezed Cesar's hand.

"That's so inspiring," Robert said. "I don't even know what to say here other than that this is exactly why I am doing this show. But Cesar, you kind of skipped over most of the details of your childhood and your roots back in Mexico. Would you be willing to fill us in on your backstory? I'm intrigued to learn about what helped to make you the man that you are."

"You want me to talk about myself?" Cesar asked, as if Robert had just asked him to perform brain surgery while riding on a motorcycle.

Irma squeezed his hand again and gave him that look. It was time.

"I'll do my best," he conceded. "You tell me when it gets dull."

It never got dull.

Present Day

Back on Jerry's porch Marisol connected a few dots. "I heard that interview. I'm a regular listener to *Borderline*, and Vallenziano is one of my favorite writers. That episode was amazing."

Cesar looked like he might be embarrassed. "Did people listen to that?"

"Oh yes," Marisol said. "Your story is inspiring many of us, Cesar. I just wonder, would you tell me a bit more about your background and history? When did you first come to America? When did you start playing music? It seems that there is a lot more to your story than we've heard."

"Oh yes. I'll tell you what I can remember. You can ask Irma about the rest."

Cesar removed his sunglasses long enough to wipe his face with his handkerchief, slide them back on his face, and then did his best to share his life's story with Marisol and the rest of the group.

Cesar's Theme

Cesar, the youngest of six children, was christened Hector Cesar Cecilio Jimenez in 1940 just outside of Nuevo Laredo Mexico, about forty miles from the U.S. border. His father, Roberto, a rancher and harvester, was a sturdy and soulful man of deep thought, quiet affection, and few words. Their family lived a traditional life. They were devout Catholics with a faith curated mostly by his mother, Maria. She incorporated every Hispanic Catholic element at her disposal, but unlike some of Cesar's friends' parents, her faith seemed to be framed more by sincere devotion than mere superstition. Cesar idolized his mother, and though he found him impossible to fully decipher, he revered his father.

Growing up so close to a border town during a time when that line was a much more casual thing meant that Cesar had a unique cultural experience. His family was as passionately in love with music as they were dependent on hard work. His father played a traditional acoustic guitar and was a devotee of the *corridos* from what he called the Golden Age of Mexican music. Cesar grew up hearing these passionate ballads with their romanticized, political stories and longed to learn how to play the accordion so he could accompany his father in the true *norteño* fashion.

German, Czech, and Polish immigrants had introduced the instrument and the polka style to that region of Southern Texas and Northern Mexico about a century earlier, so it was well rooted by the time Cesar was growing up. He could hear songs like Narciso Martínez's "El Huracan del Valle" on the radio. The sound was hypnotic.

Somehow, and Cesar never learned how, his father managed to get him a reasonable-quality diatonic accordion for his eleventh birthday. Whenever Cesar wasn't working, he had that instrument strapped on and his fingers glued to the keys. He found a local musician to give him a few orientation-style lessons, and the rest he taught himself. He played along with the radio. He played along with records. He played on his own. He played constantly.

One evening, after a particularly heated discussion at the dinner table, Hector stormed out, picked up his instrument, and started practicing.

Maria gently shook her head and offered Roberto a pinched grin. "That *acordeón* is a mixed blessing. It's so loud that sometimes I can't hear myself say my prayers. But I can tell what kind of mood that boy is in from two fields away."

Roberto nodded and offered a slight smile. "He is quite emotional, that boy. But if he keeps playing this often, he should be good before too long. It won't sound like this much longer."

Roberto was right. Hector got good fast. He was able to play along with his father within a few months. He was soon quite a bit better than his father, but his favorite music was still whatever Roberto wanted to play. The shocker, to his parents at least, came when they found their thirteen-year-old son sitting in with a local *norteño* band on a Saturday night down in a beer hall. As angry as his father was with him for being out without permission, he was even more transfixed with the sound of his son's playing. It was obvious that Hector had a gift.

Throughout Hector's teen years, the Jimenez life was a simple one: hard work, devout faith, and passionate music. He had been pulling his own weight around the family's small subsistence farm since he was little, and like many of his friends, his formal education ended when he turned thirteen and joined his father working on a local ranch. His actual education was far from over. Although he struggled to discover anything personal about his father's motivations or dreams, listening in on his conversations with the other workers taught Hector all he needed to know about politics, sociology, and history.

The radio was Hector's constant companion at home. He was attentive to current events along the border and was thrilled with the new music blending American and Mexican styles and voices. Some oversimplified this diverse cultural alchemy by calling it "Tejano," but to Hector it was magic. His accordion, which he learned had its roots far away in lily-white Europe, was able to add some wonderful brown shades to the new rock-and-roll sounds that were starting to evolve just the other side of the border. It seemed to Hector that once the music started, borders became myths. Lines faded and colors emerged...danced...blended. It was not uncommon for Maria to find Hector asleep with his accordion still strapped to his chest. When he was not asleep and not working, he was usually lost in the music somewhere—eyes closed, head moving, fingers gliding, and free.

By the time he was sixteen, Hector spent every weekend playing with multiple bands in dance halls around the area. He mastered the nuances of several regional styles, from the various flavors of traditional and contemporary *norteño*, to the more acoustic strains of *sierreño*, *conjunto*, and *banda* music. He understood that the genre distinctions between these styles almost always came down to the type of instruments that were used and the specific region in which the style evolved.

The older folks, he theorized, were much more set in their ways because they weren't exposed to new sounds and new opportunities like his generation was, and they didn't tend to pay as much attention to music on the radio and television. Now that everything was blending, anything was possible. Young Hector was a dreamer and an idealist.

While his round face favored his mother, his thick, wavy hair and sturdy frame were definitely inherited from Roberto's side of the family. He was oblivious to the attention he started to earn from young ladies when he played, unless they commented on something specifically about the music. One of the groups he played with asked him to wear a fancy jacket and shirt when he played with them, which they were happy to provide. He obliged but found the fashion aspects of the performance to be a distraction from the music.

As much as his father loved to hear him play, he worried about how invested Hector was in his music. It was time for him to focus on earning money in the fields. Though Hector showed up every day and did his work, everyone could tell that his heart was elsewhere. "Dreams get you in trouble out here on the ranch," he told his son one afternoon. "You had better make sure to keep your mind on what's important. When I was a child I spoke as a child. I thought like a child. But when I became a man I put away childish things. Your music is a wonderful thing," he said, looking Hector in the eyes with all sincerity, "but now you are a man and you have to think about paying the bills."

Hector was crushed that his father thought his music was childish. He understood that his accordion was never going to make him money, but that wasn't the point. He tried venting to his mother. Though she was sympathetic to his romantic side, there was no chance of her undermining her husband's words.

"Music makes this dusty life worth living," he told her. "I swear, the only thing that keeps me going out there on the ranch all day is knowing that my accordion is waiting for me when I get home."

"I know your father loves to hear you play. He is just concerned that you are too distracted by it. Maybe just try to pay more attention at work and it will take care of itself."

Hector's shoulders bent forward, and he turned his face toward his shoes. He was no longer looking at his mother as he spoke to her. "He doesn't understand. All he thinks about is work. He can't know how it feels to love something this much."

That got Maria's attention. She stared at the back of Hector's head. "I think you should be careful assuming that you know what he does and does not understand, my little boy. There are many things about your father that you can't understand because you have not had that kind of responsibility placed upon your shoulders yet."

Hector bristled at the diminution, but he also realized that his mother had a point. "You are right, of course. I meant no offense. But when I look at Father, he looks so much older than he is. He seems so worried, about money and about the world and about everything. I don't want to live that way. There has to be a more exciting life for me, right?"

Maria took Hector in her arms and gave him a long, gentle embrace. He melted into her.

"I hope there is, little one. But that is not a world I have ever seen. I see this world, and music like yours makes it more beautiful, but it doesn't change how hard it is for us to get by in it."

Hector resolved to prove to his father that he could do both. He picked up the pace around the ranch, but he didn't slow down his musical pursuits at all. If anything, he acted as if his father had issued some sort of spiritual challenge.

A few weeks later, lightning struck via an AM radio station out of Laredo. Ritchie Valens already had a big hit with a song called "Come On, Let's Go," and Hector had spent some time playing along with that one on the radio. But his version of "La Bamba" was so exciting that it set the dance halls on both sides of the border on fire. When Hector read in a magazine that Valens was just a year younger than him, he started to get ideas. Maybe he could make his way to California and audition for Valens' band. It was a crazy thought—more like a fever dream cooked up after a sweaty night of performing. But the thought, planted in his head like a seed, was growing like a weed.

Hector started to think seriously about making a road trip to Los Angeles. He had heard about some Tejano musicians from Laredo who were traveling to San Antonio to record. He met them after a gig one night to get names and phone numbers. There were buses and trains that connected the Southwestern states pretty easily. If he saved his gig money for about six months, he might have enough for a ticket. He heard about the growing Mexican community in East L.A. and thought he might have a shot at making a living there. Those thoughts faded by about ten o'clock each morning as the hot sun beat down on his back, but they crept back into his mind as the sun set and the music started up again.

Four months into his clandestine plan, however, Hector's father fell ill with some sort of serious lung disease. A lack of advanced health care meant limited diagnoses and treatment, but Hector later assumed his father died of either emphysema or cancer. Suddenly Hector's mother needed his help more than ever. His California dream would have to wait.

The extra hours he picked up as a landscaper drained his energy for the dance halls. He found himself playing less and less. At just twenty-two years old, Hector started to feel defeated and hopeless. Wages were going down and work was getting harder to find. Corruption and violence changed the character of their small-town life. Hector's mother's health was failing, and his brothers were talking of heading north, across the border, for better opportunities in the States.

One evening, shortly after supper, the family's priest stopped by to visit Maria. She hadn't been to mass lately, and he suspected she was ill. Hector joined them as the padre took her confession, offered her communion, and prayed for her health. When the brief religious service was completed, the pastor lingered for a moment. He turned to Hector with a warm smile. "Is there any chance you might bless us with some music tonight, Hector?"

"I did not know you were aware of my music, Padre," Hector said sheepishly. "It is not really a church thing."

"Oh, I disagree!" Father Constance insisted with a gentle smile. "This is a small community, my son. I have tried to keep a close eye on all of my flock and have been especially thrilled to see you use the gift God obviously blessed you with. I see the happiness you feel when you play, and the joy you extend to others. If that's not of God, I don't know what is. In fact, I would go so far as to say that there is nothing truly good in this world that God doesn't own, and there is nothing that brings us true joy that doesn't come from God. The only question is, do we recognize His hand in it or not?"

Hector had never thought about his music being spiritual before. He had also never felt that God saw him at all. He had belief, but it felt like a one-way thing. He said his prayers, did his religious duty, and hoped to please God. But he never sensed that God was giving him any kind of feedback. It had never occurred to him that maybe music was that feedback.

"Thank you, Padre," Hector said sincerely. "You have given me much to think about."

"Well," Father Constance said joyfully, "Might I request that you think about that later and play some music for us now?"

Hector smiled, nodded, and retrieved his accordion. He played a beautiful *corrido* he had been working on. It blended elements of a traditional Mexican *varsovienne*, or waltz, with some American country music he had been hearing recently. Though it had no lyrics, the slow and winsome melody was directly inspired by Hector's father. The tune meandered a bit, like a boy who didn't quite know where to go, but it also circled around a theme that it couldn't quite break out of.

Tears flowed down his mother's cheeks as the padre closed his eyes and took in the moment. Everyone knew exactly what the song was about. Music had never felt so holy to Hector.

A few months later Hector was playing with a small ensemble on a Sunday afternoon at a *quinceañera* in Nuevo Laredo when he met Irma, a twenty-year-old beauty with a fiery personality and a clear sense of purpose. He was as drawn to her confidence as he was to her perfectly framed face. She didn't let on, at first anyway, that she had seen him on stage at a couple of other events in the past. Their mothers were acquaintances, and after getting their blessing, the two arranged to get together.

From that point forward, everything was a formality. Hector was hooked and Irma knew it. She acted like she was in charge, and it was a good act, but she was deeply moved by Hector's quiet, thoughtful sensitivity. She sensed that he would take care of her for the rest of her life. She imagined that she would never tire of his music. The two were married four months later.

Hector and Irma were immediately thrown into the deep end of life together. She became pregnant within two months of their honeymoon. One week later, Hector found out that his wages at the ranch were being cut once again, and his mother's health continued to decline. Their situation was becoming more and more dire and their prospects in Mexico were drying up fast when an opportunity to make the move north seemed to present itself out of nowhere.

Crossing the border at Laredo was not a real problem in 1958. The Americans needed and welcomed seasonal agricultural workers from Mexico. In fact, the trouble mostly came from the Mexican government, which was afraid of losing too many workers to the U.S. Hector had been following with horror the "Operation Wetback" initiative in the U.S., where President Eisenhower had supposedly rounded up millions of undocumented Mexicans—workers that had been needed in the U.S.—and deported them in brutal ways. Hector knew several men who had been through the experience multiple times. Though he doubted the numbers he heard on the radio he had no interest in becoming a statistic.

But Hector was better trained than most agricultural workers, and he had access to musical performance visas. Irma was younger but could get a student visa pretty easily. Hector thought his mother might be able to get across the border with an old copy of his father's seasonal worker papers. No one cared about an old lady, anyway. If he could get the three of them across the border—and he had little doubt that he could—the question would come down to whether they would ever be able to come back to Mexico. They had precious little to lose though, that was for sure. Irma considered their options and showed her defiant and confident, if not also youthful and naïve, streak. They would go for it.

Hector gathered the money he had been saving, and sold most of their belongings. They would cross over into Texas and he would perform a few gigs in San Antonio. A band from California was due to be in town, and he would do his best to get the three of them some space on the band's bus for the ride to Los Angeles. If that didn't work, they'd find a train. Then he'd try to audition for Ritchie Valens. He knew that part was beyond unlikely, but he had learned enough about the growing Mexican community in L.A. to assume he could find work if his first choice didn't pan out.

They celebrated one last Christmas in Nuevo Laredo, and then a few days after the New Year in 1959 they made their move. Everything went surprisingly well. The gigs in San Antonio were exciting and provided an excellent connection to the Los Angeles musicians. Space was tight on the bus, but they made room once Hector agreed to play three gigs for no fee once they hit L.A. They even found a friend-of-a-friend with a spare room in a house in the Boyle Heights area of East Los Angeles. The ride was long, and Hector's mother was not doing too well, but the journey went according to plan. The Jimenez trio woke up in Los Angeles early on the morning of January 15 and Hector immediately started looking for both music gigs and a real job while the women went in and set up their room.

Hector looked up the address for Ritchie Valens' label, Del-Fi Records, in Hollywood and made that one of his first objectives. When he walked in, however, he forgot to consider the fact that he did not speak much English.

"Ritchie Valens?" he asked the receptionist, holding up his accordion, hoping to communicate that he wanted an audition.

The poor girl was clueless. "Please wait here, sir." She retreated deeper into the small office.

A couple of minutes later a well-dressed gentleman with a name Hector did not understand came to the little waiting room, speaking very fast. He seemed to be asking Hector who he was and what he wanted. Hector decided it was best to let his music speak for him. He strapped on his accordion and started playing his most heartfelt version of Valens' hit "Donna."

"Wow," the well-dressed man said. He said many more English words Hector did not understand, but he could tell the man wanted to know who he was and where they could reach him. Hector carefully wrote down his full name and the phone number and address of the place they were staying in Boyle Heights.

"Hector Cesar Jimenez," the man said, pronouncing it "JIM-i-nez," with a hard *j* as in *jump*. "Hector, huh? I think you should go by Cesar. I've never met an actual Cesar before!" He underlined the *Cesar* part of his name, and Hector smiled. The man pronounced it more like "see-zur"—which sounded kind of like the word *seizure* and not "say-zar," which was the pronunciation Hector was more familiar with. But he was not about to correct the man. If he thought "see-zur" sounded cool, then "see-zur" it was. He chuckled to himself when he thought about telling Irma this. She'd probably have a seizure.

"Look," the gentleman told Cesar, "Ritchie doesn't really play traditional Mexican music, you know. He plays rock and roll. I'm not sure he needs an accordion. But we'll call you if we need you." He smiled a very broad smile and patted Cesar on the back as he showed him to the door.

Cesar walked down the street, surrounded by the sights and sounds of Hollywood—things he had failed to take in on his way to this meeting—and dared to think he might have a shot at this crazy dream. From that day forward he introduced himself to everyone as Cesar Jimenez. That well-dressed man had convinced him it was a better name.

Two weeks later Ritchie Valens died in a plane crash in Iowa. Cesar heard the news on the Hispanic radio station he listened to constantly. He was crushed. Buddy Holly, who Cesar knew was from Texas—not far from Nuevo Laredo—had also died in the same crash. He loved Buddy Holly's songs. There was something so hopeful in his voice. Cesar felt that something spiritual happened when that plane crashed.

He also felt that God had just closed his imaginary door to Cesar's musical dream. He went off by himself and wept bitterly. The grief he was feeling was not commensurate with the loss of a couple of pop stars. Something else was dying, but he was so distraught he couldn't understand what it meant. He thought he was being weak, or crazy. Eventually the sobbing passed.

He remembered his father's words about putting away childish things. Cesar hoped he would never completely stop playing music, but with a baby coming, and a mother and wife to support, it was time for him to grow up. He found a job at a fruit farm outside of Los Angeles and apprenticed with a landscaper to hone his specialized arborist and horticultural skills. He had excellent talent and an incomparable work ethic. Between the cost of living in California and the suppressed wages offered to migrant workers, Hector found himself in much the same state that he had seen with his father back in Mexico. He had little time to do anything recreational and lost his appetite for dreams. He redefined himself as a man of responsibility. He saw the pride his mother took as she watched him provide for his family, and he imagined his father's approval coming from beyond the grave.

He and Irma grew closer and closer. He was more in love with her than he knew how to articulate. She came to life in America in ways that surprised but delighted him. He let her do the talking and most of the decision making, and he focused on working, disciplining the children when they needed it, and offering occasional spiritual and moral guidance when anyone was listening. He found it easier to work than to speak, and in that his resemblance to his father deepened. He wondered if Roberto had the kind of inner dialogue constantly running through his head as he worked that Cesar had running through his.

Cesar's mother passed away two years after they had settled in California. Their second baby was born two weeks later. The loss of his mother was hard, but the community they found in East L.A. was rich and deep. Irma blossomed as a leader in Boyle Heights and stayed up-to-date on all of the political and cultural happenings that might impact their family. One of those issues was the ever-changing dynamic surrounding U.S. immigration laws. They couldn't help noticing the irony when they heard rumors of deportation in Los Angeles since that area had been part of Mexico until a little over a century ago. But the fact was that both Irma and Cesar had overstayed their work visas from 1959, and under the immigration laws that passed in 1965, they were considered "illegal aliens." Their children had all been born in the U.S., and they had no ties back to Mexico other than some fond memories. But without proper papers, they always felt a dark cloud was hanging over their heads.

Irma started to think it was time to leave East L.A. "This place has changed," she told Hector one night (she never bought into the "Cesar" thing). "This racial unrest and violence is going to get much worse, I fear.

____

I have a friend with a cousin who settled in Tennessee. She told her that she found cheap housing, quiet neighborhoods, lots of jobs, and low crime there. If you agree, I can make some calls to find someone there who will help us find a place to live once we arrive. We can save up for a couple of months, sell some things, and go!"

Hector agreed. He didn't mention it at the time, but he wondered if there might be any room for an accordion player steeped in *norteño-tejano* music on that Grand Ole Opry stage he had heard so much about.

In 1968 Cesar and Irma moved their family of eight two thousand miles east to Music City. Cesar opted for the southern route so they could go back through *Tejas* one more time. They pulled into Nashville in July and had not felt that kind of stifling humidity and heat before. The little ones started complaining sometime around the Texas/Arkansas line. Irma was wondering what she had gotten them into.

The friends Irma had arranged to stay with set up canvas tents for the kids in their backyard and one bedroom in the house for Cesar, Irma, and the littlest babies. This landing pad reminded them of their arrival in Los Angeles a decade earlier. Hector needed some time to recover from the drive before he began his job search. He lay back on some cushions on the floor, looking up at a ceiling fan and listening to a local country radio station. He felt as if he had landed in another world.

Irma had done an excellent job mastering English over the previous ten years. She had taken English as a second language classes at the L.A. County Library and made sure to speak English with the kids as they learned it at school. She was fluent, though she often reverted to Spanish when the children overwhelmed her.

Cesar resisted English. He understood more than he let on, but he struggled to speak it much at all. He also often listened to American roots music, the vast majority of which was performed in English. He knew what those songs were about—and he could sing along with them—but when he tried to speak English, you would never guess that he had been in America for over ten years.

One day, after a frustrating encounter with a checker at a grocery store, Irma confronted him. *"¿Cual es tu problema?"* she demanded. "You've been here the same amount of time I have. You are one of the most intelligent men I have ever known. And yet you refuse to accept the fact that we live in a country with a different native tongue."

Hector just shrugged.

"I think you're just being prideful, or maybe just stubborn," she continued, "but it is driving me crazy. I know that in your work world you feel that you don't have to learn English, but I'm telling you, in this world"—she made a wide sweeping gesture to the streets surrounding them—"you need to be able to speak the language in order to be successful."

"Successful?" Hector sniffed. "I don't need English to cut people's shrubs and to mow their grass." He wasn't trying to be rude, though a shade of indignation could be seen creeping across his face. He let out a slow exhale, willing himself to think before he said anything else. In East L.A., the Mexican community was so big you could go for weeks, or even months, without needing English. Nashville was different. Irma was probably right. But the idea of using "success" as a reason to learn English felt off. He thought of his father and wondered if he had ever dreamed of success. Though he could not articulate it at the time, Hector had no idea what success even was. "I'm just trying to survive," he said truthfully. "I don't have time for success."

Nashville was also different in that the Mexican community was not concentrated in one area the way it was in so many other cities. Small pockets existed here and there, but there weren't many Mexican families in Nashville yet. That meant much more integration, which was still a pretty big challenge for many White folks in the South. The Jimenez family experienced plenty of anti-immigrant sentiment from certain aspects of Nashville's racist contingent, but they found the safer places to hang out and the folks they could trust. As challenging as this new frontier was going to be, they had seen and experienced worse.

Ultimately, they took to Nashville pretty well, and Nashville absorbed them into its ever-increasing and eclectic fabric with remarkable speed. Cesar found work as a high-end landscaper for wealthy clients with grand estates who were happy to pay in cash. Irma had one more baby, bringing the grand total to seven, and managed a thrifty, loving, full, and very small home in the Cleveland Park neighborhood of East Nashville. It was mostly an African American neighborhood, but Irma found the house through a friend at their church, and it was the biggest house they could afford. She was nervous about the racial differences at first, but she built relationships with her neighbors one at a time.

In the fall of 1986, two months after the birth of their first grandson and eighteen years after moving to Nashville, Hector Cesar Cecilio Jimenez and Irma Phillipe Rosario Jimenez applied for amnesty under Ronald Reagan's Immigration Control and Reform Act. They gladly paid back taxes, aced a test on American history and civics, and Cesar even passed his nominal English proficiency test. With legitimate paperwork in place, Cesar legally incorporated his landscaping business, put all of his workers on payroll, and started advertising. Irma handled his accounting and business affairs.

Within five years Jimenez Arborists and Landscaping was one of the most successful new businesses in the Nashville area, paying tens of thousands of dollars in taxes and employing over a hundred people. Cesar invested in equipment, vehicles, and once even a billboard. Ten years later, in 1996, the patriarch and matriarch of the growing Jimenez dynasty became official U.S. citizens. When Cesar stood for his citizenship exam, the test administrator told him that he understood more about both Tennessee and U.S. law and civics than most public school graduates.

None of that stopped ignorant good old boys from closing doors in Cesar's face, blocking his path when entering a bank or restaurant, or muttering racial slurs when he crossed the street. When he showed up to a construction site, it was common for a low-level worker to treat him, the owner of the landscaping firm—with the contract for the job—like he was a waterboy.

Cesar was stoic about it, though. He usually didn't let it bother him. He was quiet. He knew who he was. He knew who his wife was. He knew who his children were. He knew who his God was. Ignorant comments from racist fools didn't bother Cesar at all, but despite his financial comfort and the general health of his marriage, he couldn't escape the sense that something was missing.

The family held a backyard bash to celebrate Cesar's and Irma's citizenship. In the midst of the convivial chaos, Cesar enjoyed a long look at his wife and best friend as she moved through the space she had so artfully cultivated. He marveled at the ease with which she kept track of all of the details, from the food and drinks to the names of every boyfriend, girlfriend, or neighbor who came to offer congratulations. He enjoyed the look of her, with her long, now-graying hair flowing freely down her back and her body—older, ampler, and well cared for. He started to develop some other ideas of how they might celebrate together.

"What are you looking at Papi?" his granddaughter asked, "and what in the world is that grin on your face all about?"

Cesar had been lost in the moment and was slightly embarrassed. For a split second he worried that his inner thoughts had made their way too obviously to the surface.

"Ah, Nieta!" He blushed. "I am just, oh, how do you kids say it? Spacing out, I guess."

"Uh-huh, okay. That's not the kind of face you usually see on someone who is spacing out. I think you were staring at *Abuela*."

She nudged him with her elbow and he pulled her to his side for a hug.

"I guess you caught me, Nieta. She is something else, though, isn't she? I look around at all of this, all of you, and sometimes it can be a little bit overwhelming."

His granddaughter lingered with her arms still draped around his side. "I hope I can find something like what you two have someday."

"So do I, *cariño*. So do I."

As his business became more successful, Cesar never really changed the way he dressed or the truck that he drove. He and Irma stayed in their small Cleveland Park home long after their kids moved out. He constantly made improvements, but it was still the same four bedroom, two-bath house they had rented from 1968 to 1986 and then bought. He drove a 1988 Ford F-150 pickup when he wasn't driving one of his company trucks. Irma knew that they had enough money to cover any emergencies, and that if any of their children or grandchildren needed help with education expenses or some kind of health care emergency, she and Cesar would be able to offer it. Irma's sense of security regarding their finances was all he needed.

Their children had no idea how much money they had accumulated or how much they gave away to various ministries and charities. Both Cesar and Irma believed that it was important for their kids to find their own way.

When the tornadoes ripped through East Nashville in 1998, Cesar's company was able to donate a lot of work hours to help with the cleanup and restoration. When the flood happened in 2010, Cesar and his workers collectively spent over a thousand hours helping people demolish and rebuild their homes and yards. Jimenez Arborists and Landscaping even got special recognition from the city of Nashville for its charitable contributions and work for the community.

Irma and Cesar were seeing a kind of transformation in their community they had never imagined. Crime was down. Property values were rising. A diverse population of young and enthusiastic people was moving into the area from all over the country. Racial prejudice even seemed to be decreasing. The fact that it was causing some of his workers to be displaced, though, had Cesar thinking. He and Irma invested in an apartment building, fixed it up, and made the units available to his employees at a discounted rate.

Not that the Jimenez family was somehow devoid of struggle. Cesar could be found at St. Cecilia Catholic Church on Woodland Street several times each week praying for various members of his family, his workers, and his friends as they faced down addiction, unplanned pregnancies, financial problems, immigration challenges, incarceration, and depression. He didn't understand how some of his own children, who had seen the positive example he and Irma had set for them, could ignore that guidance and blaze their own prodigal trails.

One afternoon Father Mack, the priest at St. Cecilia, hailed Cesar as he was walking out after Mass. "Hello, Cesar. Any chance you'd like to grab a beer and talk for a while after confession and prayers?" About a half hour later, they walked to a new neighborhood brewery and ordered a couple of pints before the young priest got right to the point.

"How are you doing, Cesar? I can tell you have a lot on your mind and on your heart, and I can see that you are seeking God about some things. I just wondered how things are going."

Cesar had become so good at keeping his words to himself, and was only used to talking to Irma, that a direct question like this—from a priest no less—caught him a bit off guard. He immediately thought of Father Constance back in Mexico. But as uncomfortable as he felt at first, it was good to be seen and noticed, especially by someone in the church. Maybe after all these years, God was finally going to talk back to him.

Cesar took a long swallow from his glass, stared at his hands for a moment, and then looked up at Father Mack. "I worry about my family. I have a grandson who seems hell-bent on ending up in prison—he keeps running around with gang members and messing with drugs. One of my daughters seems to not be able to think clearly. She has been married three times and is, how do you say it, self-destructive. So many problems. So many." Cesar put his face in his hands and shook it side to side.

Father Mack nodded but made no attempt to interrupt.

"It all makes me very sad sometimes, but other times very angry. Irma and I have worked so hard to provide for them and to teach them well. We bring them to church and pray for them. I have prayed and talked to God, but I don't hear anything. I don't understand why some people just seem determined to hurt themselves. I don't know what to do, but I wish God would answer. It seems like sixty years is long enough for me to be asking questions without hearing any answers."

Cesar was worried that maybe he had gone too far. Maybe Father Mack would be offended by his frustration. He also felt a bit light-headed and exposed from all the talking.

"I agree."

That got Cesar's attention. He had been in the middle of a sip from his glass, but that caused him to stop and look at Father Mack, almost as if he was sure he had heard that wrong.

The priest continued. "Sixty years is way too long to feel like you haven't heard back from God. But in my life I have found that when I go a long time without hearing from God, it's because I'm not putting myself in the position to listen well. I think some people come by it naturally, but for me listening is a skill I have to work on really diligently. I have to put myself into the right environment, remove distractions, and open myself up. Does that make any sense to you?"

Cesar nodded.

"Can you tell me about a time you have felt like you've heard from God?"

Cesar stared off into the distance of the brewery. He noticed a song playing in the background. He wasn't familiar with it, but there was what sounded like an accordion in the mix.

"When I was young I played my accordion and felt that the wall between this world and the spirit world dissolved. I could get lost for hours—or a whole day—and feel complete peace. And when I played it wasn't just for me. I could see other people taken to that place."

"Wow. I would love to hear you play sometime. We sure need more beauty in this world. Have you ever played your prayers?"

A well of emotion started to build in Cesar's chest, throat, and eyes. He took another drink and beat it back before continuing to speak. "Many years ago I think. Many many years ago."

"Maybe sixty years ago?" the priest suggested.

Cesar wiped his eyes and locked his emotions down.

The priest continued. "Cesar, what I see before me is a man of great heart. I'm thrilled to have you join me at church as often as you want to come, but I think you should add some accordion to your prayers. It might be good to see what happens when you get your body, your heart, and your mind all lined up in that way."

Cesar nodded. He wasn't sure he agreed with the idea of getting any more emotional than he just had, but he appreciated his priest's compassion.

"But here's the thing," Father Mack said, "you might also need to follow up those prayers with some actions and words that show your love and concern for your family. None of us can control what anyone else does, and some people have to learn the hard way. But it can be impossible for us to feel peace within ourselves if we are not fulfilling the fulness of our calling to love. I think you might hear something deeper when you listen in a different way. I'm excited to hear what comes next."

"Thank you, Father, for the time, the drink, and the words." He intended to tell Irma about their conversation, but somehow never got around to it. Something made him nervous about getting out his accordion, and he was pretty sure that if he told her about Father Mack's advice, she'd have it out and on the table in a matter of seconds. He had never expected music to come back to him. Thank goodness he had Irma. When an unusual opportunity came up it was she who encouraged him to ignore his father's old advice.

"Sometimes," she said with her beautiful, mischievous, seventy-one-year-old grin, "you have to pick up childish things."

Back to Cesar's Interview on the Patio

"Who knows where I would be without Irma," Cesar said with complete honesty. His dinner guests all sat listening to the details of his life's story with rapt attention. They had heard bits and pieces over the previous months but had never heard the whole thing laid out in narrative form.

"That's just unbelievable," Jerry said.

"Unbelievably beautiful," Louis added.

Cesar was looking uncomfortable, so they backed off. But none in the group ever forgot that moment.

Recovering his presence of mind, Robert redirected to the others.

"What is the story behind the song Cesar played on, Jerry?"

"Well," Jerry regathered his thoughts, "this is hard to talk about, to tell you the truth, but I'll try."

He steeled himself. Maybe it was better that he hadn't seen this coming.

"I was married when I was very young. I was blessed with two little babies before I was even twenty years old. We were poor country people, living on a farm outside of Crossville, Tennessee. I was working two jobs and life was already kind of caving in on me. I started playing guitar a little bit when I was in high school. I loved it. My girlfriend, who later became my wife, was the only one who ever heard my music. Life was just too busy for a luxury like music. My old man had driven that into my head.

"One night, when I got home really late from my factory job, I think I must have woken up my little baby girl, Marianne. She started fussing and I didn't want her to wake up her mama. I picked her up and sang her this little song I had been thinking about as I worked. It was really simple, it just said, 'Oh, sweet Marianne, breathe it out and breathe it in. Don't be afraid, there's nothing to fear. You're not alone, I'm not much, I know, but I'm right here.'

"She quieted right down. I put her back in her little crib. But I was less than 'not much.' I was not ready to be a daddy. I was drinking too much. I was not dealing with pressure well. I already felt like a failure, and then I went and signed up for the Army, looking for a steady paycheck."

Everyone around the table was learning more about Jerry than they had known. This unexpected interview was proving to be quite an experience for the whole group. Nadia looked up when Jerry mentioned the Army part. Her eyes got wider.

"Vietnam was not a good place for me, or anyone, obviously," he continued. "The demons I brought with me just got on top of me and ate me up. I had some bad experiences there, and I came home injured—both in my body and in my mind. I tried to deal with the mental stuff by drinking more. One night that led to a fight with my wife, and I hurt her. I couldn't believe I did it, but I did. I left that night and haven't seen her or my kids ever since. I've tried. Eventually, many years later, I got some good help with my alcoholism. I've been sober for forty-three years now. I sent money for the kids and wrote to them all the time, but my ex-wife made it clear that they didn't want anything to do with me. There was no hope of fixing what I had done.

"So I guess that song is really still a prayer. My kids are grown now. They have kids of their own. I still love them and pray for them and feel terrible about what happened. Part of the recovery process we learn is to do what they call a 'fearless moral inventory,' and the next is to make amends as much as we can. I've not been able to make amends with them, and that just eats me up.

"When I was playing that song one morning on my porch, just by myself, my neighbor heard it and asked if he and his brother could play with me sometime. Something about that song spoke to them. So that's when this whole thing started. That was the song we were playing that first Saturday night when Cesar here stepped up and joined in the prayer. I think that's pretty amazing."

"Wow." Robert didn't seem to know how to respond.

"I didn't know any of that," Cesar said. "That melody feels like a prayer for sure. When I heard it I thought about my family, too. I don't know. I think that must be from somewhere else."

Robert, seeming to have collected himself, redirected the conversation for a moment. "Brother Louis, that's what we all call you, but…are you a pastor or something?"

"I'm no more a pastor than Cesar here is. The honorific was given to me as a child and it just stuck. Lately I seem to have grown into it, I suppose."

"When you heard the song, and saw that lyric, how did it strike you?" Robert asked.

"Actually," Louis began, "the whole thing is kind of a blur. I truly didn't want to sing. I have always loved to sing but have had a strong aversion to singing in public. I'm just now starting to think through where that may have come from. But that night was the first time I had ever sung in public, and I was having something like an out-of-body experience the whole time. At one point in the evening, Alex, one of the younger gentlemen in the group, asked Jerry if he would try this original song. He showed me this verse—it was just a few lines. So I just improvised around those lines. I don't even know how similar what I sang was to what Jerry wrote. But he was playing the melody on his guitar so beautifully, that I could feel that part pretty well."

"He sang it perfectly," Jerry added.

"So Cesar," Robert asked, "when you heard this country–Americana guitar player and this soulful, gospel-oriented singer playing a song you had never heard before, what inspired you to add your *norteño*-style accordion? It seems like a stylistic reach."

"It's hard to describe," Cesar admitted. "But it felt like a voice told me to. I could almost hear how the different styles of music were moving around something that we all had in common, instead of what made us all different. We all had people to pray for, regrets to ask forgiveness for, and blessings and love to extend to people around us. There was some kind of special air there, and I could hear those notes in my heart but not with my ears. So I produced them. It was risky. I didn't know how anyone would respond. But after the first few bars, I could tell that they felt it, too. Not just the other musicians up behind the microphones, but the people around me. We all felt it. It was like my mother was there, and Father Constance, and Jesus. No one wanted to leave. We stood around after the music ended and talked and shared stories. I sat and talked with some kids from a heavy metal band for an hour. It was like a small taste or, how do you say, a little sniff of heaven."

No one had heard it described that way, but everyone agreed.

Robert, once again having to collect himself, tried to find another question to ask. "One of the main themes of this show is to find inspiring examples of people overcoming the division and hostility in the world and achieving justice and peace. Do you gentlemen believe that what you are doing with this music could be a part of that process of reconciliation? Do you have plans to take this big? Where does it go from here?"

Louis seemed to be responding to the question physically before words came to him. His body was twisting a bit in his seat and he seemed uncomfortable. It was a very different posture for him.

"We have no idea what the grand plan for this is," he said plainly. "We didn't expect it to happen in the first place, and we won't say that we know where it is going. But we all agree that it has felt as if there is a hand guiding this. Like Cesar so beautifully said, we stumbled into this—I'll call it a sacred space—where we were all together. Not muting our differences but honoring them—making space for them. And we are feeling that there is a hunger out there for this kind of unity and this kind of participatory experience. So we are carefully moving forward, trying to be thoughtful about the beauty of this thing and shrewd about how easy it would be to kill it through commercial means.

"But as we sit here," Louis continued, "something else is occurring to me. Just as my brother Jerry referred to doing a 'fearless moral inventory' and then making amends where we can, I suspect that the spiritual nature of this music might, if we allow it to, help us to perform such an inventory. Jerry and I, for instance, have lived just a couple of blocks from each other for decades and yet never met. I now consider him to be family. This music did that. What else might it do? I get excited, and a little frightened, when I think about that."

"It does seem to have the power to move the community," Robert added. "And I know that it is moving me personally."

"We are hoping to put together a large benefit concert for Louis's church," Cesar said. "There are some things that a big group can do but a small group cannot. But there are also some things, like a man standing up and playing his accordion, which can only happen in a small space. We're trying to figure out how to do both."

"That's fantastic!" Robert enthused. "I certainly will buy a ticket, and I know many of our listeners will come to that. But I would also like to hear about the smaller-scale stuff. We have listeners around the country and overseas. I know they would be interested to hear about how to do what you are doing in their communities."

Louis spoke up after a while. "I am moved so deeply by my brother Cesar's story, and I am so saddened that he and his family are still dealing with the kind of ignorance and hostility that comes from fear and small-mindedness. I do hope that one of the side effects of the music we make," he added, "is that it opens some eyes and hearts to the fact that God has invested his image into all of his children, not just some of them. We want to inspire everyone to sing along—and to reject the false melodies of exclusion and hate. Like Cesar said, we get a small taste or aroma of heaven when we come together and make music. Let's make that music so loud that it drowns out the noise of hatred and violence and ignorance."

Nadia was about to do a dance. This was feeling downright revolutionary.

"I wonder if Brother Louis ever got to hear Dr. King speak?" she whispered to Kelly.

"Oh, he did," she whispered back. "He definitely did."

The Buildup

"You know what they say about great art," Nadia said, rubbing her forehead. "It's abandoned rather than finished."

She and Jerry had been working on his song for several hours, and she thought it was sounding solid. Jerry was having a hard time feeling that it was done, though.

"Is it really there?" he asked. "I mean, if you heard this and didn't know the story behind it, would you get it?"

"I think so. I really do. And I think it would be smart to leave a little space in it so when you bring it to the others, there's some room for them to breathe into it, too."

"All right, we can call it done." He leaned over to put his Martin on its stand.

"One more thought, though," Nadia gingerly suggested. "I really, really feel that you should sing this one."

Jerry looked up with wide eyes, genuinely surprised—and dismayed—at the idea.

She continued before he could object. "Just sitting here, hearing you sing, you have so much heart in it—and the lyric is all about vulnerability and frailty. I know Louis's voice is wonderful and all, and your voice is…less than perfect. But it's perfect for that message."

"I don't know." He looked as if Nadia had just asked him to walk a tight-rope between two skyscrapers. "I don't think I can play and sing at the same time, anyway."

"Well, just try simplifying what you play when it's time to sing, and then spice up the parts between phrases. You can decorate the instrumental section however you want, but while you're singing just stick to the chords. Hey, it works for Dylan!"

"Maybe. But Dylan's better than you think." He wanted to rise to that occasion. He'd work on it privately, but he had his doubts. "How tired are you?"

"I don't know," she said mischievously, "what do you have in mind?"

Oblivious to her sass, Jerry plowed ahead. "I was thinking about that poem you read at the park. I've been working on another melody idea. I wonder if we might be able to turn that into a song."

"Interesting. Let's give it an hour. I should be home by midnight or my son will worry." She still wore a sly grin, but Jerry missed it completely. "Plus, we do have the meeting at the studio with Michael in the morning."

"An hour'll be great." Jerry flipped the page in his leather journal. "Hey, how does Daniel feel about all of this stuff? We just kind of kidnapped you, didn't we? I hope he doesn't resent us for monopolizing your time like this." He looked up from the journal as his own words caught up with him. "I'd love to get to know him and his wife and kids. It just feels like things have been happening so fast around here; every day gets so busy."

"He's fine. They're all planning on coming to the benefit concert, and they're excited about the workshops at the Community Center. Honestly, they seem to just be thrilled that they no longer have to work so hard to talk me into moving here."

"Oh they don't?" Jerry tried to restrain a grin.

"Oh no. They were trying to get me to move here by next year, but I went ahead and put my notice in with my landlord three days ago. New York's going to have to figure out how to survive without me. I'm staying here."

"Wow!" Jerry said, genuinely surprised and not a little delighted. "Were you going to tell me about this?"

"Eventually. Seems like I just did, didn't I? Now play me this melody. We have less than an hour."

By ten the next morning, the whole gang had gathered at Woodland Studios. "I've always wanted to take a look inside this place," Jerry said. "This is where the Nitty Gritty Dirt Band recorded their famous *Will the Circle Be Unbroken* album. So many amazing artists have worked here, including Robert Plant, Loretta Lynn, Merle Haggard, Al Green, Aretha Franklin, and John Hiatt."

"That's an incredible list," Nadia said.

"I thank you so much for letting me tag along," added George.

"Tag along?" Jerry said. "You're not tagging along, Brother. You're on the job! We need your wisdom here, sir. You're a trusted part of this here brain trust."

"Indeed you are," Louis agreed. "And if Jerry here gets too infatuated with the ghosts, we may need you to perform some kind of an exorcism!"

They were all smiles as they walked through the doors and were struck by the simplicity and elegance of the place. Cesar held the door for the others, then gently shook his head as he followed them in. He was finally walking into a recording studio, only several decades later than he had imagined.

"Hello, my friends!" boomed Michael Thomas. "I'm so glad you're here. I want to introduce you to someone before we get started."

He walked them to a control room full of equipment, instruments, and speakers. "This is Cheryl Spree. She's the artist I've been producing this last month."

"It's so nice to meet you," Cheryl said sincerely. "I was at the event in the park, and it really touched me. I haven't sung like that in I don't know how long."

Spree was part of the new breed of female country artists in Nashville. Her fan base crossed several age groups, and her music often sounded as much like pop as it did country. She had been winning awards all over the place, and every record she released sold like crazy. Her face was on billboards out on the freeway. Even Louis knew who she was.

"It's lovely to meet you," Louis said. "Thank you for letting us invade your session."

"Oh it's an honor!" she insisted.

"Speaking of that," Michael said, "let's head over into the live room. It's a little bigger. We can get more comfortable." They went through a couple of doors into a large, open space populated with instruments and sound baffles. Michael had arranged a circle of chairs in anticipation of their gathering.

As everyone found a place to sit and Jerry continued to wander around, mentally pinching himself, Michael spoke. "Here's the thing, gang. I so appreciate you trusting me when I asked if I could record you. I want to assure you right off the top here, that I have no agenda today other than to help serve your vision for whatever this thing is, if I can. I have some ideas, but they are just that: ideas. I can get excited, and I just want to say up front that if you are not comfortable with anything, that's completely fine."

"Thank you, Son," Louis offered. "And thank you for your continued enthusiasm for this work. I have not forgotten that your words in the locker room at the YMCA were, I believe, used by God to soften me for this entire adventure. I am so glad to see that we have stayed in each other's space throughout the journey thus far."

"Well…good!" Michael said with a wide, mischievous smile. "I hope you feel that way in five minutes." Everyone now wondered what he was going to propose. "I've been thinking a lot about this. I've been at every gathering, talking with as many people in the seats as I can. I've talked one-on-one with Alex and with most of you. I've honestly never come across anything like this, so all of the old formulas fail. This requires novel thinking. So, I scrapped everything I've done before and tried to imagine something completely different."

He had their attention. Nadia took out a pen and opened her notebook.

"I believe that recorded music is ultimately going to be a small part of this story. It may play an important part—but it will still be small. Let me explain. These days the money in music comes from performing and merchandise. Next in line would be publishing for songwriters and maybe synch fees if you can get your songs placed in film or television shows. But records earn a fraction of what they used to earn because everything is streaming, and streaming doesn't pay. So, labels practically give the music away for free in order to drive the other stuff.

"But with your music, money is not the point anyway. What you are doing is spreading an idea, a feeling—something contagious. So of course you want to make the music affordable, if not completely free. But—and this is a big but—some people would still love to own physical copies, maybe even vinyl."

George liked the sound of that.

"Some will want to hold the product so they can relive the experience of having been with you in person. Some will want to learn the way you play these songs. Some will want to give you money, trusting that you'll use it for good purposes, and the record becomes almost like a souvenir of their relationship with you.

"And some might, in fact, want to put your songs in films or television shows—it's honestly that good. So here's what I think makes sense. We create a sort of hybrid album. Most of the cuts on the album would be live recordings based on tracks I have gathered from the events you've already done or future events. But for the big benefit show I'll set up a full multi-track rig and do a proper recording. But we'll also get you in here to record a song or two in the studio—just so you have something pristine and because, frankly, it'll be so much fun! We can add in some other instruments, maybe a horn section, some organ, whatever the moment calls for."

"And as far as the money goes, I'd like to propose that we set up a fund, and that you determine who is going to administer that fund, but you use that money for whatever you feel it should be used for. It could be music lessons for kids who can't afford them, or maybe a free music festival in the park. I trust you to decide. Once we take out enough money from the proceeds to cover paying the publishing on any cover songs and for the manufacturing expenses for things like vinyl and CDs, the profits can all go into that fund and you can use it however. I don't want to make a penny."

"That's an incredible offer," Jerry said. "But do you think the live recording stuff you've done is good enough to put out?"

"I'm glad you asked," Michael said with a wide grin. "Make yourselves comfortable and close your eyes, if you would."

He gestured through the large window to the engineer in the control room. "Randy, will you play back the first song, please?"

Cheryl sneaked in to watch. She was excited to see the reaction.

It was a recording of "Ain't No Sunshine" and, somehow, it sounded like they were back in Jerry's driveway. The tone was unbelievable.

"Wow." George was the first to respond. "This is amazing."

"It's a combination of these mics and the technique I've learned," Michael said. "Let's go to the next track."

Song after song, the results were the same. Though the performances on some were rough, the sonic fidelity was perfect.

"I think we could easily come up with at least one full-length album," he insisted. "And I think we could create some liner notes and supplemental materials that would include chord charts and lead sheets and short editorial pieces that would tell the story of what happened here. As much as I believe a lot of people will enjoy just listening to this, it might have an even more important role as an inspiration for replication. They say that The Velvet Underground only sold ten thousands albums, but everyone who got one started a band."

Nadia's inner New Yorker tingled at her memory of the Velvets.

"That's how I feel about this," Michael continued. "I think you could inspire people in garages around the world to do exactly what you have done."

"I like the sound of that," Jerry said. "I wonder, if we got some of this to Robert, could he use it for his podcast?"

"Sure!" Michael said. "I'll bounce him a mix today."

That made no sense to Louis, but he thanked him anyway. "This is very exciting, Michael. You are indeed one gifted young man. Would you do us a favor and make us copies of what you have so far so we can listen at home? Also, would you let us know if there was one song you think is the best to release first, what would it be? And how soon could it be ready?"

"Absolutely!" he said. "In fact, I already have CDs burned for you and a private link for streaming. And personally, I think that song called 'Marianne's Song'—the one Cesar showed up on the first time, would be a great single. That's one I'd like to do a studio version of, but the live recording is just incredible."

"We'll listen to it and let you know," Jerry said. "And like Louis said, this is amazing, Michael. Thanks so much. I am just in awe."

"Thanks. It's wild," Michael continued. "I have this feeling like I was meant to do this. It's hard to describe."

"We all know what you mean," Cesar said. "Don't we?"

Everyone nodded.

Cheryl, one of the biggest stars in Nashville, could be seen clapping giddily in the control room. The engineers were high-fiving each other.

"Oh," Michael added, "if you ever feel like some piano or organ would fit, I'd love to sit in with the band sometime. I'd love an excuse to give my Hammond B3 a workout. Just say the word."

"Count on it!" Jerry said.

As everyone else was heading to the exit, Alex and Jamie asked if they could see a bit more of the control room. "Of course," Michael said. "I think Cheryl would love to talk with you guys a bit more, too."

The three made their way into the control room, and after a few minutes of requisite gear gawking, they settled into the strangely comfortable chairs aligned around the massive console. Michael's assistant hustled into the big room to break down the chairs he had set up for the meeting and to set up some mics for the next session. Cheryl refilled her water bottle and responded to a couple of text messages before she joined the three in earnest.

"We've worked in dozens of studios," Alex began, "but this analog stuff is still kind of intimidating in a way."

"I don't think it should be intimidating." Michael jumped in. "We have a million ways to use this stuff, from fully digital, to full analog, to running tracks through an analog machine first and then into ProTools for editing. The beauty of this is that we can capture great tone much more easily and reliably than ever before. The challenge, though, is that the performance has to be there. It makes no sense to use a studio like this to record music that is basically just a mashup of prerecorded samples and autotuned tracks."

"The performance has to be there," Jamie echoed, as if to underscore the significance of that simple statement. "I think that's what has drawn me to these old guys so powerfully. The performance—and that doesn't even feel like the right word sometimes—but the way we play just feels so different. It's all so deep and true. It just makes me want to be fully there—in the pocket—in the moment—and in the group. I swear, this stuff is jacking up my head in a big way."

"I'm not sure how good it's going to end up being for our career," Alex added, "but I find myself caring less about that and more about things like what kind of person I am becoming—why I'm here and how I can grow up to be just like Louis." He laughed but he wasn't kidding.

"I know it's probably easier for me to say that I don't care about career stuff," Michael offered, "since I've had some success already. But I hear you. I think people our age have become so good at social networking and presenting a kind of filtered picture of ourselves to the world that we're just not used to this kind of authenticity. Plus, our music has become so automated, and let's face it—cheap—that we just don't have a frame of reference for stuff like this. It has weight and substance."

Cheryl had rejoined the group and took Michael's beat as a chance to inject herself into the conversation. "People feel that music is free now," she said bluntly, "so it can be tough to push through that as an artist to find the essence of the work—the part that is precious, difficult, and sometimes expensive to get to."

Everyone nodded in agreement. They all knew the temptation to cut corners and "phone it in."

"I know I have contributed to the problem," she continued, "but it feels like it's either time for me to get over this kid's stuff and take this calling seriously or to step away. I will not let this machine use me as a product any longer, and I don't want to see the listeners out there as a means to my end."

That point landed hard.

"What do you mean?" Jamie asked. "How would they be a means to your end?"

"I don't know," she stalled, "but the team constantly talks about singles and hits and what the audience wants from me. I've been reading Johnny Cash's biography and thinking about his life. I'm starting to think that if there's not more to this than cranking out product—especially product I don't believe in and can't stand behind—then ultimately, I'll end up depressed, burned out, and disgusted with myself. I'd rather quit than end up there. I hired Michael here, and we booked this great old studio, because I thought being close to the heritage, and the old-school stuff, would help me find something true."

She was making fun of herself at this point. "That was pretty stupid, actually, but it did get me in touch with Michael. It was through Michael that I heard about you all. When I heard that music, it got to a place in my heart that I can't even describe. I'm still trying to figure out what's going on in there."

"Wow," Alex said, surprised at her transparency. "I can't say I relate to the first part of what you said," he suppressed a laugh, "as I have yet to be bothered by success. But I can relate to the inside stuff going on around these guys, and now Nadia. I feel like it's probably something like faith or religion, but without the bullshit stuff that sent me running away from the church as soon as I graduated from high school."

Michael had been looking down, rubbing his chin, and listening intently. He had been wrestling with this stuff for weeks. "I can't put my finger on it either," he said without looking up. "I'm trying to. I've been trying to make sense of what it is about these people—you people—that is so freaking compelling to me. But as I get closer to what I think the answer might be, I get nervous that defining it might kill it. Somehow I'm more comfortable with this mysterious draw than I would be if it had words."

"We're just afraid of what those words are," Cheryl offered.

Michael looked up and caught her eye.

"Why are we so afraid, though?" she continued.

The room sat quiet for a few long moments.

"Louis keeps talking about love," Jamie said, "and that 'love' is behind all of this. He says love is drawing us all together and that love is calling us to be a better community. I can tell that when he says that, he means 'God.' But this doesn't feel religious to me at all."

"Maybe that's because the religion we have experienced had little to do with love," Alex said. "Our religion was about fear and power and a way of life. It was hypocritical to its core. Some awesome people were in that boat with us, but the boat was sinking."

"So," Cheryl said tentatively, "again, I ask—mostly myself—why are we so afraid of letting go? I think I'm done clinging to my sense of control and whatever else. Something is pulling me into this thing, and if it's love, and love is God, so it's God. Fine. I'm being called by God. If that's true, I'd be an idiot to fight it, right?"

They all nodded.

"It doesn't seem that the people who take love seriously and follow God on these adventures have too smooth of a ride," Michael offered. "I mean, since hanging out with you all, I have started reading things I never thought I would read, and it seems that from Jesus on down, the ones who dare to take this love stuff seriously end up having rocks thrown at them, or worse!"

"This ain't no old-time religion?" Alex added.

"No," Cheryl said. "But remember what Dylan said: 'I would not feel so all alone, everybody must get stoned.'"

They all cracked up at that one.

The next stop, for Jerry and Nadia at least, was to meet with the activities director at the Community Center. They were still trying to sort out what the weekly workshop was going to look like and where they would hold it. They left Woodland Studios and drove about six blocks west. As soon as they got in Jerry's car, he popped in the CD.

"My heart is racing," he said. "That was surreal."

"Not gonna lie," Nadia agreed. "It was good for me, too."

"So here's what I'm thinking about this workshop thing," Jerry said. "I don't expect the Community Center to understand or respond to the more spiritual aspects of what has been happening, but if we talk about the idea of a weekly time for people from different cultural, age, and other demographics to get together and listen to and perform music in the interest of neighborhood bridge-building and reconciliation, I think they'll love that."

"I think you're right," Nadia said.

"So, we'll just propose this and see what they say. Hopefully they find us some space and we can start ASAP."

They parked, walked in, and found Carol Cooper, the director of the Community Center. They made their case and she instantly agreed.

"Look," she said. "I'm a fan. I'm way into this! I went to the event at the park. I've been following this…phenomenon…online and I'm super excited about it. Whatever I can do, count me in."

"Well that was easy," Nadia said.

"We're hoping," Jerry explained, "that we can let some of the air out of the hype when it comes to the community aspect, so we don't lose that element even if the story of the music continues to grow. Maybe we can do a couple of big things but keep our home turf covered and moving in the right direction."

"This may be the 'It' thing right now," Nadia added. "But we want to build something that will be sustained long after fame fades. And one of the things we believe we are sensing in the people who have been part of it is a desire to contribute instead of just being spectators. So with things like this workshop, and maybe music lessons and such, we will open those teaching slots up to people in the community. This won't just be us doing everything."

"Amazing," Carol said. "You folks know what you are doing."

"Well," Jerry said, "I wouldn't go that far!"

A few days later, Jerry woke to another series of texts from Alex.

[Yo, JW: Check this link to Robert's podcast. It's killer. Also—his YouTube channel is blowing up with a clip he posted about your song. You ever check your FB?]

It took Jerry a moment (he hadn't had his coffee) to figure out that "FB" meant Facebook. He realized that he had not, in fact, checked his account in nearly a week. He got his coffee, put on a record, and braced himself for what might await him online. He didn't have much time this morning. There was less than a week until the big benefit show, and he had a number of things still to do, including getting ready for an actual "band practice" later, which was something new.

He was starting to get used to seeing anywhere from fifty to a hundred friend requests per day, but due to his neglect, he was startled to see over a thousand requests waiting for him. He definitely did not have time to deal with that.

Then he noticed that he was tagged in Robert's podcast release. This must have been what Alex was talking about. 5,656 likes? Hundreds of comments? He was tagged in way too many to read. What was going on? There was just too much. He didn't know where to start.

He grabbed his coffee and walked next door, but Alex wasn't home. As hard as it was for Jerry to fathom, at 8:00 a.m. Alex was already out in the world getting things done. Jerry would have to call him. He didn't have a chance before his phone buzzed.

"So you do keep your phone with you in bed!" Alex crowed.

Jerry rolled his eyes at the thought of that. "I'm actually walking back from your house. I just tried to find you. I'm shocked that you're gone this early."

"Been gone for a while already, man. So much going on it's crazy. I really think I need to find someone to help with the social media stuff though. This is crazy. I mean, it was fun at first, but I'm out of my depth and I'm having a hard time getting anything else done. Robert, the guy with the podcast, is introducing me to someone who helps him."

"Speaking of which, his show. Wow! You've got to hear it. I'm not just saying this because it's popular and thousands of people are listening to it. He did a good job with it. He respects you guys and was obviously moved by what's going on. People are responding to all of your stories."

"I've got too many comments and friend requests on Facebook. I can't begin to respond to them. If you get someone to help you, maybe they can help me, too. But I want to listen to Robert's show as soon as I can. Hopefully, I'll find some time later."

"You need to check out the YouTube clip he made of you telling the story behind 'Marianne's Song.' It's amazing—and people are feeling it. That's probably what's sending everyone to your page."

"Okay," Jerry said. "I'll look it up. See you at practice later?"

"Heck yeah! Despite all this hype, don't forget, this was—and is—all about playing music with you. I'm excited to get back to something small. I can't wait."

"Me too. See you later." Jerry ended the call and slipped his phone into his pocket.

Back at his own dining room table, Jerry pulled up YouTube and tried a couple of searches until he found the video Alex was talking about. It wasn't long—just a couple of minutes. But in it, Robert had edited Jerry's story and cut it with audio he had gotten from Michael and some of the interjections from Cesar and Louis. It worked well and was designed, he guessed, to draw people to the full-length episode. It gave Jerry an idea.

He logged back on to his Facebook account and created a post with a link to that video—a "fancy" trick Alex had taught him. In the caption he thanked everyone en masse for their love and support, reiterated his belief in forgiveness and grace, and said that he would continue to pray that we all would find a way to make peace with anyone with whom we were at odds. Once it was posted, he went back to that search bar, found Marianne and Jack, and clicked on "Request Friend." He said a little prayer and logged off. He grabbed his journal and stepped out onto the porch.

What he didn't know, was that the previous evening, shortly after the video was posted, Jack and Marianne had both heard about it from multiple friends. The name and the story seemed too similar to too many people. It had been sent to them several times and both had seen the video. They had even gotten on the phone to talk about it.

"Do you think that's him?" Marianne asked Jack.

"It has to be. I mean, you saw the clip. That's definitely him."

"But he just doesn't seem like the kind of guy I expected him to be."

"Me either," Jack replied. "But it has been almost fifty years now. Mom says people never change, but I don't know. This guy sounds like he has changed."

"And did you hear that bit about sending letters and money? Did you ever know about that?"

"No," Jack said. "Definitely not. But then again, I've been thinking about it, and if Mom thought he was bad news, it would make sense for her not to tell us that, right? I mean, it would only confuse us, as kids. We had

Joe, and for all she knew this guy was just a relapse away from who knows what. I could see doing the same thing. Take the money, put it in the bank, shred the letters."

"Yeah," Marianne said. "I guess. But this whole thing… Have you talked to Mom yet?"

"Um, no. And I'm not sure that I'm going to."

"You don't think she'll hear about it? That video is blowing up."

"Mom is almost seventy years old," Jack said. "Unless it's on the Hallmark Channel, her friends won't hear about it."

"I don't know," Marianne said. "I'll bet our kids are going to start asking about it. I think if Mom doesn't bring it up by this weekend, I'm going to ask her."

"We could go talk to her together I guess," Jack offered. "She's not going to be happy, I bet."

"But, Jack. Do you think the guy is for real? All I ever heard was how terrible he was, and dangerous, and how good it was that he was gone. I'm not sure I know how to process another possible version of him. And I'm not sure I can accept that it's real."

"I don't have any idea. I mean, I've been on Facebook for ten years, and he never once tried to contact me. He just goes out on a podcast? That seems a little odd. I have my doubts."

"Ugh," Marianne said. "I don't know if I even want this to be real. I don't think I can handle this right now. It was better when I suspected that he was just dead." She shook her head. "I guess that's harsh."

"A little," Jack said. "But I don't disagree."

Michael offered the group the use of the big room at the studio for their practice. It wasn't being used in the evening anyway, and he figured he could get a clean recording of the musicians for possible future use. They got there at 6:00 p.m. and set up their gear.

As they pulled cables, tuned guitars, and positioned vocal mics, they caught up on the recent events. Nadia updated everyone on the workshops at the Community Center. Four classes were already organized: songwriting, band arranging, vocal lessons, and a sort of introductory ethnomusicology class Nadia was excited about. Members of the community were lined up to lead the courses and all would be free.

There were already three new groups slated to meet in different homes around East Nashville, trying to do their best to replicate what had happened at Jerry's place. Jerry and the group were committed to keeping track of the challenges and needs of their groups, so that support materials and sessions could be created for them and any other groups that wanted to follow in their footsteps.

Alex and Jamie explained the increasing buzz and tried not to sound too giddy about the projections for the benefit show. Based on the online promotions, it seemed they might have up to five thousand people in attendance. Several food trucks had asked to come and offered to donate a percentage of their sales to the church fund. And the Nashville media would be out in full force. It was looking good.

Jerry brought up an unusual concept for the stage plot he suspected would not work, but he thought it was worth a try. "What if we create an area in front of the stage that is like a second stage. We run some extra mics down there, and monitors, and lights—kind of in a big semicircle facing outward—toward the crowd. Then any musicians who want to join in could go down there and just improvise. We could have a separate sound engineer listening on headphones, and if he heard that something was working, he could bring it up in the PA carefully, to blend it with us. But if not, it would stay down there in the circle. Then, at some point, we could just turn things over to the stage down there and see what happens. It would blur the lines—take some of the hype off of us."

"I can think of a million things that could go wrong technically," Jamie said, "but that's no reason not to try it. It sounds like a crazy idea. But I love it. Maybe the lighting guys could work on that area too. And if someone is really killing it down there, we could always pull them up to the big stage."

"And any of us could potentially move down there as well," Louis added. "Other than maybe Jamie and the drums."

"Hey," Jamie said, "I'll grab a tambourine if the spirit leads, man!"

Michael overheard this idea. "I love it. And I can think of one major country star who would definitely come sing a song down there on that stage, if you let her."

"Oh, we'll let her," Jerry said.

Everything was set up and they were ready to practice. But when the music started, it did not feel like a practice. It felt like what most of them thought church should be. It was intimate—just the main members and their closest friends and spouses. The sound was perfect. The performances sounded effortless, though each musician was giving it their all.

They brought forward a new version of Stevie Wonder's "Have a Talk with God," and they knew it would have to be the show opener. From there the songs flowed until the wee hours of the morning. Michael recorded the whole thing.

On show day, Jerry woke up at about 5:00 a.m. He was frustrated about that because he knew it would be a late night, and he needed his rest, but he was just too amped up to sleep. As soon as the slightest bit of consciousness crept into his mind, a flood of thoughts rushed in and chased all hope of sleep away. He stopped trying to fight it and got up.

It was a nice May morning. The heat of the day hadn't yet settled in, so he decided to take his coffee for a walk. As he strolled up and down the hilly streets, he thought of the neighbors he now knew and those he had yet to meet. He greeted a couple of fellow early risers, but mostly he had the streets to himself. The birds were up, that was certain. Their songs were loud that day.

When he crossed to the third block, where the hill became steep, he noticed the figure of a slender man coming up over the rise. It was Brother Louis. After a quick wave, the two met up on Louis's side of the street.

"You're up early," Louis said. "I don't often see you out here when I'm taking my morning walk."

"You're right." Jerry nodded. "This is early for me, but once I roused, I just couldn't get back to sleep. Too many thoughts running through my head."

"You nervous about tonight?"

"I suppose a little," Jerry admitted. "No. I'm kind of freaking out, to tell the honest truth!" He laughed and Louis joined him. "Thousands of people? A big stage? What in the world has happened here? This is insane!"

"I agree! I'll be honest too. I am both convinced that this is all a very good and important thing, and I wish something would happen that would prevent it all from taking place!"

"This morning, just before I topped that hill, I found myself remembering, almost praying, Jesus' prayer in Gethsemane. 'Father, if it be your will, let this cup pass from me, but not my will, but thine be done.' I say this almost because as the thought occurred to me, it also occurred to me how arrogant and ridiculous it was for me to compare singing with my friends to what Jesus went through at Calvary. I started laughing at myself for even thinking that, and then I saw you!"

Jerry, still chuckling but understanding what Louis was getting at, realized that he hadn't considered how challenging this whole thing must be for such a private and stage-shy person like him.

"I've got to say," Jerry said, "that the way you have embraced this whole thing, even though it makes you so uncomfortable, has inspired me. I tend to avoid discomfort at all costs—and here you are, diving headfirst into what has to be one of the least comfortable things you could possibly be doing in your retirement. While some folks would kill to be performing in front of crowds like this, I know it's hard for you. And yet you do it. I'm learning from you and I appreciate it."

"Well, thank you for saying that," Louis said. "And thank you for noticing. It's funny, but I remember seeing Dr. King speak here in Nashville when I was just a kid, and he said we would wear down the forces of evil through our capacity to suffer. I remember wondering what my capacity to suffer was. I was pretty sure it wasn't very great. I suppose God, in his goodness, is allowing me to experience some of that suffering here before I'm done with this life."

They both laughed at that one, and Louis put his arm around Jerry's shoulders.

"Tell me," Louis continued. "Have you heard anything back from your children or your ex-wife? Anything at all?"

"No. Not a thing. I did find my kids on Facebook and tried to reach out to them there, but no luck. And now Facebook is so crazy, I have to have someone else help with it. But it's in God's hands, I guess. I hope they hear my heart someday."

"I believe they will," Louis added. "And I have one more question for you, since it's just the two of us here for a change."

"Yes," Jerry said. Where could this be going?

"I wonder what it's going to take for you to build up the courage and take a risk with Nadia. It's not good for us to be alone, and everyone can see the admiration you two have for each other. What's holding you back?"

"Hmm," Jerry said. "I guess I hadn't thought of it that way." He lied. "She's a fantastic woman, so strong and independent. She doesn't need anyone. Why would she want someone like me in her life, getting in the way? It never occurred to me that she'd be interested. We're just good friends."

"Well, Brother. I think you need to start by being honest with yourself, about yourself. She may not be a woman that needs you, the way my church needed you to fix that oven or any number of people need you for this or that. And you may have some old-fashioned ideas about what men and women are supposed to be like in a relationship. But frankly, that's a load of nonsense, and you just need to get over it. Like you said, she's a fantastic woman. She respects you, and you deserve that. Wake up, Brother. Seize the day! We ain't getting any younger, you know."

"Wow. I wish you'd just tell me what you actually think!"

Louis busted out a deep, full laugh and smacked Jerry on the back hard enough to almost knock him over. "This is me being restrained! Things are about to get real between you and me."

Jerry and Louis kept walking, many more blocks than they planned.

Showtime

The "band" showed up at the Community Center at 3:00 p.m. to set up for the show that was supposed to start at 7:00. What they saw when they arrived caused them all to stop and stare. If it hadn't been for the parking spaces reserved for them, who knew where they would have put their cars. Louis and Kelly walked from their home, but it was a bit too far for the others. Fortunately, Nadia had gotten there early and thought to put some cones out.

But the lack of parking in the center's small lot was nothing compared to the scene that waited for them on the sprawling lawn. Hundreds of people had already arrived, and hundreds more streamed in by the minute. Food trucks were set up along one end, and portable toilets along the other. A huge stage, with a lower one in front of it, was set up just behind the center, facing east. Police wandered pleasantly, including several on horseback, and music was already playing on the curved stack of speakers.

People were playing games, sitting in circles singing songs, and just generally enjoying the warm spring day.

"This feels like a festival," Louis said. "We should have invited other people to play this afternoon."

"We did!" came a voice from behind them. Nadia came to join them, along with George. The two of them had set up a makeshift office in the center.

"B-Flat just got done playing a solo set," she said. "It was a last-minute idea, just because so many people were here and everything was set up. He suggested a couple of other people that he met at your place, so they are getting set up and will play a few songs here in a couple minutes."

"Family," George said, with his arms outstretched and his face already covered in sweat. He was determined to wear a shirt and tie even in this heat. "Many blessings to all of you on this auspicious day! Might you join us in this building that is being called 'backstage' today for a quick meeting before you begin to set up your things?"

Everyone agreed and followed George and Nadia into the center. A nice-sized classroom was set aside for them, and they found some snacks and water there. It was clear this was also George and Nadia's production office and they had been quite busy.

"How long have you been here?" Jerry asked.

Looking at Nadia for confirmation, George replied, "I believe we met here at about seven o'clock this morning. My team of workers from the church was here until at least midnight last night, helping to build the stage and the fencing and to set up the trash cans and more. Once word of this benefit spread, members of our family jumped into action to find a way to be useful. I believe every able-bodied member of Main Baptist is doing something here today!"

"There was also a lot of logistical stuff no one had thought about," Nadia added. "So I just decided to help with things like permits and press inquiries and the like. Like, did you know that if the mayor decides to come, it's your responsibility to facilitate that? Well it is, and he is, as well as the governor. So I've had my hands full dealing with entitled people all day."

"How is the money part looking?" Cesar asked.

"I'm glad you brought that up," George said. "We've decided to do this a few different ways. The event itself is free, but people are being encouraged to donate as much as they feel comfortable giving. They can either do that in cash or by check—and we have tables for that over by the security area. Or we have a way for people to give through an app that one of the lovely women in our church is managing. People can give from their phones. It's pretty amazing.

"So, we won't know exact numbers until we count the cash and checks, but the digital giving has already topped fifty thousand dollars!"

"Already?" Jerry asked. "That's amazing."

"And that's not all," George continued. "The community has been so excited about this, we have had other donations come in, including an electrical contractor who has agreed to donate up to ten thousand dollars' worth of labor and a roofer who has done the same. There are several calls I have not had a chance to return. Ladies and gentlemen, I believe there is a good chance that we will raise more money than we need for the building repairs. And I'm excited to say that the elders of the church have already agreed that any funds over and above what is needed will go directly toward the same fund that money from the music sales goes to. We're really going to be able to bless some people in this community!"

"That's fantastic," Louis said. "I can't even process all of this."

"Any protestors?" Cesar asked.

"Actually," Nadia began, "yes. We've had a number of complaints, including one threat of a lawsuit a friend of mine in New York tells me is a total joke."

"A lawsuit?" Jerry interrupted. "Over what?"

"Well," she gathered her notebook and put on her readers, "let me double-check my notes here. We have one group that came in demanding to set up a booth with what they called 'Immigration Policy Education Materials'—but I call anti-immigration propaganda. I turned them down and they threatened to sue me for denying them their right to free speech. Then we had an individual demanding stage time so he could promote his, how can I say this respectfully?…his 'unique' perspective on the divinity of houseplants, certain minerals, and alien life. When I told him we were not giving stage time to anyone, he said something about sic'ing some invisible spirit hounds on me. It's been interesting, let's just say that."

"And all these people are already here, but the event is not supposed to start for three more hours," Jerry said. "Do you have more people scheduled to play between now and then?"

"A few," she said. "But there's room if you have any ideas."

Cesar thought about a young Hispanic band and texted them to see if they were free. They said they were and would be right over.

Jerry texted Kyle at the same time. Kyle got right back to him.

[J: I'm actually here! In the crowd! This is awesome!!]

Jerry texted back, [K: What? Come to the Community Center and say hi.]

A few minutes later Kyle walked through the door. He was tan, his dark-blond hair was a bit longer than Jerry remembered it, and he had put on a few pounds, but he looked great.

"Dude!" He rushed in for a hug, "I leave you alone for a few months and look what you've done. This is amazing!"

"I promise you I did not DO this," Jerry said. "I'm pretty sure this was going to happen whether I helped or not."

Nadia walked up to meet this newcomer.

"Nadia," Jerry said, "Meet Kyle Smith. Kyle is an amazing artist and song-writer who now leads worship at a church in Oklahoma. I used to drive for Kyle's band."

"It's good to meet you, Nadia." Kyle grabbed her hand with both of his. "Jerry here was a lot more than just my driver. He was more than a brother to me—and he still is. How many times did I crash at your place, Jerry?" He looked over and hugged Jerry again.

"Here's the thing," Kyle continued. "When I was out singing these church songs every night and putting on a big Jesus show, it was first Jerry, and then others like him, who helped me learn the difference between what was real and what was not. He saved my life!

"Well," he corrected himself, "no… Jerry didn't save my life. But he helped me see what I needed to do so I could avoid destroying myself—and then I was able to help him a time or two as well."

"Kyle gave me my guitar," Jerry said.

"How's she sounding?" Kyle asked.

"She's still my only one. You'll hear her tonight."

"That's so cool. I just knew she belonged with you."

"Well," Nadia said, "I would love to get to know you some more, but I have work to do. I've somehow become an unpaid administrative intern." She offered a slightly weary but genuine smile. "But before I go, you wouldn't be interested in singing a few songs this afternoon, would you?"

"Yeah," Jerry added. "That's why I was texting to see if you were in town. We didn't expect all these people so early and we don't have anything planned. We're just thinking about who might be able to get up there and entertain this crowd. You interested?"

"Sure," Kyle said. "I'd love to. Just tell me when."

Cesar's friends played five songs that muddled the lines between Tejano and *norteño* but included enough Anglo folk references for Americana fans to latch on hard. They brought a tenor sax, acoustic bass guitar, and some great Latin percussion instruments that Cesar had been wanting to hear for a while. When they were done, he asked them to keep their instruments handy.

A solo acoustic guitar player filled about half an hour with nice finger-style music, and a freestyle rapper from up the road in Inglewood did some improvisational verse with mixed results. The afternoon had the feel of a ramped-up family reunion—if the family were extremely *blended*.

But the highlight of the preshow had to be when the gospel choir from Main Baptist took the stage and led the crowd in forty-five minutes of old favorites and new gospel songs. Considering the choir had no idea it would be performing, and the sound crew didn't bring the right kind of mics for a choir, and there were no choir risers, and all of the other caveats the choir director kept citing after its slot, its time was profoundly successful. Many in the crowd were only marginally familiar with gospel music, so the extended singing time opened some horizons and some hearts.

And the crowd kept growing steadily throughout the afternoon. By 5:00 p.m. the head of security estimated the audience size at close to six thousand people, with a steady stream pouring through the gates. They could safely fit ten thousand inside the fencing they had put up, but room was available outside of those barriers as well. As the sun went down and the temperatures cooled, it seemed more and more people were making their way to the park.

One of them was a nearly fifty-year-old mother of three from Crossville who hadn't told anyone where she was going that day. She wasn't sure she even wanted to be here. She hated crowds, felt too old for this, and didn't understand what all the excitement was about. She was just curious about the old man playing acoustic guitar and whether he was a fraud or not. She found a spot under a tree, set up her chair, and got her phone out to check some messages.

When Kyle took the stage, he was surprised to find that a good number of people in the crowd were familiar with him. He wondered if they would have even recognized him from his "artist days." He used to work so hard to look perfect. These days he cared a lot less about that. Plus, his career had been confined to the contemporary Christian music world. He would later find that many of the people in the park that day, looking for something real and true, were former nineties kids who had grown up in the church.

But as he gazed out at that crowd of people, he sensed that they were here for a variety of reasons and breathed a short, sincere prayer that he would be useful in that moment. That he would speak love and grace to all hearers. And, as he had seen Jerry say online, maybe welcome some wanderers back up to the porch.

He started with a Beatles song. It was a silly little song, almost like a kid's song, called "All Together Now," and he got the whole crowd singing it. Kids were dancing in circles. Adults were dancing in circles. That reminded him of an old Billy Preston song, and he segued into "That's the Way God Planned It."

Jerry was standing off to the side of the stage. He had never heard Kyle sound so soulful and passionate. He was on another level.

He did the same thing with that chorus and got the whole crowd singing along like the choir they really were.

Louis walked up to Jerry and nodded toward Kyle. "That kid is good."

Alex agreed as he gave Jerry a few pounds on the back on his way to his spot. "By the way," he said, "a friend of mine would like to come by tomorrow and ask us a few questions for an article she is working on for her blog. She's great. That cool?"

Jerry nodded absentmindedly.

Instead of waiting for Kyle to finish, the members of the main band went out and got in position behind him while he was playing. He had established a solid vibe and they didn't want to let it go. By the time he was done riffing on the Preston song, everyone in *Perros Perdidos*, or the Lost Dogs of East Nashville, were in position and ready. As the last note faded, Michael—behind a vintage Fender Rhodes, played the opening chords of the Staples Singers' "Respect Yourself," and the crowd roared. Kyle didn't even know it was coming, so he looked like a jolt of electricity shot through him as well.

Once the groove was well established, the roar had settled down, and Kyle handed Jerry's Martin back to him, Brother Louis stepped to the front microphone.

"Brothers and sisters, we are so blessed to be here with you today!"

The roar returned even louder.

"When we suggested the idea of doing a benefit concert for the church, we had no idea so many people would show up. Thank you, thank you, thank you!"

More cheering.

"But there is something you need to know about our time together this evening. Nashville is a musically sophisticated place, and y'all have all been to a million concerts. And because of that, we tend to follow certain patterns and routines. Well, this whole thing is about breaking those routines down. Whatever walls there are tonight between us and you, or between you and the person next to you, or between you and yourself."

Louis laughed a little at that line and looked back at Jerry, who smiled and laughed right back at him.

"We have experienced that music creeps under walls."

Alex laid on some extra bass groove that connected with Jamie's kick drum as if to add an "Amen!" to that line.

"We have experienced that music crawls over walls." Louis was starting to sing a bit now.

Michael laid on a keyboard riff that tumbled from the higher end of the board downward, like a person falling over a wall to the other side.

"And ultimately." Louis's hand formed a fist and his arm cocked, ready to spring—the band sensing it and beginning to pulse on the eighth notes in rising intensity.

"Eventually…"

The band was getting louder, and Louis's arm was flexed like he was getting ready to take a swing at a heavyweight champ.

"In the fullness of time, music, when it carries with it the power of love and light and truth, it will knock down every wall that man tries to build and will see the lame dancing and the dead running free!"

The crowd erupted in ecstatic agreement as the band responded in a crescendo, sustained by Louis's upheld hand for several moments, until he dramatically swiped it downward and everyone cut out except Jamie on the hi-hat, Alex on the bass, and Michael back on the "Respect Yourself" electric piano riff.

"But it starts with you," Louis added. "We can't expect to see change out there, until we see change in here." He pointed to his heart and then his head.

Then he came in with the lyric.

And they were off. Anchored by the rock-solid rhythm section of the brothers, and now with the added structure of Michael Thomas's world-class skills on piano and organ, these Dogs had never sounded better. Their set list included most of the songs they had previously performed and a few surprises.

They improvised a jam at the end of "Respect Yourself" that evolved seamlessly into a funky groove and an airy and transcendent rendition of the song they had intended to open with: Stevie's "Have a Talk with God." Years later they would argue about whether or not anyone had actually decided to start the show that way or if it had just *happened*. That night, though, they were so locked in with each other, it was impossible to tell. They were back in the flow.

Jerry's idea of the lower front stage was a hit. Sometimes it served as a place for people to merely play along with the band. Other times it became a platform for collaboration between the crowd and the band. During a version of Solomon Burke's "None of Us Are Free" when B-Flat joined them for a scorching electric guitar part, he jumped down to the lower level and happened to hear a young girl singing along. He coaxed her to a mic and signaled to Louis to give her a verse. She killed it. The communal nature of the chorus, *"None of us are free, if one of us are chained"* was particularly powerful as the line between the band and the crowd disappeared.

At one point the band recognized Matthew Clark, the host of one of the new spin-off groups, standing off to the side of the stage. Jerry had an idea. Before the band started their next song, he held them off and grabbed his microphone. "Hey, guys, I see a friend of ours over here. He has started a group that is doing the same kind of thing we did in my garage, but he's doing it up in Inglewood. How about we have him and a few of his people take a song and we take a quick break? You cool to take a song, Matthew?"

Of course Matthew was.

So, again, with no planning and something approaching eight thousand people now filling the park, three guitar players from Inglewood stepped onto the lower platform and plugged in their instruments. They began singing a simple, but effective version of the Van Morrison song "If I Ever Needed Someone" while the others took a break.

Michael could be seen texting someone.

As they brought that song in for a landing and the crowd showed their love, Michael played some chords confidently enough that Louis could tell he had some kind of plan. From the middle of the front of the crowd, a small woman in a black hoodie stepped up to a microphone. Louis smiled and nodded. Jamie and Alex kicked into a slow country soul groove until Jerry could tell that it was the Rolling Stones song "Shine a Light." They played the form one more time to let it settle in before the vocal started. B-Flat surrendered his electric guitar to a new face. He was no one famous but happened to be one of the best session guitarists in town.

Without removing her hood, Cheryl Spree stepped to the mic and sang Jagger's lyrics more mournfully and soulfully than anyone had ever heard her sound. No one even recognized that it was her. "This song is for you, Nashville."

As the song grew in structure and intensity, the crowd started grooving. By the time she got to the chorus, she flung back her hood and raised her hands like a priest pronouncing a benediction over a congregation.

Michael signaled for some extra singers to come out from the gospel choir just before the song switched to double time. He had clearly worked all this out as a surprise for the band as well as the crowd. The result was epic. Most of the crowd was so taken by the song that, until it was over, they had no idea a Grammy-winning, platinum-selling artist had been singing it. Once her cameo was done, Cheryl disappeared into the crowd, deftly avoiding drawing attention to herself.

The response from the crowd was deafening. Cell phone screens sprinkled the now-dark night. The Nashville skyline shone majestically behind the stage, and somewhere off on the side, the mayor and governor were talking about it all. Nadia met them, answered a few questions, and then left them to their chattering. She wasn't going to miss any more of this than she had to. She could tell that they just wanted to be able to say they were here and maybe to "be seen."

She could hear Jerry talking onstage again and excused herself.

"We're going to try something different here," Jerry said. "You guys know Cesar, right?"

The crowd roared again. Cesar had put on some shades, and between those and his silk work shirt, he was looking very cool.

"Well Cesar brought this next song idea to us," Jerry said. "It's from a band we both like a lot called Los Lobos."

A smaller but excited section of the crowd cheered at the mention of that East Los Angeles band.

"Cesar, what can you tell us about this song?"

Cesar walked up to the microphone like an acrobat on a tightrope. Behind him a couple of extra musicians were joining the band.

"*¡Hola, mi amigos,*" he said quietly.

The crowd roared. A group started chanting "See-Zar, See-Zar, See-Zar…"

"*Gracias, gracias*…thank you. I don't like to talk, so please stop so I can be done!"

They were laughing now.

"You might not know this, but I am from Mexico."

The crowd erupted again.

"I know, I know…" He was starting to feel it now. His heart was racing, but the adrenaline in his blood started to feel good. Instead of instilling a feeling of panic or dread, the encouragement from the crowd helped him feel excitement instead of fear.

Irma was standing off in the wings, and there were easily fifty family members who had made their way to the front of the stage for Cesar's big moment. Seeing their smiling faces emboldened him even more.

"Yes, I'm from Mexico, but I have lived in America since 1959. I have been a U.S. citizen since 1996. I love this country. I love Mexico. I love you people—even you people out by the fence with the mean signs telling me to go back to Mexico. I love you, too. I understand that you are just afraid. I know what that feels like. I have been afraid very much in my life. I am afraid for my wife's safety very often when we have lived in bad neighborhoods—like East Nashville twenty years ago!"

More laughter erupted at that line.

"But I have learned a few things over almost eighty years. Fear doesn't help me learn, and fear doesn't help me make good decisions. Only love does that!"

The crowd loved Cesar even more.

"This song is called 'The Neighborhood,' and it's a prayer that God would bring peace to the neighborhood. I have invited some friends from a Tejano band to join us, and we are going to sing this in English and Spanish, as a prayer for our neighborhood—not just East Nashville—not just Nashville—but our whole country—and our private hearts. Please bring peace to the neighborhood!"

Then the band played the song with the guest musicians, and Cesar officially became the coolest great-grandfather in East Nashville.

As the crowd was coming down from that particular high, Louis returned to his place at the front of the stage. When he felt it was the right time, he took control of the flock once again.

"Thank you, Brother Cesar!" he said both smoothly and authoritatively. "That was amazing. Peace to the neighborhood indeed!"

He glanced over his shoulder to cue the band, and they started the riff for "Ain't No Sunshine." The crowd lost it all over again.

"Thank you," Louis said. "It seems you know this song."

They cheered that they did, in fact, know the Bill Withers classic. Louis caught a glimpse of George sitting off to the side of the stage and saluted him. George returned the gesture with folded hands, as if in prayer.

With the groove playing behind him, Louis closed his eyes and raised his arm, as if conducting the audience like an orchestra. "Brothers and sisters. I must tell you that, as excited as I am about tonight, and this time with you, and the times we have had together, I am also grieved by the division we see all around us. I am cut in my heart by the pain that I hear in your stories. I know that we will have to come down from this moun-taintop soon enough."

Some in the crowd started playfully booing at this. "Play all night!" they screamed.

"Ah," Louis said. "But even if we played all night, at some point in the morning we would have to stop. We can't hold off the darkness forever. At least not for now. And it hurts me, it hurts all of us up here, and I believe it hurts each of you, to have to walk this world of shadows when we have a glimpse of the light."

"In the Bible, and in poetry and art, virtues like wisdom and grace and beauty and mercy are often personified in the feminine form," he continued. "Proverbs 7 says that we should call Wisdom our sister and insight or understanding should be like a family member to us. Brothers and sisters, let us not be naïve. The reason so many of us are here tonight, I believe, is that we are hungry for something that is real. Are you hungry for that?"

The crowd cheered.

"Are you hungry for justice and peace?"

The crowd cheered again.

"Are you hungry for reconciliation and dignity for all people?"

The crowd was getting downright Pentecostal. Their cheering in agreement was being matched, again, by an instinctive crescendo from the band.

But Louis, with a level of frustration and passion that was uncharacteristic of him, let his voice rise to the level of a shout. "If we are hungry for these things, my friends, it must be because we have not been receiving them! Let us not fool ourselves. There can be no reconciliation until there is repentance. A man doesn't seek healing until he acknowledges that he is sick! As we gather here now, tasting and smelling what is good, let us not foolishly miss the opportunity to admit to ourselves and to each other that we are hungry!"

He let those words ring out over the crowd and let the band come down a little bit before he continued. "We're gonna get back to the feast here tonight, I promise you." Louis sounded as if he might break into tears at any moment. "But this song, right now for me, is about sitting in that hunger. We pray for peace in the neighborhood because of the shootings that keep happening over in Cayce Homes, and over in Cleveland Park, and over in Inglewood, and right here in my neighborhood. We pray for relationships to be healed because we see the broken hearts and we break with them.

"The 'she' in this song, right now, is all of those things that we need in this neighborhood: grace, peace, beauty, love, mercy. There ain't no sunshine when she's gone, and we need some sunshine. Amen?"

Jerry was playing the chords, but tears were streaming down his face. Cesar was glad for his shades, too. Alex and Jamie were blubbering like babies—but keeping the groove solid. Louis had gone somewhere no one expected. George, for his part, didn't seem surprised.

Nadia was standing in the crowd now, her mouth half open. She was singing something, and her hands were half raised. She wasn't the group's manager at this point.

A fifty-year-old woman had worked her way up to the front of the crowd next to Nadia. She leaned over, with wet eyes and a set jaw. "Do you believe this stuff? Are these guys for real?"

Nadia looked over at her and could see decades of hurt, bitterness, and confusion in the woman's face. "Honey, this right here is as real as life gets. Don't let it pass you by."

"Ain't No Sunshine" was great, as usual. When they got to the "I know, I know, I know" part, eight thousand people sang it at the top of their lungs in unison—all on the same page. There would be no sunshine until goodness was back in our hearts as individuals and as a community. When the band brought it home, it seemed like it might be the final song of the night.

But someone in the crowd shouted out, "Marianne's Song!" and then everyone started cheering in agreement. The Dogs weren't going to bother doing the whole routine of leaving the stage and coming back for an encore.

Jerry stepped up to the microphone. "Thank you all so much. You sound amazing tonight, you know that, right?"

The crowd responded as if they did, in fact, know that they sounded amazing.

"If you've been following this story at all," he continued, "you know that most of us up here have never played a show like this. Most of us have never played a big show at all. That gathering that happened in the park last month was the biggest thing I had ever done."

"Me too!" Louis shouted from the side of the stage.

"I spent a good portion of my life driving artists in my bus, for crying out loud, but I never thought I'd be playing on a stage. And I don't know how long this will last or what's really going on here, but I do feel that we all knew something special was happening the night we were playing in my garage and Cesar here showed up and started playing his accordion with us on this next song."

The crowd knew what was coming and began to respond.

"But here's the thing," Jerry added. "This song started when I sang a little line to my baby girl nearly fifty years ago, but I never would have finished it—you never would have heard—and none of these amazing stories we've been hearing about people making peace and finding healing—none of that would have happened if my next-door neighbor, this kid playing bass guitar over here, Mr. Alex Palmer, hadn't heard me playing on my porch and begged, pestered, and practically forced me to play with him and his brother, Jamie, back there on the drums."

Alex shrugged. It was true. He was proud of it.

"And the truth of the matter is, I needed that. I needed someone to help me get over myself. I needed a push. And I don't know about you, but this whole thing has been teaching me something important about allowing other people into my story. I've been pretty good about helping people with their stories throughout my life, but not so good about letting people help me with mine. Mostly, I think, because I've been afraid that if anyone knew who I really was, what I had done, what I was like deep down, they'd run away. I was afraid. I was weak. I kept my guard up because of the pain I had caused other people and the pain I was trying to hide."

The crowd listened more attentively.

"I really appreciate the love and support you all have shown me. It's been incredible. And I promise, if you're one of the three thousand people who have sent a friend request on Facebook…well…I might get to those someday. But if you see me on the street and you're a part of this story, I'd definitely like to hug your neck!"

Now they were clapping again.

"So, some of you met our friend Nadia at the last event at the park."

Nadia got some applause, particularly, it sounded like, from women. One female voice shouted out, "Nadia kicks ass!" Everyone seemed to enjoy that. Especially Nadia. She waved up at Jerry, who waved back and wondered who the familiar-looking woman next to her was.

"Yes," Jerry agreed. "That she does. Well, Nadia recited a poem at the last event, and she helped me write a new original song that I told some of you about. So, we're going to try something here. This is for me, y'all. I hope you'll bear with me. But we're going to do three songs now—sort of a medley. And together, they kind of tell my story and my prayer for my two kids, but it also tells the story of all of us together, and how much we have in common. The first part is what y'all have been calling 'Marianne's Song,' then it goes right into the new song I wrote with Nadia, which is called 'Owes Me Nothing,' and then it ends with her poem set to music."

Marianne was frozen in her shoes. She wanted so badly to turn and run away but couldn't. Did he just look at her? He couldn't recognize her, could he?

Though ambitious, the medley of the songs worked well. "Marianne's Song" hit its mark, for Jerry, for the audience, and to an extent for Marianne. She held it together pretty well throughout most of the song, but when Cesar stepped forward with the accordion part and she saw Jerry's tears, her own started to flow as well. That angered her. She started to worry that someone might suspect her identity, but then she glanced around. Most people were having a similar emotional response.

She was so distracted by her frustration and her determination not to succumb to her emotions that she missed almost all of the lyrics on the second song. She pulled her phone out to detach from the moment.

"Owes Me Nothing," with its midtempo, three-four beat, was the most country-sounding song of the night. Marianne wasn't much of a country fan, which was another reason to tune it out, but up onstage, just thirty feet away from her, her father was singing the following words, having no idea that his daughter was right there at his feet.

The girl owes me nothing
Not even the time of day
I'm haunted by the knowledge
Of what I had and what I threw away
I'm the one with the matches and the gas
And the ashes on my head and hands
The girl owes me nothing
But I'd love it if she'd look my way
The girl owes me nothing
And what I owe her I cannot repay
This knowledge is my torment
And my folly is my shame
And my failure to protect
Is like an anchor around my neck
The girl owes me nothing
But I'd love it if she'd speak my name
I'd love it if she'd look my way
I'd love it if she'd speak my name
I'd love if she'd say that maybe someday
We could throw the past into
The bottom of the deep, dark blue
I'd love it if that could be true...
But the girl owes me nothing

Her heart is like a holy place
I stumble in the darkness
But her treasure cannot be replaced
Like a beggar at the temple gate
I'm hungry for a touch of grace
The girl owes me nothing
But I'd die to see her face-to-face

The audience melted into these words. Whether they understood the lyric to literally be about a girl or to be about something more metaphorical, the song landed hard. But Marianne had unplugged from what was happening in the moment and was completely in her head. What was she supposed to forgive this guy for exactly? She had never known him. Until recently she rarely thought about him. She was taught to be glad that he disappeared.

Maybe her mom needed to forgive him, but this wasn't about her, was it? Why was she even here? She had her own kids to focus on. All she wanted to know by coming tonight was whether this guy was for real or not. Was this whole thing a publicity stunt or something more genuine? She was starting to think that she wouldn't get any answers watching him onstage. This was a performance.

She missed the song completely.

But as the band segued into the instrumental backup for Nadia's poem, Marianne started to feel an avalanche of emotions she knew she would be unable to control. A few tears turned into a full-blown meltdown. She felt herself surrendering to the waves and turned to leave.

Nadia noticed the woman next to her starting to cry.

"Oh dear. Are you okay? Can I get you anything? Would you like some water or a towel?"

The lady seemed nice, but Marianne was pretty sure that if she didn't get out of here at that very moment, she might not make it. She bolted.

From the stage, Jerry noticed Nadia trying to help the woman next to her. He still thought she was familiar, but he was too far away to get a good look. He saw her leaving. Everything seemed okay. He had to focus.

After the show, everyone gathered in the ad hoc "green room" in the center. The room was full of smiles, sweat, and hugs. After getting their water, toweling off a bit, and saying a quick hello to the obligatory VIPs who had gathered, the crew made their way back out to talk with as many people as they possibly could.

Michael brought a friend over to Nadia.

"Nadia, this is my buddy James. He'd love to talk with you if you have a minute."

"Sure thing," Nadia said. "Just give me one minute to find someone." And she rushed off to find Jerry.

Meanwhile, Jerry was pushing through the crowd, taking pictures and chatting with people as he went, but the face he was looking for most was Nadia's. In the crush of people, he just couldn't find her.

He did bump into Kyle, who was effusive before they were even within ten feet of each other. "Dude, you guys were amazing! This whole night was incredible. Thanks so much for letting me be a part of it."

"Of course! I'm so glad you were here. There's no way I could have described this to you on the phone. Hey, do you want to crash in the guest room tonight?"

"If it's open, I'll take it."

"Sure thing. I'll be there in a bit and we can catch up. I just have to take care of some stuff here. You know where the key is."

A blogger pushed his way up to Louis and asked for some clarification on some of his comments. He seemed bothered or confused about what he meant by his use of the word *repentance*. Louis, sensing that it was an important question but that the moment was not appropriate for discussing it, suggested that he reach out later to find a time when they could discuss it more thoroughly. He gave the young man his business card and also pointed to Nadia saying, "She takes care of a lot of details for us. She might be able to set up a conversation time for us."

Cesar, who would rather be shoveling compost than be out in that scrum, was back behind the stage helping load equipment. He had recruited several of his sons and grandsons as crew for the night as well. But when the backstage floodlights came up, they found that all of the tires on his truck and his son-in-law's truck had been slashed and someone had spray painted the words *DIE* and *WALL* on their vehicles.

Jerry made his way back there right as the lights came up, and he found the group standing around staring at the damage. One of Cesar's sons was already on the phone calling for a tow, and George was walking up from the other side. "What happened?" Jerry asked.

"Just neighborly love, I guess." Cesar chuckled. "We were back here loading out and did not see this until the lights came up. Some folks just aren't ready for peace in the neighborhood."

Everyone was laughing except Jerry. He could not see what was so funny. He was furious. George could see the anger in his friend's demeanor.

"Jerry, my brother," George said. "We appreciate your concern, but this is a simple act of cowardice performed in the shadows by men who are either physically or emotionally children. We have faced this kind of nonsense every time we have made any kind of progress, and we will face it again."

"We laugh at these puppies together right now," Cesar said. "And we pray for them tonight. And then we forget all about them tomorrow." Everyone nodded.

"*Cachoros Perdidos!*" his grandson joked. They cracked up again and got back to work.

Lost Puppies.

Still upset, Jerry did his best to smile and shake it off and turned to search in yet another place for Nadia. He found her near the food truck area, collecting some donations. Michael and his friend walked up.

"Hey, Jerry," Michael said. "How much fun was that?"

"Pretty fun. I've never experienced anything like it. I don't know if I'll sleep for a week! Oh—that Stones song was incredible. Is Cheryl here somewhere? I want to thank her."

"Nah," Michael said, "she ducked out right at the end, before the crowd scene. That would just get crazy for her. Plus, talking in loud places like this messes up her voice. But she told me to thank you for including her and say she'd love to write with you and Nadia sometime."

"And hey," Michael continued, "I want to introduce you to a friend of mine here. This is James Miller. This was his first time hearing you guys."

Jerry looked at Michael and said, "You mean *us* guys."

"Sure! The first time he heard us. And he has an idea he wants to run by you."

At last, Nadia was free, and she and Jerry got to see each other for the first time since the end of the show.

"Jerry, that was unbelievable," she said. "I was transported. It felt like Woodstock, but constructive!"

Jerry beamed. "What did you think of the new song?"

"It was transcendent!"

They had forgotten that Michael and his friend were standing there with them.

"Oh," Jerry said. "Sorry. Nadia, this is James. He's a friend of Michael's. He has an idea to run by us."

"Oh yes," Nadia said. "We met earlier. I'm sorry I got distracted. I'm new to this whole scene and I'm kind of an old lady, so…"

"No problem at all," James said. "I'll make this short and sweet. I've never heard anything like this. It's so good. I work with the Bonnaroo Festival. We've been hearing about you from all corners. Now I've seen it for myself. We would love to have you play the festival this summer."

"Bonnaroo?" Jerry said. "Whoa."

"Bonnaroo?" Nadia said. "What's Bonnaroo?"

"You were talking about Woodstock just now," Jerry said. "Bonnaroo is like that."

"Whoa."

Michael was smiling widely. He knew, without a doubt, that this band would kill at Bonnaroo. What he did not know, was whether or not they would want to do it.

"Obviously, this is not something you'll be able to answer tonight," Michael said. "I just wanted you to hear it from him directly. I know you'll all need to talk about it. They'll send an official offer and we can get them an answer soon."

"Absolutely," James said. "I look forward to talking with you about it. You guys have such positive energy and an important message. And your music is unlike anything I've ever heard. We'll do whatever we can to make this happen, but it's totally up to you."

"Well thank you," Jerry said. "We'll get back to you soon."

Michael and James walked off and Jerry looked at Nadia for a long moment.

"You going to say anything?" she eventually asked him.

"Well, what I was going to ask you suddenly sounds puny next to that."

"What is it?"

Jerry cleared his throat, straightened his shirt a bit, and wiped the sweat from his face. Then he looked back at Nadia. "Well, I was going to see if you wanted to go out to dinner with me?"

"Like, a date?" she asked, somewhat incredulously.

"Yeah, like a date."

"Finally! If you hadn't asked me by tonight, I was going to ask you tomorrow. I've been trying to be patient because I know you're Southern, and a gentleman, and you don't take risks easily. But yes. Let's go on a date, already."

"Well okay, then," he said, smiling. "I'm sorry I took so long."

As they walked back toward the others, Nadia reached over and took Jerry's hand. "I'm going to need to hold this. I am half blind, you know."

Decision Time

Jerry made it back to his house at about 1:00 a.m. Kyle was sitting on the couch, poring through the photo album and listening to the Grateful Dead album that had been left on the player. "It's not like you to leave a record on the turntable, Brother. You must really be busy lately. And I never knew you were a Deadhead."

"It's been crazy," Jerry admitted. "And while I don't know if I've yet earned the full title of Deadhead, this experience has opened my eyes to the more communal aspects of music. I only knew that side of the Dead theoretically. Nadia brought them up once in a conversation about the more intangible value of music to people, and it reminded me that one of my old roommates had left that copy of *American Beauty* here. I dug it out and put it on, and I like it a lot. It definitely has a sort of ragged chill sound to it."

"Ragged chill," Kyle said. "Dig it. Oh, and tell me more about Nadia. She seems cool. Where did she come from?"

"She moved to town recently, came to visit her son. She's losing her eyesight, and living on her own in New York was going to be getting harder. She's a literature professor there and a poet. Smart lady, that's for sure. She was at Woodstock and all up in the whole Greenwich Village hippie scene back in the day. Good thing I didn't meet her back then." He chuckled. "I couldn't stand hippies back in the sixties."

"Really?" Kyle said. "You seem to have a very Zen soul, in a totally Christian way, of course."

"Well thank you, I guess. But we didn't go for the long-haired peacenik thing in Crossville back then." He gestured at the photo album. "I was afraid to even admit that I liked folk songs. It was always about pretending you were tough and that nothing bothered you." Jerry let out a long breath that just barely touched on the regret associated with what that pretense had cost him. "Anyway, Nadia's become a good friend, and I just asked her on an official date tonight. We're gonna see where it goes."

"That's awesome, man! I'm so happy for you. It's about time. Maybe we all should be in our seventies before inflicting ourselves on another person full time."

Kyle had a point there. "How have you been doing? How's life in the big church?"

"I don't know," Kyle said. "I think I'm done. There are a lot of people I love there. I think there are some great things that a church like that can do, but it just feels so…corporate. Everything is very brand-conscious and structured. They want me to be a worship leader, but really, I'm like the band leader on a talk show. We do the bumper music to warm up the crowd for the pastor. The service is impressive, and the people are nice—and I do believe they mean well. But the music isn't stretching me, the teaching isn't challenging me, and the whole thing just kind of feels like a job. I'm not sure that either faith or art should feel like that. But I don't know. Some people seem to need what they're doing. I'm trying to make it not be all about me, but I've been going to a little house church with about ten people on Sunday afternoons and getting more out of that than anything else. Then I saw all this stuff happening with you and thought maybe I should come back and get involved here. This looks dangerous!"

"Well, Cesar did get his tires slashed and a death threat painted on his truck tonight," Jerry said.

"Seriously? I was kidding. Wow. Did he freak out?"

"Not at all. In fact, they all laughed it off. I keep forgetting that these guys have been facing shit like that their whole lives. Good ol' boys down here in the Bible Belt threaten Cesar and his family for being Mexican, or Louis and George for being Black and daring to drive through the wrong neighborhood or walk into the wrong store, and that's just the way it has always been. This is just reality for them. We can't even comprehend it. It makes me sick."

"Yeah." Kyle nodded. "The way our church refuses to speak out against some of the political crap going on in our community—stuff against immigrants and others—because they don't want to offend the old-timers and the givers, it just drives me nuts. I see younger people leaving in droves because they've lost respect for the whole thing. I guess I have, too. But I miss the mission, man. I miss that call to love my neighbor, and my enemy. Man, that stuff Louis was saying tonight killed me. That was church!"

"It sure was. At least partly. It still seems that church has gotta be more than a concert, though. But yeah, Louis really went for it. I've never heard him like that. I sure have grown to love that man. I wish I'd gotten to know him sooner. You know, we've lived a couple blocks from each other for nearly forty years and didn't meet until a few months ago."

"Wow," Kyle said.

"He says it feels like there is a hand guiding this whole thing," Jerry said, "and I agree. I just wonder where it's guiding us. What is the end game here?"

"End game? Is there a problem?"

"Well, kind of." Jerry collapsed into the armchair and took another swig of water from his bottle. "Like your big church, this started because some neighbors felt a need to get together and make music and talk and pray together. We started to hear each other's sounds and feel them. We needed to see the walls that existed between us before we could start to tear them down. There are powers at work that thrive on our divisions. They train us to focus on what makes us different. What we felt when we got together was what we had in common. And man, it was powerful."

"And you don't think that can happen on a large scale?" Kyle asked.

"I don't know. Maybe, maybe not. I mean, I've got thousands of new 'friends' on Facebook now, and it's nice—maybe I can have some kind of impact on those people—but is it anything like my friendship with you? Is it like this right now? Too often, instead of looking at our neighbor—like the people right next to us—we see people on screens and react to the idea of people. And those ideas are shaped and guided by people with all kinds of agendas. The way we respond to them is shaped by the way we see them. It's a lot harder to hate someone to their face than it is to hate them online."

They both laughed a little at that line, at least to lighten the mood.

"At least the people picketing tonight had the courage to hold those stupid, ignorant signs up and stand there with them, unlike the cowards who snuck around in the dark slashing tires," Kyle added.

"Ha!" Jerry said. "Yeah. Props to them. But honestly, I suspect that if those folks unplugged from whatever hate machines they are connected to and came over here to the porch and had some tea with Cesar and Louis and me, they'd be looking for matches to burn those signs with. Ol' brother George could lead us all in a Bible study about how Jesus taught us to treat immigrants and what the Kingdom of Heaven is supposed to look like, and I bet if the haters were here breaking bread with us, they'd have a lot harder time hating ol' Cesar."

"True," Kyle said. "I'm just now starting to realize how subtle a lot of this disease is. I feel like Saul—when the scales fell off his eyes. But the scales just keep falling, and I don't like what I see."

"But like Louis was saying tonight," Jerry said, "we have to see how things are in this kingdom and mourn that, then catch a vision for how things are supposed to be and decide which kingdom we want to work for. I think there's good news there if we want to work for it."

"And I imagine Louis planted a lot of seeds tonight," Jerry closed his eyes as he argued this conundrum out in real time. "Maybe some people heard some things that will start them on a better path or encourage them down a path they were already on, but in my life the real change happens when people I know, and who know me, work on me up close and personal.

"When it gets all big and popular, it's exciting—and we can raise a bunch of money to save Louis and George's church. Maybe we can have a *wide* impact because of all the social media stuff and the TV stuff, but is it a *deep* impact? It feels like the bigger it gets, the less possible it is for us to do what we originally felt called to do."

"Exactly!" Kyle said. "It doesn't scale. It can get big, but it has to change to do it. And when it changes, it's no longer the thing that was so special. It sucks! I hate it. What are you supposed to do? Do you quit? How do you keep it small? Things naturally grow if they are good, don't they? Like, you can't tell people to stop coming to your shows or to your church. It's like we're doomed!"

Kyle, after having moved to the front edge of the couch throughout Jerry's little soliloquy, collapsed back, throwing his hands up in mock despair.

"Maybe," Jerry said. "But Louis keeps saying he believes that God wouldn't have brought us here just for it to either be compromised or fail. There's got to be a path. We just have to find it. They're all coming over tomorrow morning to sort of debrief on all this." He took a long draw from his water bottle and remembered the other bit of news he wanted to share with Kyle. "Oh—and we got invited to play Bonnaroo tonight. So we have to decide about that."

"Bonnaroo! That's amazing. Just think of the people you could reach?"

"See! You're part of the problem!" Jerry threw an armchair pillow at Kyle.

They both cut up again, deeply grateful for a shared history and for this time together at the end of a momentous night.

"Make yourself comfortable. I gotta take a shower and hit the sack. I have some journaling to do before I get to sleep tonight for sure." He grabbed the old leather book and headed back.

"Good night Jerry. I'm so proud of you, man. You're my hero."

"*Oy vey*! You need better heroes. Wait till I introduce you to George tomorrow."

Two hours east, Jack was scrolling through his Facebook feed. He couldn't get over how many posts he was seeing from the "Lost Dogs of East Nashville" event that his supposed "father" had put together. He watched several phone videos and read some testimonials.

I've never felt like this after a musical event. I didn't even know you could feel like this. I'm 500 pounds lighter, and I only weigh 150! Best night of my life. —MJ

Have you ever heard soul, country, Latin, rock, blues, and gospel music mashed into one new style? We did. If this is what it means to be a Lost Dog, I don't wanna be found! —JS

Best. Night. Ever! East Nashville is the best and I want Brother Louis to be my pastor! —MB

Jack wanted to figure out what the whole #BackOnThePorch thing meant at some point, too. When he got to the bottom of his notifications, he found his friend requests and there it was. "Jerry James Wesley wants to be your friend." Sent three days ago. He clicked on Jerry's profile to check him out. The first thing he saw on his wall was Robert's video that started to autoplay. He watched it again.

After some video footage of all of the members sitting around a table, and some of them in a garage playing as a band, this bit jumped out at Jack:

"I was really not ready to be a daddy. I was drinking too much. I was not dealing with pressure well. I already felt like a failure and then I went and signed up for the Army, looking for a steady paycheck.

"Vietnam was not a good place for me, or anyone, obviously. The demons I brought with me just got on top of me and ate me up. I had some bad experiences there and came home injured—both in my body and in my mind. I tried to deal with the mental stuff by drinking more. One night that led to a fight with my wife, and I hurt her. I couldn't believe I did it, but I did. I left that night and haven't seen her or my kids since. I've tried. Many years later, I got some good help with my alcoholism. I've been sober for over forty years now. I sent money for the kids and wrote to them all the time, but my ex-wife made

it clear that they didn't want anything to do with me. There was no hope of fixing what I had done.

"That song is really a prayer still, I guess. My kids are grown. They have kids of their own now. I still love them and pray for them and feel terrible about what happened. Part of the recovery process we learn when we quit drinking is to do what they call a 'fearless moral inventory,' and the next is to make amends as much as we can. I've not been able to make amends with them, and that just eats me up."

Clips of Jerry's song were cut in between the quotes. Jack felt himself becoming emotional, no matter how hard he fought it. This man was no one to him, but still, the story of his redemption was powerful.

He scrolled down Jerry's wall and looked at all of the posts. Dozens of comments and photos from people he had been working with, serving, helping, and encouraging. Jack was seeing evidence, lots of evidence, that this guy was for real. Then one particular post jumped out at him.

"Jerry, you've been in my corner encouraging me, always available for me, 24-7, for 25 years now. I'm so thrilled to see what God is doing through you, but I'm not surprised. I can't wait to see you Saturday. I'm flying in for the show." —Kyle

Twenty-five years? And that guy, Kyle Smith, he's that CCM singer who played at their church camp twenty years ago, wasn't he? Crazy.

Jack hovered his cursor over the Accept button for a good long time, then eventually pressed down. Then he went to bed. He'd check in with Marianne in the morning. They were supposed to go see their mom to talk about all of this. He'd probably not mention this Facebook thing right up front.

After the benefit concert, it had taken Marianne a few minutes in her car before she was ready to drive, but once she got going she felt fine. She talked herself out of her emotional response pretty thoroughly. Music always got to

her feelings. She was overtired. She'd been outside too long and was probably dehydrated. She just got caught up in the emotions that everyone else was feeling. There was no denying that the music was good, and this Jerry guy seemed genuine onstage, but she had known more than a few musicians and knew how different they could be when the lights were on them.

She was not looking forward to the conversation with her mother the next day.

Marianne listened to eighties pop music for the two hours back to Crossville—anything to keep from thinking or feeling too deeply. When she got back to her house, the kids were asleep but her husband, Mark, was up waiting for her. "How'd it go? Have a good time?"

She had told him she was going to see a free show with some friends in Nashville. Not a complete lie, she told herself. Everyone there was very friendly and the show was free. She had put five dollars in the donation bucket.

"Yeah, it was pretty good. I guess you get what you pay for. How were the kids?"

"Good, for the most part. Diane wouldn't go to sleep unless I sang to her, so I sang to her, and sang to her, and sang to her."

Something about that bothered Marianne. She pulled out her laptop and sat on the couch.

"Have you heard about this show in East Nashville?" Mark asked. "It was on the news and is all over social media. I guess a bunch of famous musicians were there. Cheryl Spree even sung a song there. A bunch of other famous folks were there but were just in the crowd with everyone else while this band of old people played what I guess was some kind of blend of country and rock and Spanish music or something. I don't know. Sounds pretty awesome. People were freaking out."

"Uh, yeah. I think that sounds like the same show I was at. I didn't know any famous people were there. Didn't seem like that big of a deal to me."

"Huh," he said. "I guess Spree was kind of in disguise and people didn't even know it was her. The whole thing was about, like, community power and being good people and stuff. Is that what it sounded like to you?"

"Yeah, I guess. It was weird. Seemed kind of all over the place, but the crowd was way into it. I left before it was over."

"Hmm." Mark looked over at Marianne, fairly certain that something was up. This wasn't like her. She was hiding something.

By then she had gotten her Facebook account opened and saw what he was talking about: pages of raves about this life-changing event. She rolled her eyes. But then, at the bottom of her notifications, she saw her friend requests and there it was.

"Jerry James Wesley wants to be your friend."

Holy…

She closed her laptop and told Mark she was going to bed.

In the morning Marianne decided she was going to skip church. The place was so big no one would notice anyway. Mark would take the kids, but she was going to get ready for the visit with her mom. She fixed herself some coffee, sat at the kitchen table, and opened her laptop again. The invitation was still sitting right there. She clicked on Jerry's profile. His wall was full of posts and tags from what could only be called fans. Dozens of selfies were taken just last night after the show. Jerry looked old and sweaty. She thought he seemed pretty gross.

Then a particular post caught her eye.

Jerry! You guys were so awesome tonight! I got home and saw this story on the news. Did you see it? So cool! There was a link to a NewsChannel 4 story about the band, the event, and Jerry in particular.

The story about the band seemed fine. Three old people and two college students start playing music and strike a nerve with the community. Some videos went viral. It didn't seem particularly special to Marianne until they got to Jerry's profile.

Reporter: "Guitarist, and some say founder, Jerry James Wesley, served as a bus driver and mechanic for most of his career before being forced into an early retirement late last year. Fans say that one of his original songs, a tune called 'Marianne's Song,' was specifically composed as a way to find and reconcile with the family he became estranged from over forty years ago due to substance abuse and PTSD."

Fan: "I hope his kids hear this song and realize how sincere he is. He deserves a second chance!"

Marianne felt every muscle in her body start to tense up.

Reporter: "Wesley's heartfelt introduction of the song tonight brought many fans to tears."

And then she saw video of herself leaving the concert, wiping tears from her face. "Oh my God!" she said to no one in particular. "What a load of—"

"Good morning, Mom," her teenage daughter Emily said. "Whatcha looking at?"

"Nothing good." Marianne shut her computer tightly.

Present Day

Back on the porch, the space had become a bit overcrowded. George had arrived and was waiting at the bottom of the steps for a seat to open up. Michael was there now, too. Some neighbors had spotted the gathering and come up to the porch for some photos with the group. It was sweet, but they had some important things to talk about. As much as he hated to admit it, Jerry realized that the porch was not the right environment for the task at hand. Just as that thought occurred to him, a car drove by and honked as a group of well-wishers shouted greetings to the Dogs. His expression combined a pleasant smile, some mild discomfort, and a grimace of pain, which neither George nor Nadia had previously seen on his face before.

Nadia picked up on it instantly and took charge. "Well, folks," she began, with a tone in her voice that was somehow both authoritative and graceful, "I think we'll need to move inside for the next phase of this conversation."

Marisol understood what was happening. "Thank you all so much for sharing these stories. This has been an amazing time. I have so much to work with here and I promise to treat this with the utmost care. I'll get out of the way now so you can have your meeting. I'm excited to hear about what you decide to do. Whatever it is, I know it will be the right thing." She gathered her things, shook a bunch of hands, and made her exit.

When she got to her car, she sat for a few minutes to allow what had just happened to sink in a bit. She had long prided herself on being an articulate, thoughtful, and insightful person who could capture any moment in words. But what she had just experienced defied the vocabulary she had collected thus far. The air felt different. These ordinary people, old and young, had something about them that they weren't even aware of. She felt more alive than she had in a long, long time. She started to suspect, however, that she might need to rethink some of her own prejudices and presuppositions about some things.

The crew made their way into the house and pulled chairs into a loose circle. Jamie and Alex lugged the old blue van bench in from the porch for extra seating. Jerry offered everyone coffee. George was the only taker. Jerry wondered why none of these people liked his coffee.

Louis and George had attended the early service at Main Baptist. They had hoped to have the whole group come to be acknowledged, but that would have to wait at least a week. The early returns were in, and it seemed their efforts had raised well over four hundred thousand dollars. A big chunk of that came from one major anonymous donation.

Nadia attended church with her son and his family. Theirs was a very trendy congregation that met in a former factory. She wasn't crazy about their theology, or the fact that they had no women on their pastoral team, and she wasn't a fan of their music. But she was crazy about her son and his family, and that was much more important to her than the gift she had for finding faults with churches. She was pleasantly surprised by the red ball cap-wearing gentleman who came up to her after the service.

"I heard about what happened with that fellow Cesar's truck last night," he said. "I own a tire shop. I'd like to donate a set of tires for his car and his kid's car. The way they've been treated just ain't right."

"You're right," she said. "It's not right. I thank you for that. I will let him know." She took his card and walked away. It was getting harder and harder to keep these Southerners in their boxes. She texted the info to Cesar right away, and he had already taken his truck over to the man's shop. They were happy to take care of him on a Sunday.

Cesar and Irma had attended St. Cecilia's with their family. It seemed most of their congregation had been at the show the night before. Father Mack was especially excited to see Cesar. He even brought some shades to wear in honor of him. He added some special language to their Prayers of the People, seeking "Peace to the Neighborhood," and Cesar smiled.

Jerry and Kyle had "something like church" at home and invited Alex and Jamie to join them, which they did. Neither of them had been in church in years. They called Michael and he showed up as well. Their gathering consisted of some Scripture readings, some discussion, and a couple songs that Kyle introduced them to. They had some Communion with a biscuit and some grape juice from Alex's mom's fridge.

George opened the meeting. "What a fantastic night! Four hundred thousand dollars raised, which is more than enough for the building, so our "Lost Dogs Fund" will be established. I am just beside myself. Our entire church sends their deepest gratitude and blessings this morning and invite you all to join us for a special ceremonial thanks as soon as possible."

"Of course," Jerry said. "I can't wait to see everyone there."

"Next week?"

"Absolutely," George said. "Now. What's this about a festival?"

"Yeah," Jerry said. "Last night Michael brought a friend to meet me. His name was James Miller. James works with the Bonnaroo festival. He said that they had been hearing about us, so he came to check us out. I guess we passed the audition and they want us to play."

"What would that entail?" Louis asked.

Michael stepped in at this point. Jerry had asked ahead of time if he could provide some context for this event and what the opportunity could mean.

"Well," Michael began. "You could be playing in front of eighty thousand people, for one thing."

"Eighty thousand people?" Louis bellowed. "That's huge!"

"Indeed. It could be over a hundred thousand depending on who the headliner is that day. And the crowd comes from everywhere. A slot like this means exposure to the entire country. You cannot buy publicity like this."

"Will they pay us for this?" Nadia asked.

"Oh yes," Michael said. "I haven't seen an offer yet, but it could be in the twenty-five- to fifty-thousand-dollar range. They believe that the way the buzz is building on this group, when people hear about us being added to the lineup, they'll see a bump in ticket sales. They say this is because of the message and the positive vibes. And that's part of it. But they see value in this, for sure. There's demand here."

"Fifty thousand dollars and playing in front of eighty thousand people," George said. "It doesn't even seem real. If we do the album you talked about, I would imagine this would be a great way to get the word out about that."

"Oh, that's putting it lightly," Michael said. "Not only would this get the public aware of the recordings, it would also be great in terms of press. Honestly, and guys, I'm not just saying this, this is pretty much a dream scenario. Every record company and artist manager would kill for this."

"But?" Cesar said.

Michael smiled. Then Jerry smiled.

"But," Michael said. "We do this and there's no going back to anything small and local. This will likely lead to tour requests, TV appearance requests, and who knows what else."

"No more shows in the driveway," Jerry said.

"There aren't any venues in East Nashville big enough after this," Michael said.

"I don't think it's a good idea," Jerry said. "We can just say 'no' and try to keep things manageable, can't we?"

"I agree," Cesar added. "This is too much. It sounds fun, but this becomes a new full-time life. It changes everything. Maybe not for the better."

"It is definitely appealing to have the ears, and potentially the hearts, of so many people," said Louis. "I don't want to lose what we have here in the neighborhood either, but think of the impact this could have nationally."

"This is a hard decision," George said. "Very hard. I can see both sides."

Michael had started pacing. "Look, I'm always the one thinking big and shooting for the moon. I'm the jump-first-and-look-later guy. Last night when James brought this up, I was all about it. But overnight, and this morning, I just have this fear that it's the wrong thing. Does this scale us up too big and we lose the essence of what we actually are?"

"But can it stay small?" Louis asked. "If we decided to set up in the garage right now, who thinks there wouldn't be five hundred people in this yard before we finished one song? Just saying 'no' to this isn't necessarily the same as saying 'yes' to something else."

"But saying 'yes' to this could definitely mean saying 'no' to any hope of continuing the community nature of what started here," Jerry said. "I tend to agree with Michael. I'm afraid that if we let this thing get too big, we will have to compromise the soul of what we are."

Louis stood at this point. He was staring at the floor, pulling on his chin, and wrestling in his mind and his heart. "Before I say anything else, I want to make sure that everyone here knows that I love and respect you deeply. With the exception of the gentleman standing in the doorway"—he gestured in Kyle's direction without looking at him—"with whom I am not personally familiar but assume he is a friend of Jerry's and thus is a friend of mine, the rest of you are my family. If I seem upset as I express my thoughts here, it is with this situation and not with you."

"We understand, brother," George said. "Let it out."

"Thank you," Louis continued. "I am tired of holding back. I am tired of being brought into a position where I can see what is wrong in a situation, but not be empowered to do anything about it. I was trained as an engineer. I developed specialized skills to solve problems and to build things. I went into war zones and helped design structures for getting wounded people treatment and strategies for bringing clean water and supplies to both troops and civilians. I trained my mind to see the solution in a disaster, and then came home to these streets and for over forty years drove a BUS!"

His voice was rising. Cesar was nodding along intently.

"And now I see great changes in this community. I see new buildings and lots of money and great prosperity for some, and I see increasing apathy, terrible division, and increasing injustice being not only tolerated, but in many cases being promoted by elements of the church! The engineer in me can see the mess. But I can also see at least one path forward, and that is the kind of intimate, neighbor-to-neighbor, relationship building that has the power to transform our community from one of silos and screens to one of singing, eating and praying together. And I am done sitting on the sidelines! I am tired of seeing people denied valuable resources because of their color. I feel a moment happening, and I want to use whatever years I have left to inspire and equip the next generation to invest actively in this body—both for the benefit of the community here and now, and for the purposes of the Kingdom we can't see."

Louis took a breath, then looked his new family in their faces. "I've been thinking about why it was so hard for me to sing in public," he said quietly. "I think that in part it was because I was so afraid of having my voice sidelined the way my mind was. I felt useless. I did my best to find the silver lining and to serve with a smile, but it hurt. I bottled that pain up, and when I sang was when the pain got the closest to the surface."

Jerry understood that feeling all too well.

"But now that I've found my voice," Louis continued. "Good luck trying to shut me up!" He laughed. "And God help anyone who tries to shut up or sideline any of the young people in this community if I have anything to say about it!"

"I hear you, Louis," Jerry said. "I'm not saying I know exactly what you mean, because there is no way I'll ever be able to fully know what you've been through. Or you, Cesar." Jerry glanced at both of his new brothers and then at Alex and Jamie. "But I'm still stuck on this particular problem. If we keep allowing this thing to get bigger, like taking this gig at Bonnaroo, are we working toward the goals you are talking about, or are we compromising our ability to accomplish those goals? As an engineer, if what you need is a classroom but what you build is a stadium, is that a success? Or are you setting yourself up to fail?" Jerry shook his head. "I'm afraid that we might be following the natural path that feels like success because it's what progress looks like in this world, but it might inadvertently undermine our mission."

"But what did Louis just say about making decisions based on fear?" Nadia asked. "What if the only way for us to protect the essence of what we are trying to do here is to go right into the belly of the beast and come out the other side?"

"I don't follow," Jerry said.

"Stay with me here," she said. "This might get weird."

"What if we take this gig, make this record, and use it all to build a platform, but we then use the platform to do something revolutionary? We use the system, the machinery of bigness, to promote something truly and radically...*small*?"

"I like the sound of this," Louis said.

"The sister's got my attention," added George.

Jerry was nodding, mostly because he didn't want to be left out and was of a mind to trust Nadia. He was not following her at all.

Kyle, who had been listening from a distance, was grinning. He liked where this was going. "This could be awesome. Count me in!"

At about that same time over in Crossville, Marianne and Jack were heading to their mother Susan's house. Jack picked up Marianne so they could ride over together.

"You're not going to believe this," Marianne said the second she got into Jack's car.

"Try me."

"I don't know where to start," she said, already flustered. "So, last night, for some unknown reason, I decided to drive into Nashville to go check out that Lost Dogs band thing. I thought maybe I'd get a better feel for what kind of guy this is in person than I could online."

"Wow, I wish you'd have told me. I would have gone with you. I saw a bunch of stuff about it online and on the news. Did you meet him?"

"Hell no!" she snapped, and Jack started to get a better picture of how his little sister was feeling about this whole thing. "It was bizarre."

"Bizarre? How so?"

"Well first, it was supposed to just be some little benefit show for a local church that needed money for repairs or something, but it turned into a freaking festival. There were thousands of people there—mostly young people, but all those East Nashville types. They were just throwing people up onstage with no planning. They even had that one Christian rock guy who used to play at our church camp every year, forever ago."

"Kyle Smith?"

"Yeah! How'd you know that? I forgot his name, and he never even said it onstage, but I knew I recognized him. He was pretty good. But anyway, our supposed father's band came out and played and—I guess they were good. I mean, they played every kind of music. The audience freaked out the whole time. People were singing along. They even had people from the crowd coming up onstage and playing with them. I don't know, it wasn't like a regular concert. I didn't get it.

"But at the end," she continued, "he went into the whole thing about us and regret and whatever and then played that song from the video. I was thinking maybe he was sincere. But it felt like he might have an angle, too.

"Then I got home and found a friend request from him on Facebook! Can you believe that?"

"Yeah," Jack said, allowing the question to pass.

"So I looked at his profile a little bit, and I see all this fan stuff and whatever, and there's a link to a story on the news, and all these people are putting all this pressure on us to reconcile with him and give him a chance and all this crap. Even the people on the news were on his side. The whole thing is a big show!"

"Whoa." Jack took a deep breath. He hadn't prepared himself for any of this. He knew he had to choose his words very carefully.

"Did Jerry actually say anything that was offensive or inappropriate? Or are you more upset about what other people online or on the news were saying?"

"What difference does it make? The whole thing feels like a ploy."

"I get that," Jack said. "And it might be. But just for argument's sake, maybe we should break down what he has done and said and separate it out from what other people have added to it or how they have spun it. He can't control how people react to things online."

"So you're going to defend him?" Marianne huffed. "That figures."

"I'm not defending him. I'm just saying that if this were you and you were in the position he is in, I would want to hear from you and not interpret things based on what random online fans or media people say."

She knew he had a point there.

"Look," Jack continued, "he sent me a friend request, too."

"He did? When were you going to tell me that?"

"When you stopped talking," Jack said with a smile. "I had no idea you were at that show. I got online and saw all these people posting about it, and then I saw that he had sent that request several days ago."

"What did you do?"

"I accepted it."

"You WHAT?" Marianne looked like she wanted to jump out of Jack's moving car. "Why would you do that without talking to me?"

"I don't know," he said truthfully. "When I reviewed his profile and rewatched that video, I saw what seemed to maybe be a guy who had turned his life around. He wasn't selling himself, either. It was other people talking about the impact he was having on them."

"That's just because he's famous right now," she snipped.

"Maybe some of them, but then I saw a post from that guy Kyle Smith. It looks like Jerry has been a sort of mentor and friend to him for something like twenty-five years. That's back when he was a bus driver. If you look past the recent fans, you can see neighbors and friends who go way back with the guy. He's just been living a quiet life, doing his best to help people. I'm not saying he's a saint, and I haven't talked with him yet, but the more I investigated, the more I started to think that while I might not need a father figure in my life—I mean, we have Dad for that—I could handle learning more about forgiveness and stuff. I imagine that Jerry has some stories."

Marianne was silent. She spent the rest of the ride stone-faced. She turned up the radio and changed the station to some classic rock hits.

Jack could tell she needed some space.

"I'm just saying," he tried to continue, but she raised her hand. She'd heard enough. He shut up.

The soundtrack for the rest of their conversation-free drive included "Walking on Sunshine," "Dream On," and "Another One Bites The Dust" before the computer that controlled the radio station decided to cue up Mike and the Mechanics' "The Living Years" as they pulled into Susan and Joe's neighborhood.

"Oh, Jesus!" Marianne exclaimed as she dove for the volume knob.

Her overreaction caused both her and her brother to chuckle a little.

They drove the last block in silence.

"I love you, little sis."

"I know you do, you idiot."

As they walked up to their mother's door, Jack put his arm around Marianne. He hadn't always lived up to the big brother role he had been born into. She often refused it. But this time, he was going to own it. She reached up and grabbed the hand that was draped over her right shoulder.

"Look at you two!" Susan said as the door opened. "Oh, it makes a mother's heart happy to see her babies like that."

"Hi, Mom." Jack gave her a kiss. Marianne repeated the ritual. "Happy Sunday. Got anything to eat?"

It was a silly question. They knew full well Mom would have a giant spread waiting for them.

"I've got some chicken and some biscuits and veggies all on the table. Dad has taken his lunch in to watch the game."

They got settled in and poured some sweet tea.

"I can't remember the last time just the three of us sat down," Susan said. "I mean, no kids, no spouses, just us. The original Musketeers!"

Jack nodded. "Yeah. It's been, well…have we ever done this? I mean…I can't remember doing this since we were kids. It's nice."

"Maybe we can take a trip!" Susan said. "Before I get too old and have to wear a diaper."

They laughed and passed the food around.

"Would you say grace, Jack?" his mother asked.

"Sure, Mom."

"Lord, thank You for this food. Thank You for this family. Thank You for providing for us. Thank You for everything that happened to make us who we are and to bring us to this moment right now."

Marianne squeezed his hand.

"And bless Dad in there with his food. Help whichever team he is pulling for win. Amen."

"Amen!" said Joe from the next room.

"That was an interesting prayer, dear. Thank you for that."

"Sure, Mom," Jack said. "It's kind of related to something we want to talk with you about."

"Oh?" Susan looked up from her plate.

"Mom, something has come up that we need to talk with you about." Jack was buttering a biscuit as he spoke. He hoped that the process of handling food while talking would somehow make the words seem more casual.

"We have some questions. But first we want you to know how much we love you, and appreciate you, and know that you worked so hard to take good care of us and raise us right. Being a single mom for those years before you met Dad had to be so hard. You're our hero!"

"Totally," Marianne added.

"Shit." Susan's pleasant demeanor disappeared. "That sonofabitch found you, didn't he?"

The kids could not remember the last time they heard their mother swear. It got Joe's attention, too.

"Well, kind of," Jack said. "It's complicated. We haven't actually communicated with him yet, but he has reached out to us, and we've heard a few things about his story that we want to check out with you."

Marianne leaned in. "Mom, this guy, Jerry, has been a bus driver for decades—a nobody over in Nashville. Then suddenly a couple of months ago, he got together with a couple of other old guys in his neighborhood, and a couple of kids, and started a band, and now they're getting famous. They played a song he said he wrote when I was just a baby."

"Oh my God," Susan half-set down and half-dropped her fork. "That song. It wasn't really a song. It was just, like, a lullaby he sang to you when you would fuss. All I remember was the line he'd sing 'I'm not much, but I'm right here.' Truer words were never spoken! That man was not much!" Her rage was rising.

Marianne continued. "So, it doesn't seem that these guys—and there's a lady who works with them—expected to be popular, but they are. So, we both heard about them online and figured out who he was and that he was talking about us."

Jack swallowed a bite and cleared his throat. "Mom, one of the things he says in this video is that after he hurt you, he left—and we know that part—but that he always sent money and letters back to us and wanted to have a relationship with us, but you wouldn't allow it. Is that true?"

Susan was silent for just a moment. She took a deep breath, then looked down. "You need to understand, Jerry was dangerous. He was an alcoholic and a drug addict. He was insane. He was bad before he went to Vietnam, but when he came back, he was a monster. You don't come back from that."

She looked away, seeming to be drifting into memories. "He got worse and worse. I even drove into Nashville to check on him once. He was passed out on his front porch. He stayed that way for years. Yes, he sent money. That much is true. It all went into your college funds. And he sent some birthday gifts. I gave them to you but said they were from an uncle or me. I wanted to protect you from the pain I knew he was going to cause you."

Susan was looking down at the table as she spoke. She rearranged some silverware and refolded her napkin nervously, shaking her head the whole time. "And all those years when you were little, when it was just the three of us, he didn't want to actually see you. He was too much of a mess. He just sent what money he could—which wasn't much—and stayed away. Then when you were teenagers and Joe and I got married and Joe was becoming your dad, Jerry came back around promising he had changed. I knew it was a lie. He just didn't want someone else to be your father. I told him to stay away, that you needed space, and that we were better off without him. To my surprise, he did. I never heard from him again."

The three of them sat there silently for several moments. They didn't notice that Joe had moved into the room and was standing in the doorway.

Susan was crying.

"I know; I was wrong. But I was a kid with kids. I was terrified. He terrified me. And just when I felt the ground firm up under my feet a little bit, he came sniffing around threatening to smash it all up again. I couldn't allow that."

"But Mom," Marianne asked, her head down. "Whenever I asked about him, all you ever said was how twisted and evil and monstrous he was. It would have been nice to know that at least he was trying. At least he was supporting us. As damaged as he was, at least he was trying to love us." Her tears started flowing. "I learned how to hate that man with a passion—with your passion. And now I have to unlearn that? I don't know if I can."

Joe moved over and put his hands on Marianne's shoulders.

Jack did his best to compose himself. "He says that he's been sober for over forty years now, and from the looks of it, he helps other people figure out how to confront their addiction."

"Well that's good." Susan sniffled. "I'm happy for him, I guess. At least I want to be. I don't like to think of myself as a hateful person, but as soon as he came to mind, boy oh boy…the first thought that popped up was that I hoped he was dead."

"Look, kids," Joe said. "I don't know if it helps you to know this or not, but one thing I have found in my eighty years on this planet, is that when we welcome new people into our hearts, it doesn't mean we have to kick other people out. If you feel that you are ready to get to know this guy, don't worry about that being some kind of a threat to our relationship. Getting to help raise and love you two has been one of the great joys of my life, and I owe that man a beer—or, well, a cup of coffee—for helping to bring you into existence. If he has any kind of wisdom to share with you, go get it."

They smiled at that. Joe would always be their dad and their kids' granddad.

"If you want to connect with him," Susan said, "I won't try to stop you, and I won't give you grief about it. Just be careful. Take it slow. And don't expect too much from me. I think my bitterness for that old man might be the only thing keeping my bones so strong!"

They laughed again, and Jack reached over and gave his mom a kiss on the head. "You're not that strong, Mom," he teased.

The Crescendo

"My mind, my heart…everything is racing!" Jerry could barely maintain eye contact with Nadia as he spoke to her across the table. They were sitting at one of the fanciest coffee shops on the east side. It was her favorite place to work. He had frantically texted her saying he had some news and needed some help processing it right away.

Nadia had already closed her notes and her laptop and was giving Jerry her full attention. "Calm down. Breathe. I do know that a panic attack right now will not help anything or anyone. Is this about the Bonnaroo set?"

"No!" Jerry snapped, releasing frustration that Nadia did not deserve. Bonnaroo, the band, and all of the happenings of the last few months paled in comparison to what had just happened.

She absorbed the slight and pushed on gently. "Okay. No need to bite my head off." She found his hands, took them in hers, and did her best to look him in the eyes. "Now, what—the hell—is going on, my dear?" In any other moment the gracefulness of her smile would have completely disarmed Jerry, but he was in a very different place than she had seen him before.

Jerry took the closest thing he could to a deep breath. He was letting Nadia see a side of him she had never seen before.

"Jack and Marianne…They responded! I found them on Facebook a few weeks ago and sent friend requests. They didn't respond for several days, so I assumed they wouldn't. I had resigned myself to the fact that it was official—they wanted nothing to do with me. I didn't blame them, either. I was a total piece of shit to them and their mother. Why should they want anything to do with me? Then I started to feel some real anxiety over having even sent those friend requests. I mean, real anxiety. I had a lot to keep me busy, which was good, but it was easy for me to start obsessing over that. I even asked some kids if there was a way to go in and cancel those requests."

"You started to spin out."

"Yeah," he admitted. "It was like a cyclone of regret. I regretted reaching out like that, then I regretted even being on Facebook, and then I regretted the podcast interview and that video, and I realized I had told that story and it wasn't fair to them."

"But you didn't use their names," Nadia said.

"But they would know it was them if they saw it," he snapped.

"Ah yes." Nadia nodded. "I see."

"This regret train just led all the way to, I don't know, 1958 or something. My whole life started to feel like a terrible mistake. I was a mistake. I don't deserve them, and that's why I lost them. Everything else is smoke—it's a lie I'm telling myself. I knew this was the pattern. It had been a while since I've freaked out like that, but I knew it when I felt it."

"I wish you had told me," Nadia said.

"It wasn't your burden to manage," Jerry said. "I have friends in the Program and I leaned on them. It was good. I needed that. They helped me talk and think through it. I thought I had it managed pretty well. Then the show happened and that distracted me. But today I got back on Facebook and both of them had accepted my request! I even got a message from Jack. He said they would like to get together with me somewhere in a public place."

"Wow!" Nadia said. "That's amazing. How exciting."

"Yeah, exciting. But I also think I might have a stroke. What does a stroke feel like?"

"Ah." She massaged his hands a bit more. "Now I believe I understand what we are dealing with. Once again, though, a deep breath."

Jerry breathed. He just then noticed his hands in hers and how much he liked how they felt.

"Is there a set time for this meeting?" she asked.

"I got that message, texted you, almost threw up, washed my face, and rushed over here. I haven't even responded yet. And I see that the message has been sitting there for a couple of days because I still suck so bad at this stupid Facebook stuff."

"Okay. Just relax. There is no calamity here. There is actually nothing but good stuff here. This is a good news story. Do you hear me? This is a happy day. There is no reason to panic."

Jerry took another deep breath. He hadn't considered any of those things. They sounded reasonable. He managed to gaze into Nadia's eyes for more than three seconds in a row.

"Let's just take this one step at a time," she said. "Okay?"

Jerry nodded. In that moment he hoped he would never be without this woman in his life.

A few days later Nadia and Jerry walked into Grinder House Coffee on Main Street in Crossville. It lacked the urban sophistication of the East Nashville shops but was comfortable and well appointed. Nadia said she was only mildly disappointed not to find a horror movie theme when she walked in the door, but Jerry had no idea what she was talking about and missed the reference. Because of the two-hour drive they had allowed some extra time and had gotten there early.

They grabbed some space in one of the sofa areas and ordered some coffee. The plan was for Nadia to leave Jerry with Jack and Marianne once they had made the introductions. She wanted to give them their space, and she had quite a bit of work to do related to the Bonnaroo set, which was closing in fast. Jerry had gotten a text from Jack with their coffee orders, so they were able to get those ready ahead of their arrival. As they waited, Nadia looked through Jerry's photo album, which he had brought just in case the kids were interested in seeing any old pictures.

The two walked in right on schedule. When Marianne saw Nadia her jaw dropped. "I know you!"

Nadia was smiling but confused.

"I stood next to you at the benefit concert," Marianne added. "I even talked with you."

When Nadia got close enough, she could see Marianne's face and remembered. "Oh yes! You were right there with me. I'm sorry, my vision is not very good."

"Yes, that was me. I'm sorry if I was ugly to you. I was having a hard night."

"Oh, sweetheart, I can only imagine. It's nice to officially meet you, though. I'm Nadia. I'm a friend of Jerry's. I made the ride out with him so he would have someone to talk to."

She shook Jack's hand as well.

"I don't want to interrupt your time together. I'm going to leave you three to visit. I'm sliding over here. I've got some work to take care of."

"Okay," Jack said. "Feel free to come back over and join us whenever you finish your work, though."

Nadia ducked back over to a table on the other side of the room. Jerry handed Jack and Marianne their drinks. "Here you go. I think I got these right."

"Looks great," Jack said. "Thanks."

The three sat, staring at each other for what felt like several long moments. Jerry took a deep breath, desperately wanting not to say the wrong thing. All he could conjure in his memory was regret and images of them as babies, so he worked to focus on the present. They were both fully formed adults, full of stories and questions and memories. At first glance he thought that Jack favored his mother, especially his mouth and nose, and the large frame that clearly took more after her side of the family. He was easily two inches taller than Jerry and his sandy hair was much thicker. Marianne, though, reminded him of his mother. She had a lovely face, fair skin, dark wavy hair, and a slight build. And she had the same greenish-brown eyes as he, his mother, and his grandmother all had. He thought maybe she noticed that too, because she looked away right as he thought that.

Jack and Marianne searched the deepest recesses of their memories for even the slightest spark that might connect them to the man who sat in front of them. Nothing came but questions, feelings, comments from their mother, and empty places where a father should have been. The old man sitting there seemed pleasant, relatively healthy, and pretty normal, if not a bit eager. Marianne found it difficult to look at him directly for more than a second or two at a time. Jack, deep in his own head, was searching for the right opening comment or question when Marianne jumped right in like it was no big thing.

"So," she said matter-of-factly, "this music thing is pretty crazy. You really had no idea any of this was going to happen?"

"Absolutely not," Jerry said. "And before I give you the blow-by-blow, let me say one thing. I feel real bad about how some people have taken so much of an interest in, and kind of reinterpreted, that song I wrote for you when you were a baby. I saw that story on the news, and it was over the line. All I meant for it to be was an olive branch, not a way to twist your arm. That was not cool, and I'm really sorry about that."

"It freaked me out at first," Marianne said, "but Jack helped me realize that you couldn't control how people spun that."

"True." Jerry nodded. "But I didn't have to let people call it 'Marianne's Song.' That wasn't fair. I didn't intend for that to be a title—kind of like we never intended to give this band thing a name, because we didn't think of it as a band. But when I avoid doing something because I'm afraid that doing that thing will make something official, all I'm doing is being passive-aggressive. I'm learning that now. I should have called that song 'I'm Right Here.' Then I don't think people would have connected it to you directly."

Jack smiled at that.

Jerry continued. "I also wanted to make sure you knew that I don't blame your mother at all for any of the choices she made about keeping you from me. You are fortunate to have a loving and protective mother. She is a wonderful person, and I feel terrible about what I did to her. I just was not ready for life. I failed. She deserved better, and I'm glad she got it. I feel that the way that came off in the video could be seen as a bit 'bus-throwy' and that is not what I'd intended. I deserved what I got."

Jerry held his hands palms out in a gesture of surrender, let those words settle on the table, and sat back to take a breath.

"You're very good at apologies," Jack said.

"Well, I've been practicing," Jerry admitted. "That doesn't mean I'm not sincere, though. It just means that I've wanted this day to come for a long, long time. I have had many years to think about what I would say if given the chance. So, there you go. Oh, and Nadia helped me run through my thoughts before we got here." He smiled and let out a single chuckle, but it was true and they all knew it.

"She seems nice," Marianne added. "What's your relationship with her like?"

"Um, well…" Jerry said, unsure how to answer that question. "It's in formation, I guess. She's a dear friend right now, but I'm thinking it's becoming more. She's amazing, actually."

"I've heard that seventy is the perfect age to start dating," Jack joked. "It's about that age that we start to become the kind of people others can bear."

"That's hilarious," Jerry said. "My friend Kyle just said that same thing a few nights ago."

With the ice sufficiently broken, the three began to catch up on fifty years' worth of news. Jerry did his best to be as truthful and forthcoming as possible. He didn't push for more than the somewhat-guarded answers he got to his questions about Jack's and Marianne's lives. They talked for a bit more than an hour, until Marianne needed to leave to get back home to her family.

"If you'd like to come to our show at Bonnaroo, I'd love to get you passes," Jerry blurted out before seeing Marianne's expression that seemed to suggest she was not ready for that just yet.

"I'm not sure if I'm free that day," she lied. "I'll have to check."

Her response struck Jack as a bit gruff, and he told her that with the smile on his face and his wide eyes and raised eyebrows.

"Thanks for the offer," he added, "I've always wanted to check out Bonnaroo, but it's never been in the budget."

"Tell you what," Jerry said. "I'll just leave passes for you on the guest list so if you want to come, you can just come. If not, no problem."

"Great." Marianne feigned just enough enthusiasm to be polite. "We'll see."

She and Jack got up to leave, shared some quick, awkward hugs, and then went their separate ways. Jerry just made it to his car with Nadia before he broke down sobbing. Fifty years. Joy and hurt and relief and who knows what else came flooding out.

The jungle, first love, that night in the kitchen, a pit full of bodies, and the guitar he'd smashed to pieces—lost and found love—it all swirled around in the same field. The song he was singing now and the song he'd sung in Vietnam, these adult kids and this woman sitting next to him in his car, the kid he was when he married Susan—somehow it was all a part of the same long, sad, beautiful song.

And the craziest thing was that there was—finally—*hope*. Maybe this song wasn't over yet. There might be another verse or two yet to write.

Jerry felt waves coming up from somewhere deeper than his guts. His head pounded and his sinuses emptied. There was no dignity in this kind of weeping. Just beauty.

Nadia just patted his back and rubbed his head. "Let it out. You earned this one, honey."

The day of the Bonnaroo performance had arrived. It hadn't even been two months since the benefit show, and the team had accomplished an amazing amount of work since then. There were so many moving parts, and this plan was so crazy, several times Jerry had wondered if it would be smarter to just scrap the whole thing.

"Smart? Probably," Nadia had admitted. "But we left smart behind long ago. We're heading somewhere else now."

Nadia seemed twenty years younger than when Jerry met her a few months earlier. Sure, her vision was bad, but she more than compensated for that with her other senses. She was sharp as a tack, worldly wise, and she had the confidence of a twenty-three-year-old. She had become the group's strategic manager, and she worked right alongside George, who served as the group's spiritual guide.

What had really impressed everyone involved was the team that co-alesced around the core musicians and the leaders at the top. Nadia and George had no problem recruiting social media managers, logistical as-sistants, office managers, technicians, personal assistants, and even road-ies. Everyone seemed so excited about the vision that had come together around this project.

The weekly team meetings took place in either the sanctuary at Main Baptist or the multipurpose room at the community center. As many as one hundred people from all kinds of backgrounds attended each gathering—everyone with a job to do. The core members had always said that this was not about them. They were about to prove it.

The festival organizers had agreed to pay the group thirty thousand dollars for its performance, and every penny of that would be reinvested in this project. For one thing, the entire set would be live streamed and filmed for future release. They had to agree not to announce that before showtime, ostensibly so no fan that otherwise would buy a ticket to Bonnaroo might decide to stay home and watch from his couch. That was fine. They had a PR campaign locked and loaded, and once the first note was being played, over four million people would hear about it within five minutes. They would have their own live switching system and feed. Michael had pulled together a team of techs to make sure they captured everything sonically.

Another team built a brand-new website full of resources and materials that would be launched during their set. Only staff people knew anything about it. It had been tested on a backbone that they knew could handle millions of incoming requests simultaneously. Jack had gotten his degree in computer science and owned a small web services company. His staff was eager to take on the project when Jerry had offered it. Jack found it easier to be involved when he had a job to do. Marianne was not thrilled about the arrangement.

The group scrambled to finish their album with Michael. They had cut two songs in the studio, and he had eighteen live or home-based recordings to flush it out. The packaging consisted entirely of photos taken by attendees of the events. The project was mixed, mastered, and just waiting for the click of a digital button to be released. The vinyl was being manufactured. Fans that ordered LPs would have to wait a bit. George was guaranteed to get the first copy off the line. Jerry would get the second.

They prepared an airtight set, chock-full of fan favorites, including Jerry and Nadia's originals, and a couple of brand-new covers. Since they could not do the "stage in front of the stage" thing at Bonnaroo, they decided to simply increase the size of the band that would appear on the stage. There would be a dozen or so "special guests" appearing throughout their set, as well as the choir from Main Baptist, a horn section, two electric guitarists, a DJ, and a designated spot for surprises. Since their stage at Bonnaroo would be massive, they intended to fill it to the brim. They had even hired a special sound engineer to mix for them. She specialized in Broadway shows and was absolutely up for the challenge.

Despite all of this, the public had almost no idea what was coming. The show, and the announcements they planned to make during it, would be a surprise. Their social media team met with Louis, George, and Nadia and gathered a ton of inspirational and challenging quotes. They pulled together still photos and short video clips from the previous events. Everything pointed people to this day and to their set time of 6:00 p.m. "Even if you can't be with us at Bonnaroo," one series of posts said, "be with us at Bonnaroo. Stay tuned."

Even though the show was practically local, just over an hour from East Nashville, getting there would be a challenge. Jerry worked out a deal with his former employer and secured one standard tour bus for the band and two tourist-type coaches for the staff and crew. Three buses departed the Main Baptist parking lot at 7:00 a.m. for a 9:00 a.m. load-in and sound check. Jerry drove the band bus, of course. He put his Martin on its shelf above his head. He was back in his element. But boy were things different than the last time he had his hands on the wheel!

And then…here they were, on a farm in Manchester, Tennessee. The backstage area rivaled many small towns in terms of its infrastructure and population. Very strict crowd control kept performers and techs separated from VIP fans and the general-admission crowd out front. Jerry and Nadia had come out earlier in the week to get the lay of the land with the techs, so they already knew their way around.

Jerry liked the excuse of Nadia's visual impairment in a place like this. It meant she needed him, or at least preferred to have him close by at all times. There were several artists on the bill that she enjoyed and wanted to try to catch if she could. Jerry did his best to shuttle her around when they had time. They bumped into Alex and Marisol catching a show by a band called Blitzen Trapper.

The core band gathered backstage three hours before showtime. Jerry had one challenge to overcome before he could make it to that meeting.

Marianne's daughter, Emily, was arriving and Jerry couldn't wait to meet her. He knew she was especially excited to see the Bonnaroo madness. Even though Marianne hadn't bought into the idea of any additional reunion, she gave in to Emily's pleas and allowed her to join a carful of school friends headed to the fest that day. Jack would be on-site helping with web services through his company, so Emily would have access to her uncle if she needed him.

Jerry borrowed a golf cart and made his way to the entrance where they were to meet; the deal with Marianne was that he was not "granddad" but just Jerry, an old family friend from Crossville.

It was hot. In June in Tennessee, that was a given. Locals didn't even mention it. As Jerry rounded the last corner before coming into view of the gate, he saw the gang of high schoolers walking through, decked out for a day in the sun. One of them was his granddaughter, and when she came into view it felt as if his heart moved up into his throat. He blinked his eyes a few times, grateful for sunglasses to hide his eyes and the sweat that gave him an excuse to wipe them.

"This is insane!" Emily said as they bounced up to Jerry. "We had to park in town by a Walmart and take a bus over here—and that was the VIP parking. I don't know how these people do it. So, are we going to go backstage?"

"Sure!" Jerry said with a chuckle, as he finished wiping his face with a stage towel and replaced his glasses. He wondered if he had that kind of energy when he was sixteen. "But when we play, it'll sound a lot better if you stand down front in the VIP area. The place is huge—and the stage will be so full of people you probably won't be able to see or hear as well up there. But let's go take a little tour real quick. I need to meet with the band so I was going to head back that way anyway."

Emily hopped on the golf cart, already feeling more special than she realized she was.

The team had gathered back on the tour bus and was only missing Jerry. Nadia explained the delay and that he would be there any minute. They started talking through some details.

"So," Cesar started, "even though they moved everything since we sound checked this morning, they will remember everything, and it will sound like it did before? That seems like a lot to remember."

"It'll be perfect," Michael said. "They've got the best stagehands I've ever seen. Several of these guys work at the Opry and the Ryman. They set the mix levels on the computer and have notes for everything. When the band before us is done, it'll take them about a half hour to strike their stuff and move ours into position. We'll do a quick line check, just making sure everything is plugged in properly, and then we'll go."

"It's really amazing," Louis said. "I've never seen—or even imagined—anything like it. The engineer in me is very impressed. The singer in me is on the verge of a nervous breakdown!" He was nervous, and only half kidding. Everyone was with him and he felt ready for the moment.

"In my opinion, the biggest challenge when you play a stage this big," Alex cautioned, "is not to get swallowed by the size. It can sound strange for one thing. Even though your monitor will be perfect, when you hear the echo come back from far away, or you hear the crowd singing and they are out of time because of how far back the end of the audience is, it is very disorienting. You have to just override your senses. Tell yourself what you know to be true. Those people in the back are hearing you when they hear you and seeing you when they see you. These techs even have a way of delaying the video signal for the big video wall just a touch since sound travels slower than light. That way the people in back see the image a little bit more in synch with the sound. We just need to stay locked into each other. We have our experience onstage and let the sound crew take that experience to the crowd."

"What he said!" Michael added. "Every bit of it."

The septuagenarian newbies nodded obediently.

"Louis," Michael said. "It will probably be hardest for you. Just focus on those in-ear monitors, and if you feel disoriented by what you see, close your eyes."

"Got it." Louis felt like he was about to pilot a rocket ship.

Jerry walked in right then. "Sorry, everyone. Emily just got here, and I needed to meet her and her friends. What did I miss?"

Nadia caught him up on Alex's advice. "Does anyone have any logistical questions or concerns?" she asked the group.

They all shook their heads. They had gone over everything several times. They had rehearsed. They felt as ready as they were going to feel.

"Does anyone have any spiritual or emotional concerns?" George asked. Every hand shot up at once, and everyone cracked up.

"I thought so," he said. "And I would expect nothing less, knowing how much you all care about each other and about this community. But might you indulge me in a little exercise? I know we are all kind of cramped here, but as much as possible, would you grasp the hand of the person next to you, or if that is not possible, place your hand on their arm or shoulder?"

They all obeyed and began to close their eyes and bow their heads instinctively.

"No, friends," George said. "I'd prefer for you to keep your eyes open and your heads up this time. I would invite you to take a deep breath and exhale. And again, take a deep breath and exhale. And as you do this, look around this—well—it's not a circle, but you know what I mean—and see the faces of your brothers and sisters. See them as they breathe in, and out. See their eyes and let them see yours."

Cesar took his shades off. There were a few chuckles, but everyone understood what George was doing and loved him for it.

"Keep breathing in this moment and seeing the faces and eyes and noses and mouths of your family who are on this adventure with you," he said with a beautiful, poetic lilt to his voice. A new peace descended on the bus in that moment.

"We all know, and have spoken, of a great Hand we feel has pulled us into each other's orbit. That Hand formed us before time existed. That Hand will bring us into love and light when it is our time to leave this world. Today, though, this stage, this crowd, that screen, all these workers and volunteers—this is just one more chapter in this beautiful story that God is telling. We have nothing to worry about, do we?"

"No," they all said.

"We have every reason to be excited about this, don't we?"

"Yes!" they concurred.

Only then did George bow his head. The rest followed. "Heavenly Father, Composer of all great music, Author of love, bind us together and help us to be vessels of Your grace and peace. May Your will for this story be written through us, and to us. Thank You for your goodness. Help us to be present in this moment and to take none of it for granted. You are good. Amen."

They all said, "Amen!"

"I have got to learn how to pray like that," Jamie said.

"I'm going to give Emily and her friends a brief tour," Jerry told Nadia. "Do you want to join us?"

"I'd love to," she said, "But I have quite a few things to take care of still, and Daniel and his family are due here any minute. Why don't you go hang out with them and then bring them back here to get something to eat in about an hour?"

Jerry gathered the kids and played tour guide for an hour. First he showed them the backstage area, knowing that the excitement would wear off pretty quickly. But as they were heading for the public spaces, a man he did not recognize came running up to him.

"Jerry Wesley?" he said.

"Yes?"

"Man, it's good to meet you. I'm Tom Joseph. I'm volunteering back here today, but I'm a blogger and a fan of obscure, faith-based rock and alternative music. I've been following what you're doing and it's just so cool. I don't know if you're familiar with the tradition of gospel rock or alternative Christian music or any of the other names it's been called, but it feels like what you guys are doing is kind of in that tradition."

"Kind of," Jerry said. "I know all about contemporary Christian music. I never got into it too deeply, but I used to drive for some of the artists, and there were a few I liked."

"Yeah." Tom kind of waved him off a path he didn't want to go down. "I'm not talking about CCM per se. Before CCM there was Jesus Music back in the sixties and early seventies. Artists were playing gospel funk and psychedelic music about the Gospel. And then of course there were major artists, like the ones you guys cover sometimes, who touched on those themes, too. But CCM came along and eventually kind of became a separate thing. Some of it was pretty good, but it always seemed to me that instead of focusing on making great music, that industry—or that market—preferred safe, Christian versions of whatever was popular on the radio."

"Right," Jerry said. "I know it means a lot to a lot of people. It's just not been my thing. I've got one record that a couple of really nice hippies named Glenn and Wendi gave me back in the seventies. Their band was called Resurrection Band. That should have been on the radio. They were good!"

"That's what I'm talking about!" Tom raved. "That's Glenn Kaiser. He's still making music—blues. There's this whole world of music I think you would love if you heard it," he continued. "And actually, one of the best bands in that world is a group of guys from four other obscure bands—and they call themselves The Lost Dogs!"

"You're kidding me," Jerry said. "So we stole their name?"

"Well, kinda, I guess. But I read about how you got the name, and it makes sense, too. I just thought you'd want to know. Mostly because if you heard them, I know you would love their stuff."

"Well thanks, Tom. I can't say much right now, because it's a secret. But we won't be using their name much longer."

"Really?" Tom said. "What's up?"

"Just watch the show," Jerry said. "You'll see. I gotta run, but thanks for telling me about this. I always wondered what happened to Glenn and Wendi. I'm gonna look them up. I'll look up the other Lost Dogs, too. Come see me after the show. We can get together and talk music soon."

Jerry caught back up to the others.

"What was that about?" Emily asked. "Did I hear you say something about a secret?"

"Oh, nothing," Jerry said. "That guy had some interesting information about some other music that I should hear. He says there's another band out there called the Lost Dogs. We should have looked that up I guess."

They went out front and continued their tour of the rest of Bonnaroo.

"Now listen," Jerry said, unable to restrain his latent paternal instincts. "There's a lot of crazy stuff going on here. Most of the people here are very friendly, for sure. But some folks are using a lot of drugs. You'll see some kids wearing some weird clothes, or maybe no clothes. We saw a girl earlier who just had body paint on. You gotta keep your head on straight here and realize that there are all kinds of people in the world, and every one of them is trying to find their tribe. Some just use some pretty dangerous ways to do it. We can love them, without always doing what they do. Right kids?"

Emily understood what he was getting at. Just because he was playing at Bonnaroo, he wasn't endorsing all of the behavior. Smart.

Showtime.

The temperature on the stage was a blistering ninety-eight degrees with a relative humidity that Jamie estimated to be "somewhere north of two feet up an elephant's trunk." Everyone had sweat through their clothes before the show had even started.

But spirits were high. Everyone was in place. The line check was finished. Everything was ready. Considering they had over twenty musicians onstage, and more in the wings, that was a minor miracle in itself. The entire group of musicians and crew had gathered for what could only be described as a combination pep talk and prayer meeting. With all hearts and minds clear, they had gone to their stations.

Nadia had built herself a little work space onstage left, near the monitor mix. She had quite a few management duties to take care of but was also going to be center stage at some point, reciting a poem and explaining some of the future plans. She needed to be able to move around without tripping or falling up or down any stairs. Jerry had a momentary panic attack thinking of her walking right off the edge of the stage, so he had a private conversation with a few of the stagehands to make sure they understood her visual limitations.

Because they were starting at six o'clock, the sun was still up, so they wouldn't have the advantage of dramatic stage lighting. But that's not what this day was about. By the end of their set the lights would be more noticeable. Their main concern was that people would be able to hear the music, sing along, and follow Brother Louis. This was, hopefully, going to be like no other "show" these people had ever seen.

The announcer was out onstage promoting various things, delivering safety messages, and reminding people to hydrate. The musicians were in place, constantly checking tuning due to the heat and catching each other's eyes for encouraging glances. At one point, Alex, who seemed to be standing uncomfortably far from Jerry on a stage this big, made his way over to his neighbor and mentor and gave him the biggest hug he had ever given another man in his life.

"I don't even know what to say," Alex said. "But I'd follow you anywhere, Jerry."

"I'll try not to lead you off the edge of the stage then," Jerry quipped. "It's quite a fall."

After that obligatory joke, Jerry thought better of it. He looked back over at Alex, caught his eye, and said, "You did this!" And then, "Thank you."

Alex shook his head and smiled.

Although the MC's voice was hard to make out as it bounced around the stage, they could tell he was talking about the unlikely story of three senior citizens and two soon-to-graduate college students, and a flock of neighborhood friends gathering in a garage, and then a park, to sing inspirational songs that combined genres, and about how the story had caught the attention of people around the world and that Bonnaroo was lucky to have them for their festival debut. Eventually, they heard their introduction, as Nadia had instructed it to be read.

"Brothers and sisters, please clear your throats and hearts, and howl along with the Lost Dogs of East Nashville!"

The crowd response was deafening and disorienting. For a few seconds Jerry forgot that he was supposed to start the first song. He heard the shuffling brushes on the snare, and Jamie shout out, "You with me Jerry?" and snapped out of it. His fingers found the shape of a G chord and he started strumming.

"Hello y'all," Louis said. "We thought Bonnaroo might like this song. We've never done this one, but Jerry taught it to us this week. Would you sing with us?" As the band kicked in, tens of thousands recognized that it was the Grateful Dead's "Ripple" and the cheering was back.

With a voice that sounded more like Stevie Wonder than Jerry Garcia, Louis delivered the lines. *Reach out your hand if your cup be empty…*

The crowd was already singing along. So far so good.

The band found a sweet spot to groove, adding a distinctive R & B undertone to the bluegrass-rooted Dead song. They found the zone, inhabited it, and owned it. The musical invitation had been made, and eighty thousand fans accepted it.

They allowed "Ripple" to end cleanly, before the bass and drums slid into a riff that everyone was familiar with. Knowing that hundreds of thousands of people, and perhaps most of the Bonnaroo crowd, had already watched his "Ain't No Sunshine" sermon from the benefit show, Louis kept the commentary simple this time. As the band played the familiar groove, he stared out over the sea of faces and held his hand up to them.

"Whatever you are missing—be it peace, grace, mercy, hope—whatever it is—I pray that you find her, for she is not far from those who seek her. And I know you know what I mean when I say… *'There ain't no sunshine when she's gone…'*"

Although there was a lot of applause, what was even louder were the voices of the people in the crowd who knew what was coming and were ready. They were singing along from the first note. At times, the audience was significantly louder than the band. Even with his in-ear monitors, Louis was becoming disoriented. As the famous bridge was approaching, he had an idea. He made his way down the gangway, into the middle of the crowd, just in time. And as they sang, he held the microphone out and surrendered to them.

"I know, I know, I know…"

It was electrifying. The band was locked in. The extra musicians were right in the pocket. They brought Cesar out to the gangway for "Peace to the Neighborhood" and threw a little bit of "La Bamba" in as a surprise for him at the end.

After a playful, but surprisingly effective, acoustic version of "All Together Now" that Kyle came out and led and the gospel choir joined in on, they mashed it right into the reggae feel of Van Morrison's "Whenever God Shines His Light" and then Bob Marley's "Could You Be Loved." B-Flat stepped forward for lead vocals on that one and knocked everyone out.

Next, Louis tore hearts wide open with a blistering version of Solomon Burke's "None of Us Are Free." The slow-burn groove from the band took on a fascinating dimension as Cesar replaced the traditional gospel B3 organ parts with his accordion, and Jerry found an acoustic part that added just a touch of country twang to the blues riffing. The choir stayed onstage and improvised backing vocals.

And after what was supposed to be the final chorus, Louis signaled for the band to keep playing but to bring it down. He had something to say.

"Brothers and sisters, I don't think I risk anything standing out in front of you tonight, saying that 'none of us are free if one of us are chained,' do I? You all agree with me, don't you?"

The crowd roared in agreement.

"Then I don't understand!" he practically shouted. "If there are eighty thousand of us here right now, singing in unity, saying that none of us are free if one is chained, and yet we are in the midst of millions of people in all kinds of chains—what does that mean? Am I a hypocrite? Are you?"

The crowd's cheers began to subside.

"We can say this stuff until we are blue in the face, family," he continued, a tone of lament taking over his voice. "But if we aren't going to *do* anything about it, it would be better for us to just shut the hell up and admit that we don't give a damn!"

The band was doing their best to follow his lead, to accentuate what he was saying, but he was way out on the gangway and they could barely follow him visually. This was all happening by feel now.

"We don't give a damn about the powers that keep people locked in poverty or the wasted young Black and Brown minds walking the streets of this country. We don't give a damn about the women being bought and sold for their bodies and the pleasure they can give wicked men. We don't give a damn about the lies that come from our leaders and the corruption that leads to generational bondage. No, if a group like this gave a damn, I'm telling you, something would be different tonight!"

Now the cheers began to cascade once again.

"I'm tired of singing canned songs and greeting my neighbors with empty platitudes. Are you ready to join us and make some real changes in this world, family?"

The crowd roared.

"Then let's sing this one more time and realize that some chains are obvious and others are invisible. Love demands that we lay our lives down for our neighbor until they are free from all chains. That's the world I'm looking for. Is that the world you're looking for?"

More roaring from the crowd in agreement.

"Then let's go find it together! *None of us are free if one of is chained.*'"

He repeated the line as the band faded out. Then Michael came in with a new piano riff.

"Family," Louis said. "This here thing we're doing is not really a 'band,' you understand. It never really was. This is a gathering of friends. It started in brother Jerry's garage over in East Nashville a few months ago. And you know what? I gotta tell you folks…I have to admit to you right now to all your thousands of faces, that I lived two blocks from that man for forty years and I never met him! Never once."

He moved over to Cesar. "And this fine gentleman is Mr. Cesar Jimenez!"

The crowd cheered.

"Cesar lives just a few blocks away—on the other side of Gallatin Road. He's lived there for decades. And you know what? I never met him before, either. And I'm a pretty friendly guy, folks! I really am!

"But I never met these brothers. Why is that? I think it's because we stay in our racial and cultural lanes. I see Jerry and he looks different than me. Cesar sees me and I look different than him. We eat slightly different food. We listen to different music."

Louis pulled Cesar over to his right and pulled Jerry over to his left so that the three of them were together in the middle of the stage.

"Family, if three old men like us, all set in our ways and full of habits and fears, can get over ourselves, then I bet y'all can!"

The crowd erupted again.

"You might need some young people like we did, but you can do it. We want you to do it. We're nothing special, I guarantee you that. At least no more special than you all are. We just felt the hand of Love pulling us together and decided, for once in our lives, not to fight it!"

The band was still riffing in A minor.

"So no," Louis continued. "This ain't no real band. This is like a block party that's just gotten way outta hand!"

Everyone onstage cracked up at that.

"Well, we have another friend who's going to come out and sing this next song. We hope that's okay. Is it okay if Brother Louis takes a little breather and a young lady from East Nashville takes a tune with the band?"

The crowd clapped but seemed like they would rather listen to Louis forever.

"Okay, family, please welcome our little sister Cheryl Spree."

And with that, Bonnaroo exploded. The crowd roared for several minutes, as Cheryl worked to calm them down. "Thank you. I got something to say, y'all…"

Eventually the roar subsided enough for her to speak.

"I heard this song a while ago, and I think the original is maybe a prayer for help from a junkie, but when I heard it, I thought about Nashville. This is *my* prayer for my city, and for myself."

They played the Rolling Stones' "Shine a Light." Cheryl delivered one of the most blistering performances ever seen on a Bonnaroo—or any other—stage. The lyric became a true prayer of supplication. She left it all on the stage. When she was done, she moved back and joined the choir for the rest of the set.

Then it was time for Jerry and Nadia's moment.

Jerry started playing the now-familiar chords for what had become known as "Marianne's Song," and the crowd cheered with recognition.

"Thank you so much," Jerry said humbly. "It's amazing to me that this little song has touched so many people after all this time."

The band had faded in behind him. The extra guitar players were able to pick up some of the more complicated parts so Jerry could say what he needed to say without worrying about messing up.

"Some of you know that I started writing this song as a sort of lullaby for my baby girl many years ago during some pretty dark times for me. When this group came together, this song became a sort of prayer for her and her brother—and that maybe somehow I'd be able to let them know how much I love them and how sorry I am for the failure I was as a father for them."

Jerry cut himself off and pulled away from the mic before breaking up too much. He took a breath, swallowed, and moved back into position. "I'm so happy to tell you all, that those prayers have begun to be answered."

The crowd started to cheer.

"I sat down with her and her brother, just a few days ago. It was as hard a thing as any of us had ever done. But we made it through our first conversation in almost fifty years."

The crowd erupted yet again.

"And here's the thing." Jerry tried to calm things back down. "I know that for some of you, reconciliation with the people who have hurt you, or the people you have hurt, is not possible. But for some of you it is. But regardless of that, one thing I am learning is that I will never find peace outside of myself—and I believe that we as a community will not see the kind of reconciliation we crave—until we find peace with ourselves. And like Brother Louis says, that kind of peace doesn't come from just tolerating our pain and our self-destruction. It's something deeper and truer than that. I needed good, close friends in order to find it. So anyway, thank you for your prayers. Here's a song for both of my kids. I call it "I'm Right Here" now.

Jerry turned to face Alex and, for at least a few lines, was able to tune everything out other than the simplicity of what they played together that first time they pushed their way into his house. He glanced over his left shoulder at Jamie and saw wet eyes behind the drums, too.

As that song came close to its end, it resolved into a new arrangement and a new chord progression emerged.

"I'd like to introduce you all to a very special woman. She's the glue that has kept all of the details behind this project running, but she is also a poet and thinker who has helped to guide us. She helped me finish this next song, but I wanted her to come out here and share a poem that she wrote for you and to tell you about a few things this group will be doing starting tonight. Ladies and gentlemen, Nadia Morton."

Nadia came to the microphone as the band continued to play, and a DJ joined in with some subtle beats and record scratching.

"Thank you, everyone. What a beautiful time we are having together, right?"

Again, applause.

"Like Jerry said, I do have something that I wrote for tonight, but before I share that, the group has asked me to be the one to share some news with you."

Louis made his way over to her side and put his arm around her shoulder in an authentic show of solidarity.

"As you heard before," she continued. "This is the first major concert we have ever given. And it has been amazing. What will hopefully make it even more amazing, though, is that it will also be our last."

The shock from the crowd was obvious. Shouts of "No!" and "boo" could be heard rising.

"Let me explain, and I think you'll see what I mean about this being good news. Like Louis said, this really is a block party. These are neighborhood friends. They felt a hunger for something more authentic and real than the packaged, processed, filtered music on the radio, and the segregation and division and silos being consciously or subconsciously enforced and reinforced through our social media. So, they got together in person and started making music. In doing so, they found common ground. They found a shared language. They found a love for each other and for their neighbors. And then it turned out, obviously, that a lot more of us felt that same hunger."

She glanced back at the band as the cheering continued.

"But instead of doing what they did—getting together and making music and having conversations and building community—most of us did what we have been trained to do. We consumed what they were making. We found it online or we attended their events. And as a result, while this thing has grown—and we are so honored and excited about that—we fear that it is losing the essence of what made it so special in the first place.

"We didn't even know if we should play here, to tell you the truth. Not because it's not amazing—because obviously it is, and obviously you are— but because we wondered if this would put us on a path that would lead us away from our true calling and purpose. But then we got an idea.

"So right now, we are streaming this online, and we are issuing a press release at this very moment. I just got a message that over four hundred thousand people are streaming this around the world, and that number is growing!"

More applause rocked the area.

"The good news is that we have finished a new album!"

Major applause—the crowd seemed to have an infinite amount of energy for this show.

"This album, produced by our good friend Michael Thomas, has twenty songs on it—including recordings from the garage sets, the event in the park, and the benefit show. Plus, we cut two songs in the studio. And the whole album is being released right now, for free! You can have it as our gift. If you want to donate anything for it, all money is going into a fund that will provide resources like music lessons, concerts, and instruments for low-income families in Nashville and beyond. None of us are taking a penny!

"Oh," she continued. "We are taking orders for vinyl, too. That is being pressed right now. And tonight's show is being recorded and will be released as both an audio and a video piece.

"But we are even more excited about the launch of our new website, which just went live at the beginning of tonight's show. The purpose of this website is to provide resources and help for anyone who wants to start a community group like the one Jerry, Alex, and Jamie started that led to all of this. We already have several such groups around Nashville. The website will be a place where people can find support materials, occasional live stream seminars, and even chord charts and arrangements if you want those kinds of things. It will also serve as a gathering place for these smaller communities so that occasionally we can do larger things together. We are already planning future benefit concerts, work projects, and even an international music trip this fall!"

The website was being displayed on the massive video wall. The crowd was getting into this whole thing.

"And lastly, the name Lost Dogs of East Nashville evolved because of the commonality of dogs being lost and the community coming together to find them after the tornadoes years ago. It was an apt metaphor, we thought. I worked it into a poem and people just sort of adopted it. But this movement is much bigger than just East Nashville. We wanted to find a name that reflected that expansiveness and the diversity that we are hoping to achieve.

"With that in mind, we are thrilled to announce the new name of this organization—this movement. We—all of us—are now Lost Perros!"

Right then, a new logo for LostPerros.com appeared on the screen and the crowd cheered again.

"So please, follow us online, join our movement. Start a Lost Perros group in your neighborhood. Sing with your neighbors. Talk with your neighbors. Pray with your neighbors. Until all of us lost dogs find our way back to the porch!"

The crowd broke out, once again, in an uproar.

The band took the music up a notch and Jerry nodded at Nadia. It was time. The DJ's scratching elements got a bump in the mix, and as the crowd settled in for the next song, Nadia braced herself, and then delivered her latest poem:

"Untouched by Rust"

Must growth come with scale?

What about the roots

What about the mustard seed

The kernel that must fall and be crushed?

Today we grow by shrinking

We expand within

Wither in the eye

But we do not die—Our voice is not hushed

Today we conquer by kneeling

Win by feeling

The closeness of breath

Brothers and sisters—words unrushed

Today our power is not in number

But intention

Through invention

And our treasure—is untouched

By rust

As the last line was being spoken, the band kicked off the opening riff of "I'll Take You There," and the crowd lost it again. Louis echoed what Nadia had said, referenced Dr. King's Beloved Community, and reiterated his call to action.

"I hope this has been an evening that stirred something in you," he said. "I hope we have provoked your hunger for justice and honor and goodness and all of the good things that God wants for all of us. And if we can imagine those things, and we are willing to submit to the idea that we are not God—and that our brothers and sisters are worth loving—I believe we can find that beautiful country. Are you with me?"

The crowd was definitely with him.

"Then come along and I'll take you there."

The crowd demanded an encore, and this time the band was ready. In fact, they had budgeted their allotted set time to allow for an extended encore. It was their final show, after all. They tore through raucous and celebratory versions of Wilson Pickett's "Believe I'll Run On," Dylan's "Serve Somebody," Stevie's "Have a Talk with God," and particularly fun romps through Cash's "The Man Comes Around" and Petty's "Won't Back Down."

The final song of the night was a hymnlike crowd-lead version of "I Shall Be Released."

Louis sent them off with a final benediction. "This has been incredible, my family. Now, go and do likewise. We hand this mission to you! Go find your neighbors. Learn their stories. Sing their songs. Instead of one band with eighty thousand listeners, let's have eighty thousand bands with one Listener—that good, great, beautiful Hand that formed us, that loves us, that suffered for us, and that calls us all back home. Amen?"

And the gathered throng, along with hundreds of thousands more online said, "Amen!"

When they finally left the stage, the scene backstage was absolute mayhem. Nadia had arranged for Louis, Jerry, and Cesar to take questions from a few members of the media. They took some photos and drank copious amounts of water. Emily and her friends enjoyed the revelry, and despite the fact that Jerry was sweaty, old, and gross, Emily gave him a big hug. Hundreds of phone photos were taken—and that was before they even left the backstage area.

The event's headliners found them and invited them to come up onstage for a second encore. They said they'd see if they could make it work, but they were already getting used to the idea of being off the stage and liked it.

Jack came up to Nadia and Jerry with good news. "These numbers are insane! Just since the end of the show, over two thousand people around the country have signed up for one of the online classes about how to spark community through music of their own. Forty thousand people have registered on the new portal, and over three hundred thousand have already downloaded the new album." Jack handed an iPad to Nadia with one of the charts displayed. "This is definitely a movement."

Rolling Stone sent a text asking if one of their on-site reporters at Bonnaroo could talk with Louis for a cover story. The idea that a group would intentionally walk away from this kind of hype in order to inspire people to start garage bands was just unfathomable to them. Louis agreed, on the condition that the artwork for the cover be a montage of dozens of small pictures of neighborhood groups instead of him. "I mean, you can have our band be one of the pictures," he added, "as long as it's no bigger than all the others." The editor loved the idea.

Nadia grabbed Jerry's hand. "Would you walk me to the bus for a minute?" When they got to the door, she turned and laid a kiss on him that shocked him good. "I'm tired of waiting for you to work up the courage, you big coward," she teased.

"Well, okay, then," Jerry said with eyes wide. "Is there anything else I can do for you?"

"Yes, actually. We should get married."

"We should?"

"Of course we should! Are you stupid?" she asked, with no intention of waiting for an answer. She kissed him again.

"Okay. I'd love to marry you."

"I know." She took his hand and tried to lead him back to the others, then tripped on a power cable.

"How about I lead now?" Jerry said.

"Fine, you old smartass."

Three months later, Susan was at her home, looking at an invitation to Jerry and Nadia's wedding. It would be happening in just a couple hours. Joe walked into the family room and saw her staring at it.

"That's today, isn't it?" he asked.

"Yes," she said coldly. "Seems pretty soon to be marrying someone, I say."

"Well, I keep hearing that seventy is the perfect age to start dating."

"Shut up!" She tossed the wadded-up invitation at him. Joe ducked out of the family room and headed into the kitchen.

Susan saw a new record leaning against the old record player. "Were you listening to this?"

"Yeah. It's really good. But I didn't want to upset you, so I only listen when you're not here."

"Oh, give me a break," she said. "I'm not a child. It's just a record."

She took the record out of the sleeve, placed it on the turntable, and pulled the lever to start the machine. The stylus moved into position and the needle set down on the disc. The music that came through was warm, rich, and full. It was "Marianne's Song."

Susan listened through the song, looking at the photos throughout the LP jacket. It was covered in pictures of people smiling, singing together, and sharing coffee.

Jerry's fractured voice came in:

Oh sweet Marianne
Breathe it out and breathe it in
Don't be afraid – There's nothing to fear
You're not alone
I'm not much, I know
But I'm right here

She let the song play and heard the first verse. She had never heard this section before and realized this must be the part Jerry had written recently. The vocal was not perfect by any means. She could tell the voice belonged to an old man and realized it must be Jerry actually singing.

Many the voices—many the choices
That told us who we are
Running on fumes—living in ruins
Loving from afar
There is a sound that's calling us home
Back to the light in the dark
Where we find our names
Trade beauty for chains
And hearts that carry the scars…

As the chorus came back around Susan relented. "Oh fine!" she said and got up. She started talking to Joe before she made it into the kitchen. "Let's just go to the dadgum wedding thing," she said nastily. "Let me just get—"

When she got to the kitchen Joe was already standing there with his coat on, her coat in his hands, and his keys and the crumpled invitation in hand.

"Smartass," she said. "You're a total smartass."

"I love you too," Joe said.

Coda

Fall – The Next Year

"Have you heard anything from her?" Nadia asked Jerry as they walked up the sidewalk to Cesar's patio entrance. Jerry's limp was still obvious, but Nadia called him her favorite walking stick anyway. "Any idea if they'll come?"

"Not a word," Jerry said with a definite note of resignation in his voice. "I sent her the invitation and the address, and, like usual, she said she'll 'see what she can do.' I just don't think she's interested. Jack isn't going to push her, and I don't want him to." Jerry had his old photo album under his left arm and his right arm out for Nadia to hold on to.

"Well that's frustrating." She squeezed his arm a little harder in empathy. "You've done everything you can, honey."

It had been just over a year since the big Bonnaroo gig, and the crew had agreed to grant a group interview to Marisol Knudsen, the young blogger-turned-journalist who had initially written about them after the benefit show. She had turned her earlier interviews into an e-book that had reached thousands, and now she had been assigned to write a feature about the ongoing impact of the events surrounding Lost Perros for a national publication that worked to explore the intersection of faith and social justice. The Dogs thought that was as good a cause as any to break their relative media silence.

"It's not really a 'media silence,'" Louis corrected, as Marisol began to set her recorder up in the middle of the table. "We just wanted to shift attention away from ourselves and onto the movement we were seeing around us."

"It worked, too," Alex added, settling into his seat. "When reporters couldn't get comments from us, they went to folks from the Community Center or some of the new neighborhood groups."

"But it's not like we're all that secretive." Louis poured himself some tea. "It's not that big of a deal, honestly."

The members of the original band, and various members of their extended families, had gathered at Cesar and Irma's house on a beautiful October Sunday. In truth, they made a habit of gathering at one home or another at least once a month, and this Sunday it just happened to be the Jimenezes' turn to host. Marisol had been invited to join them at noon for a conversation.

Jerry and Nadia settled at one end of the patio table, flanked by Alex and Jamie on their left, and Louis and Kelly on their right. Kyle Smith, Jerry's artist friend from his tour bus–driving days, had become very involved with the group; he sat next to the brothers, and George anchored the other end. Michael Thomas was sitting in a sort of second circle just outside of the main table, against one of the walls where an entire additional row was arranged. Cesar sat next to George and had a chair open for Irma, who was in the kitchen with a few others putting the finishing touches on lunch. The smell was wafting through the kitchen window. They all knew it would be delicious.

Once everyone was positioned and her recorder was ready, Marisol pressed Record and looked, almost reflexively, to Jerry. She noticed the book of photos in front of him on the table and remembered it from the porch. She hoped she might get a chance to peruse it before the day was over.

"Did you have any idea things would get as big as they got?" she asked.

"Are you kidding?" Jerry replied, and everyone laughed. "Not only did I not know that, but if I had known that, I almost certainly would not have risked it. This whole thing goes against so many of my instincts. No."

He pointed to the young man to his left. "Thank God I had no clue what would happen if I accepted Alex's invitation to play some music with him and his brother."

Turning to Alex, Marisol continued. "How did the hype and excitement of the Bonnaroo show impact your life?"

"Wow." Alex drew out the word as a way to buy himself a few seconds of reflection time. "I honestly don't know that the hype or the big show impacted my life nearly as much as the time I have gotten to spend with these people."

"Absolutely," Jamie agreed as everyone in the circle made gestures and sounds of both agreement and humility.

"I mean, we had played a few big gigs before—and we've backed up some big artists since. We've played on some records with some amazing musicians. We've seen hype before. Don't get me wrong, it's fun."

"Super fun," Jamie said.

"But it's like a sugar high that passes in minutes. Playing music with these people, and having conversations with them, eating meals with them, just being around them, has changed my life in a profound way," Alex confessed.

"Has it influenced you as a musician?" she asked.

"Of course, it has," Alex continued. "For one thing, playing with a guitarist like Jerry opened me up to different ideas from his side of the world, but then Cesar and Louis bring me into different places. The songs they introduced me to—and keep introducing me to—just keep expanding my vocabulary, you know? You learn a lot in music school. It's a fantastic place. We became adept at theory and discipline, but music is a language and this family has expanded our vocabulary well beyond our years. And then there's also the fact that this whole story created a slew of new relationships, which led to new opportunities for session work and live work."

"We graduated from college right around the time of that show," Jamie added. "We've stayed busy with session work, live gigs, maybe some lessons, and side-hustle things like driving for a ride-share service. That's not something most graduates can say. We've just tried to keep our costs low and keep ourselves available."

Alex sarcastically lamented, "If the rent just wasn't so damn high," and everyone laughed.

"Hey now," Louis interjected. "Don't you go givin' me no grief about the rent," he said with a smile. "You know you boys are getting a good deal. I could make a heap more money off the tourists!"

Jerry intervened with an explanation. "Shortly after they graduated, Alex and Jamie started thinking about getting a place of their own."

"Our mom said we had to move out!" Jamie clarified. "She wanted to be able to hear her TV shows instead of our music for a change."

Jerry continued. "One day they saw 'The University' up there at Louis's place. He turned his third floor into an Airbnb suite and had been renting it out like crazy. Well, they decided they needed more Louis in their lives, so they talked him into letting them rent it long term."

"I took a pay cut for sure," Louis added, "but it's fun having those boys up there. They keep me young."

"And we've gotten Louis for more than a few vocal sessions, too," Alex added.

"All kidding aside," Jamie added, "we love being close to them but still being a couple blocks from Jerry and home. We'll probably have to move away some day, but for now this feels right."

"Plus," Louis said, "those two are always over at the Community Center giving people lessons and whatnot. They give me hope for the next generation."

Knowing from her research that Nadia had been managing a lot of the details around the programs at the Community Center, Marisol looked her way. "Can you tell us about the launch of the various programs through Lost Perros, Nadia?"

"Sure. What's been most amazing is how enthusiastically the community came forward to help with this. I'd say that the current slate of activities is about 80 percent bigger than anything we had imagined, and that's because we have gladly handed things over to others. We've seen people step forward to offer private and group lessons in voice, piano, guitar, drums, bass, songwriting, production, and dance. We've started a new community choir and have volunteers going into almost all of the local schools with art appreciation programs, Introduction to Music History experiences, and several different camps and such. The talent and expertise was all right here, it just needed to be catalyzed."

"We also found out about a lot of different people who were already doing amazing things," Jerry added. "They had just never gotten any attention on any kind of larger scale. We have been able to leverage our platform to give those awesome programs some lift."

"There's one family right over here by my house," Cesar said, "who moved on to a pretty rough street many years ago, just so they could be a positive presence here. They have programs for children and have even helped neighborhood kids get to college. Because we were on the news, these kinds of people have found us and then we helped get them more support. Now I can go over and show kids my accordion or how to play harmonica. Sometimes we just watch movies and talk about them. I never even knew about those people!"

Nadia nodded. "I'm obviously the newbie to this neighborhood, but I've definitely had doors open because of that experience. I'm leading a writing workshop and hosting a book group once a week. Most of the young people around here are not from here. I'm sure it's not good for my vanity, but it's nice to have these kids see me as a source of wisdom or potentially valuable information and skill, and not just as a pathetic old gal sitting in God's waiting room."

"Tell her about your country cut," Michael chimed in from the side.

"Yes! Please do," Marisol agreed.

"Oh, that." She almost waved the suggestion off.

"Cheryl and I got together to write a song at Jerry's place just before he and I got married last summer. When she got there, Jerry had been playing an old Patsy Cline record for me. He kind of went off about these young country artists name-checking the classics as if that gave them credibility."

"It just bugs me that they love to talk about Johnny Cash, but they don't seem the slightest bit influenced by his music or his ethic," Jerry interrupted before Nadia's hand on his knee calmed him back down and he relented.

"Well," she continued, "Cheryl resonated with that. Those artists were favorites of her late mother's. We talked about that loss, and a tattoo that she had gotten, and some other stories. We ended up writing a song called 'Ghost in the Needle' that she put on her new album. It's not a single or anything, but it was fun to hear her record a song that I cowrote."

"It's a fan favorite at shows," Jerry added—clearly proud. "She plays it every night, and millions have streamed it online. It's a great song."

"It is rewarding to feel useful," Nadia added.

"I think that's the main thing," Louis said. "This whole experience has felt ordained. It feels, to me anyway, like this was going to happen whether we were involved or not. We just said 'yes' and got to be a part of it."

"And Kyle." Marisol turned her attention his way. "Your career seems to have taken a significant turn since getting involved in all of this. What was your role here?"

Kyle looked genuinely surprised at being called on, since he had never considered himself part of the original "crew." He was just here for the lunch. "Uh, I did play at the benefit show in the park, and in the band at the Bonnaroo show, but my real involvement kicked in later. I moved back to Nashville to help with some of the workshops and stuff, and to revive my own music. I was out of the whole Christian music industry, and I'd lost interest in the worship music I was hearing. But when I played at that benefit show, I connected with a good number of folks who had been fans of mine back in the day but had kind of out-grown the old-style Christian music themselves. They were interested in music that dealt with spiritual ideas and asked tough questions, though. That was inspiring. I started writing again, and I've been releasing some new stuff. It's nowhere near as big as it was back in the day, but it doesn't need to be. I'm trying to make sense of the craziness in the world, especially how divided things have gotten over the last year. Like Alex said, I keep the overhead low and try to be productive. I've got high hopes for the future."

"His music is excellent," Jerry added. "And he's going to be a great producer and mentor for the next generation of kids coming up."

"Thanks, Jerry," Kyle said. "And no, I'm not upset about having to move out of the guest room, Nadia!" That got a chuckle from the table, too. Nadia blushed a bit.

"You have to admit that it was something special that you all did here, right?" Marisol asked Jerry.

"Look." He glanced down at his right hand clasping Nadia's. "Louis said it better than I could, but yes—something special happened here. And yes, we did some stuff. And we are still doing stuff. But when I think back to all those years of Louis driving that trolley it upsets me. What a waste! This brilliant engineer, who could build the trolley *and* the road, relegated to the role of a driver because the good people of the Bible Belt, people like me, just couldn't see past his skin. He didn't let that make him bitter, though. He served and loved as best he could. Then when God had had just about enough of seeing that talent sidelined, he was practically forced into the game."

"And Cesar," Jerry continued. "Most of us see men like him and think we have them figured out in seconds flat. This guy is a giant! He has stories that would blow your mind. And his heart for his community is massive. There's a lot more going on here than we think. And when we fail to hear those stories and those songs, we lose out. It's our loss."

Jerry was starting to get a little bit upset.

"It's not that I wasn't bitter, you know," Louis said. "I just buried it deep. I was very angry. I had given up. And now I think the reason I didn't want to sing was because I knew how hard it was to have the world reject my mind. I didn't think I could bear it if it rejected my soul."

That one left the table silent for a few seconds.

"I was limited by my *own* mistakes," Jerry said. "I had healing and growing to do, and forgiveness to seek." He thought about Jack and Marianne. "And I still do! But that was all based on my bad choices. I have not had the deck stacked against me the way others have. I am learning so much about grace from these men and women, and more that I meet along the way. It's just a tragedy that it took so long for this to come together."

"But here we are," Cesar said, lightening the tone considerably. "Maybe late but here. I know I look old, but I swear to you that it feels like yesterday I was playing in Laredo. Now I understand what Father Constance was talking about. And I don't want our young people to wait so long to feel this. We need to do better—especially us men—about sharing these gifts. God knows we will always be terrible at talking about our feelings, but maybe music, or painting, or films, or sculpture can help us help them do it."

"That's amazing," Marisol said, not seeming to know where to take this conversation. It had gotten away from her. She was riding it like a stream now.

"Do you have any idea how these things have resonated outside of Nashville?" she asked no one in particular.

"A bit," Nadia said, "but again, we're not trying to control it. We raised enough money to launch the website and to seed the local community programs, and then we saw donations begin to come in. So nationally we've heard of hundreds of neighborhood groups launching. Some are a lot like the one these guys started; they focus on music. Others use film discussions as an excuse to gather, or roasting coffee, or baking bread, or brewing beer. There's a group outside of Chicago that builds kayaks together. It's fantastic! Locally we have several dozen small groups, and we all get together sometimes for larger gatherings."

"That's so cool," Marisol added. "I'd like to find someone who can mentor me as a writer."

"I bet we can find someone," Michael added with a smile, pointing at Nadia.

"It might seem like a cliché," Nadia continued, "or maybe too obvious, but I think that if we were to scroll through many people's Instagram feeds or their Facebook walls, or if we looked at the way many young artists present themselves, we'd see people with a hunger for something older than themselves. They use filters to make their crisp digital photos look older and more analog. They wear clothes from a century ago and prefer to listen to music on vinyl. Why is that? I think, at least in part, it's because they are longing to connect to something that was here before they were and will probably be here when they are gone."

As if on cue, Louis said. "And people our age are no better. Look at us with our plastic surgery and our sports cars. We want to be younger so badly—and they want to be older. We need each other. And we're right here. We just need to get out of our virtual spaces and get somewhere real."

"I remember when I was a genius nineteen-year-old." Nadia joked. "I used to have people all broken down into types. I could judge you and define you and compartmentalize you in no time flat. Now I've come to realize that we all have each of those types of people inside of us. We can be oblivious, or we can be idealists. We can be nihilists, or we can be servants. The question is, which ones will take over?"

"Sitting Bull said we each have two dogs in us," Jerry added, "a good one and a bad one, and they compete to be our guide. At the end of the day, the dog that wins is the one we feed. I've always loved that analogy. Every day we decide which dog to feed: whether it's our negative, angry, fear-based impulses, or our selfless, serving, gracious commitments. I need people around me to help me feed the right dog."

"Have you seen measurable results in terms of improved relationships between people of different ethnic backgrounds as a result of all of this?" Marisol asked Jerry.

"All I can say for sure is that this has changed me, and I'm pretty sure Alex and Jamie would agree."

They nodded eagerly.

"But honestly," Jerry continued, "it's hard to say how deep and sustained the impact of a concert, or even a few concerts, might be. At best, I suspect, those events caused people to get to know each other and to see each other up close, instead of either from a distance or from the silos we get into culturally. I mean, we didn't invent this music, for crying out loud. We just rediscovered colors and sounds that had been laid out there for us by people long ago. What changed me was spending time with Louis and Cesar and these boys. I was not what anyone would call a flagrant 'racist,' you know. I think I was a pretty decent guy, but it took a tornado to introduce me to my neighbors!"

Everyone laughed, but his point landed.

"And I might get some respect for this work online, and in the street," Jerry continued, "but for all my trying, I still can't connect with my own daughter. We've spoken now, but it's been a year and I'm just not able to bridge the gap with her. So yeah, I'd say there are some measurable results, but I still haven't found what I was personally looking for."

George, who had determined to let the others do the speaking, finally decided to chime in. "I wholeheartedly concur with my good brother Jerry. And while the music is the dynamic and obviously explosive aspect of this adventure, the big crowds and the media coverage might seem like the main story. But I think for those of us at the center of it, it's not. That stuff is like the kindling at the beginning of a fire. It burns fast and bright and the flames are exciting, but if your goal is to start a fire that will provide heat and light for a long time, you'd better engineer it so by the time that kindling has been spent—the cameras are off and the social media attention has moved on to the next shiny object—the solid wood is burning nice and warm and slow. That's what I believe our sister Nadia helped to engineer, and that's what Jerry is talking about with the changed personal relationships around town."

"But do you think that it will move the needle when it comes to the deep racial divisions we see in the country or even in the church?" Marisol wondered aloud.

"Again," George said, "all we can talk about is what we see in our personal lives and our immediate stories. Yes, as a deacon, I have seen more White kids visit our church. That's great. Do they keep coming? Some do. Is it a problem that more don't? I don't think so. Every day, as I walk around town, I am greeted by more friends of all colors—and faiths—than ever before. And this is not just the typical Southern manners thing. These are people who know me and at least part of my story. That is a change. We have young White men giving music lessons to kids of all colors. Those kids will grow up with a different sense about their neighbors, other races, justice, and other issues because of these relationships—and those young men are having their hearts expanded because of their service."

"This isn't about being color blind," Jerry added. "Color blindness is a disability. We are a body, and we need all of our senses. We need to see everything, smell everything, hear everything, and taste everything. There is a way things should be, and it is broken. 'Justice' is about repairing that breach. We don't need Main Baptist to sound less Black." He smiled generously. "And we don't need First Presbyterian to sound less, uh, *European*." Everyone laughed at that one.

"Okay," Jerry said. "Maybe they could sound a little less European. But what we need is to meet each other in the street—with music that can connect us, if music is our thing, and then go hear and celebrate the sounds and flavors that make us unique. Then, listen to the stories behind those songs. Listen to the hurt and the joy. Fall in love with the people singing those songs. That will mess you up. Then, go back to your culture and work for justice from your side of the breach."

"So," Nadia interjected, "did this moment start ripples that will change the world? I suppose that's for someone else to determine. But everyone here knows that it has changed us, and we're pretty confident that it has changed our community. We believe that love and grace and mercy and wisdom will change anyone and any community that allows it to."

At that moment Irma and several others came through the door with steaming pans full of chilaquiles, grilled fish, fruits and vegetables, and homemade tortillas. Marisol turned the recorder off. "Thank you so much for your time. This has been incredible. I'll let you enjoy your meal."

"Oh no," Cesar said. "You're not going anywhere. You stay here with us for the feast."

Marisol was hoping for that invitation more than she had hoped for anything in a long, long time.

"Now." Cesar stood, embodying his role as the patriarch and host of the home. "Who would like to say the blessing over the food this time?" He looked in George's direction.

"YOU!" everyone at the table said simultaneously and then began laughing again.

"Me?" Cesar said. "I'm not good at these things. You sure?"

"Shut up and pray, Hector," Irma said, while the others smiled their "amens."

Nadia moved even closer to Jerry, putting both of her hands in his. Michael stood from his chair for some reason. Louis removed his hat and Kelly kissed him on the cheek. Irma stood next to Cesar and slipped her arm around his waist.

Cesar removed his sunglasses, and his hat, and bowed his head.

At that moment, the doorbell rang. Cesar's granddaughter Gabriella offered to go answer it so they could continue with the blessing.

On the front porch, Jack and Marianne stood nervously. "I'm not convinced, you know," Marianne told her brother. "I reserve the right to leave abruptly."

"Of course, you do," Jack answered. "I'd expect nothing less."

"Something smells good, though. Suddenly I'm starving."

"Me too," Jack replied. "We get some food, something to drink, say hello, chat for a little bit, and then hit the highway. No one gets hurt. It's just a meal. What's the big deal about a little food?"

At that moment, Gabriella opened the door. "Hello?" she said with a warm and welcoming smile.

"Hi. I'm Jack Wesley, and this is my sister, Marianne, and we were invited to have lunch here with Jerry and his friends. Is this the right address?"

"Oh yes," Gabriella said. "You're definitely in the right place."

Afterword

One month after I finished the final round of editing on this book, another round of tornados tore through East Nashville. The storms of March 2020 closely followed the path of the 1998 storms described in this story, and the community – though very different these 22 years later – came together precisely the same way. I have never been prouder to be a community member than I was immediately following the flood of 2010 and the tornados of 2020.

It seems like we all had hammers or garbage bags in our hands when the authorities told us to go home due to the Covid-19 pandemic. But the strange silence that then overtook our neighborhoods was often broken up by songs. We heard music playing in yards and garages everywhere. The hills of East Nashville came alive even as the streets went silent during those months. I have been thrilled to hear similar stories from people in Austin, Portland, Chicago, Miami, Dublin, Asheville, and more.

Although all of the characters in this story are fictitious, they are inspired by people I have known. Most are amalgamations of several friends I met around East Nashville or the wider Music City area. A few (like Cesar and Irma) came from folks we knew from our time in Illinois. So, even though these specific people don't exist – people like this do. They have inspired me, challenged me, and caused me to rethink music, the business, and even what church can be.

This book started with an oral story I told some friends on a camping trip. I then began to work on these characters and ideas, usually when given rare gifts of time away from my busy schedule provided opportunity for reflection and a different type of creativity. Once the main story came together, and I gathered the resources to hire an editor and treat this with the respect I believed it deserved, these characters started to feel like friends. My grandmother (Nadia is named after her) got to read an early copy. She called me very excitedly, saying that at one point she was very thrilled to think that her grandson could probably connect her with one of the characters in this book. She wanted me to introduce her to Father Mack! For a few minutes, she forgot that these people were not real. That was fun, to be sure, but it did stir some feelings about how much all of us – even my 98-year-old grandma – hunger for friends like these.

The good news is, people like this are everywhere. The more time I spend talking to my neighbors and not watching my television, the more likely I am to find them. Disasters tend to pull our community together. It's a sadly beautiful thing. The storms come. Lives are devastated. We drop our everyday routines, pick up shovels, make sandwiches, and look in on folks. Everyone is our presumed friend.

What if we didn't wait for the tornados to come?

Lost Perros Playlist

- *"Ain't No Sunshine" by Bill Withers*
- *"All Together Now" by the Beatles*
- *"And It Stoned Me" by Van Morrison*
- *"Another One Bites the Dust" by Queen*
- *"Believe I'll Run On" by Wilson Pickett*
- *"Come On, Let's Go" by Ritchie Valens*
- *"Could You Be Loved" by Bob Marley*
- *"Donna" by Ritchie Valens*
- *"Dream On" by Aerosmith*
- *"El Huracan del Valle" by Narcisco Martínez*
- *"Fish and Whistle" by John Prine*
- *"Free Fallin'" by Tom Petty*
- *"Golden Road" by Resurrection Band*
- *"Have a Talk with God" by Stevie Wonder*
- *"His Eye Is on the Sparrow"*
- *"I Am a Servant" by Larry Norman*
- *"If I Ever Needed Someone" by Van Morrison*
- *"I'll Take You There" by The Staples Singers*
- *"I'm a Good Loser" by Merle Haggard*
- *"I'm Free from the Chain Gang Now" by Johnny Cash*
- *"I Shall Be Released" by Bob Dylan*
- *"Kiko and the Lavender Moon" by Los Lobos*
- *"La Bamba" by Ritchie Valens*
- *"Living Years, The" by Mike and the Mechanics*
- *"Man Comes Around, The" by Johnny Cash*
- *"Neighborhood, The" by Los Lobos*
- *"None of Us Are Free" by Solomon Burke*
- *"Peace to the Neighborhood" by Pops Staples*
- *"Respect Yourself" by Staples Singers*
- *"Ripple" by Grateful Dead*
- *"Serve Somebody" by Bob Dylan*
- *"Shine a Light" by The Rolling Stones*

- *"Stand by Me" by Ben E. King*
- *"That's the Way God Planned It" by Billy Preston*
- *"This Is My Father's World"*
- *"Walking on Sunshine" by Katrina and the Waves*
- *"What's Going On" by Marvin Gaye*
- *"Whenever God Shines His Light" by Van Morrison*
- *"Won't Back Down" by Tom Petty*

Lost Perros Playlist

Inspiration Playlist

Acknowledgments and Thanks

It took a lot of help to get this story told. I am blessed to be surrounded by many people who encourage me in my creative pursuits and come running when I need a favor. Looking back on years of work, I see a remarkable parallel between the creative barn-raising depicted in these pages and the real-life collective energy that helped birth this project.

Thank you, Michelle Lynn Thompson, my wife and primary creative partner, for all the encouragement, space, and help with early drafts and character sketches. And to my kids, Jordan, Wesley (and Jess,) Trinity, and Jesse – and my grandkids, Sammy, Margot, and John. I love the music that flows from this family. Thanks also to my parents, Tom and Barbara Thompson, for their tangible and intangible support. The first draft, only pieces of which survived long enough to make it to the final cut (which I believe was only ever seen by them,) would not have been possible if they had not gifted me two different week-long getaways in various rural Tennessee cabins. Thank you to Grandma Holton for inspiring our family's welcoming spirit and being another of this tale's first readers. (And yes, I am happy to set up a meeting between you and Father Mack.) Much love and thanks always flow from my heart to my amazing extended family – all the aunts and uncles, cousins and brothers, nieces and nephews. Much of my love of all things Mexicana certainly goes back to the adopted Guadalajara branch of our family too. Thank you, Roberto, Martha, Barbie, Robert. And thank you, Elizabeth, for reading an early draft and giving your El Guero cousin some good advice!

The editorial team on this jam was second to none. My main man, Bruce Brown, was not only my first general editor and sounding board but also one of the strongest voices encouraging me that this was a story worth telling. Thank you, Bruce, for years of work together. You inspire me to dig deep and do my best, making me look better than I am. Thank you, Julee Schwarzburg, for several rounds of intensive editing and coaching. You are a master. And thank you, Randy Kerkman, for connecting me with Julee and spurring me on creatively for thirty-some years. Even though we could not work together on this book, I will always be indebted to Ramona Garnes, my lifetime editor. Ramona was my personal writing coach and teacher for many years, and I would certainly not be doing this without her. Thanks also to Mark Kelly Hall, Eddie DeGarmo, Casey McGinty, Gwen Moore, Rob Birks, and anyone else who read an early copy of the book and gave me feedback. And thank you, Dave Schroeder, for two years of work in the canyon. Thanks for your honest feedback, advocacy, and good advice. My grandfather may have never said, "Sometimes the second-best answer is a long, slow, 'no,'" but that doesn't make it untrue.

329

And thank you, Bradford Loomis, for working so many insane hours with Bruce and me on the audiobook. Your help coaching me through the narration and editing those massive chapters was invaluable. Thank you, Kreg Yingst, for the fantastic cover art. Andy Zipf, an amazing artist in his own right, did the cover design work and all of the graphic design elements for the Kickstarter campaign and video. Andy's moral support and encouragement kept me on track and moving forward at a critical time. Marc Ludena, one of my favorite visual artists and a former member of our band, did an incredible job with the interior design. My relatively newer brother from another mother, Randy Wilcox, designed the posters, T-shirts, mugs, and other swag. Randy – who also helps with all of the design for True Tunes—is also one of my strongest cheerleaders and encouragers.

Thank you, Dan Wheeler, for helping me finish "Sweet Marianne" when I felt stuck in a box in my head. And what can I say to the amazing Phil Keaggy? Wow. Your contribution to that song and our lives is invaluable. Thanks also to our long-time friend Steve Hindalong for keeping us honest and to Michelle for agreeing to sing along.

And then there's the fact that there is no way I could have afforded to do this without financial help. To everyone who contributed your funds, either through one of the crowdfunding platforms or by just handing me some money, those votes of confidence are literally why this book is now available. I would especially like to thank Christian Cryder, Andy Grenier, Michael Bartel, Brown Bannister, Casey McGinty, Mike Beidler, Brian Palmer, Father Chris Foley, Alan Gibson, Jason Hartong, Chris Hauser, Robert Klein, Rob Cassels, Dave Meredith, Gwen Moore, John Mulder, Kevin Niesen, Tracy Smith, Chris White, Carol Wilde, Ray Wilder, Steve Young, John Rewerts, Bruce Brown (again,) David Steunebrink, Carey Womack, Paul Scott, Brenda White, James Harrington, James O'Connell, Dave Dampier, Jeremy Gudauskas, Zach Bevill, Tom and Barbara Thompson (again,) Scott Hanson, Randy Wilcox, Dave Hart, and Steve Taylor. To the fifty people who backed the initial IndieGoGo campaign so I could hire an editor and really make this thing sing, THANK YOU for your patience. To the 205 who backed it on Kickstarter, I hope you feel warm, filled, and delighted with your investment. You've got my heart here.

Thank you to all of the places in and around East Nashville that let me sit and write for hours upon hours—and then agreed to let me put up posters to promote this thing. When you come to East Nashville, be sure to stop in and show your appreciation at Retrograde Coffee, Living Waters Brewing, East Nashville Beer Works, Vinyl Tap, Sip Coffee, Riverside Grillshack, The Groove, The Village Pub,

Ugly Mugs, Bongo Java, Mitchell Deli, Grimey's, Calf Killer Brewing in Sparta, and, of course, The Nashville Biscuit House! And thanks to Chuck Beard and the lasting impact of the community he built around East Side Story and East Side Storytelling.

Thank you to the authors and artists who have inspired me to kick at the darkness until it bleeds daylight. You do it for love and encourage me to breathe deep and chase the mystery myself. If I start listing musicians here, it will turn into another book. Still, I must thank the "real life" Lost Dog: — — Terry Scott Taylor, Michael Roe, Derri Daugherty, Steve Hindalong, and the late Gene Eugene. Their music, collectively as The Lost Dogs, with their various bands, and as solo artists, changes my life daily. Terry Taylor turned me on to the fantastic authors Robert Farrar Capon, Wendell Berry, and Frederick Buechner. In an industry too often defined by clicks, follows, and other artistically irrelevant metrics, you gents have inspired me since I was about 11 years old. This story is directly inspired by the passion, chemistry, and heart you put into your work. And to the real-life Glenn and Wendi Kaiser of Resurrection Band and Jesus People USA – thank you for taking me under your wing, being such great role models, and letting me imagine you in this story. To everyone else who helped make the Cornerstone Festival possible for 28 years of my life, this crazy, counter-cultural, community-obsessed fever dream is a direct result of the Jesus magic you facilitated every Summer between 1984 and 2012. I am honored to have been a small part of that bizarre miracle.

Lastly, thank you to the mentors who inspired me—and inspire me—to dare to imagine a world in which music is bigger than the biggest hits. David Bunker, Randy Schoof, Charlie Peacock, Steve Taylor, Rich Mullins, Glenn Kaiser, Mark Hollingsworth, Chris Hauser, Casey McGinty, and Buddy Miller; I hope you see your fingerprints in this rock and soul fable. And to the many "saints in the shadows" out there writing and singing far from any spotlights, or building kayaks with inner city kids, or volunteering in medical clinics in the Mexican desert, or to those using your gifts to touch the untouchable, love the unloveable, say the unpopular thing, speak truth to power, or otherwise get into good trouble, the One that matters sees and hears you. Keep it up.

FURTHER READING AND CONNECTION...

If you enjoyed this story, please tell your friends. It would also be extremely meaningful and helpful if you would subscribe to the email list at **LostPerros.com** or TrueTunes.com (it's the same list) so you can hear about future projects. We would also love to hear your thoughts about the book.

Please forward your friends and like-minded souls to LostPerros. com where they can get a physical, digital, or audio copy for themselves or a friend. This is hopefully the first of many new books, articles, short stories, and audio experiences to be offered by Gyroscope Productions in the coming years.

The main mothership for all things "JJT and Friends" will continue to be **TrueTunes.com** and the **True Tunes Podcast**, but you are invited to connect with us on Instagram (**@TheOnlyJJT**) TikTok (**@TrueTunesTok**) and Facebook (**@JohnJThompson**) as well. Spotify users should subscribe to the True Tunes Gallery Stage Mixtape playlist (updated weekly) and the new Ballad of the Lost Dogs playlist, which will be updated periodically with legacy and new artists releasing music in the spirit of this story. (Send your suggestions through the contact form at **TrueTunes.com**).

If you have not yet heard the True Tunes Podcast, please check it out. There are over 100 episodes (and counting) currently streaming on nearly every podcast platform. These conversations have included songwriters, producers, artists, and filmmakers from a wide range of genres and generations and are designed to inspire, educate, and challenge audiences young and old.

We are currently building a new YouTube channel and there are many "JJT On Location" episodes in which you can see the various locations around East Nashville that inspired elements of this story and, in some cases, where the book was written. You can find links to the YouTube channel at TrueTunes.com or the QR code below.